The Epic Saga of Alkebu-Lan

Roosevelt Broadus

Roosevelt Broadus

New York, NY

bit.ly/rooseveltbroadus
www.thetariqsphere.com

Publishing Concierge: The TariqSphere
Cover Design by: The TariqSphere Interior
Book Illustrations by: Derrick Freeman

The Epic Saga of Alkebu-lan: 10,000 BC. -- 1st ed.

ISBN 978-1-7923-0834-5

Synopsis

The Epic Saga of Alkebu-lan
10,000 B.C.

Alkebu-lan is the Dark Continent, known for its many traditions and various shades of black and brown people. An old wanderer travels the wilderness, his eyes gazing upward during the bright sunny days and when the stars cascade throughout the blanket of darkness. The ancient communities called him Imhotep 'The Wise Man' and he lived for many centuries watching many young people transition into elders.

For years his travels led him all across Alkebu-lan, into the mountains and wide open plains. After heading north to the City of Kemet (Egypt) to visit a friend name E-Newtu, Imhotep learns that E-Newtu has many disturbing dreams filled with destruction of countless lives deep in the outer reaches of space and the information brings back thoughts of his illustrious past and an enemy more powerful than Alkebu-lan could ever imagine.

Imhotep heads to the northern mountains to search the skies; the skies reveal a burning bright light that breaks into three pieces; one part moved south, another south west and the last to the northwest. Imhotep plans to investigate the strange objects when he is attacked by beasts and he reveals his true powers.

Concerned by E-Newtu's dreams of war, he heads out to find the crash sites, meeting friends along his search route, which gains powers as strong as that in which he wields. He will need their strength in order to combat an enemy that killed everyone in his home world of Aquan; that same enemy now eyed Alkebu-lan. Imhotep and his companions combine their powers along with the armies of Alkebu-lan to prevent the Garthian from ruling the young planet.

Alkebu-lan, means the 'Mother of Mankind' or 'Garden of Eden'. Alkebu-lan is the oldest and the only word of indigenous origin. It was used by the Moors, Nubians, Numidians, Khart-Haddans, (Carthaenians), the Abyssinians (Ethiopians). Alkebu-lan, would thousands of years later be called, Africa, after being renamed by the Greeks.

Table of Contents

Chapter 1

In central Alkebu-lan a fire burns in the dark woods as a single person sat next to the fire eating. The skies above are covered with stars and beasts moving across the ground glancing at the fire before wandering off to find their next meal. Owls, cicadas and crickets, play out their neverending nocturnal tunes around the dancing flames.

A small bat flies past the fire catching insects that are attracted to the light of the fire. The lone man lies down after eating to sleep for the rest of the night. The next morning, he sets off, moving over the rugged terrain of no man's land, stepping over small bushes and stones on uneven land masses. He heads north noting that the rainy season has come and gone, leaving behind an unfavorable feeling in the air which may have been uncomfortable for some, but for him it was very pleasurable.

It was now mid-day and the sun was glaring in the middle of the sky. He looks as far north as his eyes could see, placing his right hand above his eyes in the hopes of blocking out the sun's rays. He listens closely for any sound as his ears twitched.

He moved across the hot, sun-kissed ground for several more miles before he decided to take a break, taking a seat on a large rock. Thousands of migrating animals moved slowly to the south of him while very large vultures circled high above his head.

He pulled off his sandals to rub his tired feet. From his head, hung a cloaked hood made from a dead lion's carcass with its eyes looking outward as if still alive. The creature's fanged teeth sits on the man's forehead as the rest of its body drapes down the man's back to his waistline, while his chest and stomach were bare for all to see.

Around his neck he wears a chain connected to a charm with two circular images joined by a tri-color stone. On his index finger is a ring of the same pattern. The tri-colors of blue, red and grayish-white amaze all who get a glance at it in its uniqueness and brilliance. He stands only 5 feet tall, slightly shorter than the average Alkebu-lanian. He has slightly pointed ears, a scratchy voice and over-sized pupils, which many believed could peer into a man's soul.

In Alkebu-lan is called Imhotep, the wanderer and the elders from all over the continent told stories of Imhotep's everlasting youth throughout time. These same stories, told over a few hundred years, believed he lived longer and remained youthful because he belonged to a secret society that practices the ancient and holy majestic arts. Despite this, he is well respected and often known for gazing up at the sun and stars for countless hours, seeing beyond the landscape of the naked eye. These stories about him would be passed down from generation to generation.

After resting his tired feet and weary body, he stands up, looks around and returns to his journey, setting off toward the mountains, tall and majestic in the distance. The peaks disappear into the white clouds, and he smiles to himself as he forges his path, knowing it would not be long before he reached his destination.

It had been over two years since he came through this path and before nightfall he reaches the side of the mountain, gazing upward he sees wild goats scaling the mountainside. The sight reminds him of the large catlike beast that haunts the mountain goats, a large two hundred and fifty pound predator with eight inch canines followed by much smaller cats roaming the open plains.

He traveled all through the night and half of the next day. Just as the sun began to reach the middle of the sky, he found his way out. For the first time in a long while, Imhotep heard voices. He looked up ahead of him to see a family moving up the road in a horse-drawn wooden cart with a man at the wheel; and a light-framed woman with two small children. The man appeared to be a tall, dark fellow, with a balding center patch of hair on his head. His wife was a thick woman, darker than her husband, with long braids down her back and long dangling gold earrings. The children were smiling at him. Once they pulled within several feet of him, he spoke.

"Hello, how are you doing today? It has been a long time since I have spoken to anyone as I have traveled through the mountains path."

"Good day to you. We are headed back to central Alkebu-lan. Back to our native home; there my people have had a serious drought, so we traveled through the mountains to the markets to purchase wheat and seeds, and other crops to plant," said the man.

"Be careful during your travel." Imhotep pointed upward then continued, "You do know about the large cats that live on the side of the mountain?"

"Yes." The man looked up as he continued, "I've had several encounters with the beast, mostly at night, and this is why we are traveling during the midday sun."

"Yes, that is good, but I have a question for you. While at the marketplace, do you remember seeing a physician's tent?" Imhotep asked, while brushing the dust from his face.

"Yes, we noticed the tent, and the line was long to see the physicians. Many people visit that particular tent, mostly children and elders."

Recognition appeared in the woman's eyes, she then said, "Hey, I've heard of you! You are the great Imhotep, the traveler of all lands," she smiled. Her husband held a startled look of surprise, Imhotep looked at the family, then spoke,

"Yes, that is who I am. May you and your family be guided safely to your destination."

He took his leave and began to move past the cart, looking back as the small children peered out the rear. Hearing the horse move forward, he walked on as he continued to listen to the fading sound of the horse's hooves and the wagon wheels. His thoughts drifting to his old friends he was so anxious to see.

He felt the soft dewy grass beneath his feet, and welcomed the change from the hot desert sands and rainstorms of the last few weeks.

He passed fields and homes where children were playing and men were farming the lands; while older boys tended the sheep and other grazing animals. They waved hello as he passed by. He waved back, heading towards the city of Kemet, the largest in the land of Alkebu-lan. No city comes close in beauty and structure, and the closer he moved toward it, the busier it became. Many people made their homes here, and many more came in for the trade each day.

He walked the dirt road with others leading into the city, the crowded walkway made his journey slower, another 500 yards would lead him into the main market place. Hundreds of people from many lands looked upon him in passing pointing their fingers, whispering followed, and he heard his name. It was normal for him, everywhere he went. He was used to it.

Now his thoughts drifted once again to the reason for his traveling to the largest city in the natural world. Over the last year, Imhotep was hearing sounds in the darkest reaches of space, high above him, and the only one that could help him decipher what he was hearing was his friend.

His friend had been having the same dream for many years now, and he needed help decoding it, because the sounds he was hearing could possibly be connected to those dreams, he thought.

Shortly thereafter, he reached the marketplace where people moved around purchasing everything from food, clothing, animals and other wares. Tables were set up as far as the eye could see, and items were displayed to their best advantage. High quality merchandise dotted the tables. The aisles were tight and made moving around difficult. Music was being played on a variety of instruments, and jesters danced among the people. Children danced and others performed stunts trying to gather coins for their performance.

Imhotep pushed his way through the crowded walkways, watching as a dispute escalated from waving hands and loud voices. A Kemetic guard stepped in, and the sounds blended with the pigs and other animals squealing and squawking. Bells begin to clamor as a priest, and his followers marched past wearing all white clothing. The noise of the city was a welcomed change from the quiet existence he has lived in for months. His head throbbed from the initial onslaught of sounds, but he knew it wouldn't be long before his body grew accustomed to it.

Beautiful women walked past him wearing a rainbow of colored silk see-through clothing; nails, lips and toes painted in equally bright colors. Every single curve revealed, leaving nothing to the imagination. Bright flowers adorned their hair, and their beautiful skin tones ranged from the darkest black to the lightest of tan. Some of the gorgeous ladies were as tall as he was, and all carried themselves with grace and honor.

Imhotep moved farther into the large crowd as his eyes now searched for the symbol of the medicine tent among the many that was raised. The symbol, smoke rising into the air with a red circle atop it, to symbolize the sun would be designed around the medical tent.

After an hour of moving through the market, he found the tent he was looking for; it was sitting behind another tent even large than it, so the symbol was blocked from his view at first. He smiled, noticing the people waiting in line were composed mostly of young children and the elderly, and he recalled the conversation he had with the family at the mountain path.

As he moved closer he noticed the wife of his good friend. Her name is Tu-ney. Both she and a younger man were selling healing creams and powders that relieved the common cold or headache he'd known. It had been some time since he laid eyes on Tu-ney, but to him she looked the same. She had a light brown complexion, several rings on her hands, legs and ears, and white clothing covered her body completely.

Her face sported a small nose, round eyes that spoke of wisdom and hair as black as the night sky. The young man next to her, he never met. He was a tall fellow with his reddish hair in braids; even his beard was braided, and connected to the hair on his head. He had large, solid muscles, and Imhotep noticed that he carried a spear on his right hip while he was working.

He moved past the both of them as they worked, they weren't paying him any attention. He found his way inside the tent pulling the flap back and letting it fall behind him.

The tent was much bigger than it appeared from the outside, and held three separate rooms. The floor covered in a deep green, shag-like carpet, thick and comforting under his feet. There were patients sitting on large pillows inside the first section of the tent. They all turned to look at Imhotep who was still wearing his traveling attire. The air in the room was cooler than outside as it blew in from an open section above their heads. Imhotep counted 10 patients waiting to be seen.

When he entered the next room, he pulled the thick curtains back, stepping in as they closed behind him. He noticed his good friend E-Newtu with a young woman lying before him. This room was bigger than the waiting room, and also held large pillows and carpeting, this time in blue. Tables held jars of liquid solutions in every color, and herbs and roots stored in large animal skin bags draped the walls. The third room to the far left was blocked from view by a thick curtain. The ceiling was high, and the light from a candle illuminated the inside.

Imhotep looked towards E-Newtu as his eyes adjusted to the light. His friend was so focused on his patient, and this allowed Imhotep to look his friend over. He noticed the hair on his face and head was all white; blending in with his white clothing and the only color was the touch of green at the center of the crown sitting upon his head. The man's appearance had not changed very much since the last time they saw each other; a slightly darker complexion from the sun's rays; the only noticeable difference. E-Newtu was maybe two inches taller than himself, but similar in weight.

Imhotep's eyes turned to a woman he noticed for the first time, upon her sweat covered belly a lit candle sat, soft cries fell from her mouth, and tears ran from her eyes. The candle was covered with a glass jar so that the heat would stay in place. Other glass jars full of solutions, hand tools and gentle, cotton wool lay next to her body. The room smelled of flowers. A large cat roamed around the room while a monkey could be heard chattering from behind the closed curtain.

E-Newtu looked up at him briefly with a smile on his face. He then said, "It's been a long time Imhotep. I guess your observations, and my dreams have brought you back here." Imhotep smiled broadly as E-Newtu continued, "There are not many things that could bring the great wanderer back so soon. It has been maybe two years or more since your last visit. And while your visit brings me great joy, it's really no surprise, I have already told you all that I know. My dreams have become worse than before." Imhotep rubbed his face while he listened. "Most times the dreams keep me up at night and maybe this time my dream may hold the answers to all your questions. Hopefully, now that you are here I can get some much needed sleep." E-Newtu looked

Imhotep directly in the eyes, then looked down at his patient. The spot on the woman's stomach was turning red now.

Imhotep took several moments to ponder what his friend had said. Out of all the people in this land, it was E-Newtu that knew the most about him, others could only wonder. Yes, the dreams were a concern to him; it was the sole reason he had returned. His sensitive ears had brought him sounds from the deep, outer reaches of space, and it seemed that the sounds and the dreams were connected. He had watched this man from a young child grow into who he was now. He had also watched E-Newtu's father and grandfather grow from young boys into older men with great wisdom until their time on the planet came to an end. In a sense, E-Newtu's confession of the continued dream only confirmed his suspicion of something evil.

"Can you give me details of the images? Describe to me what takes place in your mind? It will be important for me to filter through what is actually truth, and what I may consider insignificant. These things are important to the impending matter," Imhotep finished with his eyes opened wide as he waited on an answer.

E-Newtu looked up at the man who had known both his father, grandfather, and fathers before them, throughout his family's lifetimes. He thought about how his father had told him stories of Imhotep's travels. He knew that Imhotep should have died long ago, and appeared younger than he, although he spent many years traveling under the baking sun throughout the lands of Alkebu-lan on a never ending quest. But what was he searching for was the question and he wondered why his dream was so important as to bring the wise one back so suddenly.

Imhotep was the only person he could confide in outside of his wife. Imhotep believed that his dreams also suggested that what he saw was a foretelling of future events, and as a kid he believed the wise men.

In the past, E-Newtu tried to convince the city of Kemet to listen to him when his dreams told of storms, droughts and other significant events, but the Pharaoh always disregarded his words. Even when a dream came to him about the Pharaoh's impending death, his words, again, fell on deaf ears.

The High Priestess Anut Tawi believed he was a spy looking to overthrow the ruling family, and she planned to have him assassinated, but with her passing went the knowledge of putting an end to his life, in which he felt like Imhotep had kept him safe somehow. E-Newtu looked down at the woman still lying below him, then at Imhotep. He watched Imhotep breathe a ball of air from his lungs then weaved it into a circle of clear air using his hands making circular motions slowly. E-Newtu watched it break into two even smaller clear circles. Imhotep waved his fingers toward the circular sphere moving across the room, guiding them into the woman's ear softly. The woman inhaled, then a soft gasp followed, then all sound was cut off as E-Newtu made her relax a bit. When she calmed down, E-Newtu began talking again to Imhotep, noticing that he was now standing to relieve his cramped legs.

"In my dreams, which have become more graphic than the last time we talked, there are images of fires burning red hot, causing me to sweat in my sleep. The fire is from a very, very far away place. It is dark there and somewhere I know I have never been, and it felt so real. I felt the pain of millions of lives being wiped out; children losing parents, and siblings losing siblings. But the voices...they were unlike anything I had ever heard before. Not like the Alkebu-lanian people at all. I heard screaming and it woke me. I could see a man and a woman, and their anguish was so real to me. It was as if they were speaking and looking directly at me. I was shaken and my wife had to comfort me that night. She asked many questions that night while I laid there looking out at the moon above, but I know that many of the images in my dreams have come true, so I kept it to myself. So for several more days, I stayed busy and awake, hoping to never have the dreams again. Four days later as I gazed up at the evening sky, glowing with millions of stars coloring the heavens above, I ventured back into my home and fell asleep next to Tu-ney."

Imhotep sat there not moving; eyes opened wide, seeing the visions as he spoke of them. E-Newtu began speaking again, "Once again the dreams overpowered my sleep, but this time I see floating objects, these huge circles flying over where all the screaming could be heard. Flames covered the circle and I cried out in my sleep, '*Nooooooooo*', but I could not wake up. Then another circle appeared, this one much large than the last one, this, too, was engulfed in flames. Something screamed and I could see myself covering my ears, it was unbearable. Something was being chased across a large, vast space. Whatever the thing was that was being chased, entered the circle and the pursuer followed and the same destruction followed. I could hear voices ringing out clearly asking for help."

Imhotep watched E-Newtu cover his face with his hands. He took his seat again, and decided it was enough for today after seeing the effects that the dream had on his good friend. Although it was urgent that he obtain the answers before it was too late, giving it a rest was far more important at that time.

"Listen to me, E-Newtu," Imhotep said. "That is enough for today. The information you have provided is very helpful, and when you have recovered a little, you can tell me the rest of the story. I will be here to listen, OK? I will need to know every detail in order to determine what these dreams mean, and we both know they have meaning." E-Newtu agreed with a shake of his head.

"I believe the sounds I am hearing are connected somehow, and what they reveal could be very detrimental."

"Detrimental? How?" E-Newtu asked.

"I will reveal more as the information comes to me, but for now just continue your work here. There are sick people who need you. Let me think about everything you have told me." Imhotep looked deeply into E-Newtu's eyes. With a wave of his hand he retracted the pockets of air from the woman's ears. She spoke up right away.

"Ooooh I can hear again," she said. "Thank you." She flashed a smile that matched her gratitude.

Imhotep looked at the woman briefly, then at E-Newtu, he turned and exited the tent with a final wave of his hand to his friend before he said, "I will see you tomorrow E-Newtu."

Chapter 2

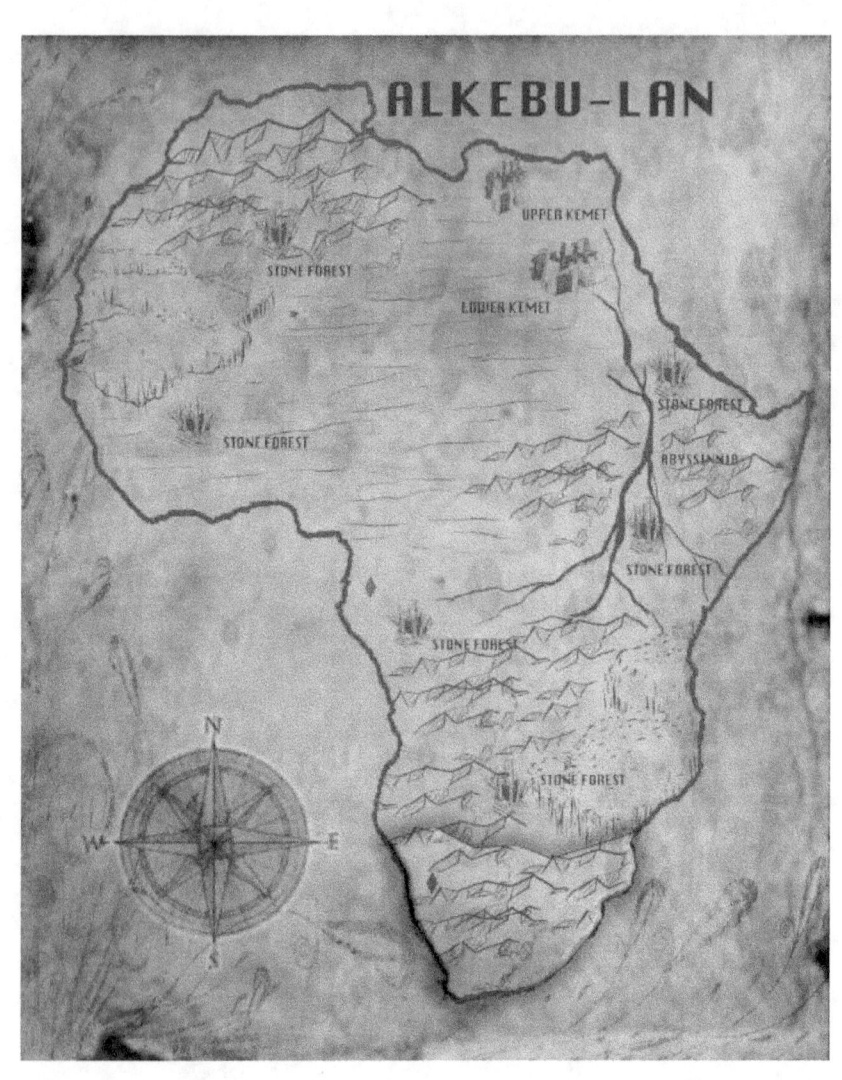

Southern Alkebu-lan

Visible through the final bend of a narrow winding gorge almost 2 miles long was the village made up of magnificent structures standing through the test of time. As if framed by a parted curtain, the most spectacular remnant of an ancient city of U-Dondo, where the homes are carved directly into the solid rock along the western coast line. Families have lived here for hundreds of years, their homes surrounded by green meadows, steep hills and dense forests, and a few miles to the south stood the tallest of mountains that overlooked the land and seas.

Women plant crops and tend to the children, the men hunted, and traded with the locals for miles around. This had been their way of life for centuries.

A dark-skinned woman wearing her hair in braids, with smooth shiny skin, full breasts, and strongly built arms, strolled through the pasture with a young boy. The woman's left hand held up her colorful dress; they descended the steep hill as she lovingly gazed down at the young, five year old child. She was called Kisse and her son was known as Tutannharmoon, Tutann for short.

The young one is already a sight to behold, having his father's distinct bone structure and muscular development. He is already four times the size of other kids his age and twice as tall. His skin is darker than his father's, who was already close to pitch black. All, in his society, have green eyes and his are a bit lighter than theirs.

He was a normal acting child for his age, wanting to play, climb trees, and play fight with wooden swords. Half of his day was spent going to the Petra, a place where all the kids were taught. Now they were heading to the river for his daily wash before his last meal of the day. Tutann has a voracious appetite and Kisse had no problem letting her only son eat as much as he liked, for his father always brought home substantial amounts of food, and the families all pitched in to help one another. Food was always plentiful; fruit trees and vegetables grew all over their land.

Kisse waved at some friends and family she passed as she entered her home. It was a nice place with several floors. As she walked through the front doorway with Tutann following closely behind her, she retrieved a wash rag and a round, large, wooden bowl from one of the many baskets around her home. Her son, Tutann, ran past her, and out the rear of the dwelling to play in their yard.

She smiled at him. The yard was huge and she and the other families had access to the river from the rear entrance. When she stepped out into the yard to her left, clothing was hanging from lines bellowing in the wind, and to her right, wooden barrels that held fruits and vegetables lined the yard. There were also large portions of meat hanging from long lines wrapped in cloth to keep the flies and insects away. She could see Tutann waiting for her at the river, just under a large tree, that offered shade from the hot, burning sun above.

The river was deeper in the center of the water, but only three feet at the shore line, Kisse stepped off of the shore line into the water, dipping her bowl under the water and placing it to the side.

Her son began to take his clothing off, and she soaked the rag in the bowl. She began rubbing his skin thoroughly, starting at his head. When she had finished, she took him by the hand so he could climb down into the water to rinse off.

"Tutann, I need you to close your eyes, ok?" Kisse said.

"Ok, Mommy," he said, while closing his eyes and placing his hands over his face.

Kisse smiled again, seeing her son as he prepared himself, she poured the water upon his head, then she dipped the bowl back into the river pouring it over his head for a second time.

"Ok, Momma, do it again. The water feels good," he said, while opening his eyes for a brief second as water cascaded down his body back into the river.

She rinsed him thoroughly before he exited the river bank, and went to the tree where several cloths hung. She took a hold of one of the cloths, and dried her son off before placing fresh clothes on his body.

"Mommy can I play outside before Dad gets home?" Tutann asked, while eyeing the small pups that entered his yard every day.

His mother noticed him looking at the pups and said, "Sure, Tutann, but you better not get dirty, understand? You just had your wash. You must be clean before you go to sleep and you know your father will be upset if you come in the house dirty."

"Yes, Momma, I know. I promise to stay clean. I just need to play with the puppies. See? They are looking for me! Look Momma, here they come!"

"Alright, I'm going in to prepare the food, it will be ready shortly," his mother said, before heading back through the door of their home.

The pups belonged to the neighbor who was training them to hunt. The neighbor also had some small cats that Tutann sometimes played with. He raced around the yard with the puppies following him, and he laughed as they tried to catch up to him.

The community loved the young child called Tutannharmoon. At the tender age of five, he was already becoming a legend. One story spoke of how one morning a woman cried out for help as she was being attacked by a black mamba poisonous snake. Seconds later she heard her back door explode open.

The woman was standing on top of one of the chairs in the room, almost climbing the walls to the ceiling because of this aggressive snake. One bite would surely kill her. Tutann heard the screams and came running. She watched as the young boy took hold of the snake, and slung it hard against the walls of her dwelling several times, so hard that the snake split in half. As one half of the snake tried to slither away, Tutann stepped hard on its head, then took both halves, and calmly walked out the door as if this was the most normal thing to do.

The young boy's father, Butann, was a thinly built man with thick muscles, who stood six feet tall. He wore a clean, shaven head and face. Another story told of his father arguing with a man about some borrowed farming tools, which led to a heated exchange of words, and then became a physical dispute. Tutann stepped in, and took hold of the older man, tossing him to the ground hard. As the man cried out in pain, he looked up and his face turned to total shock as he noticed the young boy, and realized how strong he was.

Tutann was glaring down angrily with fists balled, and he was ready for a fight to defend his father, although his father needed no help. After the altercation, the man returned the tools right away and left, never to return. It was at that moment, Butann knew his son was destined for something great.

Tutann moved around the yard laughing outwardly, and then he heard his mother calling him.

"Tutannharmoon, it is time to eat. Go wash your hands and come sit at the table," Kisse said.

"I'm on my way, Mom." He turned to the puppies and said, "I'll see you two later. I have to go and eat, but if you come to my back door, I will have something for you guys to munch on." The two puppies barked while sitting on the ground as they watched him race into his house.

Chapter 3

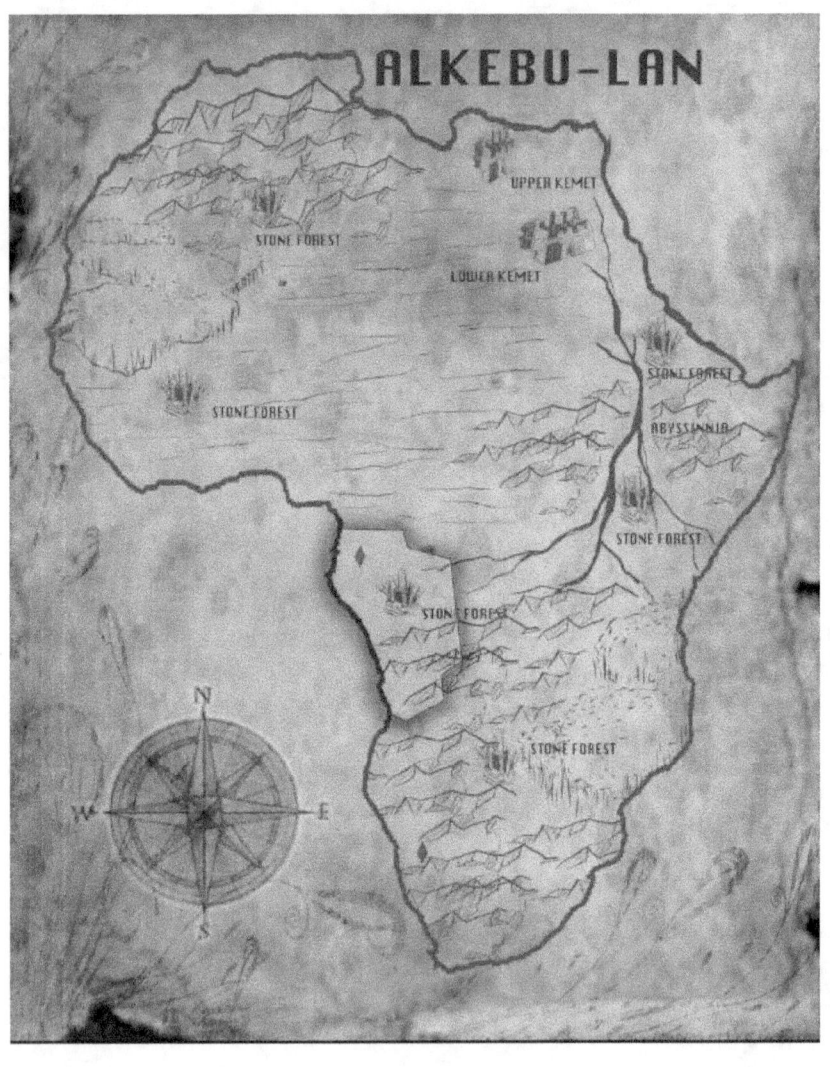

South West Alkebu-lan

The sun shined down rays of light, feeding the millions of plant life that surrounded the vast landscape. As the ocean tides crashed upon the sandy beaches in the distance, the hills rise up then slope down into gorges, where forest lay; deep dense places served as homes to antelope and other wildlife.

The homes here are made of thick mud, and were built with two levels with an opening in the roof where inhabitants could look out over their lands. There were several windows covered with curtains to prevent the sun's rays from entering, and to keep rainstorms out. You could see as many as ten fields rolling in the distance.

Mostly farmers and expert fishermen lived here in this community. Their boats lined the beaches for over a hundred yards, and the green pastures met the rolling beaches at the shoreline.

They trade with the ships from all across Alkebu-lan, especially the midlands that come to their shores just like the communities to the north, south and east. They are a proud people who are also known for their fighting skills.

A dark, smooth skinned, young woman runs across a large field in the high grass, her long dreadlocks carrying in the wind behind her. Her heart thumped inside her chest, and her long legs carried her swiftly out-pacing the three young men that chased her.

She smiles because she knew she was in much better shape than they are; for a second she stops and waits on them, breathing in easily, this only made the boys angrier. She smiled even brighter to further their anger as her long hair settled at her waist. She was fully developed at 18 years old with full breasts, a slender waist and large, rear end attached to long legs. Her eyes were small, but she had great vision, small ears with a thin nose. She hated the way the men and boys looked at her in her community because she knew what they were after, but she would hurt someone if they were being disrespectful.

She was a soldier like her father and wanted to be treated as such, but the boys had other things in mind. Being a soldier is in her blood although her father held on to dreams of her marrying, and bearing children. This idea is in fact far from what she wants for herself.

The first boy stepped in closer to her speaking loudly, "Hutapsunnimoon, why do you run from us, we mean you no harm, you act like we are your enemies," said Kutti, the largest of the three boys that chased her. The other two moved next to him, breathing in very deeply.

She smiled, showing her pearly white teeth, as she noticed they were slowly moving closer to her.

"If we are friends, why are you three always chasing me? I just don't feel like being bothered," she said, playing the helpless role.

Now crossing her arms in front of her emphasized that she was no small woman, but the three boys in front of her were much older, and bigger than she was. They stepped even closer, and she attacked, smacking Kutti across the face, he fell hitting the ground beneath him hard.

She then rushed towards the second fellow who was still winded. He swung a few punches her way; she weaved back and forth, stepping in close like her father taught her when she was only a child, then she went into a spin, sending a backhand into the taller fellow's face, connecting and smashing his nose in. He took hold of his nose as blood ran through his fingers.

The last fellow rushed away into trying to put distance between him and Hutapsunnimoon, after witnessing his friends go down screaming. She rushed after him, catching him by his clothing, and then kicked him in his tail end very hard. A blow she know he would remember before she turned and heading home.

It wasn't long before she reached home just a few miles away. Her homeland was vast, and she loved the countryside. She loved the feel of the heat from the sun while in the distance; the snow-capped mountains were still visible from many miles away.

The cool winds blew and as she looked to her right, many beautiful trees of all shapes and colors swayed from side to side; some with yellow, red, green and white leaves. Just a bit past the trees laid the ocean, large and beautiful, as it met the land.

Then she smelled the fruit trees her father, Nassir, had planted in their yard when she was a very small child. The sweet smelling fruit hung in the air and reminded her that she could find her way home in the dark by following the scent.

One of her chores was to tend to the animals every day. Their yard held several types of birds that they bred in captivity for eating and everything else could be found around them in the countryside. In their home, everything was on a schedule.

Her mother, En-Zinger, was originally from Abyssinia, farther to the north east of Alkebu-lan, and met her father at the markets for trading in the city of Kemet. Her mother's original community was a strong, organized community as well, and she hoped to visit one day.

Her father, Nassir, is a large man with thick bone structure. She and her father both stood well over 6 feet tall, while her mother stood at 5 feet 11 inches. As a young girl, she learned the ways of a woman, doing house chores, such as cleaning, washing clothing, cooking and planting crops; she was one of the best cooks among her community. But as she began to grow into a mature woman, she began to grow bored with her womanly duties.

One day, while taking a long walk, she stumbled upon her father's training camp where many of the boys were in training, and the place was sectioned off to learn various styles of warfare. Some of the young soldiers worked with knives, others with swords, and more could be found working with spears. In another area, some worked on hand to hand combat.

The clash of metal and the thumping of arrows hitting targets carried upon the air. There were sounds of men grunting as their sweaty bodies struggled to stay on their feet during combat.

Hutapsunnimoon stared down from a high place when she could be certain no one would spot her because women weren't permitted to view the men's training site.

Every day after her chores she would sneak off to train using the same style her father was showing the men. She obtained wooden weapons like the ones the boys were using, practicing strikes, blocks and memorizing the places on the body that would cripple or kill a man.

She trained herself to use a knife and spear, but she was most excited about a wooden longbow. She would practice until she could hit a target at well over 150 yards away. Every single day she made it her duty to practice and her body felt stronger and better prepared to protect herself against any opposition; she was now a soldier after two hard years.

Often, she would stroll through the valleys and rivers alone. The other women from her community laughed at her because she preferred animal skin clothing to the cotton and silk dresses the other ladies wore. She was lectured by many of the wise women of her community who felt that a woman's place was in the home taking care of family, and to them her behavior was not normal.

She was not supposed to be walking the fields alone, doing rugged work, such as fighting and using arrows; those things were considered a man's job, and she should not be acting like a man. She cared little about what they thought, although she was a woman who liked men, she wanted to choose the man she would spend her life with one day. She knew she would have plenty of time to find that special person who would accept her for who she was, and now was not the time for that.

With a shake of her head, she discarded those thoughts quickly. Now, after years of practicing, she was finally building up the courage to ask her father to join the ranks of soldiers; but each day she looked into his eyes, her courage would dwindle, so she continued to practice.

She looked as far north as she could, hoping one day to see the city of Kemet. Life to her was about adventure, and adventure was in her blood.

She heard a voice behind her and she turned to see that it was the three young men from earlier, heading home. She walked to her front door smelling the aroma of her mother's stew and whispered to herself, "Good," entering her home closing the door behind her.

Chapter 4

Kemet City

The morning air was cool, even for the city of Kemet, which sat in the east. The sun was beginning to rise in the sky and many people began heading towards the market place, pulling along animals of all sorts for sale. There was one, huge beast with long, white tusks extending from his mouth, and large ears standing about 17 feet tall. Many other merchants were carrying cages of hares or ropes with donkeys attached. Everyone was headed in the same direction. Suddenly, a blast of wind came through, and sand swirled around. Vendors struggled to hold onto their wares, while other items scattered across the desert floor.

E-Newtu exited his tent, walking to his stand to set up. His light brown shirt with matching pants blew in the wind. He placed large bags just behind the wooden stand, then walked back to his tent to retrieve the other bags of items inside to be sold. Other vendors moved around setting up their stands to attract the large masses of people that would be coming to trade or purchase goods.

He looked around to see everyone moving as one putting together their selling stations. He then began placing powders in glass jars upon the counter, the colors ranging from white to a dark brown. These items were known to treat minor aches and pains, and there were other items that were much stronger. There were also beauty creams to provide softer skin, and shaving creams for the men with a host of other items for medical or hygiene purposes.

His sister's son then exited the tent holding bamboo and sugarcane, which were each 4 feet long, he placed them just under the station out of sight. His name is Ahknonkineton, a 6 feet 8 inch tall young man of dark brown complexion. He fancies wearing his hair in braids on his head that tied into his beard and hung from his chin. He is lean and very muscular. His skin is almost transparent, and most of the time he wore no shirt, but at the moment his top was fitted loosely, draping slightly over his torso. His lower clothing matched his top, and was cut short to reveal his knees and large, calf muscles.

E-Newtu knew that the spear Ahknonkineton carried was like an extra body part. It had been given to him by his father, a traveler of the northern lands. E-Newtu also knew that Ahknonkineton had not seen his father for well over ten years, since he was only ten years old, so he held on to the last remnant of his dad. His mother died a few years back so he came to live with him and his wife, Tu-ney.

Tu-ney and Ahknonkineton's mother had been great friends. She had been in his life since he was a small child, which is, in fact, how he first met Tu-ney, and eventually married her and brought her to the city of Kemet, while his sister and Ahknon lived on the borderlands.

Now, Ahknon worked with him while learning the trade and craft of medicine. He was always more of a man of peace rather than war. He tried to bring understanding to conflicts, and had, on several occasions, solved disputes that erupted between men or women of the community. Usually after he intervened they would go their own way in peace.

A crafty builder, masonry work is his main trade, but working alongside his uncle gave Ahknon more experience in a social environment, and allowed him to meet more of a variety of people, especially here in Kemet, which he finds is full of life at all hours of the day and night.

E-Newtu smiled as he continued to watch him set up their selling station. Ahknon placed trees behind the station that bloomed with pretty flowers and the leaves used for healing. Then he called his nephew over to him.

"Ahknon, I need you to take care of the customers. I have a few things to do inside with my old friend, Imhotep. Can you handle this without me?"

"Yes uncle, I have everything in order, and Tu-ney will be out in a minute."

Then Ahknon's gaze fell upon a short man walking past the stand heading for his uncle's tent. He was wearing upon his head, the head of the large cat that roamed the lands farther to the south, and animal print covered his lower half. He remembered seeing this fellow before wearing this same attire many, many years ago and it was the reason this man seemed so familiar. Then the name Imhotep dawned on him; and he whispered, "Imhotep, the wanderer, a lone wise man, a legend, who looked the same as when he had last seen him." He watched the two men enter the tent as Tu-ney exited it after speaking with the wise man for a short spell.

Ahknon remembered his last encounter with the wise man. He had stopped by their home when he and his mother were living on the border land. Imhotep had stepped in front of him and what he remembered most was the man's eyes—they were set deep into their sockets and very large for an Alkebu-lanian. He remembered the pupils opening up to take his face entirely and on that dark patch of land, looking into those insect-like eyes. He wanted to run and flee, mistaking him for some kind of wild beast.

His polite words had relaxed him, so Ahknon knew he meant him no harm. His clothing looked old and rugged, and he had no smile on his face, but no matter how meek he looked there was no mistake about it, he had a real sense of being very dangerous.

Ahknon strolled to the tent this time carrying a glass of water for the old wanderer, and upon entering the tent, Ahknon handed him the drink. He looked up at Ahknon and said, "Why thank you. What a fine young man you have here E-Newtu! I sense something special about him, but really can't figure it out. I am sure it will come to me, one with spear," before turning around to finish talking with E-Newtu.

Ahknon turned to leave the tent, pondering Imhotep's last words, 'one with spear'. Ahknon felt like those large eyes read his mind, and knew the history of his father. For his father was also known to wander the northern lands and across the vast seas. He thought that maybe Imhotep had ran across his father, and could possibly provide the answers he needed. He would have to find a way somehow to talk with Imhotep.

Inside the tent, E-Newtu was seated just a few feet away from Imhotep. The place smelled of fresh cut flowers. Imhotep looked around seeing there was a tray of food on one of the tables, and today most of the large pillows lay along the tent walls making the room look much large than the last time he was there. A young ape moved around the room now carrying food towards them, and outside the tent the noise was getting louder as more people entered the square. Then Imhotep said, "That is a really good trick you have taught this ape. How did he ever learn to bring items to you E-Newtu?"

"Well, it takes just a bit of patience, but the creature is very intelligent on its own. It just took a little coaching, and lots of food rewards," E-Newtu said, smiling. He then took one of the fruits the ape was carrying, then the creature walked over to Imhotep making soft noises.

Imhotep looked down at the creature while taking a banana from his little arms then said, "Thank you, little one."

The creature responded with more little noises before moving to a rope that led up several feet, climbing up and perching on a seat to relax.

Tu-ney entered the tent, moving quickly. She was wearing a cream, one–piece dress, and her hair was wrapped in a matching crown with earrings of gold in her ears, with a jade, pendant bracelet on her wrist. She was carrying bags walking past the two men then continued out of the tent.

When all was quiet, Imhotep said, "First off, how have you been sleeping my old friend?"

E-Newtu gazed upon one of the only men he trusted and said, "Well I'm good, as good as could be expected I guess."

"You know I was thinking about the information you revealed to me yesterday," he said, as he pulled off his head gear.

"And what assumption have you pondered inside your mind?" asked E-Newtu.

"Well, you know me better than anyone else. I must know the full truth before I begin to speculate falsely. Your dreams could mean anything, and may have no effect here, but should it, well that is something else to think about. Have your dreams showed you those same images of the huge circles and flashing light?" said Imhotep.

"Yes, it's the same all the time, it concerns me. Sorry about yesterday, but these dreams seem more personal than any other dream I've had. The difference is I was able to understand the others so I always knew what I needed to do. But this one, whatever it is, it's very serious, more serious than the other dreams. But I have no real knowledge or clear understanding as to what it could mean." E-Newtu finished, looking down at the carpet and then over at Imhotep.

Imhotep paused after a few minutes, lost in thought as his eyes flickered from side to side. Then he blinked several times before rubbing his chin, readjusted himself in his seat and gazed about the place. E-Newtu noticed Imhotep's pointed ears, his beard and mustache was unshaven and grew in a wild bush about his face. His skin was smooth and untouched by time. He was wondering. Everything he learned told him that the likelihood of Imhotep living so long could only mean he either carried a special gift, or he is an animal of some kind. But medically he was supposed to be dead many, many years ago.

He watched Imhotep look up and say, "I need more details of the events inside your mind, we need to be prepared." Then he stopped talking.

"Be prepared for what?" E-Newtu looked at Imhotep, concerned.

"Never have I been in need of information so urgently E-Newtu. Your dream may affect me personally. Understand?" said Imhotep.

E-Newtu answered, "Yes!" But he still felt that Imhotep was holding some form of information back, maybe because he wanted to keep him calm.

Thoughts shot through his brain; the things in the dreams, Imhotep needing to know more, the seriousness of it all, more important and serious than the passing of Pharaoh. Yes, yes this feeling told him this was a very dangerous situation, but he was a patient man and he knew Imhotep meant well. So he'd wait to find out the meaning that only Imhotep could explain.

"I told you there was a huge circle then a spot covers the circle. There is an explosion of light, then screaming. And it happens again to another large circle, but the only difference is, after the second explosion, one of the spots moves quickly to the third, large circle. And it happens again. It was being chased, then the explosion of lights and more screaming. Death was everywhere. Sometimes I could feel the breaking and tearing of metal things," his voice trailed off.

Imhotep listened very carefully to E-Newtu; he sees the circles as other planets, deep in the outer reaches of space. E-Newtu would know nothing of this, or what the circle means because he has never seen his home world from outer space. The dark spots were spaceships, and the screaming was life being taken from the attack. The large explosion, of the first, second and third circle was in fact the destruction of those worlds, but what has him most amazed is the fact that one spaceship was being chased, from one planet to the other. Whoever this traveler was must have escaped with their life, and this stood out very clearly.

He realizes that the one ship is looking for help so it flees to other planets from the invaders. E-Newtu's deep feelings and visuals place him at the scene of the attack. He begins to wonder if these attacks were somehow connected to the Garthians. He wasn't sure, so for now he kept what he knew to himself.

"Listen old friend," he began, "I thank you for the information, but to be honest, it holds no apparent trouble right now. I will be leaving for a few months. I have to look into a few things. The one thing I know about you is that your dream is a prediction of future events that may or may not happen but because they are such a concern to you, I have to look further into it. I won't be gone long nor will I go too far."

Imhotep stood up and he and E-Newtu hugged before he turned to leave the tent. When he exited, E-Newtu's nephew was waiting on the other side and E-Newtu's wife was serving customers at the stand. The sky was covered with clouds and the market place was full of people.

"Hello Imhotep, I really need to speak with you before you're off again for another two or three years. You may have urgent things to do at the moment but this is very important to me, seeing as though you have more experience than most people around here. Please, I was hoping you could give me just a small piece of your time," said Ahknon.

Imhotep gazed upward at the tall man in front of him. There was something remotely familiar about this lad, in his eyes and facial structure, but he couldn't place why or where. Then he said,

"Yes I will have time for you young man, once I return. I will make sure of this but right now is not the right time."

He moved past the young man, marching quickly away. Ahknon watched him move through the marketplace marching north towards the high mountains of fire in the distance. Ahknon looked on until he disappeared from sight before heading back to help Tu-ney.

Chapter 5

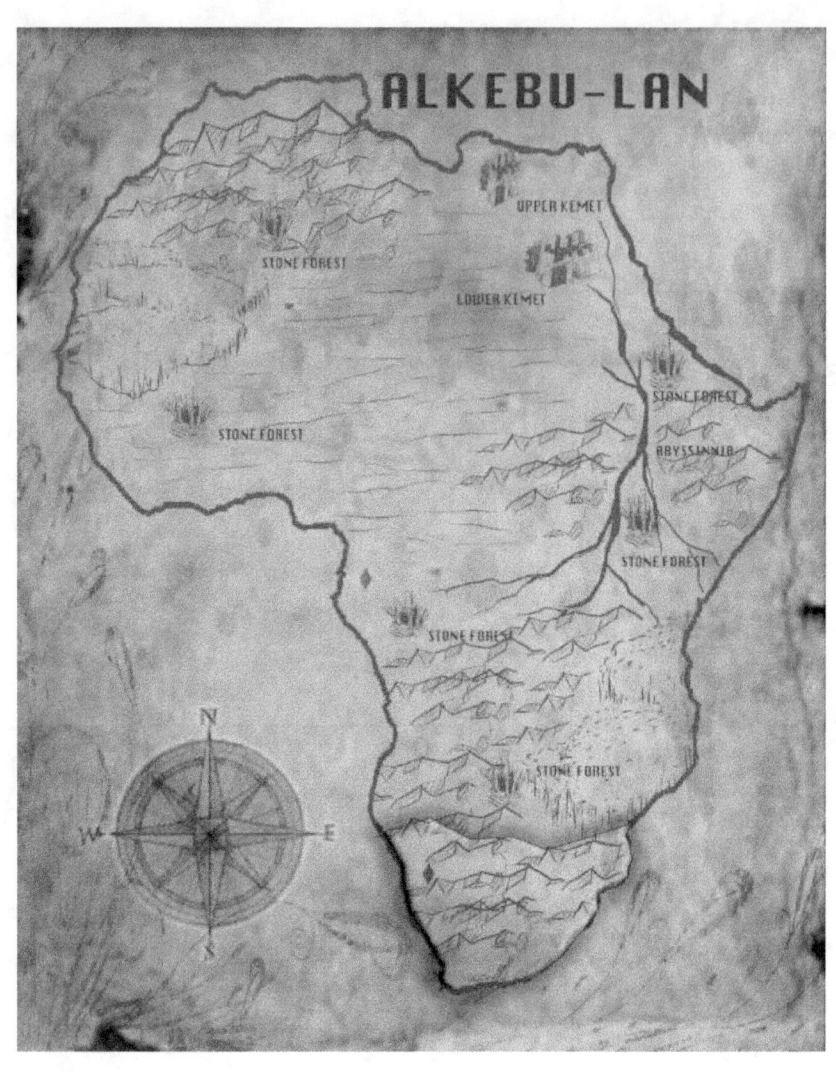

Deep Southern Alkebu-lan

A nother season has passed for the child known as Tutannharmoon. He now was even more of a help to the adults in his village by carrying blocks and toting tree logs. His black skin shone like glass. Even the top of his head had a rich glow to it because he was completely bald. He is a happy kid, especially when he could help out others in need.

It often bored him to play with the kids his own age; he seemed more excited about learning the local trades and he never seemed to tire of the things he learned. He heard his mother calling him in the distance somewhere.

"Tutann, Tutann where are you child? Don't have me come looking for you boy," said his mother.

Tutann moved quickly towards his backyard then past his mother, who was still looking around for him. When she finally saw him, all she could do was place her hands on her hips while she watched him moving towards the river bed. She shook her head then headed towards the river herself; his laughter reached her ears, so she began to jog behind him. Oh how she loved her son. He was her firstborn and besides her husband, he was her only responsibility.

He had a lot of respect for those older than him but he was a quick learner and would question you if he felt like something you said wasn't right. Some would get angry at a child so young challenging their information. He was a very good thinker. As he continued to grow, Kisse wasn't worried. His size did not concern her. She knew his growth would stop and he would be as normal as her and her husband, Butann.

Upon reaching the river she began to wash her little boy completely. She knows there will be a time, very soon, that he will become a man, so she must enjoy these times with him as a child. As she scrubbed his head, he began asking her questions. "Mommy, why is the sky so blue?" he asked as he gazed upward, pointing. She looked up also and said,

"Well, I heard from your grandfather, who is my father's father that the reason the sky is blue is because the massive oceans reflect the sunlight into the sky above and since the oceans are blue that is what we see."

"Ohhhh yes, is that large light the sun? Father told me it was. He said it creates life and if it wasn't for its existence, all life would surely perish. If that is so, I don't want to lose you mommy, nor father."

Kisse moved the cloth around Tutann's body while she tried to find an answer. Water dripped from the top of his head as she said,

"You don't have to worry about the sun going out; it will be many years before that happens. You will probably be a grandfather."

"Mother, I'm too young to be a grandfather! That will happen only when I am as old as father," Tutann said.

Kisse began laughing at her young child's remark and he began to laugh along with her.

"Tutann, you do know I'm talking about many years from now, when the season has passed you by many times," Kisse said.

"Yes, Mother, I understand," he said, looking at his mother then up towards the clear skies. He really enjoyed the moving water as it was passing over his legs. He sunk down below the surface and then came up after a short while, rubbing the water out of his eyes.

"Tutann, I want you to promise me that you will leave them snakes alone," Kisse scolded. Her smooth face turned stern but serious. Kisse hoped that it would do the job. She really couldn't be mad with her son but she wanted him to be safe. Seconds passed and then both of them broke out into laughter, again.

"Mother, I know what I am doing. Trust me. I'm smart enough to know the snake will kill me. But what will happen when father or the other village soldiers are not around, people will die and I know you don't want that to happen, right??"

"No, but I don't need my child injured or dead, understand? Be careful, the things you do for others are very dangerous, which scares me. I know you're doing the right thing but that is too much responsibility for only one small child!" Kisse said.

As Tutann climbed out of the river to dry off, he rubbed his body gently until he was completely dry then he tossed the cloth into a wooden bin off to the side.

"You are a very young boy Tutann, there is so much to learn and you have plenty of time to experience them all. OK?" Kisse said, leaning in to kiss Tutann on his forehead.

Later that night while Tutann was sleeping, his father entered their home. The first thing Kisse noticed was the concerned look upon his face. She got up from her chair to see what was wrong.

"What is it, husband?" Kisse asked, while she watched her husband pace the floor.

Butann gazed into his wife's eyes with his small round eyes; his dark, muscular body was like one of the deep, carved statues that tower over most communities, he held a sword inside his right hand, pausing for just a few seconds before beginning to pace the floor again. He stopped and looked at his wife before taking her by the arms, softly.

"Large herds of wild mammoths are headed our way. Normally, their travels led them far away from here but something has them coming straight for our community."

Kisse touched her cheeks, her eyes widened, knowing the destruction these very large creatures are capable of unleashing.

"Why haven't the men gathered and used the already tamed mammoths to help turn these wild beasts in another direction?" Kisse stated.

"Well, many men and animals were seriously injured. Three men are now dead. We managed to turn the first herd away. The other herds marched to take up where the last herd left off. There has to be something we could do," he thought aloud. "Maybe fire will turn the other herds away, it's difficult to say and we don't need any more people dying. Spears will only provoke them further," Butann finished.

"I've seen how large a herd can become; 15-20 of those large animals could totally destroy what has taken us years to create." Kisse looked around her home as she moved a few paces away to her son's room, where he lay sound asleep.

She moved back towards her husband and continued, "Do you feel we would have to leave our home? And if so, how soon will we know?" she asked.

"We have maybe a week or so. The wild beasts just may change direction on their own and if that happens, we will be free of this problem," said Butann.

Tutann was pretending to be asleep when his mother and father began talking of the dangers that surrounded his village. It concerned him that those around him could be affected by these wild beasts. His father kept such beasts around as working animals; they were very strong and powerful creatures. This wasn't a snake or mere man, like he was used to dealing with, but something one hundred times his size. After his mother came into the room to check up on him he heard the front door open then close. He snuck out of bed and moved towards the front door to peek outside without his mother seeing him. There were many men holding swords and spears. He knew they were going out to protect their homeland. He had heard his father say there were three dead and he understood what death meant and he was now concerned for his father.

Tutann closed the door, going back to his bed with concern for his father on his mind.

Chapter 6

Southwest Alkebu-lan

Inside the home of Hutapsunnimoon, months have passed since her encounter with the young men. Word traveled fast in her community, men are well aware to keep their distance. It is mid-afternoon and the weather is hot as usual, and after doing her chores, she wanted to take a stroll so she exited her home, closing the door behind her. Outside, children tended to sheep and goats to her left while the elders were picking vegetables from their gardens. She headed off to her right towards a patch of trees that provided cover from the nosy neighbors constantly watching her. She tried very hard to keep her name out of peoples' mouths…for she hated being the center of attention.

She moved swiftly to the tree line where she found a set of knives she had buried. They were old and had been exposed to the elements for many months but she cleaned them and sharpened them to perfection. She concealed them in her pockets on the side of her thighs. It was here that she also kept her long bow and arrows; these things she kept secret from her father.

She strapped the bow and arrows across her back, this time pulling her hair up then quickly braiding her dreadlocks into a single braid. Her clothing this time was as brown as the trees that concealed her.

A soft breeze passed through the trees as she walked between them, she was very muscular for a female; long, lean but muscular thighs she inherited from her father and from running chores most of the day besides practicing her fighting skills constantly. She has a beautiful face that most men find pleasant to look at. In a sense, she owes her beauty to her mother. She wore the crown emblem of her community tied around her forehead. It was engraved in solid gold.

After placing all the things she needed into her bag, she moved farther away from her home and back toward her father's training site. There weren't many things that could excite her but this was by far the most exciting, as she moved as quickly as her legs could carry her.

She pushed forward through the small streams then up large hills and it wasn't long before she reached the place she sought at a high advantage point. It seemed each week her father was changing the location for training because the conditions of the ground were different.

This training camp terrain was rockier so the soldiers were truly off balance. She admired the new place and remembered all the steps the fighters would go through. Silently, she practiced with them but she also practiced when she was alone and for hours. She learned to balance her body on uneven ground. She learned to throw her knives and make contact at fifty yards; she practiced firing off various shots, quickly using her long bow and arrows, hitting her targets dead center. She knew that practice made for perfection and she would have to be perfect for her father to let her join his ranks.

She practiced the *Kick of the Striped Horse*; it was a powerful move and could break an opponent's legs and she performed the maneuver on the side of a tree until her feet were sore or until she fell asleep from exhaustion at the base of the tree. She was born to fight and no matter what anyone said she would continue to do what she enjoyed more than anything else in the world.

Time passed and the sky took on a dark, gloomy appearance like a storm was near. She heard her father yell and she turned and dropped to her stomach to look directly at him and listened as many of the men formed a huge circle to face her father; she listened carefully.

"All of you men here have shown me these past few months your commitment and dedication to becoming soldiers. You have sacrificed and it is your duty to protect your own family as well as your community in any situation. You are to become teachers of the young, so that means humbling your emotions because who will be the thinker among confusion? Pride and dignity is very strong in the wise! This land is our home, these skills I have taught you don't make you better than any other people here in Alkebu-lan, they just make you a more experienced man!"

Hutapsunnimoon watched her father's head turn to view all the men before he finished.

"So men, in a few short days you will be warriors, and I'm proud of each and every one of you. That's all for today. See you all tomorrow."

She watched the men began to break up and go their separate ways. Many carried their weapons and shields and some wore head protection, which was something new to her. She looked around and saw that someone was looking up at her, a trainer. She began to slide backwards on her stomach. Then reaching her feet, she ran as fast as her legs could carry her.

She knew someone could come to investigate her presence there but she really wasn't sure the person had recognized her since she was so high up. She ran on and on, trying to put as much distance between her and the soldiers and her father as she could. She ran along a river bed to the high grass then up a steep, rocky slope. Animals scattered all over the place after being interrupted from taking a drink from the river.

After traveling some distance from the training camp, she slowed to a walk. She realized she was now many miles from her home as she gazed around at the beauty of her surroundings. All she could hear was the music of the many birds that lived in the trees. She saw butterflies flying around her head in many flashing colors and as leaves began falling from the trees, she heard movement to her right and it was a large, striped antelope, the kind her father hunted and brought home for food.

She pulled her long bow from her back, staying as still as possible, then notching an arrow, she took aim at her target. The creature had large antlers and it was about forty feet away. Suddenly, several more came out a patch of bushes. She released the arrow and it flew through the air, hitting its intended target with a loud thump. The animal fell to the ground as the others ran off in different directions.

Hutapsunnimoon moved near. She was very proud of her accomplishment and she also knew the meat was good eating and she could use the skin to make clothing. This would show the men she was as much a skilled hunter as they were.

Women would often capture birds but nothing as large as an antelope. She heard birds calling out but she paid no attention, so consumed with her catch. She moved in, bending down next to the animal as she took a deep breath to calm herself.

Using the knife she retrieved from a pocket at the side of her leg, she cut the animal's throat to end its suffering. The birds continued to chirp excitedly. She then heard a growl somewhere behind her and she turned quickly, knives pointing, eyes sharp to see a leopard bearing down on her. Its color mixed into its surroundings and it growled again as it moved closer to her. She was half–relieved it wasn't the huge, golden brown cat that roamed the land with its pride but still she had a lot of respect for this wild beast, for it was strong and known for killing men in her community. But she wasn't about to give up her kill to this beast, not now, not ever.

She pulled one of the arrows out, holding it in her left hand while her knife was in her right. She faced the beast, yelling, "Go on!! Get away!!!! Go somewhere else to find your meal, beast!!!!"

Her eyes closed a bit as her muscles tightened and her arms extended outward. It did nothing to deter the beast as it marched forward, growling loudly again but she was determined not to let her first kill go without a fight.

Then the beast charged. Hutapsunnimoon planted her right foot as the beast leaped up going for her neck. She ducked then rolled to her left side and as she turned toward the beast it reached out its claws, slicing a deep cut into her right arm, she screamed out.

"OOOH!! Get back beast before I have to kill you!"

Her anger mounted while blood ran down her arm, she stepped forward to protect her prize. This time, the animal circled and she readied herself, once again. She could feel the trickles of blood cascading down her arm.

She moved in a circle to keep the beast out in front of her. Her heartbeat was rapid in her chest while her body stayed tense, waiting for the next attack. The beast rushed at her, growling low in its chest. She watched the beast swipe at her using its right claw and using the arrow in her left hand, she was able to block the attack. She then thrust her right hand forward while holding the knife in hopes of injuring the animal.

It backed away quickly, growling loudly. The creature was trying to kill her but she was past the point of relinquishing her prize. This beast had injured her and now she was mad and hell bent on killing it.

She kept low in order to anticipate its next attack. Her injury was beginning to throb and she knew the blood alone was enough to make the beast attack her again so she thrust forward with the arrow, yelling loudly while keeping the beast at a distance.

It circled again, this time much quicker, and then raced in for the kill, leaping up towards her neck. She fell backwards, hitting the ground hard, but at the same time lunging the arrow upward with all of the strength she had left in her body. The arrow made contact with the beast's chest. Using her feet, she kicked the beast back over her head and before it hit the ground, she was back on her feet facing the beast with only her knife in her hand.

A few short feet away, the creature lay in its own blood and she heard it roar for its last time. She looked around quickly, knowing the conflict might attract the attention of large predators so she quickly retrieved her arrow from the antelope, discarding this smaller prey and picking up the wild beast instead, placing it over her shoulder and moving off in the direction of her home. This will be the greatest prize, especially for a woman.

It would show she is a hunter with great courage! She smiled, thinking about the looks on the men's faces as she headed home.

Chapter 7

Northern Alkebu-lan, City of Kemet. The Marketplace

Thousands of people gathered as items were being sold. Their voices carried across the winds as children ran around hiding from their parents and animals roamed freely.

Ahknonkineton worked the stand selling many items. Since early this morning, the lines had been full and as he looked up through the crowded gathering, he saw many more were moving towards his station. His uncle's wife, Tu-ney, was working the stand right next to him.

The cloudy sky above showed signs of the coming rain but it did nothing to deter the crowds still filling the market place. Hundreds come to trade or marvel at the huge, golden structures and statues that make up the city of Kemet, Alkebu-lan's most glorious city.

Visitors lived in remote places and dense jungles or mountains and valleys where their homes are made of stone or mud or were carved deep into the rocky hillside. Their clothing, their language and beliefs, all were so very different in many ways.

Their complexions range from the darkest of black to a light brown and every shade of eye color imaginable. Some wore braided hair, others no hair. Many wore designs that distinguished their community and fashion styles that ranged from high fashion, to far beyond normal.

Many of the ladies walked around with large, gold chains with charms around their necks, waist and legs. Ahknon looked on and had seen it all and nothing seemed to faze him. His uncle, E-Newtu, was busy as always, working on helping the needy people, providing service to patients and would need to make them well again. It seemed to Ahknon that the lines were getting longer as many of the sick came in calling.

One of the best-selling items is the healing roots and Tu-ney was selling them along with dried plants that numb pain. Seeing her made him think about his own mother. He then looked at the spear in his right hand, the only memory of his father which he carried everywhere.

He began to wonder where the wise man Imhotep was hiding, knowing he could be anywhere. The last time they spoke, Imhotep had promised to find time to speak with him but now it's been many moons since he last saw the wanderer. He had questions that he felt only the wise man could answer.

Ahknon remembered his mother telling him stories about his father searching the skies and the mountains across the large ocean toward the north where the fair–skin dewells live, but the only memories he has left of his father are those when he hunted with him many years ago. Ahknon remembers using his father's spear as a young boy. He was also taught by his father three basic attack formations that he never forgot.

One maneuver was spear level to the ground. It was when the spear was raised and thrown. The second was when the spear was flat and tossed, which was his favorite move and then the third was basic strikes and maneuver. He remembered his father as a very humble man so he sought to be just like him and that is why he tried to expel trouble among those gathered in the marketplace. He knew that many acted on emotions that clouded a person's judgment.

He had fond memories of the times he spent with his dad. But one of the reasons he wanted to speak to Imhotep was that he felt Imhotep and his father in many ways were a lot alike and this and could possibly shed light on some things he needed answers to.

A woman's voice brought him out of his daydream,

"Hello, how may I help you?" he said.

The woman placed her order and as Ahknon filled it, a few other customers came and he sold them what they needed. He looked over to his uncle's tent and the lines there were shorter. He wanted to question his uncle about Imhotep; the waiting was eating him up inside. Just knowing the truth about his father would bring him some closure.

The clouds opened up as the sun's rays baked the sands. It was past midday as the sun moved closer to the western skies. The entertainment tent was about one hundred feet away. There were fire eaters, dancing women, and acrobats performing the most dangerous acts for the entertainment of those that came from great distances to marvel at such a grand affair and tonight, Ahknon decided that he was going to pay it a visit.

Several hours had passed. Ahknon began to place items away in bags, helping his aunt pack things away. He gathered the animals, placing them in a small fence behind his uncle's tent. He walked just behind Tu-ney as she entered his uncle's tent.

When he entered, his uncle was sitting on a large pillow; his eyes were closed and his dark complexion shone from the large, wax candles that illuminated the inside. Tu-ney took a seat next to him and she whispered a few words inside his ear, knowing he was waiting to speak with his uncle.

E-Newtu's eyes opened and Ahknon moved closer.

"Uncle, where is the wise man, Imhotep?" said Ahknon.

E-Newtu looked at Ahknon wondering the reason for the question; he looked at his wife, Tu-ney, who got up to leave the room; when she left he said,

"Why do you want to know about Imhotep? What concern is he to you?"

"Well Uncle, before he took his leave, we talked and then I told him I needed to speak with him in private once he returned. Now months have passed," said Ahknon, frustrated.

"Well, Imhotep moves like the wind. No one knows where he goes or where he comes from but right now he searches for something and once he finds it, he will return here to see me. Do you mind if I ask you the reason for the questioning?" Ahknon paused for a few moments.

"Well Uncle, I thought maybe Imhotep would have information about my father since you know he moves around a lot. I only have bits and pieces of his life and I wanted some closure, Ahknon gazed over at several candles to his right, looking into the flickering light as if in thought.

"Well now, I can see your interest and you may be right! Imhotep sees all and if anyone may have information on your father, it's him," E-Newtu continued, "but rest assured he will be back."

Months passed and there was no sign of Imhotep. Ahknon and his uncle begin to wonder about the old traveler but the days continued like normal and Ahknon found the shows in the entertainment tent every night to be very delightful.

Khart-Haddan (Carthagen)

On the top of one of the tallest mountains in Alkebu-lan, it is also known as, the raging monster. The mountain rumbles violently, expels fire and stands at the sheer height of forty thousand feet. This land is called Khart-Haddan. The tribes who live here are sailors who travel the vast seas. They often trade with the pale–skinned people across the great seas and many other tribes along the coastal lines.

Khart-Haddan, a community of dark, almond brown people with long black, stringy hair that flows down their backs. The men often wear their hair in various styles other than just long.

The winds bellowed loudly as the snow fell, covering the mountain top. The sky was dark and cloudy and temperatures dropped to ten degrees. The wanderer, known as Imhotep, sat still upon the mountain top gazing upward, eyes focused, staring, searching the dark cloud. The loud winds screamed out blowing snow in all directions but the weather had no effect on him; the snow seemed to drift slowly away from his body. Sounds reached his ears and he closed his eyes to focus, hoping to create a mental picture inside his mind of what he was hearing.

He has been here now for well over five months, catching and eating the small creatures that ventured near, as well as plant life that grew here to keep up his strength and to fuel his body. His ears moved and twitched. He knew there was something coming, he could hear it vaguely. It was still some distance away or it could be the weather but normally the weather never made the kind of sounds he was hearing.

He looked up into the snow covered skies and in the direction the sound is coming from. To him, the sounds were getting louder but the thick clouds prevented his view. He cursed loudly as his eyes expanded to take in more of the sky above. The cold wind bellowed loudly again as snow was tossed in all directions and his keen ears thought he heard movement somewhere inside the mountain. However, he cast those thoughts aside because from his experience the mountain rumbling was a normal affair, especially when the mountain was ready to push out the fire rock, he thought.

This place was secluded from the rest of the world; no man could reach the peak of the mountain top without being subdued by the cold weather. His ears twitched and he turned his head quickly right then left. Eyes closed, he heard the sounds again. This time above his head, then he heard several, soft footsteps moving somewhere behind him. He opened his eyes looking off the side of the mountain edge and he begins to wonder what form of beast lived this far up; for sure he knew it was no man.

As the creatures moved closer and closer to him, he focused on the sky again. Then he felt the presence of five humanoids moving out of sight in different angles camouflaged by the rocky slopes and the downpour of snow. He began motioning his hands in a circle, then whispered a few words and instantly, nine glowing orbs appeared just above his head, three glowed red hot, three the color of the ocean clear and three others brighter than the falling, white snow. Still looking upward, he had no concerns; he could detect the dark arts if the creatures held any.

In his home world, he was called Aquantoria, from the planet Aquan beyond the Black Hole, an object whose escape velocity equals the speed of light, a sector that's gravitational pull drew light sounds then transferred it to a large solar system in a parallel universe with hundreds of planets, stars and moons.

His planet was composed mostly of water; the Aquanians lived an aquatic existence below the great seas and some of his people like him were called wanderers. Here on Alkebu-lan, they thought of people like him as Shamans or witch doctors.

On his planet, his powers would have grown but here, he only had the use of three of the planet's four elements; fire, air and water. His home world had been destroyed and for over one thousand years, he has lived on this new but young world of Alkebu-lan. Imhotep believed he was the only survivor. His hope was to one day return to space to exact revenge on a race called Garthian.

This three–armed humanoid, known as Garthians, saw space as a place of conquest, his past thoughts dwindled and he now focused on the beast moving in to harm him. The creature was still moving forward slowly while his eyes caught the first sight of the mechanical ship breaking the atmosphere, striking fast towards the ground. The cloudy sky opened up for its coming; it wasn't a falling star, Imhotep thought; it kept moving fast.

It was a spacecraft with large lights flashing from the metal haul. Then he watched the ship break into three sections like a small explosion; he saw the flaring lights, the ship now moving in three separate destinations. One hit the ground farther to the northwest of him, another moved towards the southwest and the last headed south; the ship's tails fire, leaving a bright trail behind it. Imhotep's heart rumbled inside his chest like the fire mountain at that time.

His thoughts quickly returned and now all his focus was on the creature that wishes to ambush him. The creature was closing in on his position.

He saw the first creature's face. It was covered in a tri-colored, thick fur. The beast blended into its environment very well. Its eyes and sharp, angular teeth are as white as the snow falling from the sky and the beast stood about 7 feet tall, hunched over a bit and it hopped rather than walked on its two legs. Its muscle tone brought images of a powerful ape that lived in central Alkebu-lan and its face was familiar to him but he had no time to remember from where.

Before he had time to think, the first beast leaped high trying to land on top of him. Imhotep's finger moved forward and one of the glowing, red hot, fiery spheres shot upward while expanding, capturing the raging beast inside. Its body moved frantically while fire was consuming it, its cries echoed then it became silent within the glowing sphere and the stench of burnt flesh filled the air.

Another creature climbed down in a rush from the side of the mountain. Imhotep sent a sphere of solid ice heading the creature's way; the ice expanded, growing to eight times the size of the creature. It collided with the beast with a loud crash, the sound echoed through the mountaintop crushing the beast between the mountain and the solid, ice sphere.

Several more creatures tossed boulders at Imhotep, the rocky structure sailed through the air, crashing to the ground several feet from him; the ground rumbled. Imhotep released two other spheres of fire and they rocketed forward in the beast's direction, expanding and rolling across the ground, brightening its path, hitting the ground with an explosion of sound.

The beasts were jumping up and out in all directions. Imhotep then released three clear spheres of solid air which collided with the huge rocky structure; on impact, the boulder was blown to pieces. Nine more spheres appeared above Imhotep's head to replace the others.

He could see the whites of their sharp teeth and their strong, powerful arms and legs were bent on killing him. He waited and waited for them to move closer; it was a grave mistake to attack him directly.

He released all of his spheres and they moved like they had a mind of their own. Fire crashed to the ground as some of the creatures screamed in pain. Then another was hit by an invisible weapon that knocked it over the side of the mountain and to the ground; far, far down below you could hear its roar. The solid, ice spheres landed on two more, crushing their bodies to the ground. When the ground was clear, Imhotep looked around for other threats while two clear spheres had captured, and was now carrying, the creatures toward him, three feet off of the ground. His senses told him he was safe, as he continued to look around.

The solid air sphere stopped in front of him. Imhotep gazed up at the large beast wondering from where did these creature come from, they towered above his head; he noticed one of the captured beasts was hitting the cell with force but was unable to scratch its surface; it struggled to free itself, looking for a way out to continue its attack. The second beast had more experience; it calmly understood its predicament. It looked down at Imhotep through those white eyes; its mouth was open. Its eyes were searching, looking for an opening.

Imhotep motioned his hand to his right in anger of the beast's reaction as both spheres moved out over the mountain edge. Now the creature was looking down, dangling forty thousand feet above the surface below them, Imhotep looked down then back at the sphere. The calmer of the two creatures watched the sphere next to it disappear and its occupant fall down to his death. It looked at Imhotep with understanding.

"Yes, you have good sense," Imhotep said.

Imhotep spoke a few words then moved his finger. He brought the last sphere down to solid ground in front of him, still encased in the cell the beast stared on at its captor. Then Imhotep whispered to the creature, which seemed to understand him; surprised the beast listened,

"How many of you are living inside these mountains?" asked Imhotep.

The creature called out in rumbling tones which Imhotep understood. He recognized the creature which looked a bit different from what he had remembered, a humanoid who was a native of his universe and solar system, whose home world was also destroyed by the Garthians a few hundred years before his planet's destruction.

What remained of their race, now lived here in these mountains he thought. Their bodies had made an evolutionary change over time and the fur had thickened but everything else about the creature was the same. Imhotep looked the beast over.

"But why have you attacked me when I mean you no harm?" asked Imhotep.

The creature called out again in rumbled tones. He was explaining that they were afraid the youngling would find out they had occupied the mountain, which in turn would cause war. It would mean they would have to fight for the survival of their race, knowing the planet belonged to these younglings.

Imhotep understood the creature and its will to survive; for over a thousand years he had roamed Alkebu-lan and never once came across this race of humanoids. But he never had to stay upon the mountain for very long.

"Listen, I'm not your enemy. Many have died. My people were also victims of the Garthians, so we have a common enemy. I travel the world, similar to your people."

Imhotep spoke in the Aquanian language and the humanoid understood; it seemed happy to finally have found someone to talk with of another race. They shared experiences and hatred for the Garthian race.

Imhotep then freed the creature and they continued their talks. The humanoid introduced himself as Kokk and spoke of his leader, named Ick, as they both entered the mountain and traveled deep into the caves. This race was called the Cravistines and they occupied the many tunnels high above the people of Alkebu-lan, in a community unknown to the world below.

Imhotep met their leader, Ick, and many young and old and told the old stories of their homeworld well into the night and following days.

Chapter 8

Southern Alkebu-lan

The rainy season had come and gone and the trees sprouted up all over the land. While in the southern lands, the clouds began to break, making room for the sun. Birds sing their songs of praise as new flowers bloomed. Women were weaving baskets and clothing, preparing flour to make bread while children laughed and played a few short feet away from their mothers.

About one hundred yards away, inside one of the homes, Tutannharmoon gazed out his front window. He smiled at the other kids running around playing. As far as he could see, the land was green in color; the rainy season brought new life to his homelands.

Several months had passed since he was able to see families gathered working together. There were still puddles of water in places but for the most part the land was dry.

Also, in these months, Tutann had grown three feet taller and his body expanded; he was now much wider and taller than his mother and weighed as much as his father; this growth was a wonder to them all.

For several hours now he gazed out of his window until it was bathing time. The older he became the more responsible and independent he felt; he was now headed for the riverbank on his own as he carried his washcloth and clean clothing.

He sat his things on a tree branch then climbed into the river to begin washing up. First, he washed his head like his mother had told him, then his neck and as he began dipping his washing cloth in the water he noticed something strange sticking out of the river surface.

He ignored it as he slid under water to rinse off a bit and then Tutann began washing his entire body, scrubbing hard. He looked at the strange, shiny thing again, protruding from the river surface, a bright light entered his mind then he saw death, images of screaming people.

The images were indescribable, nothing like he had ever seen or experienced. He closed his eyes hoping to do away with these images but images popped up inside his mind again. The things were like him but were different in appearance. They ran to save themselves but their cries died quickly as large creatures of all shapes were devouring their bodies; the young of their race was used as a source of food.

Their calls for help only attracted the beasts. Lights exploded unlike any he had ever seen before. There were flying objects above the fleeing people.

Then a loud noise sounded, then nothing. Then the words entered his mind, *Bringer of Death, the Indestructible*. The ringing in his mind became louder, he covered his ears. He closed his eyes as flashes of light exploded inside his head again but this time the bodies littered the ground, unmoving.

The fighting waged on. The men protecting their families were hard pressed to stop the invaders. Whatever the creatures missed, the soldiers found and killed, showing no mercy at all. Although he was only a young boy, he understood and he cried at what was lost…so many lives gone.

Another light consumed his entire body and he began to feel differently. His body began to change and grow and he heard the words, *"Help us, you were chosen to help us."* He opened his mouth but no words came out.

He watched his chest expand, then his hands. He began to grow taller and much bigger as he looked down at himself. The sandals he wore on his feet ripped open as his feet grew large, even his clothing expanded. The huge tree in his backyard that towered over his home was beginning to get shorter. He also felt his skin tighten and become harder.

He rubbed his fingers across his skin's hard surface, splashing water on his face before climbing out. He stood next to the tree, still amazed by his appearance, for he was now eight times the height of his father and ten times as wide. He looked behind him at the strange object submerged in the river wondering why this happened, then he remembered its words.

Then the ground began to rumble all of a sudden and it got louder and louder and then it registered to Tutann what was responsible for making the noise. His heart thumped in his chest. *Where were his mother and father*, he thought? Then his thought of the women out front with their children and his big legs hit the ground with a loud thumping, running, propelling his body forward as he leaped high into the air above his home, soaring across the sky, his huge arms spread outward.

In the distance, he saw his father Butann and the soldiers standing in place to block the stampeding wild mammoths, he headed towards them. They are huge beasts. Some standing 19 feet tall, which was much large than the animals they used on their farms and lands.

There were over fifty men holding spears or carrying swords, making as much noise as possible by clashing the blades together, screaming as well. The stampeding wild beast was heading toward his home. These were large beasts with trunks and huge, sharp tusks extending from their mouths. Their skin is coated with a thick, wooly fur and they were well–known for killing other animals that ventured too close to their pack.

Butann stood strong with over two hundred men ready to kill a few of these beasts, if it was remotely possible. He had lost quite a few men struggling with these beasts. He and his men knew that these animals would totally destroy their homes and scatter their families all across southern Alkebu-lan, so this attempt was worth the sacrifice of lives to keep their homes safe.

Butann, a tall dark man of rippling muscles, called out to one of his men. "Juiku, get back to the community and make sure everyone is prepared to leave. It's important that they get only the things they need now or it will mean certain death for many! We will continue to try to change the beast's direction but as it looks now it will be impossible. Now go!"

Juiku was one of the youngest soldiers. He was short in stature but very strong. "Yes sir!" he answered and then ran into the high grass behind the men.

Butann watched him go, hoping he reached the homes in time. The animals were right on top of them. Only months ago, these herds were many miles away. He thought the rainy season turned the wild beasts around but the ground vibrated as they marched closer, kicking up dust behind them and from where he stood, he knew it had to be well over fifty of them.

But each of his men stood their ground, shouting and blocking the path. He looked back once more and farther in the distance, he could see the families moving out, carrying items with them. He turned back and readied his men for an attack. He banged his swords together in unison with his men. He then thought about his wife, Kisse and his son, Tutannharmoon and was glad he had prepared them for this.

The wild animals were now one hundred fifty feet away and closing the distance but the men held fast, counting down until impact. They were preparing to fight to the death when suddenly a huge shadow covered the sun's light as it moved in from somewhere behind them. They looked up, startled as a large figure crashed to the ground in front of them the ground shook. The sound echoed for miles around and they looked up at a beast with skin as black as their own and a body large than anything they had ever seen appeared. When it turned to them they all backed up, afraid now of this new threat.

The ground behind the huge creature rumbled as Butann looked up at the giant. The muscle tone of its arms and legs was beyond anything he had ever seen, resembling metal found deep inside the caves to the east and the creature towered over them like they were mere ants that walked the soil.

Then Butann looked into the creatures eyes to see a face he vaguely recognized which caused him to pause. His men were all behind him holding their weapons and ready to attack when suddenly one of his men yelled excitedly, "Butann, it's your son Tutannharmoon!"

"Yes it is! He came to protect his home and community," another shouted, "but how?"

All the soldiers gazed upward, now recognizing the young child by his eyes and face while the rest of him was so different. Butann's brain knew this was his son but his eyes could only question. *How could this be Tutann, so large and powerful? How did this happen?* Butann watched Tutann turn and rush toward the stampeding animals in full attack mode, each step he took rattled the ground with force. Butann, concerned for his son, waited, their weapons raised.

Tutann was now angry as he landed in front of his father and the other men after leaping over his house into a field over two hundred yards away. His second leap brought him right in front of the gathered soldiers but with no time to spare, he turned and rushed towards the powerful, charging animals.

He faced the two lead animals with their seventeen foot long tusks extending from their mouths and completely covered in wooly hair. He crashed right into both beasts and the tusks snapped off loudly from the impact. Tutann stopped them in their tracks and they let out loud, wailing sounds.

He took hold of their heads and slammed them together. The force was so powerful that the creatures hit the ground at his side unmoving. A third and fourth were coming at him fast. *The Bringer of Death, the Indestructible* played inside his mind as the third creature slammed right into him. It came to a stop like it had hit a mountain and Tutann lifted the huge beast up over his head before tossing it in the direction of the following pride. It was twice his size but it was light in his arms. It played over and over in his mind that these beasts killed men in his community as it sailed into the air like it was a stone being tossed by a child. It cried out as it crashed into the beasts behind it and they hit the ground with a thud sending up dirt and rocks. He threw out his right hand connecting with another beasts head. Then Tutann took hold of its tusks, planted his feet and swung the beast around in a circle above his head. Then he released it and it sailed through the air until it hit a patch of trees over three hundred yards away, letting out a loud wail as dust and the breaking of trees echoed back to their ears.

Then Tutann was hit in the back and the force of it propelled him forward. He backhanded the beast; the impact and force put the beast too sleep, knocked it out and it lay cold and unmoving on the ground. He reached down and broke off the tusks with a loud cracking then flung them into the distance. He then turned toward the last of the animals and yelled loudly out over the landside, his voice growled with anger. All of the animals stopped at once, as they gazed at the creature much more powerful than them.

Tutann stomped the ground hard and the ground shook and echoed around the landside; the mammoths turn, heading off into the distance. The ones Tutann confronted were slow getting to their feet but raced off in high pursuit of their pride.

He stayed in place until they all had left his sight. Then he heard his people celebrating behind him. He turned, taking one step, and leaping back towards his home, leaving the ground and the soldiers behind as he sailed through the air and he hit the ground behind his house near the riverbed three thousand yards away.

He began to look around wondering how he became this thing. These are the questions that needed answering and then he remembered the flash of light before he changed. He walked softly towards the riverbank. The fast moving water was headed farther south and he looked at the small, shiny object still extending out of the water surface.

As he stepped closer the light from the shiny object illuminated his body. This time he heard someone or something talking. Words he could not understand and for a time he just listened. He sat at the side of the bank rubbing his head and then the sound of his mother calling his name reached him. He turned to watch her enter the yard from the rear door.

Tutann watched his mother stop and he stood up. She looked upon him with fear, hands raised before her face as she was about to scream. His rumbling voice carried to his mother's ears.

"It's me, mother, your son, Tutann." He watched his mother's demeanor change at the sound of his voice. He knew she recognized his voice somewhere within the rumbling tones.

"My son, what has happened to you?" Kisse said, tears now in her eyes; she rushed through the yard to her son. When she reached him, she watched him bend down to one knee and take her in his large arms. As the huge figure of her boy held her gently, she held his large chin in her hands.

"Here I am worried sick about you child. A soldier came to inform us that we were to leave and when I came looking for you, you were nowhere to be found. I was scared you had fled without me but I'm happy to have learned you are well, what happen to you Tutann? What is this new transformation?"

"Well, Mother, I think it has something to do with a large, shiny metal submerged in the river; it flashed lights across my body just before I became this...thing," Tutann said, pointing to the river then standing to show his mother what he had become.

"Tutann, you will always be special to me no matter what changes you go through. For a very long time now, I have known you were born to do special things. Your growth was always amazing, you have always been much large than the other children and your perception and understanding was advanced. Your father and I talked about it on several occasions," Kisse said, looking Tutann directly in the eyes. "Your destiny was written before I gave birth to you. Understand?"

"Really, Mother, where will I live? I'm an outcast! Too large to be here among my people and if what you say is true, when will these other things be revealed to me?"

"Soon, son. I will help you. You are never alone, OK?" Kisse replied.

Tutann began laughing. Low at first, then louder. His voice traveling across the landscape. Kisse looked up and asked, "Why are you laughing so, Tutann?"

"Because, Mother, even standing before you as a beast, you still love me and that alone makes me feel better."

"Tutannharmoon, you are my child, my first and only born. You are no beast in my eyes. You're still my little boy."

Then he and his mother turned at the sound of many footsteps heading their way. He watched his father walk between two homes as the entire community followed behind him and the people began to scream his name "Tutann, Tutann, Tutann,

Tutann!" Kisse smiled and held her hands together looking at the crowd of people then she turned and looked up at her huge son.

Tutann looked down at his people and they made him feel good. They were showing him that he was no outcast among them. They were praising him for saving their homes. It was a part of him to help people and they accepted that. For the rest of that night, they celebrated and sat around telling stories of how he ran the huge beasts off.

The next morning the villagers came to Kisse and Butannharmoon's home. It was a clear morning and Tutann was fast asleep in the back yard near the river. He awoke to hear his father and mother speaking of how they wished to build him a home of his own that would accommodate his size. They all agreed and were willing to build him a place among them.

Tutann then heard one man speaking.

"There's a mountain that's hollow inside and it is big enough to accommodate Tutannharmoon with other rooms inside for him to be able to move around without being cramped, also it's not far from our community." But his father, Butann, interjected by saying,

"We must let my son make the decision; these decisions could only be made by him. Yes he was a child yesterday but now…" his voice trailed off. "I would want Tutann as close as possible but the choice will be his to make."

Later that day, Tutannharmoon and the families traveled a few miles to the south where the large mountains appeared from out of nowhere. His mother and father were by his side and

Tutann was amazed at how beautiful the lands were. There were wild animals in many colors and shades and many had horns upon their heads.

He gazed about himself in wonder, it was the very first time he had been this far from the village and a new world lay before his eyes. To his right, in the distance, was a huge river, which he believed connected to the one in the back of his home. He could see large creatures in the water with large teeth and heads as well as other large, lizard type beasts lying on the shoreline with gaping mouths. Birds sang in unison with the many insects.

The splendor was a bit much to take in for one day and as they marched closer and closer to the mountains he could feel his anticipation building. Time seemed to pass slowly but it wasn't long before he arrived at his new home. One side of the mountain gave way to a large entrance twice his height.

Entering the place, he strolled through the several rooms inside. It was roomy enough and the ceiling inside was high. He felt he could be comfortable here, at least until he found out the meaning of his transformation and how to live with it. This would be a good place for him to live. He moved back to the cave entrance and stepped out to see the villagers anxiously waiting on his answer. They stood quietly but alert, searching his face for answers.

He looked at his mother and father and nodded his head up and down and said,

"This is a great place for me, just for now until I find out what is happening. I want to thank you all for making me feel comfortable. This is a drastic turn of events in my life so your kindness is what's helping me through it."

Tutann looked around at all his people that were gathered, making sure everyone understood that his words were sincere, then he looked down upon his mother and father again and said, "Mother, Father, I will be home every single day to see you." The crowd began to laugh at the fact that he was physically no longer a child but his words contradicted that fact.

His mother stood in front of his father looking up at the giant figure of her son while her husband sat his hand on her shoulder.

"Does this place satisfy you because if not, I want you to come back home Tutannharmoon?" Her facial expression softened her words and betrayed the emotions in her voice. To her, he was still her little boy, although his time as a child was cut short. She was just beginning to enjoy and learn more and more about her young child but she knew she would see him every day, that part wouldn't change. She would see to it.

"Yes it's a great place, Mother."

The community stayed until the sun began to set. They brought him food, blankets and other things he would need to be an independent man. They chanted his name a few more times before heading home. He watched them go until they were out of his sight then he entered the cave to rest for the night.

Chapter 9

Several hundred miles up north and west of Tutann

Hutapsunnimoon raced across the wide open plains; her legs carrying her on a constant path forward. She breathed in the fresh air settling deeply into her lungs as her hair drifted behind her in the wind. She passed men hunting a short distance away in a patch of trees to her left.

As they watched her pass by giving her stern looks, she gazed their way then continued on her path. Antelope, leaping high, moved quickly away from her in the opposite direction. She carried her long bow and arrows on her back and at her thigh were her freshly cleaned knives. She wore her new one-piece, cat skin outfit that covered her completely at the top and traveled down to reveal half of her thighs. It was her badge of honor.

The land she moved upon was flat for miles around and she could see it was raining to the east of her. Masses of clouds covered the sky in the north as she moved south. She felt free! Free to roam around as she wished because she had pleased her father with her hunting skills.

When she had returned that day with her kill, everyone knew that the large cat that had killed and terrorized them was no more. Now many of the women praised her for killing such a beast and protecting them. The men were another story but she did not let it bother her for she had accomplished what they did not and she knew it was jealousy.

Her father, Nassir, had always warned her about watching the men practice their war skills from a top of the range and she tried to deny it but when her father suddenly tried to attack her she reacted automatically, using a certain block formation then striking outward with her hands, more so to protect herself. She attacked using several kicks. Her father's attack was serious, although he meant to do no harm but she stayed calm and continued to fight back. Several strikes came in at her face and she blocked them, stepping in with a few strikes of her own. But her father connected on occasion and still she fought on until he stopped and said,

"Hutap, you have lied to me!!!!! You have broken every rule set in place by the elder's before me and the rules of our community!!!!"

All she could do was hold her head down, eyes glued to the floor.

"Your skills are very good daughter but don't ever let me catch you spying upon the training sites! Do you understand???"

"Yes father," said Hutapsunnimoon, her voice cried in disappointment.

She remembered her father looked down at her as she looked at the floor. He knew she had warrior blood running through her veins and he hated to admit it but he was just like her at that age and he was very proud of her advancement in her fighting skills. He began walking away from her fighting against his inner feelings. There were communities where women are warriors and good fighters but in his community women were forbidden to practice war tactic. He walked away, turning his back to his daughter, heading to his room a few steps away; he paused a few seconds then he turned and said quietly, looking around making certain no one heard him,

"Hutapsunnimoon, I will train you in private." Then he turned walking away.

She remembered watching him go and she knew he was proud of her although he had not said a single such word. His last statement said everything. They were two of the same even though she was a woman. Even her mother, Inzinger, understood her passions of wanting to explore new places and things, hunting and fighting.

She was lost in her daydreams, smiling broadly as her legs pushed her forward. Her endurance was remarkable; for over several miles she kept up the same pace in the high grass using her hands to keep the grass from hitting her face. She moved past animals lying in cover. She let out a laugh and then came to a sudden stop.

A few short feet from where she stood, the high grass sunk down into a three foot circle. She looked around noticing that only in this particular spot no high grass grew from the soil. It was strange to her because for miles and miles as far as the eye could see was nothing but high grass except in this secluded place. She wondered what could have created it.

Then something bright caught her eye and when she looked she noticed some kind of metal was sticking out of the soil. It flashed a light of many colors which brought her closer to the shiny object. It was very long and as she moved closer it was as if the flashing light seemed to call to her, she heard sounds that comforted her and she moved right up to the object. She noticed that the metal was connected to a large piece hidden beneath the soil. She stepped on that part of the ground hard then began stomping it with her feet.

Now the sound was different and she wondered how it found its way into the soil at all, she looked up then around then down on this strange object. She traveled these lands all the time and had never encountered anything like this before and she had been at that very spot. But the song coming from it entered her mind so she inched even closer, reaching out to the object. It flashed again.

Standing above it she reached out with her right hand, touching the metal; it was cool to the touch. She watched light cascade over her hand so she released the metal then turned her hand around, watching the light travel up her arm then through her entire body.

Then screaming entered her mind. She turned around quickly not understanding what was happening. She bolted forward thinking what she was hearing was someone calling for help and her legs pushed her forward at neck breaking speed. She passed the trees in seconds; everything around her was a blur.

She then passed the fastest moving land predator, a wild cat tracking antelope and it was as if the cat was moving in slow motion. Everything moved in the blink of an eye; the landside, trees, rivers. When she finally stopped and took a look around, she was many miles from her home in a place she has never been before. She rubbed her head in confusion wondering what had just happened.

Turning around she began walking home. She had to be quick. The sun was already heading west and she did not want her parents worried about her.

Chapter 10

Kemet City

The crowd was roaming around searching the market as usual. Each day brought new faces from the surrounding communities around Alkebu-lan. Ahknonkineton worked throughout the day assisting the many customers that flocked to his uncle's stand. Patches of clouds moved north and the ground was moist from the brief rain showers during the day. Day was quickly becoming night.

Ahknon placed items in a cloth bag before giving it to one of the customers. "You have a nice day, my lady," he said.

Then the sounds of laughter caught his attention. He turned to see three women walking past his stand; one in particular was looking back at him wearing some of the most revealing attire. He marveled at their smooth, brown skin and noticed their clothing was completely white. They had painted toes and fingernails and their hips and waistlines and exceptionally curved, rear ends fit well inside their clothing.

The blouses were cut short to reveal the women's mid-sections. He was captivated by their beauty, then Tu-ney brushed up against him spoiling his day dreaming.

"Young man, don't you know you can go blind staring at women like that," Tu-ney said, her hand was on her hip, her eyes searching his for an answer.

"Well, I wasn't really looking," Ahknon said, unable to come up with a better answer.

"Men will always be men, go on and enjoy yourself. I will take care of things here. You are such a good worker and a young man needs time to himself." She smiled up at him and continued, "Don't worry about your uncle. He will not be looking for you. I can handle him."

"Are you sure? I could find those lovely ladies later," Ahknon said, looking down at Tu-ney then into the crowds trying to spot the lovely ladies a few yards off walking slowly through the crowds.

"Yes! Now go. But don't let those women corrupt you Ahknon," said Tu-ney, reaching up to touch the side of his face tenderly.

He looked down at her with a smile and said, "Thank you."

Then taking hold of his spear, he rushed off in the direction of the three women, looking back at Tu-ney before he left. Carrying the spear made him think about the wanderer, Imhotep, again. Each day he had been away only reinforced his commitment to find answers about his father. It was an issue he would not stress over but when the time was right he promised that once he saw Imhotep again he would not let the wise one out of his sight without having a conversation.

After moving through the crowded square he finally caught up to the beautiful dark–skinned women strolling while talking with one another. Passing a stand that sold large flowers, he stopped to purchase a few in many colors and he carried the flowers towards the women.

"Hello ladies, I do believe you dropped these."

All three women turned to look up at this tall figure of a man. Ahknon noticed the women were impressed so he smiled and got a closer look at the women; it only showed they were more beautiful than he had first expected. The tallest of the three had to be around 5 feet 11 inches tall because at 6 feet 8 inches he towered over her and many others around the square.

Her skin was a deep, creamy brown and her hair was in braids similar to his hair. Her face appeared so young and pure and when she smiled, her teeth were as white as the ice that coated the mountaintops. He noticed they all had the same smiles and a distinct air of maturity.

"Who are you?" the tallest one spoke first. Her two companions began to giggle softly then one of them said,

"He is the one that was working in one of the stands we passed, don't you remember?" Then she held her hand out in front of her.

As he took her hand he said, "Well ladies, my name is Ahknonkineton but you can call me Ahknon," bowing low in respect.

When he rose up he gave the tallest woman the beautiful large colorful flowers, then he gave each of her companions the yellow and blue flowers. He noticed her mouth was small but she had full lips, her eyes were round and the color of the sand in the desert. He thought her to be the most perfect woman to look at, although her friends were also beautiful.

"Well Ahknon, my name is Isis," she said, touching her chest. "And these two are my cousins, Kentorey and Ethenon," she finished.

"How are you, Ahknon?" said Kentorey, waving.

"You're a very handsome man," said Ethenon, touching her chest while smiling up at him.

"I hope you three don't mind me asking but where are you going?" Ahknon said.

"Well, we are just out for a walk before it gets dark," Isis said.

"Maybe I could act as your personal bodyguard in your travels of the marketplace? If you say yes, it would be my honor," Ahknon said.

"Do you always carry that spear?" Isis asked.

"Yes, of course, it is a special gift and how else would I protect you from the bad people?" Ahknon said. That comment made the women smile.

"Yes, we would very much enjoy your company Ahknon, if you would accompany us on our way."

As they continued their walk, many of the stand owners begin to light torches as the sky began to grow dark. The music playing from the many instruments within the square is a melodious backdrop to the clusters of lights as men and women walked and talked holding on to one another but still the crowded place seemed to burst with life under the nocturnal skies.

"So are you from around here?" asked Isis.

"Well, for many years, I lived on the border lands of the city but after my mother passed, I came here to live and work for my uncle. He is teaching me the trade to become a medicine man," said Ahknon.

"Well, we are all sorry to hear about the passing of your mother," said Kentorey.

Ahknon noticed that Kentorey and Ethenon were actually twins. They were just a bit lighter than their cousin, Isis, and a few feet shorter but each of them was very curvaceous. The twins wore their hair in afros several inches thick and high, a style preferred by most women of Kemet.

"Were the two of you very close?" said Ethenon, referring to his mother.

Ahknon looked at the women in front of him and realized they must be children to one of the high officials within the city gates because of the gold around their necks and the scent of heavily perfumed oils wafting off of them.

"Yes, my mother and I were very close, especially after my father died," Ahknon said.

The women began to console him and he was surprised by their affection; soon after, they entered the wild animal tent to look at the collected species. Ahknon noticed the men inside paying very close attention to the gold on the three women's necks and he moved closer to them. A little while later they all exited the tent and Ahknon casually looked behind them, while the three women were busy talking and unaware of the three men from inside the wild animal tent following them a few paces back. Ahknon positioned himself between the ladies and the following men, his spear held firmly in his right hand. He tried to listen carefully to the men's footsteps but the women's laughter made it difficult.

"I think Ahknon has already figured it out cousins, that the two of you are twins," said Isis.

"No, he did not, Isis, but now he probably heard you and knows now!" said Ethenon.

"Yes, Ethenon you're right. Isis spoiled the surprise. Did you know, Ahknon?" asked Kentorey.

All the women turned to look at Ahknon, smiling, then Isis screamed, "Look out Ahknon!" as she and her cousin drew backwards watching three men rush towards them.

His father had taught him many things, one of the first being how to protect himself, as he heard his father's voice in his mind he yelled out, "Spear level to the ground."

Normally, he would be very diplomatic when handling issues like this but he understood there was no talking with these men. They were there to claim the women's jewelry and he couldn't have that. He went into a quick spin with his knees bent, extending his spear out and low to the ground. It came around quickly and the spear collided with the mens' legs with a loud crack. When Ahknon got to his feet the men were on the ground but they managed to quickly rise to their feet.

Two of the men were screaming from their pain but it did nothing to prevent them from moving in to attack a second time. The men wore dark clothing and had their faces covered.

Ahknon thought they wore the mask to make their escape a little easier; as he towered over the three men now with his spear firmly held in his right hand and his right leg lifted off the ground and his left arm extended towards the attackers.

THE EPIC SAGA OF ALKEBU-LAN

They stood directly a few yards in front of him and the largest of the three men rushed in first, trying to take hold of Ahknon. He yelled, "Spear toss," as he reversed his body, spinning his spear around his back into his left hand. He spun the spear above his head releasing the spear. It flipped on its end as it headed for the attacker, smashing the fellow in the face. Bones could be heard cracking as the would-be thief's body was tossed backwards and he hit the ground as his men rushed in to assist him.

Ahknon's spear bounced back into his hands after connecting with the thief's face. He then went into his next move as he called out, "Spear rising!"

The first of the two men rushed towards him as Ahknon stepped forward to meet them bringing his spear upward and connecting with the first fellow's chin. A breaking sound could be heard and Ahknon heard the women scream but did not stop. He then brought the spear back down knocking the thief off to his left side. The man crashed to the ground head first. The third man rushed in quickly, holding a knife in his right hand. Ahknon swung his spear sideways, connecting with the thief's rib cage with brutal force. He watched the man's face, contorted with pain and in one motion he quickly brought his spear in to block the thief's upward thrust, pushing the knife away from him. Ahknon quickly delivered five punches to the man's face using his left hand then used his spear to connect with the man's head with a loud crack and the thief dropped to the ground out cold.

The first man was back on his feet holding his face together and rushed in for another attack. Ahknon saw that the thief hadn't learned his lesson so he went to the spear toss again, sending his spear directly at the charging men's legs. It hit him with another loud crack as the man screamed out loudly while his body turned and twisted into the air, crashing down to the ground in an awkward position. He lay there unmoving as Ahknon's spear returned through the air into his waiting hands.

He looked around at the thieves on the ground. Two were unmoving and the third was wailing in pain. The sky was dark now and a gathering people began to move around the three men on the ground. The ladies rushed to Ahknon's side, looking down at the thieves.

"Are you hurt Ahknon?" Isis cried out with concern.

"How were you able to beat all three men?" Kentorey said in disbelief, with her eyes wide with awe and fear.

"I am glad we chose you as our personal bodyguard tonight. There was no one better suited for the position," Ethenon said, smiling up at Ahknon. Then she looked around at the people moving in to view the men on the ground.

"Ladies, you can relax now, there are no others. I spotted these men watching you closely after leaving the animal tent and you are totally safe now," he said, with a reassuring smile.

They all moved closer together and began their walk back to the middle of the marketplace towards the largest building in the square.

"Will you be at the same place tomorrow?" Isis asked, her eyes searching his face.

"Yes, Isis, I will be there, that station is where I work and live for now," Ahknon said, smiling down at the lovely women.

"We were hoping we could see you again tomorrow," said Isis.

"I heard nothing from your cousins, Isis? Is it you who wants to see me or am I just to be your bodyguard?" asked Ahknon.

"Well, we, I mean I, want to see you tomorrow," she stammered. "Will you be busy all day or will we be able to meet with you?"

Her smile was delightful and it felt good to be in the presence of such beautiful women but three was a bit much for him and he acknowledged to himself that he favored the company of just Isis and in time he will have time alone, but until then he wanted to get to know all three of these women better.

"Ok, same time tomorrow."

"Yes and maybe this time it will be a bit more peaceful," said Isis, with a laugh and a wave.

After dropping the women at the city gates, Ahknon watched the three women moving up the steps. Once they reached the top they all turned to wave their goodbyes and he in turned waved back. When they were out of sight, he turned around, heading back to his uncle's tent. Thoughts of Isis stayed on his mind and he smiled thinking tomorrow could not come fast enough.

Three months had passed and Imhotep had to move on, leaving the Cravistine race behind. Although he felt at home inside the mountain top; living among an alien being, native to his own world, unknown to the world below, he knew it was time, time to leave and find answers.

The Cravistine lived thirty-nine million miles from his native home world. They looked a bit different from what he remembered but it was normal for them to go through an evolutionary cycle, for the Cravistine had been on the young planet for two thousand years, learning how to find the right food for consumption and survive the different climate.

Their underground tunnels were no different than the ones in the young Alkebu-lan communities. Their leader, Ick, ran a tightly organized and functional colony. Imhotep thought the leader to be a person of integrity, pride and dignity. Like most of the elders from his home world, and like Ick, Imhotep aged slowly in this new world. To live twenty-five years on Aquan was living a thousand years here in this new world.

He had promised the leader that he would return soon to talk about the old traditions and Ick had passed Imhotep a jeweled amulet that each member of the Cravistine race wore around their necks, making him a member of their society; it was a brightly colored piece of glass, one thousand times harder than the diamonds found here in Alkebu-lan.

As he stepped outside for the first time in a while, the snow fell from the sky and the winds screamed loudly against the mountaintop. Imhotep turned to wave at one of the Cravistine soldiers who sealed the entrance closed behind him. He must now begin the journey to find the thing that entered the planet's atmosphere seeking to destroy it.

E-Newtu's dreams must have something to do with the fiery object, he thought to himself. He closed his eyes and whispered a few words and two spheres appeared in front of him, one see–through and the other cloudy with movement in its center.

He raced forward, moving fast across the snow covered mountain and headed for the edge of the cliff, his legs pushing him forward quickly. When he reached the edge he leaped right off, extending his arms wide and he sailed down quickly; the winds blew loudly across his face. The rocky gorge and trees below him grew as he dropped fifteen thousand feet towards the ground below. After a few seconds he whispered again and the clear sphere covered his body, sealing him inside. Then he released the cloudy sphere and it disappeared. His cell was beginning to move northeast at a steady rate and he sat down and relaxed as it moved farther away from the mountain.

Hovering while over twenty thousand feet above the ground, the cell floated forward on wind currents towards the city of Kemet. The sky was dark and fog built up below him as his cell coasted the airways. Imhotep looked down below him through the floor of the air cell. He could see glimpses of the trees through the fog as he traveled farther away from the mountain.

He was now on his way to see his good friend before heading off to find the areas of the crash sites. What he witnessed breaking through the atmosphere was too small to be a part of a large vessel and he would have picked up any sign of a large vessel to begin with, so he had no idea what this could mean. Time passed and viewing the change in the weather, he knew his clear cell was moving closer to the ground. He was now one thousand feet from the green grass below him but the fog still provided him with cover.

A dim light came from the eastern skies but Imhotep knew it was too early for sunrise; he still had a few hours to travel. He released those thoughts as his cell costed east bound at a greater pace putting hundreds of miles behind him, now only miles from the city, Imhotep needed to replenish his body with fresh fish. The Moorvine River was a few miles away and an ideal place to stop before heading on his journey. He directed the air sphere towards the river using the wind currents and force, shortly the air cell began to descend towards the ground.

The trees grew large and the fog thinned as his cell settled on the ground in a highly dense area with trees for miles around. Seconds later, Imhotep disappeared under the water's surface and the day slowly turned to night.

The next morning, Imhotep walked across the burning sands alone, heading for the city limits. He could see the buildings in the distance. It was midday and his clothing was freshly cleaned after last night's swim. It wasn't long before he entered the marketplace where thousands moved along the pathways and their voices carried all around him, along with the bellowing of the many animals.

All the stands were busy as normal and passing E-Newtu's stand, he noticed the young man, Ahknon and Tu-ney working. People gathered making purchases but Imhotep moved past the stand towards E-Newtu's medicine tent where lines formed outside. He entered the tent as normal, passed the waiting area and headed into the back to take a seat on one of the many large pillows.

Imhotep noticed that E-Newtu was working on a patient's back using a needle to close an injury. He watched E-Newtu's steady hands before E-Newtu looked up and noticed him.

"I knew one day soon you would show up, Imhotep. My nephew wishes to have a word with you. He seems to think you promised him that you would speak with him. Is that correct?" asked E-Newtu. Imhotep looked on in surprise.

"Why are you surprised? Imhotep, you did tell him when you returned that you would have a talk with him, didn't you?" asked E-Newtu.

"Yes E-Newtu, I may have said such a few moons back, but I'm on the move, it will have to wait."

"Where are you going and how long will you be gone? Does it have to do with the dreams?" asked E-Newtu.

"Yes, it does and I believe something very serious is to about to occur so while I'm gone, I want you and your wife to stock up on supplies and if you have any kind of weapons they may very well be needed," he said, forgetting that E-Newtu was with a patient. He turned to her with concerned eyes.

"Don't worry about her, she is deaf and won't hear a thing."

E-Newtu finished closing up the woman's wound then began wrapping the injury in a white cloth before sending the patient on her way.

"Well, is this all a part of what I have been dreaming?" asked E-Newtu.

"Very much so, E-Newtu," said Imhotep.

Imhotep watched E-Newtu's eyes look to the top of the tent noticing the apparent stress there.

"You need to have a sit down with the war advisor and tell him of your dreams. I'll be back but first I will go out and investigate something I saw break through the clouds a few months back."

"Don't you want to talk with these people? They will never believe me; they may even throw me in jail," E-Newtu said.

"E-Newtu you will have to try. It is better to have the armies ready here in Kemet before the assault comes and many die! What your dreams are telling me is that this place will be attacked by a race of being from far away," Imhotep pointed upward, "and this may be a fight for the entire world," Imhotep said.

"So, if that is the case, why did it take you so long to come back here?"

"One, I wanted to be sure of what I was hearing. When I watched these metal objects break through the clouds as they entered Alkebu-lan, I knew it was something from outside of this world. I've learned that your dreams have always been right and this is the first time you have ever dreamed of other life forces in distant universes. It had to mean something for all your dreams told of terrible events happening, some not as bad as others but they all had something to do with Alkebu-lan! These dreams are no different, although I had hoped so," Imhotep finished.

"What do you know of these things, Imhotep?"

"I don't have time to tell you everything my good friend but in time you will know the truth; but first I must go to find answers which may be a part of what you dreamed. You said the spot was being chased by two other large circles before the explosion of light, right?"

"Yes, that is what I dreamed," E-Newtu said, now looking directly at the old wanderer.

"Good. I will see you very soon, okay? I'm off. Maybe what I find will help. If not, I will be right back here as quickly as I can," said Imhotep.

"Yeah that is fine with me," said E-Newtu.

E-Newtu watched the wanderer leave his tent. He took a deep breath and decided he would try to talk to someone tomorrow within the city gates. He knew it was important and if Imhotep had not instructed him to try, he would have packed up everything and taken his family as far away as he could; but war is a serious event and most cannot find a place to hide because it will find you in that very hole. Tomorrow is another day, he thought, before calling another patient inside his room.

Chapter 11

South Alkebu-lan

The once young boy, Tutann, now a huge and powerful giant, traveled the woods of his native home. He walked among large, horned animals dark in color. The largest of the herd stood in position to protect the females walking with young calves.

One of the large beasts charged him as he stood his ground. Once it was within his reach, he picked the beast up. He smiled as he examined it; rubbing it on its tough hide, as if it were a pet. He was very amazed at how beautiful his homeland was. He then placed the beast down gently. It raced off back toward its herd where other bulls waited on his return.

Tutann gazed around, turning in a 360 degree circle to view the splendor of his home from all angles. When he stopped he saw some wild, large cats; a short distance away, he noticed it was hunting. He walked in their direction. He recognized the males right off because their heads were much large than the females. The group began to roar at him across the massive landslide and as he moved closer to them, the cats raced off to the east as he watches them go.

Many other herds were scattered in all directions. For the first time in his life he was able to move around alone to explore the vast landscape. He turned and noticed a tall creature with a long neck; it was eating from the tops of the trees. Several feet away lay a river and he moved in that direction.

When he came upon the water there were other animals that were new to him. A giant, lizard-like creature lived among other creatures. He stepped into the water with no fear and the large animal attacked him, taking hold of his left arm. He began to laugh while picking up the huge creature, petting the beast on its head then placing it back in the water. It moved off quickly as water splashed back into his face.

Tutann turned to take hold of another creature that was sitting on the ground along the shore. It jerked its head trying to bite him as other huge lizards entered the water quickly to get away from him. He lifted the long creature. Its hide was even tougher than the animals that grazed on the grass and it revealed rolls upon rolls of teeth in its huge mouth. Tutann found this remarkable. It shook itself violently against his hold, so he freed the animal so he wouldn't hurt it.

Birds were circling high above his head as the heat of day shone down upon him. The sky was clear as he climbed out of the water to see his home in the distance. The tall and towering structures of his community could be seen for miles around. He stepped forward, moving quickly, and as he crossed the hard ground, it shook with every one of his steps.

After picking up speed, he began to leap several hundred yards at a time and each leap he took brought him closer to the mountains that were a good distance away. For a normal person it was a day's travel.

Now only yards away from the mountain, he used all his power to leap upward. His body propelled him forward and his arms opened wide sailing through the air crashing loudly into the side of the mountain, the sound echoed loudly causing rocks and other debris to fall down below him.

Tutann wanted to see the top so he dug his hands deep into the side of the rocky structure and began to push himself upward, using his hands and feet he scaled the wall easily. He leaped upward one hundred feet at a time, from one area to another more rocks broke off at the side of the mountain.

Tutann felt good taking in the rich, fresh air as he ascended to the top. He pulled one final time and he landed at the top with a hard thump. He turned around and looked out over the side of the mountain and saw his home as he had never seen it before.

He yelled out, "Alkebu-lan, the mother of mankind!"

Turning, he raced onward toward the colorful trees high above ground; he swung his arms back and forth moving forward.

"This is my wonderful home," Tutann said with awe.

His voice was deep, loud and vibrating and his eyes searched the sky seeing the birds take to the air, wings flapping, letting out cries of alarm. He made a left turn, quickly moving across the mountaintop towards some smaller peak five thousand yards apart.

When he reached the edge, Tutann leaped high into the sky and allowed his large body to catapult across the clear skies. Tutann flung out his hands and legs, sailing through the air as the side of the mountain peak were coming up fast. He hit it with a loud boom then scaled upward effortlessly and reaching the top, he looked out for a long time. He, again, saw his community in the distance, the men and women furiously working.

He noticed a small lake out in the distance. The weather was a bit colder up here and he saw places where the ground was completely white but it had no effect on him at all.

After taking in the wonderful sights, he looked north, south, east then west, where he could see the coastline and the vast blue sea. The wind began to blow in from the west, reminding him of the lake so he quickly moved towards it.

Tutann passed green trees much taller than him and more birds took to the air as he brushed up against them. He watched as the colorful birds whirled around the summit. Small goats hovered on the side of cliffs and then he noticed a wild cat several yards away. It was hunting the goats; it peeked out from behind the large rock blending in completely with its environment.

He stepped into the water, sinking down after each step until he was completely beneath the lake's surface. He felt like he was becoming stronger and as he stood looking under the surface, he noticed a variety of creatures swimming all around him.

He smiled. Everything was new to him as he laughed at the brown colored mammals moving in close to inspect him then swimming away. Tutann moved now into the deepest part of the lake, placing his head underwater he saw a huge boulder at the bottom. He submerged under the surface, climbed up on the huge stone to have a seat and sat there looking up through the surface of the water at the bright sun shining high above.

This new power felt great and he now wondered how long he had been under the surface without a single breath of air.

Tutann began wondering about his transformation and the only thing that came to mind was the light that coursed through his body while in the river behind his house during his bath. He still remembered the images and the soft pleas for help by a race of people he did not know. Many words were spoken but he didn't understand them. He looked at his massive arms, legs and chest. His skin color was as dark as the oils that seeped from the Alkebu-lan soil. His appearance was somewhat the same but he was just so much bigger and even more powerful than anything on the face of Alkebu-lan. Then it dawned on him again how long he had been under water without so much of a thought to come up for air.

Each day he was learning more and more about his abilities. Since his change he had had no need to consume anything but being under water had the same effect as consuming food.

He stood up and turned around taking hold of the huge boulder by embedding his finger deep within and lifting it to his shoulder; it was ten times his size but he carried it as casually as he would a basket of fruit.

Moving toward the lakes surface, he exited the water and water cascaded down his body. He walked a short distance away from the lake and set the boulder down. He thought this would be a good spot to come for peace and to think. The huge boulder would be his own private seat, he thought.

Dark clouds began covering the sky and loud thunder shook the skies all around. Then lighting flashed brightly. As a young boy he had a fear of these storms but now the loud sounds and bursts of light were thrilling to watch, especially being so close to the sky from his vantage point.

Tutann began his descent down the mountain as the clouds unleashed a downpour of rain. Not long afterward he entered the large cave entrance and went to his room where a massive bed laid made from cloth and bird feathers. This had been a gift from his community and he loved it. He lay down on his back looking up at the mountain walls before falling fast asleep.

Farther North West

Hutapsunnimoon moved across the wide open fields at blinding speeds. The trees, land and animals she passed were a blur but she recognized each creature very distinctly for her eyes were very sharp. Her hair extended behind her, floating on the air as she moved and her feet barely touched the ground. She pushed forward and her arms and legs swung back and forth. She was testing how fast she truly could go and before she knew it she had moved across a huge lake that traveled for a few miles. She skimmed across the top looking down into the water to notice fish swimming below her.

She pushed herself faster forward, breathing in the fresh air. And she glanced behind her knowing she was beyond the border of her homeland and entering places she has never seen before. It excited her to explore new places and her eyesight was so enhanced that she could anticipate her own moves from three miles out in the nighttime or during the day.

She moved so quickly that those in her community would only feel the wind as she moved past them. She was as stealthy as the fastest wild cat or the fastest bird high above; none were a match for her speed.

Hutapsunnimoon's days seemed longer now and she finished her daily chores quickly in order to explore. She hid her newfound powers from her parents; for one she wasn't sure where the powers came from. When she inherited her newfound powers all she remembered was a flashing light and the next thing she knew she was miles from home in a blink of an eye. She wanted to be sure about her enhancement before she brought this matter to her parents.

Hutap ran on a straight path home knowing her father, Nassir, would be home soon to begin their training. She was ready to practice her fighting skills, her hand speed, attacks and blocks. She was ten times quicker now but she moved normally when sparing with her father, he enhanced her skill a great deal and she looked forward to their secret practices.

As she moved forward quickly, moving around trees, rock formations and rows of short bushes, she spotted a striped antelope that would be a great meal for dinner. She reached back to pull her bow and arrow out. The antelope was three miles ahead of her and it had no idea she was moving towards it. She aimed and pointed then released.

The arrow took flight hitting the animal in the heart, making it a quick kill. She smiled at the accuracy of her shot then she replaced her weapon while still moving forward.

She snatched the animal off the ground before placing it over her shoulder in one smooth motion. She moved swiftly until she reached the rear of her home. She was placing the deer on a table just as her mother, Inzinger, opened the rear door.

"Oh, there you are, Hutap! Where did you come from?" Inzinger asked, as she looked around the yard then back at her daughter. Hutap began to laugh.

"What's so funny child?" asked her mother.

"Oh nothing, Mother. I was thinking about something that happened earlier today. I have fresh meat for the night's meal," Hutap finished.

"How did you come across that antelope? Their grazing pastures are a long way from here, my child," said her mother.

Hutap quickly changed the subject. "Is father here? I'm ready to practice now," Hutap said.

"Well, yes he is and the meal will be done in a short while. We can prepare that meat tomorrow. I'll place it in the barrel," Inzinger said, as she moved out of the doorways as her daughter passed her.

Her father was tall with thick muscles and had his hair in short dreads, the color a mixture of black and brown. Above his right eye was a scar which came down the side of his face. Ever since she was a little girl her father had carried his sword, bow and arrows and knife everywhere he traveled. Even inside the home he kept his knife close by. Hutap stood in front of him looking down while he cleaned his sword.

When he noticed her, he smiled up at her then said, "Have all of your chores been completed? Did you fill the water barrels, clean the pens, feed the animals then check up on this year's crops?"

"Yes Father, I did all that and more. I even found time to hunt for tomorrow's meal, Father," Hutap said, standing proudly before her father.

That evening, they began working on mock battles, using knife strikes and going over blocks using her hands and legs. They also practiced thrusting with the knives and swords then they practiced closed hand battles using short chops, punches, and knee and elbow strikes while her father reminded her that they could be used as a deadly weapon against an enemy's skull or could break a few ribs, if necessary. After a time they stopped, they were sweating profusely and both went to get cleaned up in preparation for the evening meal. Afterwards, they ate as a family then went to bed ready to repeat the entire routine tomorrow.

\

Chapter 12

Northern Alkebu-lan, City of Kemet

Imhotep headed out early that morning, saying his goodbyes to E-Newtu and his wife, Tu-ney. The young man, Ahknon, was out doing chores for his uncle so Imhotep had no time to spend with him. Time was of the essence and whatever the young lad wanted to talk to him about would have to wait.

Imhotep walked quickly across the burning, sandy ground. His head was covered with a lion's head and he was moving steadily, northwest of the city. He had a feeling time was running out for the young planet so he marched on nonstop. He had a very good bearing on the object that broke the planet's atmosphere and he was determined to find the answers to the dreams and the crash site would be the best place to start.

He headed towards the closest site first and decided he would turn and head south to the other two locations later. His mind took a mental image of the site but once he was close the cosmic dust could still be traced in that area. Even the fight with the Cravistines wasn't enough to disrupt his memories.

Imhotep looked back and the city was now far behind him in the distance. It looked like a small speck from his view but he continued to march forward, intent on his purpose. He was moving closer to a forest of trees, about five hundred yards away when Imhotep heard someone shouting but he continued to move forward, not paying much attention.

About fifty yards from the trees the voice grew louder, someone was calling his name and when he turned around this time, a single person was moving quickly over the grasslands towards him. Imhotep heard his name being called again so he waited, wondering who this could be, as the fellow drew closer, Imhotep recognized the form of a tall man.

He was waving a spear and Imhotep thought it had to be the young nephew of E-Newtu and the closer he got he realized that it is indeed he. He smiled and waved at the young man. When he was within speaking distance, Imhotep said, "What brings you this far from the market place, young man?"

"Well Imhotep," said Ahknon, breathing hard and still trying to catch his breath. He bent over to rest his forearms on his knees.

Imhotep waited patiently, looking down at the young man.

Ahknon looked up and said "You left before we had our talk and I know there is no telling when you will be back this way. It could be a week, a few months or even years until I see you again, so I decided to come with you. Maybe I can get some questions answered while we travel?"

"This must be important to you, are you completely sure I can answer the questions? If so, I'm heading west," Imhotep said, marching forward.

Ahknon moved to the side of the wanderer. He felt he was finally going to get his answers so he kept up the steady pace, following a few, short steps behind him.

"Lad, does your uncle know you have followed me?" Imhotep asked, turning to his right to look at the tall man.

"Yes, I spoke to him and Tu-ney and they both understood what I was feeling. Actually, I got the feeling that the two of them wanted me to leave. It wasn't like they said leave but it was a funny feeling. They also gave me supplies," Ahknon said, pointing to his carrying bag.

Then Ahknon looked back at the city; he would miss the beautiful, dark woman, Isis, a woman he had been dating for the last few weeks. He hated to leave her like that but he had to learn more about his father. If everything worked out he knew he would be back soon, he thought.

The sun was now midway high in the wide open sky. A group of large birds soared high above drifting upon the wind currents. Farther north, wild pigs headed towards a water hole.

"Well lad, I hope you're up to the journey. We have many miles to travel and it will be quite strenuous on the body. It's what I am used to but it's also good to see you young man," Imhotep finished.

Imhotep looked at Ahknon briefly then moved forward keeping a steady pace.

"Me?" said Ahknon. "Before now you had no knowledge that I would be traveling here to catch you!"

His eyebrows were arched as he wondered if the wanderer truly had been expecting him.

"No, I had not expected anyone to follow me but I do believe that your coming here is truly for another reason, other than the questions you wish to ask me. That is the conclusion I have come to," Imhotep said.

Ahknon looked down at the wanderer with a curious look upon his face. He wondered what in the world could Imhotep be talking about as he gazed down. He noticed a chain with a medallion around his neck. The medallion was two circles, different from anything he had ever seen. There were thousands of men and women wearing all forms of gold, silver and bronze chains in all shapes and designs, some of landscape, and others, animals and cities. It was very different and interesting.

He continued moving behind the wanderer quickly.

The journey was very long and they walked the entire day, through the night and the next day. He and the wanderer stopped to eat but never lingered for long. Soon they were off again. Ahknon began to see sights he never saw before. As the land under their feet changed, becoming completely sand, it made their travel much slower but he noticed that the wanderer kept moving at a steady pace, focused on something. During the evenings, while sitting before a fire, he would watch Imhotep look up at the stars for hours.

Before falling to sleep he would wake to see Imhotep's watchful eyes staring and he would fall off to sleep for a second time. The days that followed were all the same as they marched farther northwest. One day turned into many as their travels continued. Ahknon began to wonder where the old wanderer got his strength.

One night, Ahknon looked for wood so they could build a fire and after returning with the wood he noticed that Imhotep was already sitting before a fire in the middle of a dirt hole. He dropped the wood and rubbed his head looking around and trying to figure out how Imhotep was able to get a fire started at all.

As the fire burned red hot, Ahknon took a seat across the fire from the wanderer. He looked around and noticed for the first time how quiet it was. Normally he would hear the growls of the huge cats hunting during the night and it all seemed very strange to him but there was not a single sound from any of the nocturnal birds or other animals. He continued to gaze around as Imhotep's eyes were closed sitting before the fire.

For the last few days it had been mostly silent between the two of them since he met up with Imhotep. He decided that he would be the first to break the silence, he was thinking about what to say.

"Well, Imhotep, what are your plans?"

Imhotep remained very still at first then Ahknon watched him open those big, bug eyes staring at him intently.

"We travel to find something of great importance," said Imhotep. Ahknon searched the wanderer's face then said, "Important to whom? It seems to me each time you leave on important business you return and there is nothing new to present to anyone. I'm sorry if you find that rude of me but I travel with you only to ask you questions about my father."

Imhotep looked upon the young lad sitting with his legs crossed. He searched the boy's face and recognized a resemblance to someone but he couldn't quite figure it out so he said, instead, "What would make you think I would know anything about your father young man?"

His eyes were focused, waiting on the young man's answers.

Ahknon looked at the wanderer unsure of how to answer but he needed closure on this part of his life in order to carry on. His heart beat rapidly inside his chest at what Imhotep might say.

"Well, my father was an old wanderer like yourself. The only difference is you traveled lands of Alkebu-lan and he traveled farther north beyond the great seas."

Startled by the information, Imhotep looked the young lad up and down then searched his facial features, he then said,

"What was his name Ahknon?"

"My father's name is Shaker and the last time I saw him I was very young."

For the very first time, Imhotep recognized the young lad's features, the eyes, nose and mouth belong to someone he loves and respects, it brought back images many years back, hundreds of years before Ahknon was born, back to a home that has been lost.

In a time when he was only a young lad himself, Imhotep's family traveled space delegates for their planet, a planet called Aquan. During these times he would stay with his mentor, Zurrorey; his guardian and teacher of the mystic arts, his powers are called hu-fe-car and those that are gifted with the abilities are called wanderers, but here on Alkebu-lan those gifted with the abilities are called Shaman or witch men and he is called the wanderer for his constant movement of the lands of Alkebu-lan.

Zurrorey taught him how to move, object, and create elemental beings and to help others heal with a slight touch of his hands, and his powers grew the older he became.

One year on his home world of Aquan is several hundred here on Alkebu-lan, the city of Aquan is located deep beneath the great seas, and although his people are aquatic they could survive on the massive but jagged landside of his home where most of Aquantanita crops are grown for consumption.

Aquan was a world of peace and prosperity, his family traveled throughout the universe, and he was left with his teacher, but no matter what, he remembered his teacher, Zurrorey, always being there. As he grew older, Zurrorey taught him skills to be a perfect Aquantanitan, Zurrorey was always there to edge him on, then he began to travel space like his family. Imhotep passes all the examinations in order to pilot one of the large ships and he became Zurrorey's copilot as they travel to three planets within the Aquan solar system, for trading purposes.

After returning to their planet's orbit, they learn that Aquan was under attack, and he remembered Zurrorey saying it is the Garthians. Imhotep watched the waters of his home world turn to flames, as explosion came from large starships shooting down upon the surface of his world. He watched his people fighting to survive as Aquanian ships tried to break its atmosphere before they, too, were destroyed.

As a young man with no experience in war he was ready to fight, but their star cruiser was little, if any, help against such a powerful war machine. Zurrorey reminded him, it was best to flee while they were unnoticed.

Zurrorey and he came to the new planet and the land of Alkebu-lan a little over one thousand years ago, their power only gave them the use of three of the new planet's four elements so they survived and prospered. The people of the land called Zurrorey, Shaker, a name he has now for some years.

Zurrorey was already becoming an elder before they arrived here, but he and Zurrorey held on to the hopes of someday leaving this world to find out had anyone survived the onslaught of his world. They decided to spit up after many years together, farther north where the lands are much colder than Zurrorey traveled.

For many years they would meet in the city of Kemet to trade what they had learned, now ten years has pass since they spoke, and Imhotep understood that Zurrorey has taken the deep sleep. It hurt to know he has lost his teacher, someone he truly looked up to, but now, this young lad sat directly across from him, gazing through the eyes of his mentor. Imhotep began to smile broadly, as he thought of his teacher falling in love with an Alkebu-lan woman and bearing child with her. He understood his teacher has found a bit of peace by finding love, after breaking his train of thought, he said,

"Yes, I know your father, a very great man, great man indeed."

Ahknon moved a bit closer, excited now. Imhotep watched the lad's eyes light up, as he was taking in deep breaths, moving around the fire.

"Have you seen him lately?" Ahknon said, optimistic.

His eyebrows were arched waiting on an answer.

"No lad, I have not seen him in many years, your father is a special man, he was like a father to me lad."

Ahknon thought he saw the first signs of emotions in Imhotep expressions, something deep was there and he wanted answers, he said,

"Well, do you think I will ever see him again?"

Imhotep noticed the young lad, Ahknon, was very optimistic about his father being alive.

"No boy, the man you know as your father has taking to the deep sleep," he finished.

Ahknon sat straight upward as he sat on the ground, he believes like Imhotep, that his father was a wanderer, who gazed at the stars for hours pointing to specific stars then calling out their names. He sat for hours with his dad finding the sky at night so fascinating, a time together he will always cherish. Then he said,

"Could you tell me what happened to him?"

Ahknon's eyes searched the old wanderer's face.

"Lad, your father passing, means as much to me as it means to you, so let's call it off for now, it's enough for one day," Imhotep said.

Imhotep thought that Zurrorey lost hope and used love to comfort him, thinking escape was futile, but for now he will hold on to the hopes of leaving here one day, and if love comes his way, so be it, love wasn't so bad.

He will look after this young lad like it's his own son, like Zurrorey had done for him.

That night moved quickly as he and the lad found a secure place to fall asleep, using one of the clear spheres. It covered a large portion of land to protect them inside a sealed space. Anything that moved to close would be tossed in the opposite direction; they had a very peaceful rest.

For the next few days they traveled directly west, moving toward a large cluster of huge stones out in the middle of no wear, colossal in size and as green as the land around it. Ahknon never being this far from home asked,

"What is this place, Imhotep, these structures are giants?"

As he looked up at the many birds nesting, some circled above the structures, insects and other small animals called, alerting others of their arrival.

"Giants used to live here thousands of years ago, it's a place called the Stone Forest, an underground world of its own, which traveled to all places in Alkebu-lan. It's a magical place that can cut your travel by days. Where we go will take us over months to travel on foot; here it may take a quarter of a day. I traverse these tunnels all the time so stay close once we are inside, Imhotep."

Imhotep moved closer to the huge structures, finding a crack in one of the stone blocks, as Ahknon stared at the design of the place. Hundreds of stones were running straight upward and closely together, Ahknon could tell that the top was flat because the other stone pillar extended outward at the top, like a roof.

Ahknon watched Imhotep step inside and as he followed he thought he saw something moving in his direction, they were very short in stature, so he climbed in behind Imhotep.

Stepping into an underground world, he noticed it had a flow system of gravity, light which reflected off the almost glass walls, and air moved through it. Ahknon kept up with Imhotep, he also noticed a subterranean lake, and the light that passed through the small cracks reflected the water surface upon the ceiling. Small animals in the background being as inconspicuous as possible, a small, dark colored bird was flying around this underground cavern.

It wasn't long before they exit the place in a wooded forest beneath a huge tree. They stop to eat a meal before they carried on, then Imhotep stopped after breaking through the tree line.

Mountains were to the north of them touching the sky and grass field as far as you could see. Ahknon watched Imhotep, looking for something, searching the ground, kicking dirt up using his feet.

"You searching for straws, there's nothing to find out here!" he said, grimly.

Kicking at a patch of grass then his foot hit something hard. Ahknon grabbed at his feet. Imhotep turned around quickly; he knew that whatever broke through Alkebu-lan atmosphere had to be here somewhere, in which he believed Ahknon had found it. Imhotep picked up on its cosmic dust, scattered on the ground. Imhotep said,

"What happened, lad?"

"I kicked a solid patch of grass."

Imhotep ran over and looked down; a shiny piece of metal was flashing colors over Ahknon's body. Imhotep began to laugh loudly as Ahknon stepped backwards away from the flashing lights.

Holding his spear in his hand firmly, Ahknon said,

"I hope you found what you're looking for, I'm ready to go back to the city."

"Lad, I suggest you step farther back away from that spot." Imhotep watched Ahknon respond to his words by moving back a good distance.

Ahknon watched Imhotep carefully as he whispered a few words indistinguishable, then out of nowhere a circle appeared inside Imhotep's hands, in the center of the circle something was alive. When Imhotep had released them, the circular outer shape had disappeared, and a spinning whirlpool of air was now in its place, it begins to grow larger than large as the force grew much stronger, and the wind, as if it was alive, moved over the metal, shiny object below the soil.

Ahknon stepped further back as the wind tunnel picked up momentum on top of the object and he watched as the swirling air grew large yet again, pulling up dirt, grass, and rock. Ahknon noticed the shiny object was much larger then he had expected, it seemed to grow larger as the soil cleared. The wind current was growing, tugging on Ahknon's clothing; he was in shock that Imhotep held control over this powerful force of nature.

The powerful wind tunnel uncovered the object, which changed colors; it was clear as the air then as brown as the soil of Alkebu-lan.

Imhotep, looked down on the ship, then lights were flashing, he watched the light pass over Ahknon's body several times then a sound came from the spacecraft.

"Did you hear that?" said Imhotep

"No, I heard nothing, Imhotep."

This time, Imhotep watched the flashing light cover Ahknon completely. Imhotep knew this spacecraft had no intention of doing anyone harm but it had made a choice.

"The craft has chosen you Ahknon."

"What has chosen me? What is this thing? I've seen enough this very day, from you and this strange thing." Ahknon now glared at Imhotep who was unmoving, staring towards the strange object.

Imhotep noticed it was a small, transport spacecraft, there were solar panels and a cloaking device, so it would blend in with whatever the environment it came in contact with, then transparent screens pop up, of an alien race, and there were two more creatures sitting just behind the first one that was talking, and the two were from a place totally different from the one speaking, the screen blinked off then on, then to Imhotep; shocked he understood the words.

"If anyone out there could hear these words, I'm a Saggurdian; my world was attacked by a race called Garthians. I have escaped to find help, but now it's too late. I'm the last of my kind; the ship was crafted to choose a champion to help defeat this evil race. We had once combined our powers with the Qcbekans and the Kuiflard. The battle would have been won, but the pride of our worlds prevented us from putting our difference aside and because of this you see all that is left of our three races. The Garthians are heading to the new planet. There are three crafts bringing the new planet the combined D.N.A. of each of our worlds; the chosen will gain powers far beyond what the new planet has ever seen.

The flashing of the lights indicate that the person who is chosen is good in heart and holds its people before their self. The chosen maybe the only thing left to stop these beings. Learn to use your powers, learn of your abilities, because it will help you defeat the Garthians, this is one of three ships, find the others too, don't make the same mistakes we have."

Imhotep now watched the screen vanish and he thought about the dream E-Newtu was having and how they are related to the words of these foreign beings. Now Imhotep was angry and worried it was time for war and this time he will be ready, he looked over at Ahknon then said,

"Ahknon come here now and touch the object."

Ahknon looked at Imhotep in shock, at that very moment his life has changed; everything he has been raised to believe was now in question.

Ahknon spoke up, "I'm not touching that thing. Why is this important?"

Imhotep grew angry, his eyebrow was arched as his hands began to motion into circular movements, then he whispered words and a clear sphere appeared within his hands; he watched Ahknon closely.

"I said touch the craft now boy!!!" Imhotep screamed this time.

Imhotep looked at the boy's stance and noticed it's one of the fighting stances of his people on Aquan, it validated who his father actually was; Imhotep yelled again.

"Your father was my teacher; I would never put you in harm's way unless it was something that endangered the people here on Alkebu-lan.

Your father and I are not from this world, Ahknon; we are from a place far away, far beyond any place you have ever seen. Our world was destroyed and this place may soon be, if we don't stop this evil race called the Garthians."

Ahknonkineton looked at the old wanderer, shocked and surprised by this new information his body softened, his father was the great Imhotep's teacher. That made him feel good. It also gave him confidence in Imhotep's decision, but anger was there also. Hearing that someone wished to harm the people of his home land didn't sit too well with him; he always stood up against evil. Something about the old wanderer rang true, everything began to reveal itself, Imhotep never aged and was always on the move looking to the stars.

Ahknon even noticed Imhotep's clothing, clothing he wore over and over again but they seemed clean.

Imhotep watched Ahknon begin to believe in him, it began to settle inside his mind, when Ahknon marched towards the spacecraft then bent down and touched it, the light cloaked his body entirely, Imhotep covered his eyes from the bright light, when the light dwindled, Ahknon was standing there glowing of bronze, even his eyes expelled light.

His spear tip was as bright as a small sun, it eluded heat; he seemed more muscular and Imhotep was very impressed and eager to see what new talent Ahknon now possessed.

"Let me see what you can do, Ahknon."

Imhotep begin casting then raising his hands, gusts of wind carried Imhotep over seventy-five feet away from Ahknon and now several glowing spheres appeared above his head, flashing glowing lights dangerously.

Ahknon reacted to Imhotep's threats, the tip of his spear shined a blue flame, and it flashed its warning. Words entered his mind, "Sun Spear" and energy radiated throughout his body. He felt amazingly powerful and warriors from the distant past, who souls were within the Sun Spear, those who claim the spear when the universe was young, begin to impart those skills within his subconscious mind.

Ahknon's brown skin shined of gold bronze, his eyes were shaped and he gripped his spear tightly and he ready himself on the field of battle; a fireball rocketed in his direction, expanding in size as it gained speed cascading across the green field.

Ahknon leaped high into the air slinging the Sun Spear at one of the moving flames. The Sun Spear turned on, cutting the flames in half, drawing the flames inside of its tip. The Sun Spear spent quickly, moving towards the second flame, ripping through the air at ten times the speed of the flame. When it had made contact, it exploded through the second, huge flame; the flame parted then was also absorbed into the sun spear. The spear flashed back into Ahknon's hands, but before he could celebrate, the ice block was upon him; he had only second to respond.

Ahknon leaped upward in a half twist, towards the threat kicking outward with his strength and power. On contact with Ahknon's feet the ice bolder exploded, Ahknon spun while in the air. He brought his right arm around to his left, making contact with the ice bolder in mid–air—it exploded in to millions of raindrops.

When Ahknon touched the soil he wasted no time, he looked over to Imhotep then quickly slammed the flat end of his Sun Spear into the soil with force in front of him, then an explosive sound evoked around the open valley as the surface of Alkebu-lan tore open and the landside shook violently.

Imhotep was very impressed by Ahknon's powers. Large waves of soil rolled his way and he was almost toppled and fell into one of Ahknon's deep cracks. Because he responded so quickly, his air sphere carried him up and over the rolling soil and Imhotep watched several of these wave pass beneath him. When he had touched the ground softly more spheres of ice appeared, rocketing towards Ahknon; they grow up to eighty feet in diameter, large enough to crush Ahknon, Imhotep knew.

But Imhotep watched Ahknon point his powerful spear and bright lights lashed out of its blue flame tip, tearing into the solid ice bolder like a flash of lightning. It turned the massive ice bolder into a small ball. The second one Imhotep watched in awe as Ahknon leaped up, spinning around, kicking out with force, connecting with the second ice block, catapulting back towards Imhotep.

Imhotep prepared himself but heard something cutting the air behind the ice bolder coming his way. He knew it was the sun spear and Ahknon covered the coming of a powerful weapon; he felt it was a smart move.

Imhotep released the wind sphere throwing them to the ground in front of him, in seconds they rose to over one hundred feet and they begin to expand pulling everything around it inside. The powerful winds took hold of the bolder and slung it off to the ground over a mile away while the powerful spinning tunnels were also able to deflect Ahknon's Sun Spear off course just a bit. Imhotep watched the sun spear reappear inside Ahknon's hands.

Everything went quiet as Imhotep began to clap his hands,

"Now that was good Ahknon, your newfound power will be needed. I can't image you at your full potential, remember to always focus, come on now."

"Where are we going now, Imhotep?"

"Well lad, we got to find the other two crafts before it's too late."

"You mean there are more metal things out there, and if so, what kind of power will they have, what will our powers be used against?"

"In time, Ahknon, I will tell you everything."

They headed back to the stone forest and they began their long walk south throughout the night. By morning, they exited the stone forest, hundreds of miles to the southwest; they sat down to eat a bit while Imhotep's sensitive ears carefully combed the skies above. Then they began their march southwest under the baking sun. Ahknon wiped his face but followed Imhotep steadily, the sun sat in the middle of the sky and there was no shade for the next several miles. Ahknon wondered how the wise men, like Imhotep, stay in these wastelands for so many years, but now he had a profound respect for the old but wise wanderer.

The skies above begin to darken, small insects began their mating calls while the nocturnal animals awaken from their day slumber in search of their next meal, the moon was shining brightly in the eastern sky while patches of clouds move north.

Imhotep's ears began to pick up sounds in the outer reaches of space, sounds which only he could hear. Something started moving; it was a dark image, a huge shape which blocked out a part of the glowing moon. There was no eclipse of the moon. Imhotep awakened Ahknon from his nap. Ahknon was slowly moving to his feet while Imhotep picked up the pace heading through the woods, then through the tall grass, they marched on.

Chapter 13

I n one of the outlying, spiral arms of the Milky Way Galaxy, an inconspicuous, solitary ship, moved at the speed of light. The huge vessel is a Garthian Battle Cruiser, as dark as space itself, its circular shape offered the look of an asteroid moving through space, the ship was heading to what the Garthians called the new world.

There was a small blue planet that is one of the satellites of the sun, among the planets and bodies in the family of the sun; it is only on this planet that any complex, enduring life has ever developed.

The last time the Garthians were on the new world orbiting position, great reptiles of fearsome power had just begun to establish their dominion on the world.

Their race, a race of conquests, searching to control dominion over the universe, their spacecraft contains a number of captured species of life from other worlds, mostly used as soldiers, but the new planet was unlike the intelligent life on other worlds, the Garthians looked at the young planet as being what it was; a very young planet who held no real threat.

Commander Iou controlled the huge star cruiser with an alien race of creatures with human-like features, their eyes are normal with small, round ears, a round but long face and round like chin, small mouth with large teeth, the shortest Garthian stands at the height of seven feet tall, three strong arms and a second limb just under the left arm.

Thick bone structure, it carried two hundred fifty pounds at the least; a fearsome fighter, with thin skin, their strategies of war has overwhelming numbers and surprise attacks; to win it is a tactic which hasn't failed them yet.

Captain Iou knew it would only take one star cruiser to take the new world and control its occupants; a battleship with over forty thousand ready, fighting soldiers.

Iou commanded the ship to hover in the new world's moon orbit. Captain Iou prepared his forces to descend to the new world surface, orders were called over the ship's intercom, Garthian soldiers began moving around the ship frantically. Iou glared through his screen at the new world's surface, leaning to the right of his commander chairs, as sirens sound the alarm, on then off, the sounds echoed throughout the entire starship.

"Arkadim make sure you use any number of the large beast, to roam the lands. The sight of these beasts would spread terror all across the land below. The fire breathing beast, several large worms, and choose a few others; make sure many of these beasts is to secure my high ranking official," Iou said.

"Yes, commander," Arkadim said, bowing slightly.

"Sipck, you and a few men release several of the large giants and two-headed cats."

The Garthian soldier reversed his hand in front of his face as a sign of saluting, he then moved off and through a doorway and down.

"This world should take the least of our effort to control, it has no weapons to counter our own or the technology, the occupants here may have swords and a few of them would rather die than to be controlled, but my soldier will not hesitate to kill," said Commander Iou, but he continued.

"Kill anyone giving trouble. Officer Acee, you will be the commanding officer on the floor of the planet, you override all orders on the ground floor and report directly to me, let loose the flying beast and also the armor drucular lose on the lands; twenty thousand soldiers on the ground is all that is needed."

"Commander our descent will begin before the next moon passing," Acee said.

"Yes, that will be good. We travel to another world soon after the conquest of this world, this one will be spared, now be gone," Iou stated.

He leaned further back in his chair, his third limb rubbed his stomach, the other two were crossed over his chest. He is an overweight, aged military strategist, and a killer once placed in his leadership position; now he presses buttons and sends soldiers to do the work for him.

He watched his view, screening very carefully, looking at the surface below and the movement on the space dock, as large beasts are being brought up in cages from many of the lower levels of the star cruiser. Large, thick wire held some beasts at bay; many were being ushered into smaller star fighters. Iou look at all several screens, viewing every level of his star cruiser, Iou settled down as two Garthian females brought him a refreshing drink, he took in a deep drink then looked around his command center, as time passed his soldiers began their descent to the planet floor.

Chapter 14

Imhotep and Ahknon marched southwest; it is where the traces of cosmic dust had the highest reading. Imhotep has been seeing smoke in the eastern skies now for two days, then signal smoke floated upward from the northeast skies a day later. Large groups of soldiers were moving in the direction of the smoke, Ahknon looked around wondering what was happening. There were hundreds of men carrying swords, spears and a host of other weapons; they rode on animals with armor covering their skin.

Ahknon noticed that Imhotep had picked up his pace. Imhotep moved quickly across the dry lands. The message from the ship and E-Newtu's dreams played inside his mind; flashing images of his past, the destruction of his world. Since than Alkebu-lan has been his only home, it hurt Imhotep to think what the Alkebu-lanians would lose. He thought of the Garthian ships firing down upon the surface, within his mind he watched many of his people dying, but now he wondered why they had chosen this world, a world so young.

Then it dawned on him, and he whispered,

"They believe this world has no power to stop them and if so, it maybe their only chance at defeating the Garthians." To him, he saw only one ship, although that one ship was enough to take the planet, especially if the star ship fired down from outer space. He marched forward quickly, focused on his mission, Imhotep begin to wonder about the other two crafts, and understood that the crafts may have chosen it's next champions, but he also understood from the images of the holograms inside the spacecraft that the chosen champions would have to fight together in order to win, independently they would lose.

They passed several hundred heading eastbound, they were called to war through the smoke signals; they wore marching farther north. Imhotep was elated that he informed E-Newtu to speak with the leader so they would prepared for war; he smiled while him and Ahknon pushed further southwest.

Ahknon could feel something was happening, as many people that travelled the Kemetic market each day by the hundreds, it was nothing in comparison to the number of soldiers heading to the northeast, all men of all ages were taking up arms, hundreds carried shields while many were covered with animal skins.

Ahknon begin to wonder, with the powers he and Imhotep possessed, could it be enough to inflict major damage to the enemy? But he began to think otherwise, why else would Imhotep be seeking out the other two metal objects so passionately, unless he knew it would take their combined strength to defeat the enemy. Ahknon continued to follow Imhotep's fast pace, then he found a question to ask,

"Imhotep, what if we find the crafts and it has chosen but we are unable to find the chosen one, than what, what are our plans?"

Imhotep took a few moments to ponder Ahknon's question, he had thought of all the possibilities, even the question that is being asked at that very moment, he looked behind him and simply said,

"We travel to the next craft further south, than we return here if we have not found any of the others; it only means they have already traveled to the northeast. Hopefully, we can catch up with them before they do something that would get them killed."

Ahknon had accepted the answer moving behind Imhotep, more soldiers passed them and he looked down at the many shining weapons the soldiers were carrying, several hours later he heard Imhotep say,

"Here we are Ahknon, this is the place."

Ahknon watched Imhotep moving among the tall grass searching, he looked out on the vastness of it all, it was the perfect hiding place an army could be among the grass and you wouldn't even know it.

He now followed Imhotep, searching as well, for it was him who spotted the first craft by accident. Then he heard Imhotep say,

"I found it!"

Ahknon looked closely and noticed it was the same form of craft; its outer hide shined brightly, as the sunlight reflected off its surface.

He looked at Imhotep, who stood up sensing something, so he asked,

"What is it, Imhotep?"

"The ship has made its choice and it's our luck that the person is not far away."

Ahknon looked around, then said,

"How far and how do you know these things?"

"I can sense the slightest signs of powers and it radiates strongly from this direction."

After a few short miles, they arrive at a large community. Ahknon watched Imhotep pause for a bit then he looked around, then he moved toward one of the doors in the community. Ahknon had never been this far south, and he thought the land and people were beautiful. He watched the children play out front while their mothers planted crops.

Imhotep stopped at a door then knocked firmly and Ahknon stepped just behind him looking around, moments later a woman answered the door.

"Hello my name is Imhotep and this is my friend, Ahknonkineton."

Imhotep noticed the look the woman gave him, it was the look he was very familiar with, "Hello, my name is Inzinger, what brings the great Imhotep knocking at my door, and a hello to you, young man." She then turned her sights back to the wanderer.

"Imhotep, my husband speaks of you often."

"Is your husband home, my lady?"

"No, he and the men of this community traveled north, they say the communities of Abyssinia are in war! Abyssinia is where I was born, all of my family is there, do you know anything about this Imhotep?"

Not wanting to cause concern Imhotep lied,

"No, I have heard tales, though."

Imhotep used his powers and he sensed the powers coming from someone at the rear of this home, so he said,

"I need help, I'm on my way further south; do you know anyone who could show us the quickest path through or around the river heading south?"

Inzinger smile then stated,

"The rumor has it that the great Imhotep walked the Alkebulanian plains for hundreds of years, when the elders were babies and so on, so how does the great Imhotep get lost? Maybe what they say about you is untrue, but I love the stories. Wait a moment," she continued,

"Hutapsunnimoon!"

"Coming, mother!"

Hutap walked inside the room to find out they had guests, she looked at the old fellow with the lion head upon his head then at the much taller fellow just behind him, then to her mother.

"Hutap show these fellows the best path around the river, they are heading south, they are very good friends of your father. This fellow here is the wise men they call Imhotep, and this young man's name is Ahknonkineton."

They each bow in respect of one another. Imhotep noticed the weapons at her legs, the long bow and arrows on her back; he sensed a power resonating out of the woman's body.

Hutap looked at the older fellow, she heard of him, so many stories about the wanderer, she thought he may have the most exciting stories to tell and she wanted to hear about all of them.

She always wanted her life to be of adventure, and seeing other lands, suddenly a form of excitement overcame her but she kept her composure. She even wondered if he would have the answers to her newfound strength, than she began to wonder what brought the wise man, Imhotep, to her doorstep. She began to believe that this was no chance meeting.

She knew all the stories, so why would Imhotep need to find a shorter route around the river? She will go along with it for now. The other fellow was even taller than her father, she noticed something about him that read powerful, as if the spear was reaching out to her, she quickly stated,

"I can show you a path to travel which will cut your time in half as you head south. I'll be back shortly mother."

They left her home and community behind, moving through the dense trees as they begin to walk south. When Imhotep felt they were alone, a solid sphere of air expanded up to sixty feet around, sealing them inside; an invisible cell invisible to the naked eyes. Then Imhotep stopped to speak with her,

"Right now we need your help, we both know you heard there are wars going on in Abyssinia, well Abyssinia is being attacked by a race of creatures."

Ahknon was now paying close attention to what Imhotep was saying. This is the part he was unaware of; he was now eager to hear more so he listened carefully.

"From the dark reaches of space," Imhotep pointed to the sky, "where the stars shine." He watched the woman look upward then all around her. He continued, "Alkebu-lan will be destroyed, starting with Abyssinia. Abyssinia is being invaded as we speak."

"Why haven't you explained this, Imhotep?" said Ahknon.

"And why would you come to me out of everyone else?" said Hutap.

Imhotep looked upon the young born of a true warrior's blood and said,

"Because you hold a very powerful secret." Then he turned to look at Ahknon and said, "The craft said it needed you, Ahknon, to fight together or you will fail."

For the first time, Hutap looked around, her eyes were sharp and she just noticed some kind of wind cell spinning, which was supposed to make her a captive. To most, the cell was invisible to the naked eye, but her eyes aren't normal. She gazed around quickly then back to the old wanderer, she had no concerns of being caged in, for the wind cell had pockets in which she could make her escape, and free herself through the opening; because of her speed it would be an easy task to escape.

Hutap believed if Imhotep meant her harm it would have happened already. She stated,

"What secrets, and how do you know these things?"

"Let's just say I have a talent of understanding these things," said Imhotep, who was now looking at the young woman, noticing her long, dreaded hair falling down her back and skin as brown as the bark on the large fruit trees. She was very beautiful with a rugged exterior, and warrior spirit.

"So why do you hold me inside the cell?" Hutap asked.

Before Imhotep could get his next word out, the woman disappeared completely. He, and now Ahknon, looked around quickly, they both noticed she was standing outside of the air sphere enclosure; she then reappeared back next to Imhotep.

Well, Imhotep, you have found me. I will follow you to help save my land and my people from these foreign invaders. My father and his men joined the war leaving me behind. These Garthians are real trouble if the armies all over Alkebu-lan are on the move."

"Hutap, you inherited your powers just as Ahknon has and you must learn to fight as one."

Hutap took a second look at the tall fellow. He has inherited some form of powers, as well, that is why she felt something powerful which stemmed from that powerful spear he carried. She took a closer look and she noticed warriors standing around this tall fellow in some kind of alternate dimension. She believed she was the only person that could see them, things unlike she has ever witnessed. She also felt a power coming from the old wanderer, then she heard Imhotep say,

"What changes have been made in you besides your speed?"

"Well, my eyes can see at great distance away, at night or during the day, and I'm fifty times faster than any animal that runs or flies."

"Yes, you are," Ahknon said.

Imhotep touched his chin then said, "Well I believe there's more."

"What do you mean there's more?" said Hutap.

"I think you left so soon that the craft wasn't finished with you, we need to go to the craft then continue on our way. The craft in which you inherited these newfound powers has chosen you as its champion."

"Is that what happened? Now I do feel special. This thing I stumbled upon was buried in the soil, when the light flashed, I just ran."

"Yes, I understand. Let's keep it moving, we are almost there," said Imhotep.

They returned to the high grass and moved deeper into the center where the craft was located. Each of them moved close, looking at its outer shining haul, Ahknon then looked at the beautiful landside in the waterfalls and valleys, with thick, green pasture; it was a welcomed site from living in the desert sands for so many years. Then he looked to Hutapsunnimoon, she was rather beautiful and just a bit taller than his queen Isis, and with a more muscular build. Her brown skin had a healthy shine and her dreadlocks fell down her back. She had the powerful legs of a horse, built for running, but the curves of the Kemetic dances, while her eyes had a bright glow to them like one of the powerful, predatory birds.

Imhotep brought him back to his senses.

"Hutap, I want you to reach down and touch the craft."

Hutap looked at Imhotep, and then to Ahknon, who was standing just beside the wanderer. She stepped right above what Imhotep called a craft; she noticed it was flashing colors when a second ago it only shined brightly. She reached down and her hand felt the cool metal. The craft turned as blue as the large seas and the light consumed her, she looked over to Imhotep and said,

"Well, Imhotep, I don't feel any different." She looked around at herself, then to the men and she noticed the awkward looks they gave her. She heard Ahknon speak.

"Look Imhotep, her bow, arrows and knives at her thighs have transformed, such as my spear."

Hutap reached back to pull her long bow from her back, looking at the bow in amazement, the design and color was beautiful.

"Never have I seen anything like this one and I have seen many bows and arrows."

The color was a dark black, but the string to the bow was as blue as the skies above. She turned the bow in every angle to get a better look, and then Ahknon said,

"She only has ten arrows, and they seem to have no tip. What good are ten arrows against many?" He was now looking at Imhotep.

"If you and Imhotep want me to go to war with ten arrows, you both are crazy," Hutap stated. She stared at both men angrily.

She reached back, pulling out one of the arrows, laying it in place on the string of the bow, she noticed the craving and design on the side of the arrow, it read *shooting star*. The wording was from some other place and time. She had no knowledge of how she understood, she just did.

Hutap pulled the arrow and string back, looking at a very large but old tree one thousand yards away, and then she heard a click, as she watched long blades extend outward from each side of the arrow forming a crescent moon blade. Hutap noticed the tip of the arrow was turning into a blue flame, like that of Ahknon's spear tip.

When she released the arrow it struck across the landside in seconds. She witnessed the tree falling but nothing else, then a fast, moving light came toward her and she ducked.

"Wow that was amazing! Look Imhotep, the arrow returned to its quiver," said Ahknon.

"Did you see how much easier it went through the tree, like it was made out of paper? As quickly as you pulled and released the arrow it returned," Imhotep stated.

"Yes, then the ten is all she would need, sorta like my spear," said Ahknon.

"Yes, let's see what you have Hutap," Imhotep stated. Right then, Imhotep's body rose of the ground ten feet, hovering in place, and then twenty glowing spheres appeared above his head, some white, red and clear. Imhotep focused on Hutapsunnimoon.

Hutap stared at Imhotep hovering above her head, then she watched Ahknon.

Ahknon leaped up and backwards forty feet. He understood the speed of his adversary and he prepared for battle.

Two fire spheres crashed to the ground, burning the area where Hutap was standing. She raced out of harm just in time. She was moving away from her opponents. She was elated to have found someone she could practice her skills with. She would use everything her father has taught her.

Her heart beat rapidly inside her chest. She turned up her speed, everything was blurry but she concentrated on her two opponents. Then she vaguely saw something cutting the air, screaming, and coming her way with force and power. She leaped up and over the powerful spear, it screamed past her. She hit the ground with a roll, raising up and pulling out her bow and arrows, releasing five at Imhotep. Then she spotted Ahknon and released another five at him. The arrow struck toward their target, lighting up their path.

Imhotep noticed the flaming arrows coming his way. He sent two large, solid ice blocks her way, as his body rose further off the surface, then he released two fire spheres to follow the first two.

Hutap moved towards her attacker noticing the ice block which collided with her arrows. She was upon it and leaped up and to her surprise two balls of rolling fire followed. She grabbed her legs spinning, she came out of the spin sideways slipping between the rolling fires, hitting the ground, she was on the move.

Ahknon saw the arrows coming his way. The sun spear was already inside his hand, he instantly went into the style of the spear toss. The sun spear turned on, flashing across the air at its target, connecting with the arrows then there was a loud explosion. When the sun spear returned to his hand he noticed more arrows striking his way.

He, right away, began turning his spear out in front of him in a 360 degree spin. He was screaming, not sure of the outcome. The sun spear deflected the arrows and they sliced through trees. A few trees fell on his left and right and Ahknon witnessed two other arrows were deflected straight up into the sky.

Ahknon was now beginning to know how powerful he truly was; he was ready for more. Imhotep cast a pocket of air followed by fire that was as large as two houses. They rolled, heading for Hutap. He was hoping the fire cloaked the air; he wanted to see how good her eyes were.

Hutap raced forward cutting the distance between them. She saw a fireball coming her way again, it hit the ground and exploded scorching everything around it. Then she noticed something, and when she realized what it was she was almost too late to react. She hit the ground with a roll and the pocket of air smashed against her body. She screamed out, but kept moving. She released ten arrows at Imhotep while closing the distance between her and Ahknon, she was one hundred feet away; in seconds they met in hand to hand combat.

After blocking the last of the arrows, Imhotep watched in awe at the blinding speed of these two warriors. He watched how swiftly Hutap moved her legs, kicking at Ahknon's face and legs, then their hands, and speed. He smiled as Ahknon's sun spear was there to block at every thrust. He watched Hutap press the attack.

He sealed them in a cell of water, then air followed then solid ice large enough for the combatants to move around without injuring outsiders. He was very impressed by Hutapsunnimoon's attacks. He know she would be a great asset in helping him win this war, and Ahknon's powers continued to grow and he was now beginning to learn this about himself.

"Hey, that is enough," Imhotep said, loudly.

Both champions stopped and looked at Imhotep then at each other. "Very good fighting style you got there Hutap," said Ahknon.

"Well, thank you, Ahknon. I learned my skills from my father; his skills with added speed and power," she laughed.

They both stepped to Imhotep's side, who they found smiling, the barriers were removed and Imhotep noticed Hutapsunnimoon's mother, Inzinger, standing there with a sword, she begin to speak.

"When I heard all the commotion I thought you were in trouble, Hutap."

Hutap rushed to her mother's side, "Mother I have something to tell you." Then Imhotep began speaking,

"Yes, your child is needed. What Hutapsunnimoon does now is for you, her family and the survival of this world."

Inzinger and Imhotep talked for some time before he explained they had to leave.

"Imhotep, I have to go home to collect a few items, it won't take me long. I'll catch up to you and Ahknon. I want to make sure my mother knows I'm alright. You are heading down south?"

"Yes we are and we will be expecting you. This world depends on us; the armies of Alkebu-lan are depending on us."

Imhotep and Ahknon watched her go. They had one more stop then he will confront the Garthians once and for all, even if it means his death. He began to wonder what powers will this last chosen one wield and for the first time, he felt that the Alkebu-lanians had a real chance.

Hutapsunnimoon grabbed a few items, placing them in a carrying bag, while her mother brought her food, water and a few other items to carry on her travels. Hutap tossed everything inside her backpack so she only carried one bag; shortly afterward they hugged and said their goodbyes.

Hutapsunnimoon was sad leaving her mother behind all alone but she knows she will be safe here for a while; she had to go and help her people and especially, help her father win the war.

All her life she wanted to travel and see other lands, she will finally get her opportunity, not sure where the roads will end or if she will ever see her home again.

She stopped to look at the place she has called home one last time before she caught up to Imhotep and Ahknon; they all headed south, quickly.

Chapter 15

Northeast Abyssinia

E-Newtu and his wife, Tu-ney, lived inside one of the large medical tents a few feet from several other tents that housed Kemetic forces. Shortly after he spoke with Imhotep and was informed by Imhotep to speak with the Pharaoh of Kemet, E-Newtu sought out the High Priestess, Kahare; he waited patiently for days until word came back that he was declined an audience. More days passed and he pressed on, expressing the importance of his information to the high priestess, Kahare but word came for him to never return. Two days passed and E-Newtu heard the call to arm and word of war in Abyssinia. Only then was he granted a hearing by the Pharaoh.

He entered the big palace where the wide floors were clean. The walls revealed large images of the Pharaohs of years past with many family members. The halls were majestic as gold and silver figures stood holding spears. Women carried baskets and animals walked beside the figures, their dark skin ranged from the black night to golden brown. He passed several guards carrying swords with golden crowns upon their heads and many servants walked the many walkways in see-through attire with beauty paints on their eyes, hair in braids. They continue to look back at him as he passes by.

Once entering the Pharaoh's hall, E-Newtu looked up and the Pharaoh was sitting several feet away in a chair that sat higher than anyone else inside the room. The room was filled with many of the Pharaoh's advisors. His queen sat in a chair lower than his own and the high priestess Kahare was present, who bowed her head as he stepped near; he bowed slightly in return.

E-Newtu stopped before the Pharaoh and looking up into his eyes he began telling the stories of his dreams and images of death of men, women and children. He continued to explain to the gathering, and especially to the Pharaoh of the wise wanderer, known as Imhotep, and his visit with him.

At that moment, he had everyone's attention. Some whispering could be heard until the Pharaoh silenced them. E-Newtu continued once there was silence. "The wanderer and I sat together and he wanted to hear every detail of the dreams I have been having. He believed it revealed information that was somehow connected to Alkebu-lan and its future. After speaking with Imhotep he left and then he returned a day later and more of my dreams were revealed. He seemed to have more knowledge of what was to come then I did."

"He instructed me to bring this information to you, Pharaoh, to inform you to gather the forces." The Pharaoh thought on this a moment and shortly war signals were sent up high into the day skies for all nations to move northeast. Men were coming from all across Alkebu-lan, the largest gathering of men E-Newtu had ever seen. He was then instructed by the Pharaoh to aid the soldiers with his special training and he agreed. A few days later, he and the forces traveled to Abyssinia where they found that the word was true; creatures from another place came and began attacking, and soon injured men and women were being brought to the tents after suffering massive injuries.

E-Newtu and his wife, along with many others, worked extensively on the injured. E-Newtu worked on those with severe injuries, such as crushed limbs and amputations of limbs, while his wife, Tu-ney, worked on closing gaping injuries and the minor problems were taken care of by the workers.

The fighting was so intense with the large creatures with deformed faces and three arms. These creatures called themselves Garthians and from what E-Newtu was hearing, the third arm was smaller than the other two normal sized ones.

Legions of fighters came from far and wide to enter the war. One messenger brought word of the Garthians asking the people to bow down to them and the war would end but the warriors fought on, pressing the three–armed creatures. As E-Newtu reflected on the carnage, a thudding in the distance brought him back to his senses. The fighting was intensifying. He reminded himself to stay focused on the task at hand.

Days passed and soldiers brought a dead Garthian to his medical tent. He examined them extensively to learn some secrets of the beasts. Upon examination, he learned that the ribs were covered by large, thick, flat bones that could deflect a sword's blade but the bones in the back of the creature were thin and it would allow the best access to killing the beast. He passed this information on to the soldiers. "When you fight them, aim for their backs. Pierce their back with swords and that will ensure their death."

More days passed and E-Newtu received word that his advice worked. The men began celebrating victories against the Garthians. E-Newtu was happy but it was short lived when new information came in about large, fire–breathing creatures, so large they swallowed several Alkebu-lan warriors at one time. It was said that others had a wingspan that shaded the ground over six men when it flew over. E-Newtu heard talk of one-eyed beasts carrying a large club–like object and it was large enough to kill five men in a single swipe.

E-Newtu is thankful that the tents they had set up were among a thick, dense forest and would provide cover for them from the large beasts. The enemies used other four–legged creatures to search for Alkebu-lanian forces.

More soldiers moving into the tent brought E-Newtu back to his senses. He moved towards the injured warriors, noticing that one of them is a young boy of about thirteen years of age. The child had been cut by a Garthian warrior in the lower stomach region and the boy was crying softly. He was losing a lot of blood. E-Newtu cursed under his breath because he knew that with an injury like this the young boy would be dead soon and it hurt him to see such a young boy his age fighting to be free. He made the young child as comfortable as he could until his eyes froze in place. He then covered the kids face with a blanket while letting out a deep, mournful breath and rubbing his tired eyes.

He began to think about his dreams again then his mind thought of Imhotep and where he might be. He hoped his old friend had an answer for these creatures. He went back to work, keeping his mind focused on the tasks ahead.

Forty miles to the South

General Nassir commanded the forces to the northeastern parts of Abyssinia, having taken control of the soldiers coming from a number of lands after leaving his home moons ago when smoke signals appeared in the sky, alerting all communities of the trouble in one of the largest city in Alkebu-lan. It has been a call to arms that he along with others answered. The Pharaoh placed him in charge, knowing of his reputation for strong leadership and success in defeating attacking forces. He was somewhat of a legend.

He now commanded over one hundred fifty thousand soldiers and for weeks now the fighting continued. He had buried many of his finest warriors but the beings known as the Garthians were dying as well, but in lesser numbers. Several of the bodies were brought back to the campsite, where a physician examined the remains and would report to Nassir the best tactic of killing the creatures effectively.

His tactic was to pair one of his large and more skilled, fighting soldiers on the field of battle with a smaller fighter of the Zukufu tribe because this tribe was one of small people who at full maturity stand only four feet tall. Their homeland lay farther to the southeast among the cliffs high above the ground. The Kemet fighters boasted strong bones, large feet and hands and they wear bone earrings and nose piercings of colored stones. The men's facial hair is grown around their faces while the women cut their hair to show their faces.

By pairing the fighters, the large Kemet soldier could engage a Garthian fighter directly while the Zukufu solder could attack the enemy soldier with a javelin from its most venerable place, in the back.

When the war first began the soldiers were adept, longbow men who rained fire and arrows down upon the Garthians, killing many, leaving their blood to stain the ground. But the strange looking creatures pushed forward; however, Nassir's tactic of the partnered soldiers eventually began to turn the tide.

Although the Garthians fought to win the day, Nassir and his men engaged the enemy directly, metal against metal, clashing of swords and shouts rising from every space of the huge fields. Nassir swung his sword upward to deliver a devastating head injury but the huge creature blocked the blow and the Zukufu soldier struggled to get to the rear of the Garthian beast.

Nassir stepped inward, landing several blows to the enemy's body before switching the sword to his left hand and slashing the Garthian's neck.

With no time to gloat in this kill, Nassir engaged another beast while assisting the soldiers under his command. His eye gazed sharply around the field and sweat poured from his head. Screams and shouts came from both the enemy and Alkebulanian soldier, clashing metal continued to ring out over the fields. The brave fighters continued to do battle with the three–armed humanoid. His gaze falls on that of a female, Zukufu fighter who has now come to partner with him. She is covered in hardened brown leather to deflect enemy swords. She correlates her movement of attack with his. Lunging forward from the right, she attacks from the rear and they felt the Garthian coming towards them.

Suddenly, they saw a large metal form moving across the sky like a bird and they hear a loud, blaring horn coming from it. The thing lands and from inside, large Garthian beasts began to rush into the fighting frenzy. He stares in shock at the ugly beast standing about twenty feet tall, some other beast behind the first seeming even taller.

The first giant beast grabbed the closest Alkebu-lanian soldier and tossed him a great distance. The solider went screaming across the field in the air, falling to his death. Another creature with eight arms moved across the field like an insect, trampling some of his men while consuming others with its large teeth. Right away Nassir removed his javelin from the dead Garthians body and tossed it directly at the huge beast. It made contact with its head and it let out a chilling cry of pain, Alkebu-lanian soldiers attacked it, hacking it to pieces.

Nassir noticed another beast to the side of him. This one had one eye and carried a huge, wooden club with jagged knife-like edges. It swung its weapon through the crowd of fighting men and made contact with the Alkebu-lanian soldiers. The soldiers were being tossed into the air in all directions, screams could be heard and others stopped to gaze backward at this new threat. Another giant beast with lepers-like sores, smelling of liquid death, laughed a hideous sound and swung a huge ax, cutting many of his men to shards.

Concerned with the lives of his fellow soldiers, Nassir yelled out, "Fall back now!!! Fall back! Take cover!" He waved his hands as many of his men passed him or stood at his side holding spears, poised to throw. Once most of the men were safe, and out of the way of the beast, Nassir rushed behind them as his female counterpart tossed her spear, hitting the one-eyed giant in the arm. The beast tossed its club in anguish which nearly killed her; it rolled across the ground killing several Garthian soldiers. She then turned and followed a few short steps behind Nassir. His forces moved across the hot ground until they had reached a safe location away from their enemies.

Nassir looked around and his count of fighters was down; he lost a lot of men on the field today as the Garthians pushed forward extending their territory. *"Tomorrow is another day,"* he thought. They had to stop this race of alien-beings; Alkebu-lan was their land and they refused to hand it over to anyone without a fight.

He took a seat between the trees as the sun moved toward the western skies after dispatching guards to various sentry points as lookouts. His weary warriors began to settle in. Some ate, while others were cleaning injuries; a few attempted to sleep. He and the female warrior, Titi fell off into a light sleep for much needed rest.

General Butannharmoon commanded the soldiers in the Southeast of Abyssinia. He had started with over one hundred thousand under his command; that count has been cut by half in the past weeks.

He looks down at the bodies that littered the ground below him. Garthian blood was spilled as well but the number of his men lost was astronomical. It was two to one! His Alkebu-lan soldiers' blood mingled with the enemies and that caused a deep sadness within him.

Young, strong soldiers gave their lives for the freedom of their homeland and Butannharmoon was consumed with the thought of the power that these beings controlled at the moment. But he also knew that he would continue to fight until his last breath. It was just the way things had to be.

Every life was in jeopardy, especially that of his wife, Kisse and his son, Tutann. Whatever they accomplished here would affect the outcome of life, they had to be strong and continue the fight, it is the way of life here in Alkebu-lan, he thought. Then he thought of Tutann; his son could have been a great asset against some of those huge creatures and their new weapons but he was thinking about himself and wanted his baby boy safe, when he should have been thinking about the safety of his land. He moved away from the battlefield to find cover for the night. Tomorrow would bring more fighting and he needed to learn more about the beings called Garthians.

Suddenly, a messenger from Commander Nassir brought word of an effective tactic to kill these foreign beings. This new information gave him hope and Butannharmoon looked down on the bodies of his brothers one last time before finding a place to rest.

Central Abyssinia

I nside one of the tents, Captain Acee, spoke with Gl Commander Ior. His image appeared on a large screen in the control center of the star cruiser that orbits the new planet's moon.

"Well, Commander Ior, the youngling have taking up position to fight against our demands to be controlled in a peaceful setting! Their futile attempts to wage war have cost them dearly. It will not stop our march across the planet and take what we want," Acee said.

He held his hand to his chest in a gesture of honor and respect while standing with legs together but feet turned outward. "Well we knew to expect some form of rejection and rebelliousness. They have come a long way since our last visit here and they have developed into an intelligent race of beings."

Acee watched his commander rub the top of his head then lean back farther in his seat while others worked around the control center. Several Garthian females walked past carrying equipment and other items to the doors just behind the commander. He focused and began to listen carefully while the commander continued.

"I want you to slowly take the eastern area of their homeland, making your way north and then swing around to the south. Kill everything if need be until every life form on this planet complies with our wishes. Kill the troublemakers. Also, I wish to see what these beings look like."

"Yes, I know you have spoken of them but I wish to see their ugly faces myself and maybe have them examined from the inside. Do you understand?" said Commander Ior.

Leaning closer to the screen, "Yes commander, we will kill all hostiles and bring other captives to the command ship. We have some soldiers collecting water and various foods that were found to be edible, some even tasty."

Commander Ior replied, "Yes, I am looking forward to tasting different and strange foods but remember...I WANT THOSE CAPTIVES!!! Maybe there is a soldier we could send to complete our conquest? What do you think about that?"

"Well yes, I believe some of them would be a good addition to the ranks. They exhibit a great deal of war skills but not enough to win against an army as powerful as mine," Acee said, smiling.

"Keep your confidence, you may need it. Remember, no use of the laser weapon, only use the swords. This experience will be great for the men for fighting above ground or below because there is no telling what we will find on the next planet."

Then the screen went blank and Acee moved to his command room inside the smaller star fighter.

Once inside, many soldiers waited on his orders. He began to debrief his men on the information from Commander Ior and after the meeting the highest ranking officials moved off to other parts of the ships to inform the others. He picked up his remote control and pushed a few buttons. It beeped and flashed a few lights before someone on the other end picked up. He began to relay his instructions.

Chapter 16

Deep Southern Alkebu-lan

After traveling for a day, Imhotep, Ahknon and Hutapsunnimoon exited the stone forest into the bright lights of day. The birds were singing as small monkeys roamed the branches of some of the largest trees Ahknon and Hutap had ever seen. They gazed upward in amazement; butterflies in many colors floated in the air, some using the men's shoulders as a place of rest.

The companions moved through the trees stepping on roots and they could see large fruits hanging from many trees. Imhotep walked up to one of the trees, grabbing a fruit then taking a bite. He looked back at Hutap and Ahknon and nodded toward the tree then moved to his side and began eating their fill.

They all moved forward through the trees several steps behind Imhotep. It was still early and the sun moved slowly from east to west in the sky, heading towards midday. They traveled another few miles and they walked down a steep hill and into grassy lands that rolled in every direction. It wasn't long before they came across a community of people, many of the families living there greeted the old wanderer like a long-lost family member and the kids reached out to touch his clothing, as he smiled down on them.

Ahknon followed from the rear but to him, there was no mistaking the love the members of the community had for Imhotep. He smiled at all the joy and love from the communities. The village huts were made of mud with hay covered tops and there were at least forty homes in all. There were fires burning in the center and men with swords and spears standing around smiling. Some shook his hand and greeted him in a peaceful manner as he bowed slightly. Several women looked his way and gave light waves. A few men of the community pointed at Hutap, then said a few words to Imhotep.

Ahknon watched Imhotep smile then said a few words in a dialect he couldn't understand and all the men turned looking at Hutap. He figured they were surprised to see a female warrior and as he looked around, most of the ladies did motherly type things. He gave a big smile then looked at Hutap who gave a shrug of the shoulders.

Ahknon learned this was the elusive Tonga tribe that moved like the wind. The men gathered around Imhotep and the looks on their faces became very serious.

Ahknon watched them move their heads up and down and then he heard Hutap say to him, "Do you think Imhotep told them of the war?"

"Yes, I'm sure that is what he is telling them now. You can tell by the changes of happiness to looks of worry and fear on their faces," Ahknon said.

"Good, the more warriors, the better. I heard a lot about these people. They are very dangerous but they seem to love Imhotep," Hutap said as she gazed around the place.

"Yes, they all seem to love the great Imhotep. He has been around for many, many years," Ahknon stated.

Soon after Imhotep received gifts to help him on his journey, the people waved their goodbyes as the companions headed further south. The sun was now in the middle of the sky as they marched closer towards another large community just beyond the forest trees. There were huge mountains just a bit to the south of their position seeming to reach up to touch the blue clouds.

Imhotep moved closer to the community and he turned and whispered, "Keep your eyes open, we are in range of the third craft and even closer to the last chosen." Ahknon and Hutap shook their heads in agreement as they casually strolled forward.

Imhotep used his power to search for the spot where the craft was located. It led him to one of the many homes there and it was quiet as they entered the yard. He moved towards the back where a river appeared. He stopped at the river's shoreline, looking into the fast moving water and a flash of light came from under the water surface.

Then a woman's voice came from behind them. They all turned toward the voice as one and saw a family gathered staring at the old wanderer. A middle-aged woman stepped towards them, and then stopped.

"Hello Imhotep, my name is Kisse, I bring you all greetings," she finished. Imhotep bowed showing the woman respect, and then others from her communities spilled into her yard as they began to cheer a name loudly, "Tutannharmoon, Tutannharmoon!" They stood listening and then Imhotep turned to the woman who called herself Kisse.

"Who is Tutannharmoon?"

She replied, "It's my son. He lives in the mountains. Maybe you could help him? You are the wise man, Imhotep and maybe he would listen to you." She points in the direction where the mountains rise up in the distance. "My son lives three miles that way."

Imhotep realized that this is the last choosing as he said, "I will check and see what I can do to help your son, Kisse." As he turned, he was followed by Hutap and Ahknon and the crowds opened a path for them to pass through, heading toward the large mountainside directly in front of them.

It wasn't long before they reached the side of the mountain and towards a large cave opening in which they were instructed to enter. The entrance was about thirty feet tall and eighty feet wide. Imhotep looked around, thousands of wild animals roamed the land in all directions, it was migrating season in southern Alkebu-lan.

"What else could be living in there?" asked Hutapsunnimoon.

"I really don't know but whatever lives in there has to be big," Ahknon said.

"It's just a cave opening. Over the years, the weather created these natural openings and if you look closely you could tell the sides are very old and not freshly created. You would be able to tell the difference between the rock patterns," said Imhotep.

"Hello is Tutannharmoon in there?" said Ahknon. His voice echoed back to him through the large cave opening. There was no answer.

"I guess there is no one inside," said Ahknon. He looked over at the wanderer who then looked over at Hutapsunnimoon. She recognized Imhotep's jester; in a flash, she raced inside the cave entrance to search. Her eyes were the best among them. She exits as quickly as she entered standing next to Imhotep, eyes looking into the large cave.

"Whatever lives in there is very big. You should see the size of its bed. The person has to be fifteen to twenty feet tall and as wide as one of the houses we passed," she stated, looking from Imhotep to Ahknon then back at the entrance.

All of a sudden, Imhotep's ear picked up the sounds of a loud beast coming from the community. He and his companions had just left and thought it must be Tutannharmoon, whom they were looking for. But the loud-pitched sound hurt his ears. Then he heard a loud sound coming from somewhere at the top of the mountain, different from the first noise.

Tutann was ready to settle down into the deep lake high upon the mountain top when he heard his mother screaming and even at this distance, her voice reached his ears. He raced to the side of the mountain and looked out towards his community. In the distance, he saw a large beast unlike any he had ever seen before and a deep rage took over him. The beast was spraying flames from its mouth, burning his home. He leapt outward away from the mountain and down the side, screaming loudly and sailing downward quickly.

Imhotep, Hutapsunnimoon and Ahknon were all looking upward after hearing the loud, rumbling cry coming from above them. They watched something huge leap off the top of the mountain top. Its body was moving quickly towards the ground from thirteen thousand feet up. Imhotep cast an air pocket around the companions lifting them up off the ground thirty feet. When the huge beast hit the ground, the ground shook and a sinkhole was created. They watched this huge giant leap high over the land heading towards the community. His power carried him swiftly away from them, over one hundred yards away.

Imhotep knew this was the son of Kisse, called Tutannharmoon, coming to his mother's aide. Imhotep allowed them to settle back to the ground quickly and released the cell but Hutap was already on the move as her eyes spotted the threat. Her body was propelling forward with force and speed and she passed underneath the huge giant called Tutannharmoon. And when she was a safe distance in front of Tutannharmoon, she looked forward and saw that it was some sort of large lizard-like creature, breathing fire from its mouth; it had red skin and large points extended from its wings. It had to be over twenty-five feet tall and made her wonder where such a creature came from. Once she cut the distance down she pulled out her long bow and arrows.

Her keen eyes also noticed scales covered its body as arrow after arrow she released on the new threat. Arrows exploded into its flesh as the creature screamed loudly and turned in her direction. She moved around trees then cut quickly to the right, releasing more arrows into the back and side of the beast, causing large wounds to open across its body. Its fire burned red hot, incinerating trees and brush. As more of her arrows entered its neck, stomach and arms, it turned away from the community, Hutapsunnimoon allowing it to find safety. Hutap came to a sudden stop, for the one known as Tutannharmoon was upon the beast.

Tutannharmoon was really angry as he lifted off the ground one last time, extending his arms as he sailed into the beasts causing their bodies to collide with a loud boom. They tumbled across the ground for several yards while the beast was screaming out, loudly.

Trees, shrubs and bushes and anything in their way were crushed under their combined weight. Once he made it to his feet, Tutannharmoon lifted one arm and slammed the beast in the head, hard and it crashed to the ground loudly. Taking a hold of the beast, he spun it around, tossing and spinning the beast two hundred yards away; the creature hit the ground like a quack. Tutann leapt in the direction of the beast, hitting the ground on top of the creature, dirt flying everywhere making sure that the beast did not get to his feet.

Hutap watched in awe at the power of this giant after the one called Tutannharmoon tossed the beast aside. She was already upon it, releasing her shooting star arrow that burned a blue flamed tip, and the beast screamed as it cut large patches from its flesh, exploding out the opposite of its body, the blue flamed tip lighting up the sky as they returned to her. She watched Tutannharmoon land and grabbed the beast's arms; she stepped back quickly.

Tutann snapped the beast's arms and the crack was so loud even Hutap turned her head. She watched Tutann take hold of the beast's head forcing it together. Fire blew into Tutann's face but it had no effect on his body that shone of dark, black oils.

With tremendous force, he crushed the beast's head and she heard the skull explode as the side of its face sunk in. When its body was unmoving the giant beat its huge fist down upon its body until every bone began breaking.

Hutap watched the giant look down at her. His facial features changed and were now softer. She said, "Well, I guess that did it for that beast. It will not burn any more homes again."

Hutap looked up into the giant's face seeing only a man, and for the first time in her life, she saw a face that she felt was very attractive. They both gazed at one another for a long while before she heard the giant say, "Thank you."

"Oh you're welcome big man. I have to say the jump from the mountaintop was very impressive. Maybe you can show me how to do it one day," she said, smiling up at him.

Tutann smiled down at the pretty woman, then he turned around remembering the houses in flames. He leaped away landing in front of the burning homes. As he touched the ground with a loud boom the woman he was talking to a second ago was already waiting on him to land.

Tutann noticed people gathered but he frantically searched for his mother. Then a smile crossed his face as Kisse raced from around one of the homes. When she reached him she looked up and said, "Are you ok Tutann?"

"Mother, I was so worried about you! Did the beast hurt you in any way?"

He was examining her to make sure she was unharmed when he immediately recognized two strangers; one, an old man with the head of a wild cat upon his head and the other, a younger man carrying a spear. Then he wondered who the woman was standing next to them.

He lifted his mother off the ground to see if she was okay. He had no concerns for her safety now that he was there. She kissed him on the cheek and he gently placed her back on the ground but slightly behind him. He turned his attention to the strangers and said, "And who may you be, old man?"

Hutap stepped forward again and Tutann gazed down at the warrior woman.

"Well, we came looking for you Tutann. The tall fellow here," she pointed, "his name is Ahknonkineton. My name is Hutapsunnimoon, similar to your own. And this is the wanderer, known as, Imhotep," she finished while she pointed at each of them.

"Yes," said Imhotep. "How are you Tutannharmoon?"

"And like Hutap said, I'm Ahknonkineton. It's good to have finally found you."

Ahknon looked up at the huge giant. He was a normal man of Alkebu-lan descent but his size and overly muscular body was unimaginable compared to Tutann. He stood at least fifteen feet tall and his body was as wide, if not wider and his feet and hands were like nothing he had ever seen.

Tutann towered over the three strangers and he remembered stories his community had told of the old wanderer, fascinating to hear even for a boy of five. He was the helper of the needy; he heard nothing but good things about him.

"So you are the great Imhotep," Tutann said, as a smile appeared on his face. He reached down opening his large hand in a greeting to the strangers.

Imhotep touched his hand then Ahknonkineton touched his hand as well. Hutap touched his hand and stayed there next to him. He felt a deep connection to this woman he had only met today. It was something he couldn't explain.

Then he said, "What brings Imhotep this way? I heard the one called Ahknon say it is good to have finally found me so there must be a purpose as to why you are here."

"My purpose was to search for you. What has happened to you has also happened to Hutap and Ahknon," Imhotep stated, pointing at both Hutap and Ahknon. Tutann looked at the both of them.

"Your transformation is the result of the ship in the riverbed behind your home. It is where you first noticed your change, am I right?"

"Yes, you are correct, Imhotep."

Hutap watched the giant who seemed humble and smart. She rubbed her hand inside his own and he looked down at her briefly. They both smiled and she felt close to this giant Alkebulanian. No one had ever caught her eye before this so she listened patiently.

"The large beasts are something from another place and were brought here. It is just one of many from a large army of visitors from space," he said as he pointed to the skies. "All of the communities are engaged in war with them, just look around. "Where are the men of your community?" Imhotep finished.

For the first time Tutann gazed around to search for the men and he noticed only young boys and very old men remained.

Then he thought of his father and he looked down at his mother, Kisse and said in a deep and emotional voice, "Mother, where is father?"

"Butann and the men went off to fight a war in Abyssinia; word came from the city of Kemet to the various communities to move northeast. Your father felt you were too young and he asked me not to tell you son," Kisse said, looking up into her son's eyes.

Tutann then looked at the wanderer and said, "Are there many beasts like the one I killed back there? And if so, what can we do to stop them all?" asked Tutann.

"The ship that sat at the bottom of your river was just one of three. It transferred special powers to Hutapsunnimoon and Ahknonkineton, powers that if used together will be an effective tool in defeating this army. Each of you, independently of the other, will lose the war. I also believe there may be more to your powers than you know right now," Imhotep said, looking up at Tutannharmoon.

Tutann's eyes widened as he wondered what more could there be.

"Follow me," Imhotep stated.

Everyone followed the wanderer to the rear yard and stood at the side of the riverbank.

"Go touch the ship again."

Tutann stepped into the water, trusting the old wanderer and when he did; his body began to feel different. Light cloaked his body yet again and he felt himself getting stronger. And there was something else. It felt to him like a small creature was running through his skin, then a dark sword appeared and he pulled it up out of the ship. When he raised it to the air it took on the color of his skin completely and he tried to drop it but it moved to clamp itself to his back, melting within his skin. He pulled it out again. It was huge in size but very light in his hand. He marveled at its design and craftsmanship. He began to swing it lightly back and forth then he sat it on the ground. The sword rose up from the soil to again attach itself to his back. All those gathered began to whisper.

Imhotep was the least surprised at witnessing the weapon's connection to Tutann. Then a screen popped up above the spaceship and his eyes were glued to the message beginning to play.

He listened carefully while everyone was speaking to Tutann. He looked at Hutap then at Tutann and after several more moments passed, the images disappeared and he thought about the message.

Imhotep decided to keep the message to himself for the moment, the day was turning into night, everyone was tired and began to leave to get a good night's rest.

The next day, Tutannharmoon dug out the insides of the cave he lived in, making enough room for his entire community to be safe should it come to this. He then created a line that could send water to the cave entrance and lastly he blocked the front entrance to the cave with a huge boulder making it only accessible to normal people.

Later that night, Tutann said his goodbyes and his mother, Kisse, cried.

He promised to bring his father back safely and she believed him but she was also frightened for him; she kissed him gently. Shortly afterward, he set out with Imhotep, Ahknonkineton and Hutapsunnimoon as the three companions headed toward the northeast.

Hutapsunnimoon realized how serious the threat was and she decided to head home to warn her community first. A day later, she caught up with Imhotep and the others during the night. They were gathered around a fire and she took a seat next to Tutannharmoon. Imhotep spoke to them of the alien race as they all listened attentively. He talked on and on as stars lit up the sky. Imhotep was glad that the three were getting along for they would need to be in sync and rely on one another in order to win and Imhotep was bent on winning this fight.

For the next several days, they traveled by foot seeing some of the great sights Alkebu-lan had to offer. Large green pastures, colorful trees and millions of migrating animals. Imhotep gazed back seeing the gleams in their eyes for all of this was new to them. These were things they would never see if they did not have the chance to travel beyond their homes. They spoke about their backgrounds and learned they had many things in common and he was glad they were getting better acquainted.

The bond between them was needed to overcome the advancement of the Garthian race. He looked back while they were unaware of his watchful eyes, knowing one or more of them would probably die to win a victory. But in war, it was to be expected. He continued forward as he listened to their conversation.

"What was it like for you Ahknon, when you first learned of your powers?" asked Hutapsunnimoon.

"Well for me, it was different from you and Tutann. You two happened to stumble upon the craft which gave you your powers. It seems as if the craft understood your daily routine. Tutann went to the river for a bath every day and you, Hutap, always went out to hunt alone but with me it was different. I live in a major city, for it to crash in the city it would have probably been picked up and sold to anyone who deemed it worthy to purchase and I would have never found it unless it fell on my uncle's tent. I was chasing Imhotep for answers and to be honest it took me months to catch him but in my pursuit I left the city behind and that is where I stumbled upon it."

"The spacecraft!" Tutann and Hutap exclaimed together.

Tutann thought about the power of a race of people capable of sending a spacecraft somewhere deep in the outer reaches of space and to choose an individual among so many. It was the most spectacular thing he ever heard of and he looked at Hutap and realized she was thinking the same thing. They both continued to listen.

"Yes! Imhotep made me touch it. He wanted to see what I would gain."

Walking on the path behind Imhotep, Hutapsunnimoon was on his left side while Tutannharmoon was bringing up the rear. Tutann began to speak, a deep, rumbling sound left his lips,

"Yes, in a sense, Hutapsunnimoon's situations and mine are alike but there is one big difference, I was only 5 years old!"

Imhotep, Ahknon, and Hutap stopped in shocked, turning to face the giant Tutann as he continued to explain.

"I was transformed from a young child instantly to what you see now. Not only did I change physically but mentally as well. All of a sudden I knew a lot about the things around me."

"Well then, it's even more amazing that the craft chose you out of all of the people in your community. Your mother and father probably never even spoke to you of this war and suddenly you are transformed from a boy to a man. To both of them you are still their young boy inside this huge outer shell," said Imhotep.

"Is it possible that these other races are so advanced Imhotep, that they had the intelligence to choose us before any of us were born? Is it possible that these crafts were dispatched many years ago?" asked Ahknon.

"Yes, from the things you have all explained it has to be the case. Right?" Hutap said, looking at Imhotep. She then looked at the very handsome Tutann as she touched his arm softly and he looked down into her eyes.

"Well yes, it is possible. The ship may have held androids which are artificial life forms that could live thousands of years after we have perished. The life forms may be able to calculate or program a computer to find distinct forms of life and a particular person that would meet a certain category. So yes, it is very possible to have chosen you while each of you was still in your mother's womb. They would have made an assessment of your parents to gain the knowledge they needed. You would be very surprised at the things I could tell you about," explained Imhotep.

They all settled back into silence. For days they continued to the northeast. They entered another stone forest down the middle, southern region that would provide some cover as they marched steadily on.

Chapter 17

Captain Acee towered high above the normal Garthian soldier. Their uniforms were deep gray in appearance. Each soldier carried double swords as well as a double, short–bladed weapon in a side pocket just below the short jacket. The weapon was full and powerful but he was ordered that the weapon wasn't to be used. He agreed with Commander Ior but he wanted his men wearing the weapon just in case.

To Acee, it would secure the win against the enemy. Out of the ten thousand original men, he was now down to nine thousand. The beings of this young planet fought hard and he learned that they had found an easy way to injure or kill his soldiers with rear attacks.

In the weeks to follow, he ushered in many of the large creatures and he brought in the land surfer. It was a craft that hovered from three to fifty feet above ground and could carry three Garthian soldiers at a time. There were light cannons aboard. It was a craft that was twenty feet long and eleven feet wide, effective on any type of terrain and it was quick and fast. Between the land surfer cannons and the huge beast's consumption of this new race of people, he felt he had them on the run. They were powerless to stop them and he refused to look bad before his commander; a win here was a step in the right direction.

A large group of soldiers was headed north with several one–eyed creatures, a large serpent moved across the ground ahead of them and various select other large beasts followed suit.

Acee then looked to the south. He had dispatched four thousand soldiers to the north and south. He was leading the army heading south, sitting inside his hover craft that was being pulled by two large one–eyed giants. Their lower bodies were covered in thick fur with wide noses and a mouth with large, flat teeth. They stood twenty feet tall and it pulled the craft forward as Acee yelled out, "Move it now!"

As his forces pushed through the trees, two of his main security to his left held chains attached to a large, lavender two-headed cat with spots across his coat and large sharp claws. It stood at over twelve feet tall and twenty feet long and its tail swiped back and forth viciously. Just below the surface another huge beast followed. Captain Acee relaxed a bit, eyeing his men entering the tree line. They began to disappear inside; several minutes passed and still nothing. He was really enjoying the slow taking of this planet. A win here most certainly meant a promotion, he thought.

The clash of metal sounded followed by the sounds of shouting coming from the dense stand of trees. His men had found the rebels. He was excited as more of his troops rushed into the wooded area. Acee could tell from the shouts of his men that the fighting was intense but the trees cloaked the actually battle.

He grew concerned as the battle went on longer than he had expected. His view was obstructed and that further angered him. Normally, he would send one of his flying beasts but they were with his forces in the north. He heard screams from his men and the soldier of the planet so he screamed out, "Release the cat beast!" As the chains released the beast it catapulted forward, its feet kicking up dirt in its forward motion.

Butann and his men had been hiding throughout the large, dense trees for weeks now, since their last battle. They moved back south to this area and learned the invaders were headed in their direction. Here is where they lay a trap; thousands of his men lay in wait. Some were in tunnels below the soil. Others were up above upon branches. Their bows and arrows ready.

It was virtually impossible for the Garthians to see his men posted above them holding weapons because of the amount of leaves covering them. He watched closely as the Garthians marched closer. Butann noticed the leader being pulled along the ground by two large one-eyed beasts and on the left of the metal object being pulled was a two–headed cat beast measuring five times the size of the brown cat that lived here in Alkebu-lan.

Butann watched as the strange creatures and men moved toward them. They were only one hundred yards out now and closing in fast. He let out a bird call to alert the men in the trees and underground. As they approached the tree line, he moved farther back behind a large tree that provided cover.

Butann noticed just a few at first and then many Garthians moved in among the trees. When hundreds had entered, he yelled out, "Kill the enemies now!"

Hundreds of arrows rained down from the treetops, connecting with throats, heads and shoulders as Garthians yelled and screamed from their injuries. Many of the Garthians turned and looked upward, throwing large blades up at their attackers but the Alkebu-lan soldiers exploded out of the underground tunnels, attacking from the rear. The clash of metal rung loudly in the air as Garthians littered the ground. Butann had chosen this patch of trees knowing it would be difficult for the large beasts to maneuver; they would be less mobile than his smaller fighters.

More Garthian fighters moved in and his archers released more arrows at their targets, killing many more. Butann pulled his sword out and entered the heat of the battle, moving in to assist his men. His blade moved swiftly, cutting into the first Garthian he saw, severing its arms then cutting deeply into another's neck. The clashing of metal sounded all throughout the trees.

Then a patch of trees to his right exploded inward; it was the large, cat beast. Butann watched it leap upward and take hold of a few of his men, killing them instantly, each of the beast's head bit down upon his soldiers, slanging their bodies off to the side. Then it leaped to the next tree, biting down on several other Alkebu-lan soldiers. He listened to his men's screams for help as the beast roared loudly. Butann rushed into the beast's direction banging his swords together and yelling loudly to get the beast's attention.

The large, two–headed beast turned quickly in his direction and stomped his way forward, knocking trees down—Butann readied himself.

Further to the north, Nassir viewed the military force of his enemies. Three large, metal birds were stationed seven hundred yards from where he and his men stood, ready for their next attack. These large, flying objects were the key; if somehow he could take these crafts, he felt he could win the war, he was wondering how Butann and his men were making out.

A large force of Garthians headed north towards Kemet, but Kemet military forces were even greater the farther north the Garthians traveled. He noticed another force of Garthians moving among some trees and the sound of fighting among the trees had Nassir's attention.

Then Nassir watched as a huge, cat beast was released and it moved across a field rushing into the large forest. He heard branches breaking and snapping as the cat beast knocked down the first tree. His eyes widened, knowing that Butann and his men were among the trees waiting.

As clashes of metal and shouts rose up to the sky. The Garthian general's metal craft with the two one-eyed creatures attached to it on chains begin to move and Nassir noticed the sand moving like waves headed for the trees.

Nassir screamed out, "Kill our enemies!"

Every one of his men charged into battle with swords drawn, spears held high and arrows ready to fly. Nassir led his men with both swords aimed to kill; his body tense with anticipation for the coming battle.

Captain Acee stood now in his hovercraft and viewed the trees from a distance. He gave the order to one of his soldiers standing beside his craft to release the sand beast.

He watched as the huge beast moved across the field towards the trees. The soil rolled like a huge wave. He smiled knowing now that his enemies had set a trap.

But it was the least of his concerns, as he watched the large waves enter the tree line and trees were uprooted then crashed down to the ground. He noticed there were enemy soldiers high in the branches; some fell to their deaths. He turned around quickly after hearing shouting behind him and saw another army of enemy soldiers heading his way.

Acee pressed a lever on the cart and it released the large one-eyed beast. They turned around and moved towards the charging army, their feet hitting the ground loudly with every step and their arms open wide and mouths roaring loudly.

Butann screamed out! His swords banging together as the cat beast moved in for the kill. He raised his swords up high and watched the powerful cat move forward with a loud roar. Its muscles flexed, as it leapt high into the air to pounce and Butann leapt at the same time, latching on to a tree branch and swinging up and over the head of the cat. He heard it land with a thud behind him.

All around him his men were fighting but he focused on this predator. He turned as the large cat headed his way again. He bent down low and raced forward. His heart was beating quickly inside his chest and sweat poured from his head as each step brought him closer and closer to the beast.

He faked a jump to the right knowing the beast was smart enough to anticipate his next move. It leaped and he pulled back, moving under the large cat. He kept moving forward, not once looking back but knowing the beast was close upon him. His feet hit the dark soil and he breathed deeply; if the beast caught up to him he was a dead man.

Butann saw a break in the trees and he smiled. He was almost there.

He began to shout, ""Ha Tom Ba, Ha Tom Ba!"

As he broke through the tree line the cat beast exploded through right behind him and large war elephants rushed towards the cat beast with their tusks pointed forward; their loud bellows reached the skies above. The war elephants collided with the large predators as other war elephants moved in to join the attack as Butann stood far behind, watching with his sword firmly in his hands.

Butann watched the large cat swipe at them using its left paw and connect with the side of the elephant's head as it hit the ground, bellowing loudly.

An even larger war elephant rammed the cat with its head. The cat beast tossed it several feet away to collide with the trees and it hit the ground hard. Butann watched as his war elephants stormed forward for another attack and the cat got to its feet and began circling.

Keeping his war elephants at a distance, they moved in close together. His war elephant rammed the cat one last time and it roared in pain then leaped up over the gathering beasts and broke for the tree line back into the woods.

Butann heard more screams as his men moved towards him leaving the forest behind. Hundreds screamed, looking behind them and pointing as more and more men followed. Then Butann notice the trees were being uprooted and sailing through the air. He called to his elephants and they rushed towards him.

Then he knew the reason the trees were being torn apart as he saw a huge beast rise up high above the trees. Its mouth revealed thousands of teeth, millions of small legs extended from its bottom and its skin was like armor. It turned to look at him then a wet substance rained down out of the creature's mouth. Butann turned when he and his men and the war elephants moved away, putting distance between them and this new threat. The beast hit the ground and moved to follow them but they all ran across the ground quickly, leaving the huge beast behind.

Nassir and his men killed one of the large, one-eyed beasts but before its death it was able to kill a large portion of his men. The last beast fought hard as his men rained spears into the creature's side. The beast ripped the weapon out then stomped forward, taking hold, crushing and biting his soldiers. Nassir was surprised at how quickly the creature could move. Its body was now covered in its own blood.

Then Nassir heard the sounds of another large creature and when he turned it was the two–headed cat racing across the field to assist the one-eyed beast. Nassir reached down to pick up his spear and when he looked up, he heard a loud thump and the cat was standing in front of him.

He called out, "Men, retreat now!"

He took a lunge toward the cat but something took hold of the spear and when he looked up, the one-eyed creature towered high above his head. It reached down and grabbed him, lifting him off the ground, carrying him towards the craft where a Garthian was waiting. Later, he was restrained and laid in the back of the moving craft. He could not remember how long the ride was but once reaching the huge, metal bird he was ushered inside to a holding pen with many others, some women and children, that the Garthians had collected.

After settling in, he noticed there were other cages with a huge selection of animals from Abyssinia; birds, cats, apes and more. Nassir began to wonder what their plans were for these creatures and his people.

The cage was large enough for all inside to have room to move around and he checked to see if everyone was doing well. He learned they were given food and water daily. He was now out of the war but not out of the fight. Nassir observed everything about the strange metal bird. Days passed and then so did weeks. Time kept moving but he never gave up the thought of freedom.

Far North Abyssinia

"What should we do now that the Garthians are moving this way?" asked Tu-Ney.

"Well love, I guess we will just move to another location."

"These men may need us. We cannot go too far away," said E-Newtu.

E-Newtu watched his wife rubbing her hands together and then she rubbed her face.

"I'm very scared E-Newtu. What will happen to us once they find out where we are hiding?" Tu-Ney asked, this time looking her husband in the eyes.

E-Newtu looked around the room as his eyes fell on the thousands of men who had fought to save their homelands and then his eyes looked at his wife and he said,

"I understand your concerns, we are of the same mind in that regard but look around you; thousands are fighting to prevent these beings from controlling us. Who knows what they really came for? Maybe they need the land and we will all die at their hand, who knows. Nothing will be revealed to us until it is too late to do anything about it. Men and boys are dying out there in the field," E- Newtu pointed then continued, "the least we can do is continue to help those with injuries." He took Tu-Ney in his arms. "I know it's tough but it will all be worth it, we will win as long as we stay as one. Alright, you have to trust me on this one Tu-Ney," said E-Newtu.

"Yes, my love, I trust you," Tu-Ney said and then she embraced her husband tightly, when they had released each other they kissed briefly.

More injured men moved into the tents as Tu-Ney and E-Newtu moved apart. They moved around the tent, closing gaping wounds with needle and thread, placing splints and bandaging other body parts. E-Newtu moved to another soldier's bed and saw that this patient was in his late seventies, his hair was completely gray and his skin was a leathery brown, dry and wrinkled. In his right hand was his sword and tears shone in the soldier's eyes. Even this old man wanted to do his part in the war but after E-Newtu examined the patient, he explained to the old fellow that there was to be no more fighting for him. He had sustained an injury to his right lung which made his voice sound raspy and made his breathing difficult, so E-Newtu injected the old man with a painkiller.

"Well old timer, you have fought your last fight. It's time to let the younger men fight. I know your heart is there but you need some much needed rest, ok?" E-Newtu said. He took his eyes off the old fellow for a few seconds and when he turned back around the old man's eyes were frozen in time as death crept in suddenly.

E-Newtu closed the old fellow's eyes as sadness consumed him. This was an elder, a man who would normally be found resting at home, being pampered by his family but he had been compelled to fight. He pulled the covers up over his head and looked around as a new wave of men entered the tent with fresh injuries. A young woman walked his way so E-Newtu asked her, "Find out who this man is and where he comes from so we may send word he fought hard and will be remembered."

The woman found some assistants to carry the body away to be buried. A tear fell from his eyes but he wiped it away quickly. He knew he had to be strong for his other patients; he could show no sign of weakness. He moved around the tent finding his next patient and sat down next to her. She was a small woman with a golden brown complexion and she was holding her ribs so E-Newtu offered her comfort and aid.

Chapter 18

Farther South

Imhotep lead the companions at a steady pace, moving through the scorching heat. Imhotep created cool winds to cool and comfort them as the sandy hills rose up and down for miles in every direction.

Vegetation was at a minimum and small rodents and insects found the sands to be a luxury home from large predators. Tumbleweed bounced around on the barren sands.

They moved on until the sun sat directly above their heads, then Imhotep noticed an oasis of several large trees with plenty of shade. He also noticed that the trees held fruit and there was a pond large enough to have a nice swim in. As they got closer to the oasis they began to hear and see birds of all colors and rich, beautiful tones.

Each of the companions found a nice spot under the tree. Tutann was the least affected by the heat so he began to move towards the water. As he stepped in, snakes and other small sea animals scurried out of his way. Tutann sunk below the surface as his companions watched him go.

"What is this place, Imhotep and how could it survive out here so far away from everything?" asked Hutap, looking around at the place in wonder.

"I've seen places like this before not far from the Kemet city. It seems to be a wonderful place. It is just strange to see it out here in the middle of nowhere," said Ahknon, while looking at Hutap swiping at the flies around her head.

"Well, nature has a way of providing for its creatures even in a place as barren as this. See those birds up in the trees? I noticed them miles back heading in this direction; they are migratory birds and I often follow them when I find myself in the middle of the hot desert because I knew they would lead us here. During the changing of the seasons you can spot them moving in packs across the hot sands and they have saved many lives. So remember the things you learn for you may need them one day," Imhotep said.

Ahknon and Hutap stood up and began eating fruit from the trees. There was a long yellow fruit that was very sweet and tasty. It was mostly eaten by the large apes found farther south but there were also fig trees, so each of them had their fill, including Imhotep.

"It has been a good while since Tutann sank below the water's surface," Hutap said, moving to the water's edge. She gazed down into the water to see Tutann lying on his back looking up at her. She smiled then looked back at Ahknon, then Imhotep and said, "I wonder how long he could stay under the water without one breath of air; this is really amazing."

There was a sudden movement, as Tutann broke through the water's surface and water splashed everywhere. Hutap moved quickly, putting distance between her and the water. Imhotep was sealed inside an air cell while Ahknon stood there soaked.

"Ha-Ha Ahknon, you have to be quicker than that!" said Hutap.

Imhotep was also smiling as water ran down the outside of his air cell.

Ahknon looked down at his clothing then at Tutann, who was smiling a large smile and he said, "Well, the water felt great, especially with all this heat bearing down upon us!" Everyone laughed.

Hutap moved to the water's edge. In a flash, it caught Tutann by surprise as he stumbled back a step.

"How did you hold your breath for so long?" Hutap asked.

"Well, I don't know," Tutann said, rubbing the top of his head in confusion. But he continued, "I guess it was a part of what I received from the craft."

Imhotep interjected by saying, "Hutapsunnimoon, you and Tutann's powers are related, you should be able to survive under water in the same fashion. Your powers are derived from a race of beings called Saguardians, Tutann holds the totality of the male genetic structure and you the female, so go ahead and try it."

She stared at Imhotep for a long while then looked at Tutannharmoon as she stepped into the water, moving in until her body was totally submerged. Maybe this is the reason she had such strong feelings for him, she thought to herself.

Tutann followed her down. Ahknon watched the two disappear underneath the water's surface then looked at Imhotep and asked, "There is more to those two than you are telling us, isn't there?"

"Yes, there may be more but you do not need to know the answer, not yet at least. It's very important that you don't bring this question up in front of them, understand?" Imhotep said, whispering.

Imhotep moved to the water's surface and followed the other two in. Ahknon moved away from the water's surface and lay down in the soft sand enjoying the heat of the sun. His clothing was quickly drying and time passed but neither of his companions came up for air. He thought of the beautiful woman called Isis and wondered if she and her cousins were safe. He really began to wonder how things would have turned out between the two of them.

Then he thought of the war and wondered how many people would die. He wasn't worrying about dying; he would do what was needed against the invaders. He stood up and went through several fighting motions as he became one with the war spirits living inside the sun spear. He spun his spear around in a circle from side to side as an ancient voice played inside his mind. He opened up to them as he threw several attack jabs, some chops, several kicks and elbow strikes then he made a right step and threw his spear as hard as he could.

It cut through the air, moving to somewhere off in the distance. Voices entered his mind again and he moved his legs forward quickly, jumping as high as he could as the spear re-entered his hand. It carried him across the ground at amazing speed and he extended his left arms as he coasted on the winds. He was flying across the ground, his clothing bellowed against the wind.

As he continued to soar, he pointed the spear down as his body moved quickly towards the ground. Now he was only a few hundred feet from the ground so he pushed his arms forward as his body moved faster, quickly locating the oasis and he landed gently just below a large tree to rest a bit.

Ahknon looked around and noticed that Imhotep, Tutann and Hutap were still under water. He took a seat below the tree, wondering what else this new gift would reveal to him. He looked up and imagined being in the clouds; the view from up there would be breathtaking. He was wakened from his daydream by Hutap, Imhotep and Tutann exiting the water and coming to lie beside the tree. Imhotep then said, "We leave when the blanket of night covers the sky when the air is cooler. We are so close to the stone forest; it won't be long now, so you all get some rest."

Time passed and the bright stars covered the skies above. The next morning the clouds moved in on the western winds and lightning flashed. Suddenly, the rain came down, lightly at first, then it began to pour. Imhotep cast out three spheres that sealed Hutap, Ahknon and himself from being soaked by the rain. Tutann fancied the rain water and followed several feet behind his companions enjoying it. For the next several miles they walked until the sandy ground turned into rocky terrain. They moved up a steady slope and kept climbing until the sandy ground was far below them all. The rain stopped and the sun was beginning to shine. The walkways were narrow but the companions moved forward following behind Imhotep.

Trees were growing along with thorny bushes and colorful flowers along the side of the high cliffs. Large, ground rodents peeked out from burrows as they passed. Several paces up, the companions passed some large, flightless birds of with long necks and large feet.

Hutap looked down below her in wonder. The trees on the ground were so small but she could still see very clearly. Ahknon focused on the mountain itself, a place he would love to visit on his own or maybe with the young lady, Isis.

Shortly afterward, Imhotep led them to a high cliff. They looked on in wonder as rivers of water in a huge circle came together in one spot as a waterfall and at the center of the fall were what Hutap and Ahknon noticed was the stone forest, just several feet from the cliff's face.

"Yes, it's the stone forest that will take us to Abyssinia. In my long travels I have been through this place twice; it will take us only a day to reach our location," said Imhotep.

Tutann spoke up in his deep, rumbling voice,

"How is it possible that water is moving from every direction to this one large center down into a hole? How deep is that fall to sustain the amount of water entering it?" He said in wonder, as he continued to look down.

"This place is beautiful; the water so blue and clear," said Hutap.

"Are we to enter that stone center? But how is that possible? And you told me that the stone forest was a place where giants traveled," said Ahknon. Eyebrows arched now, rubbing his head.

"Well, I would guess from their size it was possible for them to leap out catching the center," said Imhotep.

"But what happened if they missed?" said Hutap, watching the water fall down seemingly without end.

"You know what happened; it was the end of their life," said Tutann.

Ahknon, Hutap and Tutann watched as Imhotep whispered a few words that none of them could understand and then a very large sphere appeared above their heads. It was huge and clear and made them wonder what Imhotep's plan was. Then they watched the sphere fly into the huge circular river, submerging itself beneath the surface where it exploded out of the water. It was full of very blue water and the sphere began to elongate as Imhotep motioned with his hands. It reached out to touch the center of the stone forest and extended to reach the cliff's face.

Tutann, Ahknon and Hutap looked on in awe as the sphere expanded to accommodate their passage through, then they watched the blue water turn into solid white and extend into the stone forest.

"That's ice. We can walk through it to the stone forest," said Imhotep.

They all looked up at him as Imhotep began walking across as the other three soon followed.

"This is truly amazing! Where could all of this water be traveling to? The water is travelling at 360 degrees to enter this one opening," said Hutap.

The sprays of water drifted upward into the air leaving a moist, clingy feeling. The companions followed Imhotep over the ice into a large entrance way at the center of the falls. Its opening revealed a large mountain structure sunk down in the middle of the falls. There were letters outside the cave as Imhotep entered first; followed by Hutap, Ahknon and finally, Tutann.

After climbing down several hundred feet, Hutap moved in front to lead the way and they kept following the path leading down to level ground until they begin to see some light at the end. They continued to follow the path, unaware of the time below. They came to an opening sometime later, exiting and moved out into the wood lands.

They marched across the open fields where wild antelope roamed the land. Hutap noticed something to her right, a large opening leading down into the soil even larger than the entrance to the stone forest.

Imhotep headed in that direction. Then he stopped at the tunnel entrance while a strong smell drifted to his nose. In all his years he has never smelled anything so pungent and he and his companions had to turn away. Imhotep said,

"A tunnel leading out into the open could only mean that the Garthians are on the move. This could be the burrow of one of their pets; whatever it is, it's huge. It may be some kind of worm so we have to deal with it first."

Imhotep moved inside the burrow and stopped to listen. His ears picked up movement a great distance away so he marched right inside and Ahknon followed him with hands firmly on his weapon with Hutap and Tutann following closely at the rear.

Imhotep looked around at the walls; they were circular and thirty feet wide and thirty feet tall.

"Listen, there is something really big down here. Let's find and destroy it and continue on our way. Whatever it is, sooner or later, we will have to face it. Why not face it now?" he said, looking back at the companions.

Each of them agreed with a nod of their heads.

Imhotep led them further down, at least another one hundred feet. They came into a passageway that travelled into three different directions. Imhotep listened carefully as Hutap's eyes searched the burrows farther down in every direction. Imhotep continued to follow the burrow, time was ticking and it seemed as though they had been walking for days when they came across what looked like large, green eggs.

"What are these?" asked Hutapsunnimoon.

"These are the eggs of the creature that traverses these burrows. See the silk webbing that protects the eggs?" Imhotep said.

"What manner of beast lays eggs as large as me?" said Ahknon.

Hutap was gazing steadily down the long burrow as Tutann stood directly behind her.

"A beast that is trying to make this place its home," Imhotep answered.

He began whispering some words again and this time a clear sphere appeared and expanded, enclosing the eggs inside. A fire began to burn, consuming the large eggs inside and the light glowed brightly, giving the companions a good view of their surroundings. After completing this task they marched farther into the burrow as smoke moved upward towards the surface.

Hutap took up lead again since her eyes were the best among them and after another several hundred yards Hutap gazed down the dark corridors stopping in her tracks—Imhotep, Ahknon then Tutann stood still.

"What is it Hutap?" Imhotep said.

"I see something moving up ahead," she said.

"I heard something a while ago but I did not know what direction it was moving in," said Imhotep.

"Tutann, stay in this corridor to the left. I will stay here and Ahknon will be on your right. Hutapsunnimoon, since we are in close quarters, we need you with your speed to flush out the creature. Send it this way towards us, understand? Tutann, I need you to try and hold the beast while we attack it," Imhotep said.

Tutann took to the corridor to the left as Imhotep moved into the deep passageway. Hutap and Ahknon were directly across from Tutann.

Hutap moved down the dark corridor quickly, her heart beating loudly inside her chest. This would be her first time using her power against the enemy and she hoped she was ready. She moved closer to where she had first seen the movement. She passed another large passageway. This one had four different paths going separate ways then she noticed large bones and some skulls littering the ground.

She reached back for her long bow as her body moved steadily forward. She smelled the beast's stench. It was suffocating. She then reached for her arrow, called a shooting star, and seeing movement ahead of her, she released several arrows in that direction. They moved quickly lighting up the dark passageway and when it reached its target, a howl burst through the corridor.

Hutap stopped moving and began to release more arrows in a steady stream, their flames lighting up the tunnel then exploding into the creature's side. A green fluid poured out of the creature's wounds and she watched as it turned to look at her. She noticed its head filled the corridor and its teeth were jagged but razor sharp. It began to move for her as the corridor shook then a toe-curling scream of pain blasted through the passageway hurting her ears.

Hutap turned quickly, heading back towards Imhotep up the dark corridor, her feet digging into the soft soil and the huge beast, which she thought looked like some kind of huge grub worm, was moving behind her. Her speed left the creature far behind.

Hutap passed several cross pathways. Suddenly, out of nowhere came another beast. It lunged from a corridor on her right and its large teeth snapped at the air loudly. She barely avoided the attack. She turned quickly to her left down another corridor moving faster. She could hear the beast moving behind her. She had to find another path back toward Imhotep, so she slowed her pace as she came to the end of the passageway; a wall of soil. There was no way out. She turned quickly and the huge beast was moving closer to her so she began releasing arrows one after the other. It's fiery tip sailing through the air making contact and tearing through the beast's head.

Its cry of pain did nothing to deter its movement. As quickly as she could, she notched arrows letting them fly ripping chunks of flesh from the beast. It was now only one hundred yards away and closing. Desperately, she continued to let arrows fly.

Tutann was waiting on Hutap to pass by but she never came. The beast's screams reached his ears and then he heard a second scream, much different from the first. A short while later he watched Imhotep looking down the long passageway as a globe of fire appeared inside his hand lighting the dark corridor. Then he watched Imhotep's eyes open widely in alarm. Another sphere quickly appeared inside his hands, then words fell from his mouth.

"Tutann! Hutap may be in trouble, get that beast!" Imhotep screamed.

Anger exploded inside him and a roar louder than the one that came from the creature blasted down the corridor. His feet stomped the ground as his body moved forward and words entered his mind, *The Bringer of Death, The Indestructible,* with fear, the powerful Tutann raced towards the creature.

Imhotep and Ahknon moved behind the large Tutannharmoon and Imhotep noticed that there were two beasts. He quickly cast two spheres over Tutann's head and they expanded, growing large as the fiery sphere rolled down the corridor to its target, blasting the beast in its face with rippling fire. It screamed again from the double explosion.

Tutann was now in total rage as his skin began to crawl but he paid it no mind. He was concerned for Hutap. He turned right at the end of the passageway taking hold of a large creature by the rear end, holding tightly to stop the creature's forward movement. It screamed trying to free itself but Tutann dug his feet into the soil and began to pull with all his strength.

He felt the creature giving way as he pulled backwards. Then bright lights flashed behind him as a second beast was being attacked by Imhotep and Ahknon but he was focused on what he was prepared to do, so he kept pulling.

Ahknon threw the sun spear at the huge beast and on contact it exploded through its skin and the beast cried out in pain. When his weapon had returned to him he tossed it again as the tip turned bright white, slicing through the beast's head. Imhotep followed Ahknon's attack with two large blocks of ice as large as the corridor itself, and they collided with the beast's head, crushing its mouth and part of its skull.

As they moved closer to the creature, they noticed Tutann fighting a second beast, dragging it backwards as it fought against his powerful pull. Imhotep smiled. Tutann's power was too great for the large beast. Ahknon noticed Tutann's body seemed alive with movement and his skin seemed to move on its own.

As he and Imhotep took a closer look, huge insect-like creatures crawled around his body. Some were devouring the rear of the large beast Tutann had taken ahold of. Then Tutann disappeared into another passageway dragging the beast with him. Then the beast's head appeared and it looked at Imhotep and Ahknon before disappearing up another passageway.

Imhotep moved quickly to the passage the beast was pulled from and out came Hutapsunnimoon.

"Are you alright?" Imhotep said, as a sphere appeared inside his hand, lighting up the passageway with fire while his eyes searched her body for injuries.

Ahknon smiled down at her and said, "That was very close."

"Yes it was. That passageway I ran down is a dead end. It was the only option I had at the moment. That creature's teeth came this close to me!" Hutap said using two fingers to show the distance. "I hit the creature over and over again in its big head but it still came for me. It stinks too." She stopped talking to look around. "Where is Tutann?"

"Oh, he is fine. He just dragged that beast away from you all by himself," said Imhotep.

At that moment, Tutann came back down the corridor towards them. The fiery glow of light from the fire that burned inside Imhotep's hand revealed Tutann's skin and the spider-like creatures swarming across his body erratically.

Imhotep, Hutap and Ahknon all stared at the insects. As Tutann began to relax, the insects that were as large as Ahknon's hands, moved towards the vein–like openings in Tutann's skin. For the first time, Tutann looked down at his own body, rubbing his chest as the last of the insect-like creatures disappeared. They did not concern him. He actually liked the ugly looking things because in a sense they helped him prevail and were just another part of his powers.

"What was that?" said Ahknon, pointing.

"I guess it is another part of the powers I received when I touched the craft the second time. I was wondering why the worm-like beast's rear end was being consumed. I think the creatures understand when there is a threat. Did you get a look at that beast? It had several eyes and small legs all around its entire body. There is nothing left after those creatures got a hold of it," Tutann said, pointing to his chest.

He looked down at Hutap then he asked, "Are you alright?"

"Yes I am, thanks to you," Hutap said, moving close to him and touching him on the hand.

"We have to move. If these creatures are this far out, then Kemet and Abyssinia is in need of our help," said Imhotep, turning to move up the large corridor. The last beast moved slightly and Imhotep stopped.

Tutann stepped in front of the others and said, "This creature may have been a peaceful beast back where it came from before the Garthians caught it but like the other creatures it fights because it must. I will take its life quickly. Now I understand the laying of the egg. It was to keep its kind alive. These two may be the last of its kind," said Tutann.

Tutann took hold of the beast's head and the insect-like creature inside him smelled the stench of blood and rushed out to devour the beast. In a very short time, there was nothing left and the companions moved off quickly, following behind Imhotep.

Imhotep decided it was best to continue through the underground passageway without being seen. The companions continued with Hutap taking up the lead, heading down deeper beneath the Alkebu-lan soil and disappearing totally into the dark passageway.

Chapter 19

Eastern Abyssinia, Command Center of the Garthians

"Well Captain Ior, these rebels are showing signs of being a tough adversary. The forces are pushing farther north toward their main city and the southern forces have the rebels on the run. Also, there are several creatures missing that were sent out on a scouting mission. They have not returned which is unusual, the large, red flying beast Gedoe, two of the very large, ground dwellers."

"Even if we are controlling the ground attacks, we are still losing a great deal of our soldiers, especially now that more rebels are getting involved. How is team leader Tigr making out?" asked Ior.

"Well Captain, he is moving his army towards the main enemy farther north and the people called Abyssinians. But we also experienced another loss," said Sith, a small Garthian soldier with missing teeth at the front of his mouth.

"Well, I expected loss. Death is normal in war; as long as they take the greater loss. I have asked Commander Acee to block the land of Abyssinia and to prevent outside help from reaching them. This will help keep the resistance from escaping or expanding their forces. They will run out of supplies, there will be nowhere for them to turn and their fighters will be too weak to fight," said Captain Ior. He now looked up at a large screen just above him as personnel moved throughout the ship.

"Thank you, Sir. With this new information, I can continue the advancement of my forces. It will be sometime before the rebels know about the new perimeter," said Sith.

"Have you any captives? You know that Commander Acee wants prisoners?" asked Captain Ior.

"Yes, I have caught a select group of males and females as well as a few little ones," Sith said, bowing to his superior officer.

"Well, you're doing very well. I'm looking forward to seeing what these creatures look like," said Captain Ior.

I have also captured a wide range of animals for scientific research. You would be amazed Captain, at the similarities in the species of life to the Garthians. Do you think the commander would like to look at them?" asked Sith.

"Yes, Commander Acee would like that very much. In fact, the commander gave me specific orders to ship these creatures to him," said Captain Ior.

"Well, they can be shipped after they have been quarantined. No one can know what kind of infectious bugs this race carries and I won't be the one to blame for the death of any of the staff on the star cruiser," said Sith, saluting his commanding officer then taking his leave.

Captain Ior turned to his right to see his second highest ranking officer, Tigr, coming towards him. Tigr was a younger version of himself. Tigr was raised in the military back in their world of Garthian. He came from a long line of fighting Garthians who traveled the eleven dimensions of the multiverse, winning victories over many worlds.

The Garthian planet in the tri-sector of the known universe is a planet whose occupants live below ground in a city of rock and metal. Garthian revolves around twin suns that raised the heat far beyond normal conditions on its surface. There are five moons that rotate around Garthian and when each moon is in a particular orbit, their position blocks out the rays of the twin suns. During this time, the temperatures are much cooler, the Garthian beings move to the planet's surface for long periods of time.

Thousands of years before the Garthians had set out to conquer space, they lived a very peaceful existence. The people of a planet called Tariath, which sat one million miles from Garthian, were the original ones who migrated to the Garthian planet. Hundreds of years passed and Garthian became independent of Tariath's rule and over another one thousand years their appearance changed. The Tariathians warred with them to regain control of the Garthian race but discontinued the war after their world was hit with an asteroid a quarter the size of their planet.

After the Garthian's experience with the Tariathians, the younger generation developed and evolved to exact vengeance upon the known multiverse. They began construction of bigger and better fighting, space vehicles that could store solar power for over hundreds of years. The solar panels could absorb the slightest glimpse of light from any of the millions of known suns throughout the multiverse.

The Garthian race was certain that at least forty percent of the stars had orbiting planets and that many of these planets had, at some time in their history, atmospheric and thermal conditions conducive to the formation of amino acids and other organic chemicals that were necessary for any biology. As a race, this was something they could reasonably hypothesize.

Captain Ior was brought back to the present as Tigr stood before him.

"Captain, you were saying?" asked Tigr, standing straight and tall.

"You are to march your forces to the north and take up control of the forces there entirely. The main city must fall! From what Officer Sith said the captives call it Kemet. I have set a shield in place to keep the rebels inside and to also prevent any help to assist them during our ground attacks. Understand?" said Captain Ior.

"Yes, I understand, Captain. I will move out right away," said Tigr; each of his three limbs reaching for his chest in salute. As he turned to walk away, Captain Ior called him back.

"Listen, show no mercy! Once we assume control over this place the shields will expand to further our reach, so kill everything out there. We have enough captives and have no need for more," he finished.

"Yes Captain!" said Tigr, as he turned around to exit the captain's station. The door closed behind him and he moved quickly to his hovercraft.

Inside one of the dozens of large holding cells, Nassir moved around. It had high ceilings with metal boxes pushing air into the enclosure. The metal boxes moved in all directions above their heads and large, metal gates held them inside but they could see everything. Nassir looked back as the group laid side by side watching his every move. Children were playing, others cried and some talked of their families. He gazed upwards several times. After being captured, he was brought here by the large, one-eyed beast and he entered the large, flying, metal bird; it was large than his whole community. Every day since, he had been watching their every move. Women consoled their children, offering comfort and looking to him for hope. A few men stepped near.

"What are your plans?" asked Bugo, a tall, dark fellow. Other men looked on waiting for his answer.

Nassir looked at the men then around the room before he said, "First, we must make sure the women, children and especially the elders, are safe. I do not want to launch an attack on these beings who call themselves Garthians and they use those weapons at their belts. I've seen how they work. Should they begin using them inside this cage, no one will be safe. The main guards will be easy to take out and extract those metal things that unlock the doors; the only problem is that we will need time to get everyone out. And from the way things are looking, we may just have that opportunity but what still concerns me is, are we going to be able to get everyone out?" He looked at every man around him.

"Yes, you're right, even if we free ourselves, we will still be out in the open after leaving the iron bird," said Bugo.

"Now, what I suggest is a few of you should climb through the air passageway and once you're inside, you can try to either find a way out or just leave and lead soldiers back here with weapons so they can help us all escape," said Nassir.

They all agreed it was the best plan to save them all and after things had calmed down, Bugo and a short man of even darker complexion scaled the high pillars. One Garthian soldier had his back to the cage watching the last of his army leave the metal bird. Nassir looked up quickly to see them disappear inside the large, metal, air passage. He was smiling, thinking there was still hope.

Farther to the Southeast

Butann and his men moved down the face of a cliff on a very thin landing. Far below the jagged rocks appeared next to a river and as they moved around a bend, a large waterfall appeared. White water cascaded down to the river below and a light mist rose in the air. The gray rocks were covered in green moss and yellow and white flowers sprung up between the cracks in the stones. The sky was a light blue as the sun moved towards the west.

They moved closer and closer to the waterfall, taking hold of the rocks as they stepped closer and the landing changed, moving directly under the waterfall. Butann disappeared as the falls blanketed his entrance. The men followed one after the other behind Butann and entered a huge cave. All his men found spots and settled in to get some much needed rest. Many began to fill their water skins as others placed their heads under the steady flow, cooling them off from the hot sun or allowing them to wash up a bit.

Just before scaling down the side of the cliff, Butann had directed that the war elephants be kept in a dense forest several miles away. Ten rode off in that direction; two had been killed in the attack against the large, two-headed cat beast.

As he stood looking through the waterfall at the western skies and the bright star, he thought about his elephants and their safety. None of the Garthians had seen his pets so he felt they would be safe but the huge, cat beast knew him on sight. He thought of trying to put distance between him and the Garthian army but as Butann looked back into the cave, there was food, weapons and other supplies that would aid them. He watched his men rest in every corner or sat eating bread, fruit and beans.

Some of his men were very young boys but they were fighting for the survival of their race. As Butann looked through the waterfall again, thinking of a way to crush the invaders, he heard footsteps and he quickly raised his sword. A man appeared; it was a messenger. The soldier was breathing hard as he entered the huge cave, bending over to take in more air after the long run he had just made.

"Are you alright? Catch your breath," Butann said.

The soldier sat down below Butann and looked up at his commanding officer before saying, "I was heading south to assist you but on my way, I witnessed a battle between Alkebu-lanian soldiers and the Garthians. Many were injured and a few were captured."

Butann looked down on the young man. He wondered for what reason was the Garthians taking prisoners. Would they be used as soldiers? He was silent as he waited to hear more.

"The Garthians took General Nassir, the commander of the forces to the North," he said, still breathing hard.

Butann clinched his teeth and hit the cave wall with his right hand. Nassir was an experienced war general and he worried about who would take his place. They had been waiting for the arrival of another fifty thousand men from the west lands. Word had traveled fast about the need for more forces. Men from communities all over Alkebu-lan were on their way to join the war; there could be well over a million ready and able men willing to fight. He looked out into the falls again then down to the tired soldier beneath him.

"Go find something to eat and get your rest for tomorrow. I will need you to travel west as far as you can travel. Men should be coming our way and you will need to lead them back to the falls but be careful, there are some very dangerous beasts moving into Alkebu-lan."

"Yes, I know a creature with a single eye took General Nassir. It was standing next to a large, two–headed, cat creature," the soldier said, before moving deeper into the cave to find something to eat and a place to rest.

At that very moment, Butann wished he could have killed that beast. His mind drifted to his son's power; powers he could really use now to make things easier. If it was meant for him to die, at least he could die in battle; fighting for his people at his father's side.

The skies above were completely dark now. Butann turned and moved farther into the cave to find food and rest. Tomorrow is a new day and he only had a few hours to rest. He was determined to be ready.

Chapter 20

The companions moved through the huge tunnels underground heading east at a steady pace. Hutap was leading the way, followed by Imhotep, Ahknon and bringing up the rear was Tutann. They traveled through the twisting turns in several directions. Imhotep would stop and listen carefully then point out their path. They continued northeast and they picked up the pace and found an exit out. The moon was fully glowing above their heads and Hutap pointed at another dark object beside the moon.

"What is it? Is it the ship you spoke of, Imhotep?" Hutap asked.

"Yes, it is the ship used by the Garthians. They are the race that seeks this planet's downfall," Imhotep said, glaring at each of the companions around him.

"Wow! Things have changed so quickly for all of us. Normally, I would have paid it no mind but life is so surprising, but the way I perceive things now is so different. There is so much more to learn and now my mind is open to anything," said Ahknon.

"Everything I see and experience is showing me the reality of my life and the possibilities in the dark reaches of space. There is so much more to life and I'm ready to learn if we just survive this invasion," said Tutann.

"Hey, look over here. I just noticed something else," Hutap said, pointing up and all around them.

Imhotep looked in the direction she was pointing to but he saw nothing, so he said, "What do you see Hutap?"

Tutann looked upward to where she was pointing and said, "Well, I don't see anything either."

"What does it look like Hutap?" asked Imhotep.

"It kind of looks like the pocket of air you seal us in but this thing is huge!" Hutap said, looking all around her. "It is travelling above our heads into the sky in all the directions."

"But what is it Imhotep?" asked Tutannharmoon, looking down at the thin figure of the wanderer.

Ahknon gazed upward, looking around to try and see what Hutap was seeing. "You have great eyesight because I can't see a thing."

Imhotep looked around then up at the starship in space then back towards the invisible barrier then over to the huge underground tunnel he and his companion had just exited, then spoke,

"What Hutap is seeing is a force field used by the Garthian's starship."

"What is a force field?" asked Ahknon.

"A force field is a clear barrier that is often used as a means to keep soldiers in or out; in this case the Garthians wanted to keep the Alkebu-lan forces out. It's a viable tactic of war," Imhotep said. Each of the companions looked amazed as Imhotep continued.

"What I'm figuring is that the Garthians are attempting a total take over and they wanted to separate parts of Alkebu-lan to be more effective. It must mean Alkebu-lan soldiers are putting up a good fight and the force field is their only means of control because it prevents other communities from entering the war."

"Well, I can understand that. But you told us the Garthians are a powerful race! They should be able to come in and take the lands by using their powerful weapons," said Ahknon. Each of the companions looked to Imhotep.

"Yes, they should, they have the power to do so but I think it's more of a sport if they fight a world with less chance of prevailing against them, so they are fighting in the old ways, which takes longer. But this is also something that we could use against them; they are underestimating the people of Alkebu-lan," Imhotep finished.

"So, tell me. If the barrier is to keep those in with nowhere to go and others out with no way in, then how did we get through the force field?" asked Ahknon.

"Yes, how did we enter?" Hutap said.

"There are only two rational explanations; one, is that right after we climbed out of the underground tunnels the force field appeared and we were already in it. The second reason could be that the tunnel is far below the force field and we bypassed it altogether," Imhotep said.

"So, which do you think it is?" asked Ahknon, looking from Imhotep to the tunnel.

"Let's find out," said Imhotep, moving toward the tunnel exit. It was huge and able to accommodate the huge creatures that passed through it. He began to mumble a few words and a sphere appeared inside his hand. He cast it toward the tunnel entrance and the others watched it grow into a spinning tube of air visible within the clear globe. The sphere disappeared and the spinning tube was left. Imhotep motioned with his hand and the spinning tube entered the tunnel very quickly.

"Well, we will know shortly. The air tube will hit every tunnel inside the underground passageways. If it returns shortly, then yes, the force field extends far below Alkebu-lan soil and we were lucky to have made it through unharmed. The force field has the power to crush us and we would be dead. But, if the air tube does not return, it means that these passageways extend far below the force field and that means the Garthians are unaware of this opening and the huge beast acted on its own without orders from the Garthian army," said Imhotep.

"Well, if this hole is the only place for Alkebu-lan people to join in the war, it has to remain hidden. Only we can know about this place," said Ahknon.

Hutap was looking at him as Tutann moved toward a forest thick with trees, then they heard a loud noise as if something was breaking.

When Tutann returned he was carrying a tall tree with its roots still attached in his left hand and in his right hand was a large stone about four times his size balancing on his shoulder. He came to the exit of the tunnel and paused as Imhotep cast another spear and it expanded to the size of the tunnel entrance. It was a solid block of ice but Imhotep left enough room for the soldiers to come through. Suddenly, air came rushing through, pushing soil on top of the ice and in seconds, Tutann had created a hole and pushed the tree down into the soil and placed the huge stone next to it, giving it the look of a natural setting.

The companions set off moving in a straight path toward the northeast. Hutap, again, moved ahead followed by Imhotep and Ahknon with Tutann taking up the rear.

After several miles, Imhotep said, "We are now in Abyssinia so keep those eyes of yours sharp, Hutapsunnimoon, and each of you remembers the location of the tunnel; it's vital in this war. Understand?" Each of the companions agreed, pressing forward. They did not stop for the next two days and rested on the third before setting out again, moving at a steady pace.

Northeastern Abyssinia

The hot sun burnt down on the soil. The medical tents were among a large cluster of trees, spread out for miles. The large foliage camouflaged their location and grass grew like thick rugs across the ground and a river ran past the forest a few miles to the east.

For several weeks now, the tent city had many close encounters with the enemy. Injured men were arriving daily. Several days passed and then information came in that the Garthians soldiers were on the move but more days came and went and nothing happened. A scout finally arrived, bringing news of a large army moving towards the tents.

E-Newtu was sitting with patients. He looked around, shaking his head, knowing they would have to find another location. It was a lot of work to move everyone but it had to be done.

Men from all areas of Alkebu-lan lay in the makeshift beds.

E-Newtu looked over to his wife, Tu-Ney, working feverishly to close a soldier's head injury while another assistant moved to usher more of the injured to beds. Other workers carried supplies to feed and provide medical attention to those suffering from pain.

E-Newtu thought about his people and how the Garthians were holding captives. All good men, some he had become very close to. A woman stepped to his side tapping him on the shoulder, breaking his chain of thought.

"E-Newtu, we may need to open another tent. Men are coming in great numbers," the woman said, with concern apparent in her eyes.

"I don't know how long this place will last," said E-Newtu, touching the young lady on the arm to console her.

"We have to do something. This tent and the second tent are not enough to accommodate all of the injured soldiers," the young women replied.

E-Newtu understood the woman's frustration. The woman's father and brother were right in the middle of the war and she felt helpless.

"There is only so much any one person can do."

"Things are going to work out as they always do," he said to the young woman as tears shown in her eyes. E-Newtu continued, "Do not stress yourself too much, OK?" He looked up and noticed his wife coming over to console the young woman.

"Come along dear, I have you now. Get your things together. We are about to move to a new location and time is running out," Tu-Ney said, as the loud breaking of trees somewhere in the forest reached their ears.

It became louder and louder as everyone sat still and very quiet. They listened as more trees were being crushed and the women began crying softly. Suddenly the loud roar from some kind of beast shattered the quietness. E-Newtu looked at his wife and took her by the hand. She held tightly to his hand with tears in her eyes. He put his finger to his lips and he closed his arms around her. They had done their part to assist in the war and now in the backs of their minds they knew the inevitable was coming.

Tu-Ney kissed her husband on his lips then held on tightly to his shoulders while he was looking up at the tent roof. Their world, the place they were born and raised, was being taken away from them.

Suddenly the tent disappeared upward as screams came from those inside the tent. Another loud roar sounded as a 30-foot-tall creature stood over the tent, its mouth agape, showing long, curved teeth and large eyes staring down at them. Its body was green and scaly with large pointed fins running down its back. Its feet held four talons. The sight had some frozen in place.

Terrified screams came from every direction as the creature's mouth opened wide and clamped down on patients lying in beds.

It raised its head and began chewing. E-Newtu looked on in sheer terror. Soldiers and staff scattered in all directions as the beast swiped its claws at them, killing some of the people.

Two hundred yards away, moving up a grassy hill, Imhotep heard the screams sailing on the winds. He ran forward passing Hutap and the others ran up the hill behind him. When he reached the top, he looked around quickly and noticed an army moving among the large forest. Several large beasts moved out in front of what he thought were about four thousand Garthian soldiers. His anger heightened at seeing the Garthians again after so many years had passed. More screams came and he looked at a large, snake-like creature with wild, wide open eyes.

He then heard Hutap say, "That beast is killing Alkebu-lanians!"

"What should we do Imhotep?" asked Ahknon, still staring in horror.

Tutannharmoon's anger built and his heart thumped wildly inside his chest. He looked down and screamed, "My father is out there! Those beasts are killing our people!"

"For us to win we must hit them with a powerful attack. Tutann, you and Ahknon attack the beasts directly. Hutapsunnimoon and I will destroy their military forces; we don't want any information traveling back to the command ship. No creature is to survive! Understand? And we must protect each other. It will take our combined efforts to defeat this enemy, understand?" Imhotep said. More screams reached their ears and Imhotep commanded, "Move out!"

Tutann left the ground swiftly and was several hundred yards away, sailing through the air in no time. Ahknon trained his sight on the beast and pointed his sun spear then he launched it outward with force. It sliced through the air with speed, screaming towards its intended victim, as Ahknon bolted forward across the green grass. In seconds, the spear made contact, exploding through the creature's neck. The beast roared out loudly in pain as Ahknon took two more steps, leaping up into the air. Turning his body as the sun spear reappeared inside his hand, he flashed across the ground putting miles behind him.

Tutann took one last, giant leap and rose to meet the large beast head on, smashing the creature with his right hand. The immense power sent the beast crashing to the ground and Tutann was on top of it. They rolled around on the ground for several moments before Tutann got to his feet, looking around quickly. He was aware of his people running in all directions but he focused on his task. He grabbed the huge beast around the neck and tossed it one hundred yards away to crash into more trees. The ground shook violently and he jumped into the direction of the reptilian beast, trying to keep his people safe; another large beast came running across the ground in his direction.

Ahknon's spear carried him over the landmass in seconds. He landed in front of a huge, one-eyed creature with graying skin, several horns protruding from its skull. Another creature rushed at him in rage. Using his fighting technique of the spear leveled to the ground, Ahknon swung the spear for the creature's legs and it connected with a loud cracking sound as the one-eyed beast was tossed several yards away; hitting the soil head first, its leg was in an awkward position. Ahknon then threw the spear and it exploded through the creature's stomach before returning to his hand, it stayed their unmoving.

A second, one-eyed creature moved up behind him and Ahknon rose from the soil turning into a 360 degree spin and smacking the new threat across the face. The sun spear ripped into its skull causing half of the creature's face to dangle down. It cried out loudly, holding its face together but Ahknon held no remorse for the beast. He rushed in leaping upward, kicking the beast in the face, then smashing the creature on the top of the head. The sun spear severed its head and cut the creature's body down the middle as several more huge beasts rushed at him as he touched the ground.

The ground shook as they marched toward him. Ahknon was now smiling at the various creatures; some were tall, others insect–like and even more were one-eyed beasts. When the beast was within a few feet of them, he slammed his spear into the ground causing the Alkebu-lanian soil to rumble and shake violently. Then a crack appeared in front of him, it raced in the direction of the creatures, opening the soil and swallowing the beasts' whole—the soil soon closed. Ahknon turned quickly as he heard thundering footsteps coming his way; his heart pound inside his chest, he was in his element.

Imhotep was sitting on Hutapsunnimoon's back as she raced across the land with blinding speed. He had asked her if she could carry him and when she said yes, he was amazed to feel how fast she travelled upon the surface, even with his weight. They were moving closer to the Garthian military force. When they were five hundred yards short of them, Imhotep said, "Thank you."

He raised himself into the air and a clear sphere appeared beneath him as other spheres appeared just above his head—he floated in place. They were flashing red, white and blue as Imhotep begin whispering words, and then smiled. This is what he had been waiting for, for over a thousand years. These creatures had cost him his life, his home, his world, his family and his teacher!

Imhotep released the fire sphere as it moved through the air, expanding as it moved closer to the main hovercraft in which the commanding officer was stationed.

The sphere of fire gained size as it moved closer to its target. Hutapsunnimoon reached for her long bow right after Imhotep released himself from her back. She was now angry but silent and the military force had not seen her moving towards them.

Hutap released ten shooting star arrows and they sailed across the green land several feet off the ground—their tips burned white fire. She followed behind them with her arms moving back and forth. She watched the arrows slice through several dozen heads, one after the other, and kept moving as heads toppled to the ground next to their standing bodies.

Hutap sent another round of arrows their way. Each arrow moving side by side, this time making contact, slicing bodies in half as the creatures lost arms, legs and many died before they even know what hit them. Reaching the line of Garthian soldiers, she noticed how ugly the beings were but nothing was going to stop her. She released another round of shooting star arrows, which chopped down the numbers by the hundreds, she noticed the third line of their military force approaching.

Hutap replaced the long bow and pulled out her comet blades. They shone brightly in her hands as she quickly moved among the ranks of thousands; thrusting, kicking, spinning, jabbing as soldier after soldier began to fall, screaming out in pain. Hutap continued working at blinding speed as her long, dreaded hair moved wildly about her shoulders.

The Garthian's commanding Garthian Officer Tigr controlled the forces to the north and after obtaining information of the whereabouts of the rebel camp he pushed his forces farther north to a large forest. One of the beasts caught the scent of the rebels and Officer Tigr sat back in his seat waiting on the events to play out. He knew their main city was only miles away and after crushing his rebels he would move to take over that city.

Tigr gave orders for all the beasts to enter the tree line as one of the large serpents led the way, crushing trees in its wake. Shortly, he heard noises that could only mean the rebels had been found and they were now a meal for the large beast. They had been hiding among the trees and Tigr laughed outwardly, thinking about this first victory.

The four thousand Garthian soldiers waited in line formation for him to give the order then Tigr heard something cutting the air, then he saw a flashing light as many of his soldiers' heads fell from their shoulders leaving their bodies standing in place. Surprised, he reached for his light caster, a weapon he was ordered not to use.

With his swords in his right and left hands and the light caster in his third small arm, pointing forward, he listened to the screams of pain coming from his ranks of soldiers as they continued to fall to the green soil. It must be an invisible attacker, he thought, decimating his ranks.

Suddenly, he felt a great heat and turned left and noticed a huge ball of swirling light. He tried to leap out of the craft just as the huge light blasted the craft and he screamed loudly before the blaze consumed his body.

E Newtu and his wife Tu-Ney moved out of the tent holding hands, scared for their lives as they raced through the woods. They noticed another huge beast circling, waiting on them, but there was nowhere to run so they stayed quiet. Then they heard the breaking of air somewhere above them and they turned to see something hit the huge beast and its blood rained down over the trees and them. E-Newtu and Tu-Ney covered their eyes.

The beast let out a heart curdling scream of pain as a giant dark-complexioned man appeared and crashed into the beast, taking hold of its head, and both the giant and beast tumbled to the ground as the land shook while dust carried in the air. E-Newtu felt that the giant was there to protect them but did not know who it was. E-Newtu watched as several other beasts charge through the trees and realized these were the ones that had been waiting on him and Tu-Ney to exit to ambush them. They stood still, waiting on the outcome of this battle.

Tutannharmoon landed on top of the huge, snake-like beast, smashing his fist into the creature's eye as his skin came alive, the spider-like creatures entered the large beast's wound. As they begin consuming its host alive the beast's body jerked back and forth knocking down trees.

Something took hold of Tutann from behind in its large hands. He turned to see a one-eyed beast as large as himself as it reached for him and lifted him off the ground. Tutann swung his arms down breaking the creature's hold and swung his right hand around connecting to its head. It sailed across the ground to his left knocking down a tree as a second, one-eyed beast took hold of his neck from the side.

Using his left hand, Tutann reached over to catch the beast by its horns and swung the beast over his head and down to the ground with such force it shook the ground all around. Tutann rained massive blows down into the one-eyed creature's face until it lay unmoving. A huge, two-legged beast with short arms and a large head, standing twice his size, stormed through the pathway charging at him. Tutann grabbed the one–eyed creature by the leg and flung him in the direction of the large beast. The creature caught it in its mouth and shook it like a rag doll. Tutann, again, stormed in the creature's direction grabbing its left leg. The beast's large teeth bit down missing its target and Tutann used all his strength to pull it down. It crashed to the ground and he dragged it away from his people who were now gathering around. Tutann jumped straight up into the air and with all his force and power he landed on the beast's second leg; it broke with a loud snap and then his skin came alive as millions of the spider-like creatures rushed out of veins within his skin. He looked around to see if there were more to fight as the creatures' bodies were being consumed. He took in deep breaths of air; when he knew everyone was safe, he walked among his people hiding in the woods.

E-Newtu felt someone tapped him on his shoulder and when he turned he smiled widely, for it was his sister's son who had run off with the old wanderer, Imhotep, several months ago. As E-Newtu and Tu-Ney gazed upward into the tall man's eyes, E-Newtu noticed a change in the young man's demeanor and he noticed that the spear looked different as well; it radiated power and shone as brightly as the sun above.

Tu-Ney was the first to hug him and he returned the gesture. "Ahknon, you had us so worried. Where have you been? Is Imhotep with you? I am glad to see you but we will have to talk more later. The enemies have found our location and brought large beasts unlike we have never seen before," E-Newtu said, looking around.

At that very moment, Tutann crashed to the ground next to Ahknon. Towering over those around him he caused many to begin to run deeper into the woods and E-Newtu and Tu-Ney backed away in fright as the huge, muscular giant gazed down upon everyone.

"Everyone come back, calm down. He is with us! This is my friend Tutannharmoon!" Ahknon called out, loudly. Tutann spoke up. "How are you all?" He spread his arms widely, looking around smiling, so everyone would know it was safe to come out. Many of the survivors gathered around and some recognized both Ahknon and Tutann as the ones that battled Garthian creatures. Others were slow to step near but recognized the Alkebu-lan names, so they began to relax.

"Everyone listen! Collect everything we will need to set up camp elsewhere and help the injured get ready to travel. We have a lot of work to do and our men need us!" E-Newtu said.

Many of the staff began to tend to the patients as the soldiers began gathering the necessary items and moving through the woods.

Shortly after, Imhotep and Hutap moved through the trees to where a group of people were gathered. They noticed the huge Tutann first and moved towards him. At the sound of footsteps, E-Newtu turned and he smiled upon seeing his old friend as Tu-Ney rushed over to give Imhotep a hug. The others gathered and begin whispering at seeing the old wanderer.

"Well, well, I thought I would never see you again old man," E-Newtu said.

"Well, you're a vision of life and yes, we need to talk. I want to know everything that has been going on and it is important if we are to win this war, but right now we have to move," Imhotep replied, looking around at the gathering of people.

E-Newtu notice a large female standing behind Imhotep, Imhotep noticed the look and said,

"Well now, this is Hutapsunnimoon, a brave and powerful warrior, but there are others. Your nephew is another and the giant, Tutannharmoon, in which I will explain, but first we must quickly bury these creatures; you and the people go, we will catch up with you all.

"Yes," E-Newtu stated.

Chapter 21

Star fighter UV1

I nside the large holding cages, prisoners moved about and General Nassir could only shake his head in disbelief. He held onto the thoughts of freeing his people but the thoughts begin to dwindle rapidly as time passed and no word came from Bugo after he and another soldier climbed up through the metal squares above their heads and had not returned. A female warrior stood at his side now and she looked up at him for answers but he had nothing to say.

Weeks passed and nothing happened. Nassir noticed that the Garthian soldiers moved out each morning in full force and reentered the ship after dark bringing new prisoners. He spoke with them and they explained that the Alkebu-lanians continued fighting and had some success against the Garthians. There was also more disappointing talk; Nassir learned of the thousands of men cut off from joining the war by the Garthian race.

Nassir understood that without a steady supply of more men to join the fight they could lose but the name Butann brought him some comfort, for he knew that General Butann would continue the war to the best of his ability along with the other forces.

Early this morning Nassir watched a large force move out with a large group of beasts but this force never returned. Nassir began to pay very close attention to the gestures the Garthians were making to try and find some form of answers to what was really going on. Their words were mostly grunts and Nassir moved through the crowded cage to get closer and to see them more clearly. He took a seat. Some Garthian soldiers stood several feet away and the commanding officer he recognized by the way other Garthians acted around him. He took special notice of him and by their erratic movements he could tell that something was not right. He continued to watch unnoticed.

"Captain Ior, I have lost contact with your second in command, Tigr. It appears that hours ago his military forces found the rebels hiding among a large growth of trees and Officer Tigr began his attack but since then we have not heard a single word from him, Captain," the soldier said, nervously.

"You lost contact with the Captain?" Angered now, Captain Ior continued, "Do you know Captain Tigr is a man of extraordinary skills? This planet is no match for a soldier of his caliber. Give him some time and if it is still a concern, send one of the flying creatures to investigate his location to the north," said Captain Ior.

"Well, it has been some time already," said the soldier, with uncertainty in his voice.

"Well, relax a bit. There is still plenty of time for Tigr to return and I'm sure when he returns he will have something very special for all of us. It will be the reason why he is late," Captain Ior finished.

Captain Ior turned around, moving back to the command center of the star fighter. He was now concerned as well but he refused to reveal any emotions to his soldiers. As he passed the cages, he looked inside at some of the rebels that had been captured and wondered how these creatures fought so hard. He had fought much stronger enemies in the past with no problems. Even with the shield up preventing others from joining the battle, they were worthy opponents protecting their native home. His forces had already chased the rebels to the south across the landside and when he felt he had them trapped, they seemed to vanish.

Tomorrow his military forces would fan out and crush the remaining rebels. They would kill every single living being here as a reminder that the Garthians were here to stay. The images of the dead would serve as a reminder of what could happen to all living here upon the surface.

Leaving the cage behind, he walked through a doorway and it closed behind him. He took a seat on one of the large chairs in the command center and looked down at a map of the surrounding land. Ior let his thoughts go back to Captain Tigr and the four thousand Garthian soldiers and many beasts Tigr had led into the field of battle. Were his forces destroyed, he wondered. If this were the case it would mean that Commander Acee would have to begin using their most advanced weapons. *Would Commander Acee look at him as a failure?* He shook off the thought and decided not to question himself. *How could such a young race of beings fight so strongly against a race so much more powerful, could these being have real hopes of prevailing?* Ior's face contorted in anger as he thought about these young beings defeating one as great as Tigr. *No,* Ior thought, *he will return shortly in victory.* He went back to viewing the map of the young land, planning his next attacks.

Southeastern Abyssinia

Butann and his men moved constantly across the colorful landside to the southeast. After a full day of being chased by the enemy, Butann broke his forces into three fractions to lure the Garthians into breaking their forces up to follow. Each time the Garthians thought they had the advantage. He and his men would simply disappear, upsetting the Garthian forces further. As the large beasts closed in on their trails he switched tactics and moved in another direction so that the beasts were ahead of them and could not thwart their plans. He and his men kept moving westward towards a community that had denounced entering the war.

Butann and his men entered the community cautiously as they noticed the place was burned to the ground. All the homes were black from smoldering fires and there was no sound or sight of anyone. Months earlier this place had been alive with life and as they turned into a large pasture they all looked in total shock as some men covered their mouths. There was a pile of bodies, one on top of the other about fifteen feet high and twenty feet wide. Flies and other insects were thriving among the dead and large birds took to the air circling above the pile of bodies.

Butann recognized young children among the pile. Some of his men began to cry for the innocent lives stolen. They turned and left the community behind like they had found it, knowing if they took the time to bury the remains the Garthian army would know they had been there. They headed back to the waterfall where all the men were to meet.

After reaching the falls, Butann had to think of something fast. He had no supplies, no extra men to resupply his ranks and he could not afford a major battle now. He was planning to send out a message to see if he could contact the Alkebu-lan forces to the north hoping they were still alive when a young soldier moved towards him. Butann whispered a few words to the thin but strong, young man. When he finished whispering in the young soldier's ear, the young man raced out from under the falls to the rocky ground above. Butann watched him go, moving swiftly, the dark skies glimmering with stars as the falls cool streams of water cooled his body.

He watched the messenger until he was out of sight. Images of the dead played inside his mind and he looked up at the stars thinking of his own family. High above the night skies, Butann didn't see the several ships moving towards the surface of his world but another pair of eyes had been watching very carefully as the ship moved closer to its destination.

North beyond the city of Kemet

Nassir heard enough to know that his people were waging a serious battle against these beings. From the erratic behavior of the Garthians, he realized that at least three to four thousand Garthians and their pets had not returned and were now considered missing. His hope is to be able to get free to help continue the fight. He watched the commander of the Garthians move towards a door and enter but not before looking inside their cage.

Nassir stood up after hearing noises above the cage and he looked up to see the young man, Bugo, returning. Nassir hoped this meant they would be able to free all the captives but Bugo and the other man climbed through the air passageway and down the pillars to the ground below. Nassir and the men took a seat out of view of the guards and began talking. Nassir touched Bugo on the shoulder as he began speaking.

"We found a way out but we crawled on our stomachs for several days. Do you think some of us could leave first and then come back for the elders? I don't think they can make the trip," Bugo whispered, quietly.

Nassir rubbed his chin as he looked at the young lad and then looked outside the metal cage for any sign of Garthian soldiers.

After pausing a few moments to think, he said, "If too many of us leave the cages they may notice and torture those left behind. That would end our chances of leaving here safely. I will stay behind. What I want you two to do is leave and head north to the city of Kemet. There should be huge forces there and you can explain to the commanders of our capture. Explain to them that I believe the Garthians are going to transport us all to another place, maybe to be used for something and they need to be stopped. I want you two to eat something and be off again, as quickly as possible. You must get out! Only you can make a difference and bring the help we need."

Bugo and his friend agreed and moved off to get food before moving up the pillars again and back through the passageways. Before they moved out of sight, Nassir and others saluted the departing men by placing their right hand over their heart. Even the young boys followed suit.

Chapter 22

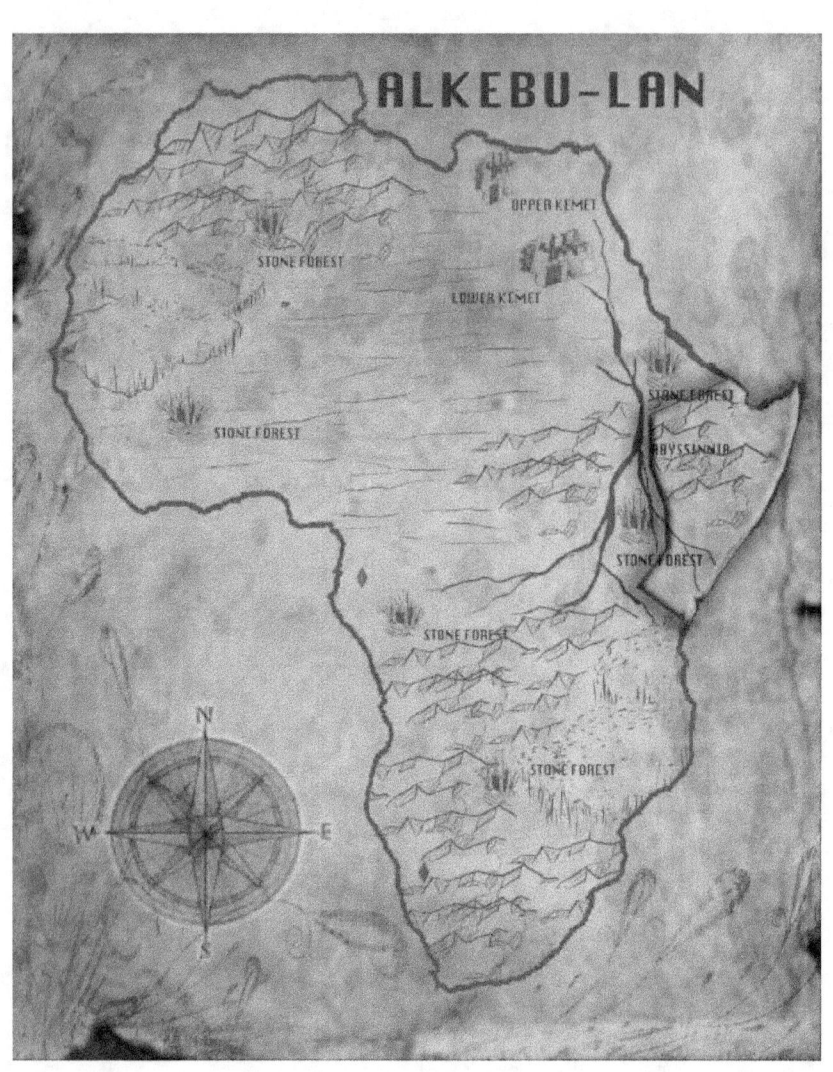

Farther to the north

A week had passed since the companions saved the many lives in the woods and they left scouts to pass on information of the soldiers' new location. Imhotep took command of the forces and he talked with many of the soldiers and began to set out a plan of attack upon the enemy. He spoke with them each day and they coordinated their attacks so that all the men would move as one.

Just fifty yards away sat Ahknon with a lady friend. The cool air blew in his face as clouds began to cloak the skies in darkness. The landscape was beautiful, Ahknon thought.

"I was wondering where you went Ahknon. Since the day you left me, I have returned to your uncle's tent daily looking for you to return," Isis said, while rubbing Ahknon's braided hair.

"I thought about you too, Isis," Ahknon said as he watched Isis smile. "Since the first day we met, I can't get you out of my mind but I was compelled to search for answers about my past and my father. It led me on a journey with the wise man, Imhotep. I have not learned the truth about my father but look at what's happening now in my life. If it should lead me away from you again just know that you are a part of me inside here," Ahknon said, pointing to his heart.

"How am I supposed to feel if I'm unable to see you again Ahknon? My heart couldn't bear that," said Isis, laying her head on his shoulders.

Ahknon wrapped his left arm around her shoulder, kissing Isis on the top of her head, then he said, "Nor could my heart bear it. But what kind of life would we have if we let these strange beings from another world take our freedom. If we let these beings take our homes, our world, our lives, we could not be together happily. These tender moments are what I cherish; it is what I fight for, for all those who made the sacrifices for their families so they could live in peace. I do so now so one day we, Isis, can live together in peace," Ahknon finished.

Tears appeared in the corner of Isis's eyes and Ahknon kissed her forehead. Isis turned as their lips met and stayed that way for a time.

One hundred yards away, Tutannharmoon sat beneath a huge tree as Hutap sat next to him. Tutann noticed the sad look in her eyes after learning of her father's capture. Her demeanor saddened him. For some reason, out of all the people around him, he felt very close to Hutap and the feelings were beyond anything he had ever felt before.

"Hutap, I know how you're feeling after learning about your father. From what I hear from the people, he is very brave and I promise you if there is anything we can do to save him, we will. You and I are dealing with similar circumstances. My father is somewhere to the southeast but no one has heard anything from him in weeks and that is a great concern to me but just being concerned won't help the problem."

Hutap looked up at Tutann and for the first time she saw a kinder, softer edge about him. Since they first met, she had this strong attraction to him and always wanted to be next to him. It was a struggle for her to hide what she was feeling. She loved his very dark complexion and his deep, rumbling voice. He was the first male she sought attention from besides her father. She loved looking at him when he thought she was not looking.

It was funny to her that at one point she almost hated men, especially those in her homeland, and yet without warning this big, strong giant fell into her life. When they were alone she wanted to reach up and kiss him and she wondered if he was feeling the same way. She thinks so but she wanted him to say it. But right now, he seems so concerned with how she is feeling that she quickly changed her thoughts, trying to focus on other things.

She said, "You are right, Tutann. We both come from warrior fathers. One of the reasons your father, Butann, left you behind is because he fears even with your size, you would be killed. That is also the reason my father left me behind. Our fathers needed to focus on the problem. I will let it go for now but thank you for your willingness to help me free my father." Then she looked up into his eyes and they stared at one another for a long while.

Tutann opened the palm of his hand and Hutap placed her hand in his, unspoken words passed between the two and they sat there for a very long time. Then, in the distance, she heard Imhotep calling out her name. "I'll be right back," Hutap said.

It took her no time to reach Imhotep who was standing with two other men: one tall fellow with a dark complexion; the other much shorter.

Imhotep turned to see Hutap standing behind him and said "This is Bugo and his friend Goin. This is Hutapsunnimoon." The two men turned to greet her as Imhotep continued, "I need you to explain to her what you just told me," he finished.

Bugo, the taller of the two soldiers, went on to explain their capture by the Garthian beings, the cages that held them as captives in one of the large, iron birds and how many others were captured and held inside. Hutap listened carefully as the hair on her neck was standing on end and her blood pressure was rising with each new word spoken. She remained quiet as she listened to the soldier go on to explain that the Garthians were setting up for a large-scale attack. The highest-ranking officer in captivity felt he could not leave the families behind so he stayed to protect them.

Hutap wondered why Imhotep had called her over then she asked the one named Bugo, "What is the name of the General?"

"His name is Nassir," Bugo said.

Hutap's eyes widened and her mouth dropped open before she turned, lowering her head and whispered "He is alive!" She then turned back to face the two soldiers and asked "Is the General healthy?"

"Yes, he is fine. He just needs help to free him and the other captives," Bugo finished.

Hutap was so happy to hear the news of her father alive that she wanted to hug the two soldiers but she thought better of it and shook their hands instead.

"Thank you for bringing this news. Do you feel we have a chance of get back inside?"

"Well, yes, but I witnessed two more iron birds come flying out of the sky to land beside the one we escaped as we left. More

Garthian soldiers and beasts arrived to replace the ones lost in battle. It seems the commander of the Garthians is frustrated.

"Nassir believes that the Alkebu-lan forces somewhere to the south are becoming a real thorn in his side. Where are the supplies and the other communities of fighters?" asked Bugo.

"It is why they put the force field up around Abyssinia to keep reinforcements out! The Garthians see the Alkebu-lanian fighters as a real threat. It is a sure sign of resistance. Hutap, I need you to go back to the underground entrance and show the soldiers looking to join the war the way inside. You are the only one who could lead them through without aid of light. Return here in a few days' time," Imhotep said.

"Ok yeah, I understand. The soldiers may be looking for a way inside and I must lead them to the only way in. Yes, I can do this but one thing, Imhotep, what of my father? Who will help him before it's too late?" asked Hutap, her eyes clear and focused.

"I'm already making plans so leave that to me," said Imhotep.

Hutap agreed by shaking her head then she said, "I trust you, Imhotep. I will leave now. The sooner I leave, the sooner I will return. Just let me collect a few things," as she left and walked among a group of men.

Bugo looked shocked at the thought of letting a woman travel the dark lands by herself. He watched the female soldier move back into the circle.

"Imhotep, tell Tutann I will see him in a few days," then she disappeared from the men's sight. Bugo and his partner looked around wondering where the woman had gone so quickly. They rubbed their heads looking around and behind them. Imhotep began to laugh at the two men.

Hutap moved quickly across the dark landside with blinding speed. She moved like the wind as her feet lightly touched the soil. Hutap's eyes lit up in the blanket of darkness that covered the skies, her pace was steady. Her hair cascaded in the wind behind her. She pushed forward moving at a much faster pace, quicker than she had ever moved before.

Hutap knew the importance of her task. It was a matter of life and death and she would do whatever she had to do to keep her people from suffering the same fate of the beings whose lives were taken by the Garthians, so many millions of miles and lifetimes away, deep in the outer reach of space. Those thoughts alone propelled her body forward. She noticed the green of the landside which changed to lakes and mountains as colorful flowers rose out of the ground. Nocturnal beasts moved across the land as she moved past them, picking up even more speed as she moved around trees and large rock structures up and down the hilly lands; she looked right and left then up ahead, knowing she was on the right course.

She thought about her father's sacrifice and his commitment to his people. She felt that same bond in her heart and knew she was doing the right thing. She wondered how her mother was doing as everything she passed by was a blur now and only what she could see in front of her was clear.

She moved across the top of a large river stepping across the animals that lived there and then she left the river behind still pushing forward. She recognized landmarks as she turned a bit to the west. She passed more landmarks she remembered and knew she was almost there. The moonlight disappeared and she breathed in deeply but kept pushing herself on.

Imhotep talked with Bugo and Goin for a good while before the men were startled by the sound of loud footsteps coming their way from somewhere in the darkness. Just as the two men were about to take cover, Imhotep said, "You are safe. There is nothing to worry about," as a giant beast emerged from the darkness. Bugo and Goin looked on in fright as the giant of a man questioned Imhotep.

"Imhotep where is Hutapsunnimoon? She told me to wait but she never returned," said Tutann as he looked around. He noticed Ahknon talking with a woman while other soldiers moved around among fire.

Imhotep looked up at the powerful figure of a man who was only a boy several months back and realized that indeed desperate times calls for desperate measures; an essential key in a battle against such a powerful enemy.

Imhotep remembered the message from the race of beings called Saggurdians. It was one that only he could understand and the message explained the powers of Tutannharmoon and that of

Hutapsunnimoon are in fact related. The information went on to say that Tutann and Hutap both received the totality of the male and female D.N.A of the Saggurdian race and as Imhotep pondered these thoughts, he also knew they would develop a strong bond that could never be broken. He kept this information to himself. He felt that telling the two any of this would do more harm than good and wouldn't help in the battle.

He needed Tutann and Hutap to focus on the war rather than the well-being of the others, so if he could, he would keep this information to himself.

"So," he said to Tutann, "Hutap will be back. I sent her off to scout the tunnel to lead the troops through. It is important to resupply our forces and Hutap was the only one who could get there and back the quickest."

Bugo and Goin watched as the huge giant's facial expression showed a bit of concern and then they looked at Imhotep.

"Will she be back in a few days?" Tutann said, his voice a deep rumble.

"Of course," Imhotep responded.

Bugo and Goin watched the huge beast leap upward into the dark skies and vanish. They heard him hit the ground somewhere in the distance and looked back at Imhotep in amazement.

Bugo whispered, "Where did you find that?"

"Well, you will learn there is a lot here that will amaze you. Just be ready to fight when the time comes. You can find food, beds and weapons and anything else you may need in those tents.

"Help yourselves," Imhotep said, before he turned and moved off into the darkness.

Chapter 23

Southern Abyssinia

Early the next morning, just before the sun began to rise, Butann and his forces pulled out of the falls, carrying as much supplies that his forces could carry. Being in the falls for weeks now placed his men in grave danger; he knew sooner or later that location would be found, although the Garthians passed up that place on several occasions, but to be trapped inside the falls was certain death.

After a night of rest his men pushed on, the last messenger Butann send out never returned to him. It was a sign to Butann that his messenger was captured, it was a task each soldier was willing to take for the protection of his people; each soldier fighting understood their position and the struggle, the beings known to them as Garthians was not to be trusted.

Butann still thought about the images of the dead bodies, even children lying dead. He watched his men move past him heading southwest. Even now, Butann avoided a direct attack from the enemies. Out of a hundred thousand men, he now commanded a few thousand. Thousands of Garthians littered the battlefield, many more than they had imagined, Butann realized that these creatures were very powerful.

Creatures that traveled the skies above clouds and the stars, he was also pretty sure they had advanced weaponry, but for some odd reason, the beast they controlled was a total treat to their existence. To have gained control over such predators was a sure sign of their power. Butann watched the last of his men moving passed him. He quickly moved alongside his forces keeping an eye on the land side. They walked a half of a day, approaching a huge riverbank, as others searched the skies. Some of his men began to quench their thirst, until all had their fill. Butann led his men west, moving into dense trees for a walk in the shade, they continued walking until the day was fast becoming night.

Early one morning, Nassir was awakened by the movement of large groups of Garthian soldiers. Large beasts were being ushered to large cages, some growled, others roared loudly. Nassir noticed the commander of the iron bird stood several feet away from the cages, talking with several high–ranking soldiers, he looked down at Fertari, a female Zukufu solder, watching intently, then he noticed that the commanding officer was walking past him. Nassir listened as they communicated their words sounding like pops and clicks of some of the insects that live in and around Alkebu-lan.

"Get a good look at the weakling of this race, this is what you will be fighting, don't take them for granted, they have won victories on the land, more than we had first expected. Commander Acee insisted that our soldiers take this world without the use of technology. He is strongly against using powerful weapons against these young beings, and I quote, 'THE USE OF HIGH POWERED GARTHIAN WEAPONS AGAINST THIS YOUNG RACE IS A STRIKE AT THE INTEGRITY OF OUR PROUD MILITARY,' but also underestimating one adversary could mean defeat, so we are fighting in the old traditional ways," said Ior. He continued,

"I want half of these prisoners taken to the star cruiser right away. Get them ready for transport. Commander Acee is persistent in seeing what these beings look like, to me, these beings have nothing of beauty."

He then moved closer to the captive cages.

"Open the door here," thirty Garthian soldiers surrounded their Captain, "bring out a large group of these ugly creatures."

Garthian soldiers moved inside the captive cells carrying swords ushering a ground of Alkebu-lanian rebels out, mostly women and children. Nassir and Fertari moved among the group exiting the cage. He knew he was their only hope to keep them strong. The ones left inside their holding cage was sure to be free and somehow he would free the group he now followed, women and children looked back at him and he silenced them. They moved down a large path inside the metal bird, various doorways revealed other Garthians talking inside, they moved inside a large, square room and after the door closed, Nassir felt the room moving upward, slowly at first then faster.

Garthian soldiers held their weapons dangerously circling the group, when the doors opened they entered a large room with cages that held all forms of beasts and machinery. Shortly, they were inside another iron bird and strapped down before large, glass windows. Slowly, Nassir and the captive watched their world seem to grow smaller; women and children began to cry softly. He viewed the large city of Kemet, then further to the east, the huge ocean. Fertari gazed out at the huge blue circle in which she realized was her home. Nassir's thoughts were of freeing his people. He had to find a way or he will never see his home again. He continued to look through the large windows, no one inside the room made a single noise.

Hutap made it to the dark pathways, into the tunnel. Her vision was as clear as if it was daylight. Hutap remembered every step she took, re-entering the path she traveled, moving deeper and deeper into the dark passageways leading upward then down deeper. Around several turns and more hilly grounds, her eyes scanned every small detail and she smelled the stench of the dead, she passed some of the remains of the beast they had killed, time passed and she found the exit.

Looking outward very carefully, then racing west until the sun reached mid sky, she slowed, and to her surprise, there was a huge gathering of Alkebu-lanian soldiers. Hutap noticed carts of supplies, she headed straight for the gathering, and soldiers begin looking her way pointing, as their voices rose. Two large, brown skin soldiers moved in her direction, their heads was shaved clean, animal printed clothing, swords, bows and knives was attached to their clothing.

"Where did you come from?" asked the older of the two soldiers standing to Hutap's right.

"Listen, many of your questions will be answered later. I'm here to show you away inside. I know most of the men here tried to gain away inside, but the enemy has put up some kind of shield from what I have learned from Imhotep."

The soldier's eyes widened at the mention of Imhotep's name. She noticed their reaction,

"I have away inside, but we will not leave out until dawn or the enemy will kill us all and destroy the only access inside Abyssinia," Hutap finished.

Both of the soldier's listened intently and shook their head in agreement, the oldest soldier begin to speak,

"My name is Jophe and this is Ziko, the armies are joined together, once we independently tried to gain access to reach Abyssinia, we gathered here together hoping to find a way to enter the war."

"How are the armies making out?" asked Ziko.

"Strange things and very rough, let's find a place so I can prepare you for what we now face so there won't be any surprises," Hutap said.

Jophe and Ziko signaled out for every soldier to find cover, the men responded, moving to a hidden location. The men began to diminish as they moved into the thick, tree line.

Hutapsunnimoon sat and explained everything to the commanders. She also expressed the capture of her father and many Alkebu-lanians by the enemies. She talked about General Butann leading soldiers to the south, and she watched them also recognize that name. She continued by explaining her meeting with Imhotep, and others who fought the powerful enemies. She noticed that they had doubt, but after a showing of her powers and weapons, the generals were excited about the idea of having a powerful weapon against powerful enemies.

Hutap finished with a description of some of the large beasts and talks of the Garthians with three arms. General Jophe and Ziko was eager to finish what these beings had started. The general left Hutap to inform their men of the dangers that lay ahead. More soldiers were arriving from all over Alkebu-lan, as the sun moved to the western sky; large clouds gathered above, darkening the skies as the rain came down.

Hutapsunnimoon felt the rain was an ideal cover for the large forces to move out. General Jophe and Ziko called out loudly and men, one after the other, shouted down and the shouting continued a ways down for over three thousand yards, and now thousands of soldiers were moving out behind Hutapsunnimoon, while General Jophe and Ziko moved just beside her. Hutap began to speak,

"Listen during our travels through the dark corridors, you must spread the word using your messengers, a third of the forces will follow me north, another third will go south, led by you General Jophe, to meet up with General Butann and the last third will be taking eastern central, led by you, General Ziko. Ziko, you will keep your forces west so we can attack the enemies from three sides."

A short time later, Hutap led the Alkebu-lanian forces inside the deep corridors; many soldiers began lighting torches as they moved steadily through the winding tunnels.

Jophe walked beside Hutap.

"Well, this is the place you killed the large beast," Jophe looked around at the high ceiling, "it had to be something huge living down here carving out these corridors."

"Yes, there were two of these beasts the Garthians let loose upon our world." She continued to move forward as the entire force entered into the dark corridors, they marched onward.

Butannharmoon moved his forces into the cover of trees and the shadow of the mountain, he notice that the enemies used a flying craft that hovered above ground; fast moving metal birds much smaller than the iron birds the Garthians travel within.

Yesterday, he came across some kind of clear wall. He noticed the grazing animals eating grass just twenty-five feet away, it was a barrier, and a tactic to keep the soldiers of Alkebu-lan from entering the war. His men were now low on food, but they could survive off the land. He needed numbers to win against this enemy, he thought. After a few days of walking, they started to rest as the sun begins to set. They hid among a large forest. Shortly after, they begin hearing footsteps. This was no normal sound, it was hundreds of footsteps, each of his soldiers began to rise up looking around, weapons firmly inside their hands. The footsteps were getting louder and louder, then they found the direction of the sound and sat still waiting.

About two hundred yards away Butann saw movement, it wasn't too clear; it was near a tree and a large stone. Things started appearing from beneath the ground, not too sure, Butann moved closer to get a better look. Four of his top soldiers moved with him, Butann's swords were in his hands now.

Hutap climbed out of the deep corridor first, followed by the generals, and then the soldiers began pouring out. She looked around then to the sky, then to the landside noticing Alkebu-lan soldiers a short distance away. She understood it was difficult for them to determine whether they were friends or foes.

Hutap began to wonder was this the southern forces. The main forces have lost contact with, led by General Butann, Tutannharmoon's father. In the time it took Butann to blink, Hutap moved across the field, pulling Butann's swords from his hands. He turned then looked in shock, wondering where this female had come from. His soldiers began their attack, but Hutap interrupted them, stating,

"These are Alkebu-lan soldiers coming to resupply your forces against our enemies." Hutap looked at the men around her, Butann relaxed a bit. He knew she knew who he was, it was obvious, but he still wondered how she was able to sneak up on him.

Soldiers hearing the commotion rush out towards the sound with their weapons raised; General Jophe and Ziko led the way.

Butann's force rushed out from a patch of trees in response.

Butann yelled, "Stop now, these are our men!!!"

His soldiers slowed, taking easy steps towards their General, while Hutap stopped their largest forces, led by the generals.

Butann turned, looking at Hutap and said,

"How did you move so quickly?"

She responded, "It's a long story, General Butann."

"Then, who may you be?" asked Butann.

"Well, I'm Hutapsunnimoon. I'm with your son Tutannharmoon, the wise man, Imhotep and another friend, Ahknonkineton. We came to support the war, and I led these men here to resupply our war efforts."

Hutap noticed General Jophe and Ziko step near,

"This is General Jophe, he was taking his men to meet up with you in the south."

Hutap watched the two men shake hands. Butann looked at the tunnel and was delighted to see soldiers pouring out by the hundreds, he had lost hope but now they could crush the enemy and run them out of his world.

"How are you, General Jophe?" asked Butannharmoon.

"Feeling better, now that these new soldiers can assist in the struggle."

Hutap noticed the resemblance, Tutannharmoon was the splitting image of his father, Butann was an older version but handsome like his son. Butann turned to Hutap and said,

"How is my son doing?"

"Your son is a force to be reckoned with. He is the beast against the creature they unleash against our people, he will be very happy to know you're alive," Hutap said, emotionally.

A smile broke out across Butann's face, he was glad his son came to fight; they needed his kind of power on the battlefield, as well as the power this female exuberated.

"Has anyone seen my father, Nassir?" asked Hutap. Her eyes searched the men with General Butann, she had hoped her father had escaped and headed south, no matter how slight the chances were.

Butann looked in surprise, he and Nassir talked before the war commenced, they talked about family and their children. Butann remembered Nassir talking of his soldier daughter proudly, but refused to bring her along for fear of her safety, it was the same reason he left his son Tutann behind. He spoke up,

"I know your father very well, good man and even better General, one of the messengers brought information of his capture, since then we've heard nothing."

"Thank you, General Butann."

General Ziko stepped near and Jophe introduced them to the generals, then Butann stated,

"I guess we should be off, we have a war to win," as he stood watching a large mass of soldiers moving to the north, while another large mass of soldiers moved directly to him. Butann shook Ziko's hand and said,

"We will stay in contact using messengers in order to coordinate the attacks," Butann said, looking at Hutap then to Ziko but he continued, "Tell the wise Imhotep my forcers will be ready, and Hutap, tell my son we will meet in the center."

The forces broke up into three groups. Butann led his large forces back south. Hutap watched him go, fading into the darkness, she whispered, "I guess we will meet in the center."

Many more soldiers were moving out of the lower tunnels, moving into line formation. Down below, soldiers at the rear of the line waited their time to exit, the very last of the soldiers are old men but very strongly built with graying hair. Each of the two held torches inside their hands, the fire light flickered brightly, and further down the tunnel was nothing but darkness. One of them turned quickly, raising his torch high to get a better look, his iron sword held firmly.

When he was satisfied it was nothing, he placed his sword back in place, then he turned, ready to exit. The line moved and they moved along and out of the darkness, looking to the skies of Abyssinia.

Back inside the dark tunnel, several pairs of eyes gazed out upon the dark landscape, watching the soldiers moving among the forest heading west. The largest group of soldiers were heading north, after a final look, the beast sunk down below the surface moving quickly through the passages ways. As they moved as one, remembering their way in and now back through, knowing the trial by scent, they had followed the soldiers through the maze of twists and turns. The beast's powerful legs propelled him forward, breathing in deeply the stale air, growls escaped their mouths, yet they moved on non-stop. They reach the entrance way, peering out, then fast across the green landside heading northbound, determined in their path, they continued.

Chapter 24

Farther to the north upon the northern mountains

Ick, the ancient leader of the Cravistine race, voice travelled around the deep corridors of the mountain. Inside Ick's hands were two swords; attached to his waistline is a large, headed axe; right next to his Quastor light blaster, in which Ick was saving from times like this.

He stood high above his community barking out orders. The leader of the Cravistines was now angered while he prepared to go to war against an enemy that wiped out everyone in his home world and chased him across the universe to this new world he now lived upon. In the course of weeks past, his scouts have reported information on war farther to the east.

A week later, news of a large ship hovering near the moon and ships entering the Alkebu-lanian atmosphere spread throughout the community; then word came of a force field to the east around a place called Abyssinia. Ick learned the people of Alkebu-lan were fighting for the survival of their world from a powerful race called the Garthians; the same beast that attacked their home world.

Ick looked around the huge hall at his underground hive. His soldiers were moving franticly. Many of his kind rushed to gather the things they would need. His mind thought of the peaceful life he has enjoyed here for well over two thousand years.

Ick looked up and noticed his kind was awaiting his further orders. He looked around at all his people in the huge halls carved deep into the mountains as he began to speak in his native language, loudly stating,

"What you have been seeing are our enemies! Many of you here are too young to remember your home world of Cravistine because so many of you have been born here!!! But your ancient fathers and ancient mothers have been killed by this race of beings that are now here to kill this world. I say, there is no more running! His soldiers cheered loudly!" He continued as his eyes scanned the faces of everyone there.

He stated, "Take a good look at what we call home when there are better places. This may be the last time you see it because as of today, the Garthian reign of terror is over!!! We will kill them to the very last soldiers! Remember, your ancient mothers and fathers who have been slain. Remember our people built this world and ships, but we were forced to live here and the reason is out there where we go. It's time to put an end to this." Ick raised his hands above his head.

Shouting came from all around the hall. Growls and barks, Ick turned and rushed through one of the large tunnels of the mountain top. Ick's powerful limbs propelled him forward. He snuffed the scent of the pathways for the last time. The wall was high and jagged. The corridors long, some smaller than others. Ick began to move down, descending from the mountaintop. The rumble of thousands of his kind followed behind their leader, huge beasts possessing extraordinary power, moved through the large raceways. Ick rushed out of an exit into the cold air where the skies are a blanket of darkness. Only the moonlight shines in the middle of the sky. Ick leaped outward and down the side of the mountain, hitting a small cliff below; turning backwards as he began his descent to the mountain floor.

Thousands rushed out to cover the mountainside for over a thousand feet. Their powerful hands take hold of the solid rock. The mountain rumbled and shocked violently. Hundreds passed their leader, leaping from one rock to another, until they began hitting the ground, hopping quickly south. Thousands Cravitines moved as one hitting the ground every several feet. Scouts scanned the skies above as others watched the tree line for danger.

They pushed on, rising into the air then hitting the ground. Several huge Cravitines surrounded their leader, Ick, on all sides. While the most experienced moved ahead, leading their forces to the underground tunnels.

The Cravitines moved all through the night and much quicker during the day. They stopped only to drink. Then they continued.

On the third day, they reached the tunnels, two large Cravistine soldiers stood outside as thousands entered, moving down the dark passages. Ick was ready but so were his people. In their hearts and minds was the enemy. It was the passion that drove them forward. They continued as one.

Northern Abyssinia

For weeks now, the wise man, known as Imhotep, spied on the Garthian force, as they increased in sizes, Garthian star fighters traveled from space to the surface from the main vessel. The power of a star fighter alone could help give the

Garthians a win. Other land machines were being added to the Garthian's arsenal; hover crafts, which carried large explosive cannons and powerful machines, Imhotep knew.

Imhotep plans his tactical maneuvers to strike out at the enemy. A messenger was sent south and west central Abyssinia, where the Alkebu-lan forces gather in those areas. He planned to attack the Garthian forces, where they are the strongest.

Imhotep understood that the Garthian forces still believe that only a few hundred soldiers were out and about but once the Garthians see the battle field with hundreds of thousands of Alkebu-lan soldiers, it would then be a difficult task to win. He sat down on the ground next to a small fire. His tactic is to send Tutannharmoon south to meet up with his father to lead the forces to the battlefield. After speaking with Ahknon, Imhotep sent Ahknon to west central Abyssinia as a weapon to protect the soldiers there, while Hutapsunnimoon attacked from a northern position with the total forces. His own plan was to enter the star fighter ship and free the captured Alkebu-lanian people. In his heart, he was pressed to do so—he left his people of Aquantanita to die alone, so many years ago. He would not leave the people who he calls his own. All details of how to enter one of the star fighters was clear. He was awakened from his daydreaming by someone's voice. When he turned around, it was Hutap.

She walked up to him,

"Are you sure you won't be needing my help?" asked Hutapsunnimoon, her eyes searching the wonderer's face.

"No, Hutap, you are needed here. I will take care of the problem and bring our people back here. I just need you to focus your attention on the field, understand?" Imhotep said.

Hutap's sharp eyes noticed the twitching of the wonderer's ears and recognized that he was looking southwest into the darkness; eyes frozen in time. Hutap quickly turned and her eyes expanded widely, in surprise. She reached for her long bow, pulling out one of the shooting star arrows.

Imhotep stopped her by using his hand, then asked,

"What do you see?"

"I see hundreds of beasts moving in our direction, still way off. Different from the beast we fight now, we have to gather the soldiers.

They are coming fast, leaping off the ground. Large beasts that kind of look like the large apes that live in Central Alkebu-lan, in the forest near the mountains but their faces look like the wild dogs that run the wide open plains. Large teeth and claws; powerfully built, they carry swords and a host of other weapons," Hutap said with her weapon aiming.

"Don't attack! I have a hunch," said Imhotep, then whispered a few words and a large pocket of air covered the entire army, spinning rapidly.

Hutap moved around, getting the men ready just in case. She moved back to Imhotep's side as men all around reached their feet, weapons ready for war.

Imhotep gazed outward to the dark, landside. He was thinking it was possible being called Cravistines. There was no doubt they had seen the ship flying through the atmosphere and back to the large, star cruiser docket at the side of the moon, or the force field that surrounded Abyssinia. One of Ick's scouts found their way in, Imhotep thought. The Garthians are the arch enemies of the Cravistines. If the Garthians win here there will be no place for them to hide.

Imhotep had lived among the Cravistines for a short while. Ick, a well experienced leader, kept the life of his people reclusive. It wasn't until Imhotep travelled to the top of the northern mountain that he learned of their presence. A powerful leader that only wished to live in peace, Imhotep remembered the fire power Ick held onto for so many years; weapons that would be very effective in killing their common enemies. Their neatly organized communities are vast, deeply embedded in the many large tunnels. The Cravistines have created over the years, many of the males, females and younglings that live, learn and prosper among the mountaintop, never once giving up on the hopes of going back to their home world; similar to his own thoughts and dreams.

Hutap stood at his side ready for war; she noticed nine spheres hovering above his head; three raging fire, three blue ices and another three, air swirling in the orbs center. His arms were placed behind his back, patiently he waited. The large group steadily moved closer and closer.

"They had to stop; now they're looking at us. They could see us clearly now. One of the beasts is moving forward, holding something inside his hand," said Hutap.

"What does it look like," asked Imhotep, looking at Hutap.

"Well, it looks like some kind of stone on a rope around the creature's Neck," Hutap said.

Imhotep reached for the chain and stone, inside his pouch, he received from the Cravistine's leader, ICK and raised it for her to see.

"Does it look anything like this?" asked Imhotep.

Hutap looked down on the stone in Imhotep's hands, then said,

"It's exactly like that stone," she finished.

The large being moved closer and Imhotep moved towards it; Hutap at his side, within feet of one another. Hutap heard Imhotep's barks and calls to the large beast as it responded to his calls, then she watched them communicate while in a deep conversation.

"Well, it's you, Ick, my good friend. Glad you could make it," Imhotep said. He took a deep bow in respect as Ick bows in return.

"I could see the trouble we are in and had to come to support the Alkebu-lanian people; so help everyone including my people. Did you really think that I would let you do this on your lonesome," Ick asked.

"Well, I almost forgot about you. The powerful Ick, living up there in the mountains, but we could sure use your strength," Imhotep expressed.

"Well we are here, my entire force. The actions my race has been seeing lately, I knew it only meant trouble. I brought my soldiers as quickly as I could. The Cravistines are here to fight and die if necessary, but there will be no more running," Ick said, looking Imhotep in the eyes. Then he pointed up to the sky and smiled.

"Yes, I understand, but it brings me joy to see your soldiers prepared for war. Now bring them in, all is welcomed," Imhotep said, then released the air seal that protected the Alkebu-lanian forces.

Hutap moved around the soldiers informing them of their new allies so there would not be any surprises. Ick called to his people waving in; the Cravistine beast moved among the Alkebu-lanian soldier towering above their heads. They were greeted with pats on the back, as Imhotep and Ick moved off to talk a bit in private.

They settled in the distance away, stopping near a large lake. The crickets let out a mating song as insects buzz over the lake and over the glow of the moon. An owl sat on a huge tree branch looking down.

"Ick, you are a bright star for sore eyes. Well, I need to tell you, I'm leaving right away. I have learned the Garthians have captured men, women and children. They're being held in one of the star fighters and I know I'm needed here but your appearance reinforced my decision to go. I must free the captive, and bring them north, then I will meet you all on the field of battle," Imhotep said.

Ick towered over the small frame of Imhotep; he rubbed his chin, reliving the Garthian attack on his home. Alkebu-lan was his home and to do harm to its people was to do harm to himself. He looked up at the starship near the moon, then he gazed down at Imhotep and said, "Yes, go and free the Alkebu-lanian people, you may be the only one here that could get inside and out without harm," Ick finished.

"I need you to break your forces up into three parts, send one force to support General Butann and his son, the giant Tutannharmoon to the south; another to the west central, where General Ziko and Ahknonkineton will move on the command center from that location and I need you to command the army here, leading the northern forces to engage the enemy," Imhotep said.

"Me, why me?? How would the soldiers feel about me and how would I communicate with them?" asked Ick.

"Well that won't be too much of a problem, just use hand signals. It is easy for the soldiers to understand, especially Hutapsunnimoon. Listen! They will respect my judgement. You are the most experienced general on this field. Who else knows the Garthian forces better than you and me? The Alkebu-lanians and Cravistines are counting on you," Imhotep replied, looking into Ick's eyes.

Ick looked down on the wanderer and said, "I will carry the forces to victory, while beating his hand on his chest."

"Go now, send your forces! In two days, we will attack! We carry enough power to crush the enemy," Imhotep said. His eyes looked around, he spotted Hutap a few feet away but so were two of Ick's main security.

"Yes my forces will be in place, and I will command the northern forces," Ick said proudly.

"See this woman here?" Imhotep pointed at Hutap. Ick looked back to see the young woman. Imhotep continued, "Her name is Hutapsunnimoon. Any instruction you feel you may have a problem with she could correct also."

Hutap walked to Imhotep's side while he continued to talk, "When you make the call to attack, she will be a very effective weapon, she is the only one to fight on her own, everyone else follows orders."

"Yes, I see something very special about her," Ick said.

"Get your soldiers ready to move out as I find messengers," Imhotep explained.

Ick moved to his personal body guards, a huge beast towered above his large body as they begin to talk, then his guards barked out orders as the Cravistines moved in close.

Imhotep turned and began speaking with Hutap.

"Listen I'm leaving, I have spent too much time here already. I'm leaving Ick in charge of the forces."

"Why him I don't know these creatures," Hutap said.

"Do you trust me?" Imhotep asked, touching her on her shoulders, looking her directly in the eyes.

"Of course, Imhotep, but..."

"Then trust me now and my judgement. Tonight I leave to free your father and the others who are trapped inside cages aboard the ships. There will be no other opportunities, once the attack commences, I can bring everyone out safely."

"I can come along to support you," she stated, "He is my father."

"I'm very well aware of him being your father Hutap, but the Garthians have added more strength to their arsenal. You are needed out there on the field, without you most of the men and Cravistines will perish. What are swords and bows and arrows compared to explosive weapons? You, Ahknon, as well as Tutann, will be the power out on the field. The Cravistines also brought powerful weapons, the Alkebu-lan soldiers will listen to you. I'm counting on you, Hutap. Ick is sending his soldier's to support Butann and Ziko, send messages to each of their forces tonight, so they could expect the Cravistine's arrival. I will free the captives then come back to help you in the war," he said, as he touched Hutap on the shoulders briefly, and looked around at the men.

"I will focus my attention on the battlefield and I trust you will bring my father and our people back," Hutap said, then hugged the old wanderer.

"I will try to be in and out before the battle begins. If I can destroy most of their weapons and communication equipment, I will," he finished.

Then he paused in thought.

"What is it?" Hutap asked, noticing the curious look upon Imhotep's face.

"It's nothing, remember, two days. Ick knows the plan, see you in two days."

Imhotep turned around, moving a fast pace heading southeast. Hutap watched him go until he was out of her sight. She turned around, moving toward the men, calling out as they gathered around her.

West central Abyssinia

Following day

Ahknon and General Ziko talked underneath a large tree, going over plans for engagement of the enemy. Ziko turned and noticed one of the scouts to the west moved towards them. Ahknon turned to look as well, but someone walked with the scout that caught their attention; now several feet away Ahknon recognized the soldier as one of their messengers.

Ziko and Ahknon approached slowly.

"General this is Nefie, a scout bringing you a message from Imhotep," the short soldier said.

Ziko and Ahknon step closer to hear the message.

"I bring help sent by Imhotep, and word from the military commander to the north, by the name of Ick," said the messenger, a brown skin fellow with long hair—he was thinly built.

Ahknon looked on in surprise, and Ziko was as surprised as him.

"What happened to Imhotep leading the northern armies to the battlefield and who is this person called Ick who leads the northern forces?" asked Ahknon, looking down at the messenger, leaning over a bit.

"Ick is the leader of a race of beings called the Cravistines, and a good friend of Imhotep, Hutapsunnimoon stands by Imhotep's word," the messenger paused for a while then continued, "Imhotep traveled to the iron bird to free the captives held by the Garthians. Ick was instructed to break his soldiers up into three groups, one was sent to General Butann, one here to join up with the forces General Ziko commands, and the last to support the forces to the north," the messenger said.

Ahknon looked on, nothing surprised him when it came to the old wanderer, he held many tricks, as well as many friends. He watched the messenger, as General Ziko asked, "Where are these soldiers?"

Ahknon and General Ziko looked at one another, and then back to the messenger, as the messenger waved his hand behind him, then a large number of Cravistines moved towards Ahknon and General Ziko, Alkebu-lan soldiers quickly moved to their feet, weapons ready inside their hands. General Ziko looked back behind him waving his soldiers off as they relaxed but stayed on their feet looking.

"God where did the wanderer find these beasts to help in the war?" asked General Ziko.

Ahknon began laughing out loud then he said, "The wanderer has many friends and there is so much you do not know about him, leave it to him to find help and these creatures are welcomed, a powerful ally."

Hundreds moved among the ranks greeting General Ziko and Ahknon. Ahknon could only smile, in his mind he was thinking he was going to give the Garthians hell in another day, as the huge furry being moved into their ranks to relax a bit.

Southern Abyssinia

A tall, lean fellow moved into the campsite of Commander Butann, where his son, Tutannharmoon stood right beside him. Tutannharmoon noticed a messenger walking beside one of their scouts. Butann looked up wondering what his son was looking at, and noticed the messenger also. The messenger stepped in close to speak with his general, he stated,

"I bring word from Imhotep, he sends help from a race of beings called Cravistines to assist in the battle, a very strong ally," the messenger said.

"Where are they?" asked Butann, looking at the messenger then around the landside.

"There back among the trees, a group went to General Ziko and Ahknon, their leader commands the northern forces. Hutapsunnimoon stands by Imhotep's word," the messenger finished.

"Why isn't Imhotep commanding the northern forces?" asked Butann. Tutann looked in wonder.

"The wise man, Imhotep traveled southeast to free the captives inside the iron birds, then he will return to help put an end to this race of beings," said the messenger.

Butann looked up to his son and said,

"Imhotep will free the captives, this I know for sure. We do our part here, he will return and assist in this war," Butann finished.

The messenger waved his hand and the Cravistines moved toward the Alkebu-lanian soldier's powerful beast. Butann whispered then he smiled, looking up to his son, Tutann, who was staring in awe. One of the beasts greeted the general and Tutannharmoon, as his group moved in to rest after there long trek south.

"The more, the better," Tutann said, smiling down at the added fighters.

He noticed that each of them carried swords and some form of powerful weapon which flashed a light at their waistline; to him they are powerful looking, they will compliment there attacks, then the messenger caught their attention yet again.

"I also bring word to you Tutannharmoon."

A surprised look came over his face but he hoped the message was from Hutapsunnimoon, he listened intently.

"Hutapsunnimoon sends her thought, be safe out there. She will see you on the field of battle in one piece," the messenger stated, looking up at the giant.

Tutann smiled down on the messenger, then began laughing outwardly, his deep voice rumbled loudly. Butann looked up at his son wondering what had his son so tickled, then it dawned on him that his son was very fond of the female. Butann begins to smile, then he heard his son say,

"You tell Hutapsunnimoon I'll meet her in the middle and will have her in mind and heart."

"Yes, I will tell her and I'll leave right away, my animals are resting under that patch of trees," said the messenger, pointing as he watched the last of the Cravistines marching into the ranks of soldiers. "Imhotep showed me a quicker route to make the journey back north, ok now I'm off."

Command ship in the moon's orbit

Down below in one of the lower levels, Nassir with Fertari, moved through the miles of metal shaft that circulated air through the large ship. Fertari was keeping up with the amount of time they traversed the air tunnels knowing Garthian soldiers counted the captives every few hours.

They have found the landing dock, where the iron birds comes in but they have been unsuccessful in locating the weapons room, weapons that will be needed if they wished to escape. He crawled forward, moving pass the room that Garthians occupied. Fertari is several feet behind Nassir, after carefully moving down to a lower level, and looking inside many of the rooms, he found what he'd been looking for. Nassir looked back at Fertari giving her the thumbs up, as she smiled in satisfaction.

Nassir moved passed the room as Fertari moved forward over the square opening that looked down upon the room. Nassir turned around and moved back towards the opening, watching as Fertari placed her ear to the opening to listen carefully.

She looked at Nassir and said,

"I think it's clear. I don't hear any signs of movement, there are swords and other weapons down there but I noticed that the Garthians carry a very powerful weapon at their waistline, more powerful than swords. If we plan to leave here, its best we take the powerful weapons," she finished.

"Yes, get them as well," Nassir said. He then pulled the square box to gain access to the room. Fertari climbed down with the help of Nassir, dropping to the floor quietly, she moved to a rack that held the hand weapons. She looked up at Nassir then pushed a chair below the air passageway.

Fertari found a large pouch and began placing weapon after weapon inside. They were strange to look at, a red light flashed on the side of the weapon. She also placed many swords inside the bag, moving just under the square passage where Nassir waited. Nassir noticed that the room held many metal boxes. He believed in those boxes were many more weapons. The room held chairs and a desk like those in Alkebu-lan; it amazed him how similar these creatures are.

Fertari passed him the bag after standing on the chair; he reached down, taking hold of the bag and lifting it up, placing it in front of him inside the air passageway. He watched Fertari push the chair back in place so the setting inside the room would seem normal.

Fertari climbed upon a table, she suddenly heard footsteps coming in her direction. Nassir heard the steps also. When she looked up his hand was dangling down from the passageway, she leaped upward catching his arm as he held on tight, pulling her small body through the air passageway, then closing the entrance way. Nassir followed Fertari back in the direction they came, they heard a door open up below them inside the room, they crawled forward moving quietly, heading back to their confinement, better off than when they left.

Chapter 25

Universe 1(UV1)-Commanding star fighter

Captain Acee moved through the star fighter, heading down just one of the many walk ways is the vessel, he moved to a pair of doors and they opened, as he passed through they closed behind him. The next pair of doors opened as he entered taking a seat at his post, many soldiers gathered around him as he began to speak.

"Is everything ready for a full–scale attack, we don't need any more soldiers coming up missing. I want these beings to conform to our every wish, and if not, kill them all; we captured more than we needed so there is no reason to take any prisoners. I want the beasts to be the first line of our defense. The land cruiser will support the beast's advancement, but if not, their cannons are ideal to clean a path. I only want three men to the land cruisers," Captain Acee paused for a short while in thought.

"Remember four thousand Garthian soldiers are heading north and the other four thousand are heading south. Whoever took out Captain Tigr will be held accountable, we will torch many of these rebel's homes and entire communities, then we will find answers. Have you deployed the last of· the rebels in the cell?" Acee said, now looking at one of his officers standing to his left.

"No Captain, we are in the process," the soldier said.

"Get the captives up to the main ship. I hate the smell of the beings. I want those cells cleared, understand?" Captain Acee said, looking down on the Garthian soldier.

"Ok Captain, right away, sir," the solder said, heading through some doors.

Acee watched the soldier go. He then said,

"We win tomorrow, then we extend the shields over a large part of the planet. These ugly little beings, with their ancient weapons, will never prevail." He stood up at his chair.

"Captain Acee, shall we begin setting up the beast and land cruiser in preparation of tomorrow's advancement upon the new planet," asked one Garthian soldier with a deformed third arm where its finger was now nothing but a nub.

"Yes indeed, begin the process, that's an order." He turned, walking past several soldiers, then passed the cells where the captive rebels were being held. He watched them as they looked at him in passing, he held his nose.

The Alkebu-lanians held on to the hope of being free; women comforted children inside the large cages. It's been days now since General Nassir was carried away and even longer since the two Alkebu-lanian soldiers made their escape. Many fell in to a depression, while others continued to believe their freedom was near.

Then noise above them all caught their attention, many begin to whisper while many moved to the cage door to carefully watch the guard's every move, as others stood up to prevent a clear view of the inside of the cage. More of them begin to wipe tears from their eyes, as more whispered, looking upward.

The entire room began to stare upward, as they noticed an old face peering out through the opening, excited smiles crossed every single face at the recognition of the old man their people called Imhotep. They begin to celebrate quietly, hugging one another as the wanderer floated down from the top of the ceiling to touch the floor softly.

Many gathered around him, touching his clothing, feeling his skin, while the elders hugged him with affection. As he greeted the people he has lived among for over one thousand years, some begin to whisper his name, he spoke,

"You have to be very quiet," now waving his hand to settle the crowd but Imhotep continued, "I'm here to free you all." He looked around the room carefully, searching the large gathering but there was no one there that appeared to look like Nassir.

Imhotep thought for a moment, then he bent down to speak with an elderly woman with graying hair, very dark in complexion.

"Where is the one called Nassir?" Imhotep asked.

The old woman looked up with a smile and said,

"They took him, and now we are to follow. They come for us right now, Imhotep."

Imhotep patted the woman on the hand, then said,

"We will be home soon, I promise. I will go to where they took Nassir and then I will bring you all back," Imhotep said.

Everyone inside the room heard the legends of Imhotep and how he lived for so many years. He was considered a person of great power and skill. Their concerns are now washed away; they held great faith in the wanderer. By the wanderer's side, they all could meet any challenge, they celebrated quietly.

Imhotep's first option was to free the captives; even doing so would not end the ship's docket near the moon, there his powers would grow far beyond anything the Garthians have seen in over a thousand years. If he can take the star cruiser then he could end the war. The people of Alkebu-lan need him; the dead souls of the Aquans need him.

For over a thousand years, he thought of plans of revenge on the Garthian race, here and now was his final chance, Hutapsunnimoon, Ahknonkineton and the powerful Tutannharmoon was more than a match for the forces gathering here on the surface, including the Cravistines, a powerful ally.

Imhotep pondered his decision, knowing if the main ship turned its main fire power upon Alkebu-lan from outer space; it will destroy the people and the planet, like the Garthians have done to his native home world of Aquan.

Imhotep watched his world be destroyed inside of his mind as a tear ran down his face, images of his mother and father hunts his memories. This is his only chance at it, and it would be the only chance he needs. He smiled when he heard the soldier's coming to the cages; they begin yelling out orders, pushing everyone in line.

He stepped in line like he was the most humble person among them; he was now in his element.

All the rebels were placed on another star fighter called UV3, each of the captives was placed in a cell location as Imhotep watched everything around him excitedly, his demeanor made every captive around him comfortable.

After being strapped down, the star fighter lifted off, moving quickly, his balance was off, the feel of the ship's movement was new to him but something he could get used to again. Gazing through large windows looking at the planet grow smaller, then even smaller, it was a wonderful view and he now relives how much he truly missed space travel.

Imhotep looked at everything like he was a small child learning for the first time. More tears filled his eyes and he blinked them away. The planet was moving away, as the spacecraft rocketed towards the moon. The Alkebu-lanian people aboard, pointed at their home through the square window as it began to get small amongst the black of night.

Imhotep could feel a shift in the star ship's speed, knowing shortly they will be docking. Through the large window, he noticed bright, blinking red lights, then the spacecraft entered a large docking area and for the first time, Imhotep sees what he had been seeing now for months up close.

He had forgotten how large the main ship could be, nothing of this magnitude or structure, even in his home world of Aquan, could he remember weapons of such size. Imhotep felt the starship touch the docking areas softly, as the window revealed the inside; the outer space dock doors closed as Garthians begin moving around in all directions.

Shortly afterward, Imhotep and his people were led out of the star fighter to the landing bay floor, where many Garthians were there holding weapons. Imhotep felt his power growing now that he was away from the planet's surface, powers he has not felt since arriving here at the new planet. At that very moment, he knew he could wipe out everything on the docking stations.

Still amazed, he followed the Garthian soldiers as they were being led to another cell location. Many star fighters were upon the landing deck, soldiers stopping to look at the captives, others working on the dock stopped to get a view as they passed.

Imhotep's mind took a mental picture of everything he had plans of destroying. He and the others were being led through some doorway over two hundred yards away. He looked up and around the large dock at the wonders of the ship's creation. Moving through the metal doorway now and down into a corridor, it was a wonder how clean the place was, Imhotep thought.

They moved among some other door and entered a large cage with several Garthian soldiers holding weapons. The doorway to the cell was open and Imhotep noticed many others inside the cage, as he and others moved inside. All the captives inside got quiet after seeing the likes of Imhotep being brought inside, but the Alkebu-lanians that followed, all appeared to have smiles. When the last captive entered the cell and the door was locked, the soldiers all moved away.

Everyone inside the enclosure surrounded Imhotep, others cried, as if their saviour heard their calls, "Imhotep, Imhotep," they all shouted.

Garthian soldiers moved away, paying little, if no attention at all, to the commotion.

"Listen, everyone here quiet down, we don't want to alert the soldiers of my presence," Imhotep said, looking around the huge cell.

"Are you here to take us home, Imhotep?" asked a young woman, holding his hand, then kissing it, laying her face against his hand.

All those around waited patiently for his answers.

"Why else would I travel this far?" Imhotep said, as his eyes scanned the large group of captives, then Imhotep continued, "Is the general, Nassir, here?"

A tall fellow walked through the crowd towards him and Imhotep noticed the facial features, the likeness of Hutapsunnimoon, while a Zukufu female soldier walked at his side.

"It is me, Nassir, the great Imhotep, how have you found yourself in these conditions, were you captured?" asked Nassir, looking down at the old wanderer.

"Well, I was under the impression you sent two soldiers to bring the northern forces a message of you and other captures," said Imhotep.

"Well that's good, I'm glad they were able to get free to alert the forces. So you're telling me you crawled through the air tunnels within the iron birds?" asked Nassir.

"The life of one Alkebu-lanian was enough to bring me here, but let's not forget about you, there are people worrying about you, especially, a young, powerful woman named Hutapsunnimoon," Imhotep said.

Nassir's eyes spread wide; he moved closer to Imhotep and then said,

"You know my daughter?"

"Very well, she is a skilled soldier indeed. I had to do everything in my power to keep her from coming with me," said Imhotep.

Nassir remembered the story of the old wanderer but what is the story now that they're millions of miles from home up against an enemy with power far beyond anything he has ever seen. He said,

"Well Imhotep, look around you, it will be very difficult to leave this place. We just found weapons, but neither of us could fly the large iron bird," he finished, but the look in the wanderer's eyes told him that Imhotep was the least bit worried about escaping.

"Well, is that right?" Imhotep said, looking at all those around and then at Nassir. Imhotep continued, "You leave the flying up to me, but we need those weapons for the war in Abyssinia, once we are back on the ground."

"What about the fighting up here? How will we defeat the Garthian soldiers?" asked Nassir, looking as if the old wanderer is losing his mind. What is a little Voodoo, Nassir thought.

"You leave everything up to me," Imhotep said, smiling brightly, and continued, "We are going home!!! Everyone gather around, gather your things we are going home," he said, looking around the room, the crowd gathered closely.

Chapter 26

Star fighter, UVl, Command ship

Three star fighters were several hundred yards away near a huge lake near the eastern shore. Large groups of Garthian soldiers stood ready in line formation, each carried swords, a small shield and other weapons to be used on the battlefield. Twenty land surfers hovered four feet in the air awaiting orders to move out. Over twenty large beasts, some exceeding thirty feet tall, waited for the order to move out, many with wings to carry them through the air, others with horns protruding from their head walking on all four legs, and giants, some with a single eye, holding large clubs.

Back at the star fighter, Captain Acee stood with several large, personal body guards, looking out at his spectacular force; he was very impressed at the powers he wheeled. He looked right at one of his soldiers and asked,

"Are the forces ready to pull out…" his words were cut short, as they begin to hear the ground rumbling towards the south. Acee turned to look out in that direction, he covered his eyes from the sun, a large, dark shadow moved across the ground then into his view, the large beast turned to look at the incoming forces, letting out ear– piercing roars.

Excited now, the Garthian soldiers looked on, swords dangled down in their hands, as the large, land surfers turned toward the marching forces, all cannons aiming at this new threat.

One of Acee's prized soldiers said, "Make the call, its good we don't have to go out and find them. Its better this way, make the call. Set the beast to attack," Acee said, taking a seat, leaning back farther in his chair.

"Yes Captain, a horn was blown across the land side; two large beasts took to the air, one, a huge black dragon, its scaly skin dark as the night skies, scaly with sharp claws, teeth and spikes exiting from its back, a long neck, and wings that pushed it upward into the sky. The second, huge insect– like beast with armored skin, red in color with six legs and clear wings, its mouth is huge with several rows of teeth. It took to the air behind the dragon, wings moving quickly, carrying it over the ground."

Two land surfers moved high off the ground about twenty-five feet. Their cannon pointed at the incoming enemy force. Three Garthians maned the flying craft, as it moved behind the huge dragon. Down below the soil something moved like a huge ocean wave, other beasts begin roaring, outwardly across the land side.

Captain Acee patiently waited for the war to begin, he opened his mouth to yawn, showing his jagged teeth, many of them broke with a fork shaped tongue. He wiped the dust out of his eyes, crossing his hand over his chest while the small limb held his powerful weapon; he spoke in mumbled tone and clicks.

"Yes, I like this, come to your death you ugly looking creatures. "Ready the soldiers for the attack on my word."

"Yes Captain," one of his main guards said, holding two swords in his hands, looking out in the distances to where the rebels moved closer.

The powerful giant Tutannharmoon walked beside his father, Butann, leading the southern forces to the battlefield. Butann held swords in both hands, bracelets of armor tied to his wrist, thick, raw hide, and animal skin covered his body from the protection of swords. Upon his head is a head band, the color, a mixture of brown and black, are the colors of his people, the Alkebu-lanians, and red, symbolizing their blood; it symbolized the fighting warriors of his community and many of his men wore the symbols of their communities in colored headbands. Thousands carried hand axes, swords, composite long bows, flight arrows, and daggers in many sizes, including a backpack for secondary weapons and water.

The Alkebu-lanians marched forward behind the large Cravistine being, whose angler swords was half their body size with double– edged ties, at their waists were powerful light weapons that will be used in close battles.

Butann marched forward, the Cravistines began barking loud, and the Alkebu-lanians yelled to the skies as their voices carried on the winds. Many soldiers begin banging their swords together, and the sound rang across the field.

Butann looked up to his son, Tutann, standing on his left and noticed something was different about him, he flinched backward a bit, there were creatures, large, scorpion–like moving around his huge body franticly, eerie looking insects, as large as his hands.

Butann said, "What are those strange creatures?" His eyes wide, watching the insect move quickly over his son's skin.

"I am Tutannharmoon," his voice rumbled loudly across the plains so the enemies could hear his words, the indestructible, the bringer of death, Tutann said. Looking now at his father, as he stepped ahead of his military forces, quickly leaping away to put distance between he and his men, hitting the ground hard as it shook.

All his men cheered loudly behind him, their voices raised to the air. Two flying beast moved towards him, one looked like the large reptile that lives on the water's edge and the other, some kind of oversized insect, Tutann thought. Two flying iron crafts moved passed the beast moving quickly his way. Tutann raced forward, legs hitting the ground one after the other, propelling his body forward. The flying craft unleashed its weapons down upon him, an explosive sound came. Suddenly, explosion after explosion rained down out of these crafts tearing in to him and the ground. The power was so intense, the fire and smoke covered his body completely, tossing soil rocks in every direction.

Butann screamed out,

"Noooooooooo!!!" Raising his hand to the air, wondering why Tutann left formation, nothing could withstand the force the iron birds was unleashing. The iron birds continued to release its weapons upon his son's body.

Every Cravistine and Alkebu-lanian soldier covered their eyes from the debris and flashing lights, everyone was quiet. Soiled, thick clouds covered the ground where Tutannharmoon was standing. All his men waited to see what was left of the large Alkebu-lanian giant. Then the clouds cleared and every single soldier, including Butann, began yelling to the sky. While they watched Tutann leap upward, smashing the first craft using his left hand, it exploded loudly, killing its occupants. He took hold of the second craft, bringing it to the ground, then ripping it in half and slinging it at the Garthian army a mile away, Garthians dived out of its way, as it crashed to the ground killing many in their ranks then exploded, fire spread across the ground, screams could be heard from the enemy ranks.

Butann and the force of Alkebu-lan rushed out to the field to engage the Garthian forces. Tutann was already on the attack running across the ground, he leaped upward with his arms extended, these beings wanted to take his world and he couldn't have that. He was now mad; he took hold of the insect– like beast, his finger broke through its outer shell, as a blanket of fire consumed him and half of the large insect–like creature. Tutann climbed to the large beast's back, taking hold of its wings then ripping them apart. He and the beast hit the ground loudly, a cloud of dirt and rock rose from off the surface. The crawling parasites creeped upon his body, erratically entering the insect–like beast's injuries by the millions to feast as they began to devour it alive. It screamed out it pain, kicking its leg wildly. The reptile smashed into Tutann's body, forcing him to the ground, its claws tightened its grip as Tutann's body was being lifted into the sky. The ground was quickly moving away, as the beast took to the air roaring loudly.

Tutann turned, taking hold of the beast's feet and with his strength; he squeezed with his hand until the bones cracked loudly. The beast shook its legs, trying to free itself; it looked down letting out a stream of fire that covered Tutann's body. And the scrolling move upward to feast on the beast as it cried of pain, its large wing moved back and forth.

Tutann climbed up the large beast's chest, pounding the beast's body until his hand exploded through its chest. Tutann's left hand dug into the beast's skin. Then the cracking of bones was heard as Tutann continued, he and the dragon fall out of the sky, hitting the soil hard, the ground shook.

Butann and his soldiers rush quickly to meet the Garthian soldiers, as they continued to cheer, witnessing his son's raw power against some of the enemies' most powerful weapons. They knew they had a chance; he was the equalizer on the field and they will win the day.

To the north, Hutapsunnimoon moved over the large, hilly land side, as she crossed the last of the large hills moving to the top. She noticed that the fighting has already begun, as Hutap watched Tutann in full battle with some large beast, she screamed out.

"We must attack now! The soldiers are under attack," Hutap finished, waving her hand back and forth.

Alkebu-lanian soldiers and Cravistines raced upward and down, moving into the direction of the battle. The Cravistines took the lead, hopping outward several yards at one time, Ick was leading the pack. Hutap dashed forward, in blinding speed, across the hot soil, the northern forces were already in the distance. Every step she made brought her closer to the fighting soldiers. Her long, powerful legs pushed her forward at greater speeds. Several metal crafts were moving in to engage the northern forces.

The enemy had not seen her coming. Hutap pulled her long bow, placing her shooting star arrows in place, still moving forward across the burning sands, it extended outward into a crescent moon as the blade burned a hot, white heat. She released it.

As it cut through the air heading for its victims, one after another, she pulled arrows from her pouch at her back and released them. The shooting star arrow lit up its path to its target exploding through ranks. The Garthian soldiers died instantly and the star arrows flashed back in place; after making contact it reappeared inside its holder.

The next metal craft moved quickly, it was hit dead center; the shooting star arrows cutting it in half, the craft crashed to the soil.

Hutap watched it explode into fire. Two more crafts move her way, within feet of her enemy, she released three arrows into the craft on her right. The arrows strike across the field tearing through its target. The last craft that carried the enemy soldiers was headed directly at her. Hutap leaped off the ground and over the last craft, she turned her body around to look down into the craft. She released three arrows that cut through the craft as it exploded. She turns around while still floating in the air to hit the ground running toward the Garthian forces.

She moved forward, releasing several arrows as they sailed across the field, cutting into the ranks of Garthian soldiers. Their bodies were cut in half while others lost legs and arms; their blood covered the ground below them. Still a short distance away, she headed toward a large beast swinging a club.

A hknon and Ziko led the forces, moving further into center Abyssinia from the west. The soldier was about two miles out when the sounds of war reached their ears. All the soldiers begin to pick up there pace knowing their fellow soldiers needed them. Ahknon remembered what Imhotep had told him, the words played inside his mind, *"Together you could defeat the Garthians, without the others it could only mean the end."* Ahknon's heart thumped inside his chest, he had no more time to spare.

Ahknon looked back at General Ziko and said,

"I'll meet you all on the battle field," as he propelled his legs forward, moving away from the moving forces, extending his spear outward in his right hand he leapt upward to the air, as his body took off, leaving the ground behind. He sailed through the air quickly; the ground moved away below him he passed the trees and soil in the blink of an eye. The closer he got the louder the fighting became—in seconds he landed. He looked to his right; Tutann was in battle with several large creatures. Then he quickly looked to his left, Hutap just killed some form of giant and was now taking down hundreds of Garthian soldier's and their hover crafts, bodies were being flung airborne and in every direction.

Ahknon turned back toward Tutannharmoon, he was fighting several beasts. He watch Tutann smash one across the face and it went airborne, another, Tutann ripped the horn from its head while stabbing another beast with it and another large giant moved in to hit Tutann in the head with a large axe. Ahknon pointed, took one step and threw his sun spear at the beast's head.

The spear rocketed across the brown soil, cutting the air with sound and force, then exploded through the head of the huge giant; its body hit the ground, still holding its weapon.

Ahknon raced forward leaping up into the air as his spear reappeared inside his hand. He flashed across the air to land among hundreds of Garthian soldiers moving out to attack Alkebu-lanian soldiers and Cravistine fighters.

Ahknon slammed the sun spear down into the soil as the Garthians turned to attack him; the ground shook violently, causing his enemy to topple to the ground, while others were catapulted in the air, the soil opened up in all directions as a huge crack appeared. The soil consumed many of the Garthian races. Hundreds fell to their death then the soil closed. Ahknon pulled the sun spear from the soil.

Ten flying crafts moved towards him, pointing their weapons. A loud noise flashing of light moved at him, words entered his mind, and he turned toward the fire power of his enemies.

Ahknon raised his sun spear above his head, looking to the sky, words passed his lips, as lighting flashed downward in seconds like a thousand arms burning the weapons and machines; explosions soon followed, one after the other.

Ahknon was hit hard from the rear, his body sailed across the ground, making contact with several trees. The impact caused the trees to fall. Ahknon got up, looking at the trees in wonder, any other men would have been dead, then something took hold of him squeezing, forcing the life from his lungs. The creature had eight arms with two legs, it looked like some kind of aquatic beast, its suction cup held him in place, as other limbs wrapped around his small body. Ahknon watched as the beast opened its mouth to consume him. Ahknon called out a few words of an unknown language, this time the sky above rumbled loudly as thunder and lightning flashed violently from the sky, crashing into the beast's body. It screamed, as it blood poured from it and its body exploded into nothing—it dropped Ahknon.

Ahknon reached his feet; he turned and threw the sun spear at another beast. On contact it exploded through, as the beast crashed to the ground, holding its chest, killing several Garthians in its wake, as the spear reappeared back inside Ahknon's hand.

The fight was pandemonium, now that all Alkebu-lan's forces reached the field. Clashes of metal and loud grunts rose to the air; all around, Garthians, Cravistines and Alkebu-lanian soldiers fought side by side. Ahknon turned and moved quickly into the heat of battle.

Imhotep's power grew before sending Nassir, Fertari and a few other soldiers through the air passageways. He looked deeply into their eyes for several brief moments, when he broke contact he was able to see through each of their eyes as if their sight was his own, they moved through the airway looking at every part of the ship for Imhotep's knowledge.

Nassir thought all this was a waste of time, but he keeps his thoughts to himself. The wanderer was very sure of their escape, he looked through all the rooms in the lower levels of the huge ship, it was a word Imhotep has called it.

He moved on, taking in as much of the ship as he could. It was eerie knowing that Imhotep was watching through his own eyes. He began to wonder how he could hear what he was thinking. It was even eerie that the wanderer was able to do this trick with many others, all at the same time.

Nassir moved through the ship quickly, it was time for the Garthian soldiers to count his people. He headed back the way he came.

Imhotep sat in the room, legs crossed in meditation. Several soldiers and a host of women was there to keep an eye on him, others watched the cage door as he instructed them.

Quietly, he sat in that very spot and turned his head, although his eyes were closed, it appeared to them the wanderer was looking at something, then they hear d him whisper, "Yes."

The captives watched over the old wanderer like their lives depended on him, in which was true. While many others secured the air passage way listening for the General and other soldiers, others keep a sharp eye out for Garthian soldiers by the cell door.

Imhotep smiled brightly at the images appearing inside his head, several screens appeared deep within his subconscious mind, images of things his hosts are viewing. He gazed from one screen to the next, taking as much information he would need, learning every single aspect of the ship, the space docket reappears in his mind and he looked around to see all the things that would be important. Other images showed him large computers that ran the star cruiser, images of the engine room, the Garthians living quarters and the large weapons bay.

But what he watched most importantly was the ship's power cannons that could destroy the planet from space. He would have to seal that area off from the Garthians completely. When he was satisfied that he saw everything that needed to be seen, he opened his eyes, knowing he would have to put an end to those aboard the ship, then get back to the surface to help destroy the Garthians there.

Inside the room Imhotep stood up, then he looked up at the air passageway, hearing the soldiers making their way back, after a short spell, men begin to exit the passageway climbing down to the floor. The last to come through was Nassir, touching down then moved to stand by the wanderer. Imhotep said,

"I've seen all the things that was needed, the areas of importance, places that need to be sealed off, so I thank you for your patience, you can gather your things now," he finished, then he moved his hands in front of the face of those with his visions.

Nassir rubbed his eyes feeling the disconnection of he and Imhotep, he had underestimated the old fellow who talked of being free. He now understood why he was known for traveling Alkebu-lan for some hundred years. He was truly a powerful shaman with enormous powers and if he had any doubts of going home now, he discarded them.

"Everyone step back a bit from me," Imhotep said, looking around the room as everyone moved toward the wall away from the cage.

Imhotep began mumbling words, then a flash of light and five replicas of him appeared in a circle, looking at the original image of himself. Imhotep stated,

"Each of you have been created for a special purpose, you are a part of me so what I have done is equip you with some of my powers to finish what I command of you. Each of you are programed for a certain mission, once it's completed, your physical state will be drawn back to me, where ever I am on this ship," Imhotep continued.

Nassir and the captives looked in awe at the few images of Imhotep in deep conversation with himself, whispers came from all around the room, as Alkebu-lanians looked and pointed, many others gathered the children and prepared to leave. The legends were reinforced about the wanderer, a new story would be told, greater than the last.

After talking with the visions of himself, each one disappeared as Imhotep closed his eyes, seconds later the alarm sounded around the huge ship. Imhotep turned around to face the door entrance, turning his back to the Alkebu-lanian people; several spheres as black as space itself appeared above his head.

Imhotep looked back at Nassir and said,

"Get ready to move, make sure you all stay together," while the black sphere moved and expanded its casing around the entire group into its center.

Nassir gazed out the dark circle that covered the captives; it was clear from the inside. They watched as Imhotep tossed the dark globe at the cage door, it spread out, eating away the door in seconds.

Imhotep moved out the doorway looking back at the dark circle that followed him, it was called dark energy, the energy of empty space, it was very cold, colder than the artic place in Alkebu-lan, it would devour anything that came in contact with it and was unseen by the naked eye.

He was making his way toward the space dock; the alarm was going off in every location aboard the ship. He smiled knowing he was capturing Garthians all around the ship and sealing off dangerous locations. He moved forward down the corridors, while images of himself, entering the weapons bay, the engine room, the control center of the large cannons outside the star cruiser, pointed at Alkebu-lan. Several Garthians rushed up the hallway toward him, Imhotep captured them in a large pocket of air then squeezed the life from their lungs, sending the sphere on its way around the ship to capture more. Imhotep began to release more and more circular spheres to move around the ship; invisible spheres to the naked eye to capture unsuspecting Garthian soldiers and staff. He input these thoughts through to all his replicas. He turned the next corner as spheres moved down the corridors on their own, floating several feet off the ground.

Imhotep remembered the way to the space dock but he truly needed to take control of the command center of the ship, where the Commander could be found. Alarms blared in every direction; lights flashing off and on, staff were running down a passageway ahead of him through crossed paths.

Imhotep released more and more clear spheres, as he moved towards the space dock. He moved quickly up flights of stairs, behind him the dark energy followed. He heard screaming as Garthians unaware of the sphere, ran into it, and was captured inside.

Imhotep grabbed at the railing of the stairs as he pulled himself upward. He turned to move up the next set of steps and so on. When he entered a door way, several Garthians turned his way rushing in his direction. The sphere of dark energy raced forward as they expanded, devouring its host, screams raised from their mouths, as Imhotep marched forward.

Imhotep made it down the next corridor and noticed hundreds of clear spheres had captured many Garthians inside, understanding that the replicas have followed his instructions. He passed many more spheres in the large corridors holding up to ten Garthians at one time. He passed them moving away, the dark sphere moved behind him quickly.

Nassir led his people behind the wanderer seeing all the turmoil all around the ship. He noticed Garthians being captured in a clear cell, many of the occupants were forced together, tightly inside these clear cells. He looked behind him as the large group moved down the very large corridors.

Ior, the commander of the star cruiser, sat back waiting on communication from Captain Acee about the war ethics on the planet's surface, then the alarm rang around the ship, he looked to his staff next to him and said,

"Find out where the alert is coming from."

One of the staff sitting at a computer several feet from Commander Ior's seat, said,

"Well Commander, looking at the main computer, the alarm is coming from several locations."

Ior turned his chair towards the officer and said,

"Do you think we have a problem with the computer system?" Ior said.

Rubbing his eyes, he then looked around the ship's control center as lights flashed brightly, off and on as the warring horns came from all over the huge ship. For the first time Ior realized how serious the matter may be.

"Call the control room at the space dock and everywhere the alarm is tripped now!" Ior yelled around the room.

A female sitting several feet away said,

"Yes Commander, right away."

The female staff placed the call then placed the speaker over the intercom, a voice spoke loudly.

"Commander!!! We are under attack, the weapons bay, engine room, and many of the rooms that control the ship are being closed off," the Garthian staff finished, he pushed several buttons, as Commander Ior's large screen shows five scenes from around the ship. He looked up from his seat, concern now apparent in his eyes. The Garthian staff continued,

"Large, circular spheres are moving around through the ship at all levels, capturing hundreds of soldiers aboard."

Right then the commander heard screams and the intercom and viewing screen went dead.

Ior screamed, "My personal guards follow me!"

Several officers followed Commander Ior to retrieve weapons from a side panel several feet away inside a locked metal door. After arming his men, he wanted to investigate these mishaps, and at worse he would move toward the space dock, where the dock control room offered the detonation of the entire ship, but while there, a small ship awaited his escape. A star fighter could be moving toward the door to exit the control room; Ior looked back and said,

"Stay where you are, make sure no one gets inside this room no matter what, you hear? No one goes beyond these doors."

As he moved forward, he begin thinking how could this happen, could one of the planet occupants manage to cause so much turmoil or is the problem timing from the captives? His ship was now branched, and for the first time, Ior had to question himself, wondering what kind of powers do these beings wield? He underestimated their abilities, he hoped he was wrong.

The exit door slid open as one of the guards peered through, Ior looked out behind the guard as he noticed a being from the new planet moving farther down the corridor, to him the being was strange, it was wearing some kind of skin of a beast above its head. Ior rushed down the other end of the corridor, his guards rush out behind him. They turn around and begin firing concentrated beams of lights towards the rebels.

Ior rushed down the corridor looking behind him for a split second to see the rebel moving behind him, he turned right at the end, moving to another door then down some steps. His guards followed quickly, Ior noticed not a single soldier or staff was moving in any direction, the stairwell was dark and he continued to move quickly.

Heading down to the space dock, Ior stopped and noticed, for the first time, a large sphere moving up the steps towards him, several soldiers were trapped inside the large circle, as it moved forward, Ior climbed over the railing to drop down four stories to crash to the floor below, he heard his men screaming then nothing.

Ior looked up to see a fiery elemental being and another wearing a beast upon his head, looking down at him. He moved to his feet, now realizing he hurt his leg, he hopped up quickly finding a door, when he opened it, he was shocked to see some of his men.

"Set up formation at this door now, whatever comes through it kill it!" Ior screamed.

As the Garthian soldiers took up position and readied their weapons, Ior moved through another doorway inside the room, which led to another way out, he heard his men let out screams behind him as he moved forward.

Imhotep was on the commander's heels, Imhotep had to capture the commander before he does something that will kill everyone on board the ship. The ship was branched and because so, and to protect his planet, Imhotep believed the commander is heading somewhere to release their powerful cannons upon the planet's surface but to also detonate the ship. The sphere he has created continued to move throughout the ship's levels, consuming everyone on board, pretty soon they will have captured all and what the sphere won't find the replicas will, as his powers continue to grow, he created fiery elemental beings.

Imhotep and the Elementals moved though the doorway the Commander went inside, a group of Garthian troops opened fire, the fiery elementals raced forward taking hold of the four Garthian soldiers, the clothing turned into flames as they screamed trying to free themselves, their entire bodies caught fire and they eventually succumbed to their death.

Nassir and all the captives watch the struggles from within just behind Imhotep, invisible to those around them all. When the last of the soldiers was down, Imhotep was moving through the doorway, followed by the Elementals and the large sphere of dark energy, they moved quickly after the commander.

Central Abyssinia

Butann swung his swords from left to right, sweat poured from his skin, the clashing of metal was heard all around the large field as Garthians, Cravistines and Alkebulanian soldiers fought hard around the field. Butann pushed through, slicing through the neck of one Garthian soldier, then jabbing his blade into the back of another. Butann moved through the crowded field slicing and stabbing every single Garthian soldier that came into view, all of a sudden he heard a growl, he turned quickly, it was the huge two-headed cat beast, from the woods weeks ago. Butann lashed out in its direction, cutting one Garthian soldier across the chest, ducking another, thrusting forward, sticking the blade threw the body of another Garthian soldier, he dove just in the neck of time, just before the huge cat beast leaped upward. Grazing his right arm, blood spilled from the injury, with no time to wrap it Butann turned, but the loss of blood made his movements slow, his eyes closed a bit, knowing his body wouldn't react quickly enough. The cat beast leaped and Butann could only watch as its huge body was coming down upon him.

Tutann was battling several large beasts and for a split second he recognized the two-headed cat beast that tried to kill his father. He noticed it was moving in to kill his father, anger took him, he landed a punch, smashing his fist through the face of a one-eyed giant, it fell to the ground. Tutann raced toward his father, each ground shaking step brought him closer. He leaped outward, arms extended crellings by the millions covered his skin, they were agitated, the large two-headed cat beast moved through the air.

The cat was upon his father when he slammed into the beast, hitting the ground, the sound echoed around the battlefield. Tutann took hold of the large cat as its sharp teeth bit down on his tough, outer skin, knowing the other beasts was making their way to him. He heard the thundering of footsteps he leaped away one thousand yards, carrying the large cat with him to put

distance between he and the other creatures, and the Alkebu-
lanians fighting on the battlefield, hitting the ground a distance
away.

Tutann held the cat beast up above his head by one of its
necks. It raked its claws upon Tutann's face and bit down on
Tutann's left arm, as its sharp claws sliced away at Tutann's skin,
the ground rumbled behind him as other beasts moved closer.
Remembering his talk with his father, when the Alkebu-lanian
soldiers were attacked in the woods, and how the cat could have
killed his father, this angered him totally. He looked into the large
cat's eyes, the one he was holding around the neck, his finger dug
deep, his powerful hand squeezed tightly.

Tutann turned around using the huge cat as a weapon,
knocking down a creature his size with sores across its body. He
used the cat several times with all his strength, rose up and
slammed the cat beast against the giant on the ground, the cat's
body changed, as sores appeared across its skin. Tutann realized
it was some kind of infectious disease, his skin came alive as the
insect-like parasite rushed towards his hand and began eating
away at the disease. Tutann spun around catching another huge
insect-like creature around its neck with six legs and a large
mouth, long but angled body, hairs were sticking out at every
side, he held it in place tightly.

Tutann swung the two-headed cat beast smacking the insect
creature in the face, sores spread across its body, it cried out in
pain. Tutann, with both hands, ripped the cat beast in two, and
slung its body away angrily. Other beasts charged him from all
angles.

Ahknon's spear reappeared back inside his hand as large groups of Garthian soldiers rushed at him, he was more concerned for Tutannharmoon, it seemed like all the huge creatures brought down by the Garthians are targeting him.

Ahknon tossed his spear at an insect-like creature standing above Tutann, it exploded through the creature's face, as its body goes limp. When his spear reappeared back inside his hand, he spun around, leaning low to the ground and every Garthian soldier rushed his way, Ahknon's spear made contact with their legs as they surface one after the other, then the sun spear exploded through several hover crafts then into more Garthians.

With each contact of his weapon bones was breaking, as he moved through the ranks, Ahknon looked over and Tutann was now fighting a three–headed scaled beast, it towered above his powerful frame, then another four-legged beast with horns sticking out of its head rammed Tutann from the back and was now dragging him across the ground.

Other beasts raced behind it to attack Tutann. With two steps, Ahknon threw the sun spear, making contact with the beast that followed, their bodies crashed to the ground. After the sun spear entered the beast's back then exited its chest, he ran as quickly as he could, leaping up into the air. The spear appeared and his body rocked across the sky rising higher above the ground, flying passed the scaled beast, Ahknon noticed the beast took to the air quickly, its wings lifting the beast upward not far behind him. Ahknon then looked down to see the beast dragging Tutann.

The ground is a dust trail kicking up behind them as Tutann smashed the beast in the face. They enter a large patch of trees as trees crashed down to the ground from the impact of their body weight. A pathway was being made as trees continued to fall. Ahknon's body now floated in the air, his spear reappeared inside his hand, the large scaled beast was moving closer to him. He faced the beast, its three heads looking directly at him. Then the beast opened its mouth, the first head let out fire, its face large with straight but large teeth a single eye upon its face.

The second, Ahknon noticed it was different from the other two, the skin was a glowing green, it's mouth larger than the other two and head even bigger, it released a black, toxic gas from its mouth, and the third head, its skin was the color blue; a white substance released from its mouth, its head was narrower than the others too, the power of their breath weapon combined as one. Words of a foreign language entered his mind, and Ahknon raised the spear, and in seconds, lightning exploded out of the bright skies, entering the spear, electricity surrounded him like a million thin lines, the creature's breath weapon collided with the electricity and a loud explosion came after, like a thousand thunderstorms all at once.

From the center of his electrical cage, Ahknon pointed his spear and a powerful lace line of lighting and thunder raced towards his attacker, catching the beast in its chest, its heads froze as the power shook its body violently. Its body began its decent to the Alkebu-lanian soil, the beast's contact with the surface shook the landside from miles around. Ahknon turned around then pointed his spear, his body moved through the air toward Tutannharmoon, as the battle wage on.

Just a few short miles away, Hutapsunnimoon moved like a shadow of death in the mist of the large forces, thrusting her comet blades into their necks, stomach, and backs; massive blows to vital organs, leaping over others, tossing Garthian soldiers off to the side after killing them, sweat passed through her pores, as her hand and legs made contact with blinding speed. Hutap saw a group of soldiers moving to take hold of some form of large weapon, instantly, she pulled her long bow and released several arrows in that direction, the arrows heads turned white moving towards it intended target. The arrows made contact exploding through the weapons destroying them completely, several large pieces fell to the ground. Hutap went into a 360 spin releasing several arrows, that destroyed the hover craft shooting down on Cravistines and Alkebu-lanian soldiers, their bodies were tossed backward to their death.

The crafts all around crashed to the soil, then exploded, she replaced her long bow, retrieving her comet blades, Hutap was now angry, seeing the bodies of her comrades. A huge, one-eyed beast with rippling muscles like Tutann, began swinging a huge, spiked club through the crowd, bodies were being catapulted through the air. Hutap headed straight for the large beast, she watched as it lifted its club to swing down at another group of Cravistine soldiers that surrounded it. She leaped upward, sailing through the air, standing the huge beast in its neck several times, in one quick motion she pulled her long bow out before she hit the ground and released several shooting star arrows, on impact it severed the huge club, then the creature's arms, it screamed of pain.

Hutap could feel the huge beast reaching up with its left hand to take hold of her, she moved, pulling her comet blades out, plunging the knife into the beast's single eye. It roared, clapping its hand to its face. Hutap leaped off the giant's head. The beast hit the ground on his back as the soldier pounced on top killing the large beast. Garthians, Alkebu-lanians as well as the Cravistines, were falling around the field of battle as yells, and painful cries went on and on, as the clinging of blades and small explosions by weapons the Garthians and Cravistines were using against the other.

Hutap turned, another iron hover bird was shooting a high powered weapon in to ranks of Alkebu-lanians, many men and Cravistines were being torn to pieces. She raced through the crowd, rising up from the soil, using head of a soldier to move quickly. Reaching behind her, pulling her long bow, she released three shooting star arrows, one severed the arm of a Garthian. Shooting the weapon again, the second cut straight through the weapon and the third, cut the iron hovercraft in half. The Garthian soldiers inside fall to the ground where they were mobbed by Alkebu-lanian and Cravistine soldiers, who hacked the Garthians to pieces.

A second iron craft moved off fast, and Hutap moved behind it as it gained speed hovering five feet off the ground, it made a sharp turn and picked up speed. Hutap turned and picked up speed moving faster behind it, for the first time, the Garthian had spotted her, the Garthian was pointing back at her now, she stepped quickly behind the craft as it picked up more speed. The soil behind was being kick up into the air, the faster she traveled, her dreaded hair floated behind her cascading in the wind.

Hutap followed the flying craft away from the fighting, now across a large barren field, the Garthian turned the craft's cannon directly towards her, she smiled, the craft cannon blasted away as she moved quickly out of the way, dirt exploded in those areas.

Hutap broke right then left as the ground exploded upward yet again. She made a sharp turn, barely evading an explosion. She pulled her long bow again as the iron hover craft moved ahead of her, turning a steep left then right, she moved steady behind it taking aim. The explosion of the hover cannons caused her to move quickly and out of the way, the explosion rocked the landside. She noticed the craft was heading to a high cliff wall. She released several shooting star arrows that moved quickly out in front of her towards its target. She watched as the craft rose up as the star arrows passed beneath the fast moving hover craft. She replaced her bow while her eyes continue to watch the hover craft move higher off the ground. Hutap's legs propelled her forward, everything around her is a blur. She noticed that the craft was rising higher to reach the top of the cliff.

She pushed forward, moving fast below it heading for the cliff wall. She looked upward as a Garthian looked down with what she thought was a smile. She moved directly beneath the cliff wall, in seconds she hit the side of the wall ascending to the top. The iron craft disappeared, moving over the top and out of her sight. She knew it was a few feet away. Hutap's feet dug into the side of the cliff as she moved up its side, moving quickly, when she reached the top, her body sailed skyward.

Her eyes made contact with its target, she pulled the long bow quickly, noticing the lack of attention the Garthian was paying her, she now smiled, releasing twenty shooting star arrows, five just above the craft, five to its right, another five to its left and the last five below it. She froze for a short while, as her body continued to rise upward through the sky. Hutap smiled, her eyes noticed the concerned looks on the Garthians' faces. She reversed her body turning into a somersault moving down toward the side of the cliff, she then heard the explosion, her legs made contact with the cliff wall. Reaching the ground, she headed back towards her fighting men quickly.

Star cruiser near the moon's surface

Ior locked the huge door behind him, depressed now, he was thinking, he has never suffered a loss in a war at any time, but the tactics he used on the new world was unlike any tactical moves used anywhere else. Normally, he would bomb the planet's surface from space, then send down his men when he thought it was clear. But this new world is very young, with no known advanced technology that truly offered a resistance to a greater power such as his Garthians. Ior moved through a large room to find another doorway out, he could hear banging then an explosion as the beings gained entrance to the large door he closed, after a while he heard footsteps moving somewhere behind him, tracking him down. He questioned himself, could the new world's beings have been smart enough to stage their imprisonment for the taking of the command ship, it was hard for him to fathom, but it was exactly what was happening.

The command ship is a powerful and effective weapon, Ior was thinking, once he could get to the lower space dock station, he can gain access of the weapons there, fire down upon the planet, killing millions including his soldiers, but he thought it was a price they all had to pay for such a grave mistake. He began to wonder how the clear sphere went up unnoticed by his staff aboard the command vessel. How could such a few take control so quickly? Ior exited down a huge doorway, closing it behind him, then looking around quickly for the large sphere, never knowing where they may appear. There was a chair in the corridor. Not sure, Ior took hold of the chair and moved forward, holding it out in front of him running now down the halls which angled right, he was almost there. First he will initiate the self-destruction codes, then destroy the occupants of the planet by activating the star ship's main weapons, then escape using one of the escape vessels. Before the ship exploded, he moved down the halls quickly.

The fire element exploded through a doorway, it caught the scent of the Garthian commander as Imhotep moved two steps behind it, as they moved down the hall as quickly as their legs could manage. The large, circular sphere followed several feet behind Imhotep. Down an angled hall they went, Imhotep caught the glimpse of the commander's back, much farther ahead of them, then Imhotep watched the commander turn up ahead out of sight.

Nassir followed right behind Imhotep within a cell of safety, he was angry because he knew he could help with the fighting on the ship. He moved forward as his people followed. The cell Imhotep created seemed to elongate so that even the young or old would easily find their way unharmed, within the sealed cell. Nassir has been watching closely, as the fire elemental being Imhotep has created killed many Garthians around the ship. While in pursuit of the iron bird, Commander Nassir watched the commander turn and disappear through one of the doors ahead, he screamed, hoping Imhotep could hear him.

"Where do you think he is going?" He watched Imhotep look back at him and say, "I think he wants to destroy the ship killing everyone aboard, then flee, we have to be fast in order to stop him."

THE EPIC SAGA OF ALKEBU-LAN

The fiery elemental beings outpaced Imhotep; they turned through a door far ahead. Imhotep was fast on their heels, followed by Nassir and the group. Imhotep rushed through the doorway onto the landing deck of the space dock. He noticed a huge sphere that held hundreds of Garthian captives inside, they were as large as the star fighter on the landing dock, scattered in every direction as more moved into sight. The Elementals were now several yards behind the commander of the vessel, which was moving up steps leading to the control center high above the floor of the space dock. Lights flashed of alert, sirens blast through its intercom, as Imhotep moved to catch up with the commander. He was very tired; he had little, if no rest, within the last few months, sweat poured from his skin, his clothing bounced up and down all around his body. The space dock landing was huge, as Imhotep looked around, the ceiling was over two hundred feet upward.

Imhotep noticed the commander moving to a doorway at the top of the stairway, the Elementals were one stairwell behind the commander when he closed the metal door behind him. Making it to the steps, Imhotep ascended upward, breathing heavily he pushed forward, he could hear the Elementals banging at the door trying to gain access. Imhotep knew he had only one option now, to perform a trick he used years ago on his home planet of Aquan. A trick he could not perform if down in Alkebu-lan. He was hoping he could remember the words exactly, he understood the protocols of being a commander and the sacrifices one in that position has to make. He began concentrating, once making it to the top landing in front of the large metal door.

Imhotep began whispering words quickly, the Elementals continued to kick and bang on the doorway, Imhotep's body begin to fade becoming transparent. The Elementals moved to the side as they watched Imhotep's body disappear into vapor. Now the size of a molecule, the smallest part of any pure substance, Imhotep looked around at the Elementals then noticed the sphere of dark energy that protected Nassir and the group of Alkebu-lanians. His body drifted upward above the doorway to the large window that looked down over the space dock landing. It's been a while since he traveled in this form; it was strange, but he needed to stop the commander of the vessel.

Floating before the large glass window Imhotep noticed the commander, a huge Garthian soldier moved around turning switches, moving to another part of the room, as Imhotep watched him pushing buttons, slowly he moved through the tiny opening in the glass window, so small only something his size could pass right through. He moved away from the huge Garthian commander, he needed a bit of time for his body to regain its natural form. He is vulnerable in this state, so he found a corner a short distance from the commander, who was concentrating on other things. His body slowly was taking form, when all of a sudden, he felt hands taking hold of him, forcing his body hard against a wall, knocking the air out of his lungs. Imhotep, connected to the huge Garthian's face but it did little, if no damage, to the commander.

Commander Ior began his sequence of numbers to begin the unleashing of the large cannons outside his star cruiser. The weapon was now motioning towards it target from the computer reading, then he noticed something to his right, he turned quickly to see someone standing there—he rushed in for an attack. Slamming it against a wall, what looked like one of the creatures from the planet's surface, taking hold of the small being around its neck, he began choking it.

Ior then slammed the being's head against the wall several more times, and it scratched at his eyes. Ior faintly remembers seeing this creature before and he tried to remember from where, it was a bit different now that it wore another form of attire. Slamming the being on the floor he began landing crushing blows to the being's face. He knew how serious it was to take his ship so quickly and he wanted to put an end to it, but it fought back, after the second and third crushing blow to its head its body weakened. He lifted the badly beaten being above his head as its life forces drained from its face and head, onto its clothing, Ior began to choke the life out of it.

Imhotep realized he was in trouble, the beating he was taking was brutal, he came too far to fail so he fought against being unconscious. If he got one second to whisper a few words, he could capture the ship's commander who continued to beat down upon him. He was bloody but he tried to fight back. The Garthian soldier was five times his size, Imhotep used his hands and arms to block the powerful blows raining down upon him, his eyes begin to close; to never open again.

All the noise was gone from his ears as the blows continued. He looked deep into his subconscious mind, his thoughts were on how the Garthians had killed his people. He watched the fires consume his planet as he traveled away to safety across the universe to the new planet. Now these same creatures wish to destroy his new home, his new family. The people down there looked up to him, depended on him, and he promised them he would take them home.

So close to victory, the blows kept coming, he can't let them down or the souls of Aquan, words escaped his lips as Imhotep's body transformed to solid ice. The commander smashed down with his fist again but this time stopped, as Imhotep climbed to his feet. Ior begin looking around for something, he remembered his weapon at his waistline, he pulled it out and fired, Imhotep's body turned to water splashing down over the floor. Ior's eyes opened wide, now remembering a race of beings his soldiers conquered more the a thousand years ago, because of their use of special powers; a people from a place called Aquan but how he thought. More words fall from Imhotep's mouth as a clear sphere appeared.

Imhotep watched the commander pushing what he knew was the detonation sequence of the command star cruiser. The sphere moved forward capturing the commander, he fought against his holding cell, trying to shatter it. Imhotep reformed his body, climbing to his feet badly beaten. He moved to unlock the door, the Elemental beings moved inside looking into the clear sphere at the Garthian leader.

Nassir climbed the steps and now was looking at the badly beaten Imhotep.

He asked, "Are you alright?"

"Yeah I'm fine, nothing a little rest can't fix," Imhotep said. His left eye was closed and swollen, his neck was also swollen and bruised, other bruises appeared all over his face and neck.

Nassir noticed that the wanderer was tired, so he asked, "Can you walk?"

"Yes, although I will find it very difficult," Imhotep said.

Nassir, Imhotep, and the fire elementals climbed down the steps, as many of the Alkebu-lanian people begin to cry after witnessing the bloody and beaten vision of Imhotep. Imhotep was able to calm the gathering down after reaching the space dock landing. His people gathered around him reaching out to touch him, he spoke,

"The ship is now under our command," he smiled.

"We have to get home to assist the forces below," said Nassir.

"Yes, we will be there shortly but I need to see into a few things before we leave. Nassir I ask that you take the family through the door, there," Imhotep pointed, but continued, "I don't want any of them to see what i must do next," Imhotep said.

"Yes, I think I understand," Nassir said.

Moving a hundred yards away and into a large doorway, the huge group followed him through the door as Imhotep watched Nassir close the door behind him. Other large, circular spheres entered the space dock, carrying Garthian soldiers within, then through many other doors came the replicas of himself, each one stood at Imhotep's right as well as his left. Thousands of circular spheres Imhotep faced, all the Garthians inside look upon their capturer, many worried faces, others stood tall with pride. The sphere took up a quarter of the space dock, Imhotep looked to his replicas and said, "Thank you."

Each of them bowed in respect as each of them moved inside of Imhotep to become one again, when it was completed Imhotep turned his eyes back to the captured enemies, his arms extended, as the last of the sphere floated downward carrying the commander of the Garthian ship, it floated out in front of them all and several feet from Imhotep. Imhotep began, in his clearest Aquanian language.

"You all have traveled the universe on a conquest to control and in doing so millions were killed, their lands, homes, and planets destroyed, and for that you will die!! Yes, many of your hearts may be in a good place, maybe those who kept quiet among you after witnessing some of the most horrendous crimes, did so to keep from being targeted, but still many died for your silence. I say I'm sorry to all of those who had compassion in their hearts, but not the courage to act upon it."

Imhotep looked around to each sphere and a Garthian woman was crying. Imhotep whispered a few words and the woman was cast inside a single sphere, separated from the one she occupied at first and she was pulled away. Then he looked to see a young Garthian male and he repeated his method, pulling the male out of his enclosure. Their bodies floated down toward Imhotep, then the sphere became one, male and female inside one sphere, they found comfort in one another's arms, looking to their capturer, then the sphere rested just behind Imhotep.

"I want you all to know, I will travel to your home world with an army to destroy it completely and what you see behind me is a new beginning of the Garthian race. I will be monitoring their teachings as well as power, and your people will continue without all the evil. I gave your people an opportunity, then you gave nothing and took everything. You took my homeland, and killed my people. I watched my planet turn to fire, from the weapons you have unleased, you spared no one!!!! And before you die I want you to know my name, it's Aquantoria, from the planet of Aquan, far beyond the Quasar, or the Pulsar, a planet that was composed mostly of water, we, Aquanians, lived an aquatic existence below our great seas, so now what you see here," Imhotep pointed around to every sphere, "You have created!!! But first I want you all to watch you commander die."

Every Garthian's eyes turned to their commander, as his sphere filled with water until the commander was submerged. They watched their commander fight to breathe hitting the side of his death chamber, until his body stopped moving and his body floated around lifeless.

"Your death will be quick, I will release your bodies into a dark space and there you will drift until one of the planets or Suns draw your body to it," Imhotep said.

Imhotep now looking at one of the Elementals and said, "Do you see the red handle over there near the door?"

The Elemental moved his head up and down looking in that direction.

"I want you to turn that switch left, it will manually open the space dock's doors," said Imhotep.

The Elemental moved towards the large red lever, Imhotep summoned a sphere of dark energy around the Elementals and everything he needed to protect on the dock, the opening of the space dock will drag out everything through its opening. Imhotep looked back at the doorway; he wasn't worried about Nassir and his people of Alkebu-lan for they were, just in case, in a sphere of dark energy.

The Elemental reached the manual switch and turned the lever as Imhotep instructed, warning lights flashed as the sirens blared loudly throughout the large star cruiser. The space door opened and the sphere begin to shift.

Imhotep spoke, "I sentence you all to death!!!"

Large and small sized spheres were being pulled quickly through the space dock doors. One after another, hundreds begin to fall outward, floating at first then the air disappeared around its captive and their bodies moved swiftly through space, every single last sphere exited the doors. The Garthians behind Imhotep watched in fear as each cell exits the huge ship until the very last one falls from its space dock.

Imhotep turned and look at the two left alive and said, "Do you understand why your people died?" His eyes red and injured.

The male and female Garthian consoled each other; a colored solution fell from their eyes as they understood his words and answered by moving their heads up and down.

"You will lead me to your planet, and in time, what I have done here will happen upon your home world. I suggest you follow my orders completely. I chose you two out of everyone else because I could see the compassion in you to teach your people a better way. Your future depends on what you do from here on out, understand?" said Imhotep. The two agreed.

"I will free you both after I have completed my mission."

Nassir appeared from an image through the dark matter noticing now that all the captured Garthians were no longer around.

"What are we waiting on now, Imhotep?" Nassir asked.

"Take our people to the star fighter over there," Imhotep pointed.

Nassir looked in the direction where many of the large birds were stationed. He guessed Imhotep was talking about the one closest to them; he called behind him as the large group of Alkebu-lanians moved behind Nassir.

Imhotep turned again to the Garthians inside their clear holding cell, and said, "Where do you hold your prisoners?"

The two looked at him sadly and then the female said, "They are held in level seven."

Imhotep turned around moving off towards a large doorway. The clear sphere floated behind him. The space dock doorway was closing as the flashing lights stopped, as well as the loud sirens. He entered the doorway; he moved inside and the sphere followed behind him. Imhotep looked at the colorful buttons inside the square room, he looked to the Garthians and they pointed to what button should be pushed. Imhotep pushed a yellowish button, and the square room began its descent downward.

The door opened as Imhotep stepped outward; there were large captive cages, for as far as he could see, he had to be fast because the Alkebu-lanian people needed him. He moved quickly, looking into several cages at alien beings, we will get to know soon enough. Most of the cells were to his right, the other side held cargo to be stored inside the huge ship.

He passed a large cage that held a huge horned beast, the size of Tutannharmoon, pops and clicks spilled from its mouth. Imhotep understood the creature and vague memories of a beast that lived among the Cravistines in their home world, he and the beast communicated as Imhotep released it, it followed behind him as if it was his protector, its feet shook the ship's floor. Imhotep released several more captives that he remembered, then he came across one cell. It held a sleeper box, it was sealed tightly. The large beast and other alien forms waited patiently at the cell doorway. Imhotep moved towards the strange object, he noticed the sleeper held a dark, colored metal surface; it was long enough to fit a person as big as himself.

The closer he moved to the object, he noticed the top of the sleeper held a window to look inside, he moved closer and closer until he was right upon it looking down into it, seeing a sleeping figure inside, the glass window was covered in frost, he wiped it using his hands. A warm feeling began to seep into his blood, a cold chill traveled up his spine, as he looked down at a beautiful woman, eyes closed sleeping, and his one injured eye widened at a sight he thought he would never see again. His heart raced inside his chest as he breathed in deeply, it was a female Aquanian, trapped inside a sleeping cell, frozen in time. He looked around to see a release button on the wall of the cell, Imhotep pushed it and the door unlocked with a loud click, and a cloud of cold air rose from the box. Imhotep whispered a few words and a small sphere of water appeared. He released it inside the sleeper cell as he watched her vitals on the computer screen, to him everything was normal and he knew she would be up shortly.

Then Imhotep thought, he had to get back before the captain on the planet's surface learn they have lost contact with the main ship, he would have to hurry. Her face balled up as if in pain from being in a stiff position for so long as she tried to move her limbs. She looked up at him surprised, as her large eyes focused and a look of shock showed on her face, her hands moved to her mouth, and a visible, tear spilled from her eyes, as Imhotep smiled. She rose up and climbed out of the sleeper cell stopping two feet in front of him, there she looked at him, as if he was a vision of a past dream. She touched his hands, then his face, shoulder, then hugged him softly around his neck, as Imhotep hugged her in return. She had so many questions, but Imhotep quieted her and whispered softly,

"I will tell you everything but this isn't the time."

He took hold of her hand and moved quickly back to the space dock. The elemental fire beings secured the dock, waiting on orders, the other alien beings stood behind him and the female from Aquan stood, holding Imhotep's hand on his right refusing to release her hold. Imhotep whispered a few words then pointed, ten more Elementals appeared just to his left behind him, Imhotep spoke to the one standing before him and said, "You are in charge here; these are your men, as well as these beings behind me, they will follow your instructions to protect this ship, I'm leaving for the surface."

The Elemental understood, moving his head up and down, Imhotep moved to the star fighter where Nassir was looking out of the doorway. Imhotep made his way to the ship, entering with the female Aquanian at his side, Nassir looked in surprise at the young woman but the image of Imhotep, he smiled as the woman entered the iron bird. Imhotep looked around at his new wonderful star fighter. Making his way to the captain's seat, he began punching buttons as the ship came to life; he looked back at Nassir making sure everyone is strapped down in their seats.

Nassir moved off through some doors, the Aquanian female instantly took a seat near one of the control panels, as if by instinct. The dock door opened as the ship floated ten feet off the floor, when the door completely opened; the star ship exited the space dock moving quickly for the planet. The large image was growing every second, Nassir found his home a wonderful place and he is glad he had an opportunity to see it from afar, but now he was on his way home, he was ready to continue the fight.

Chapter 27

Abyssinia

Screams and shouts rose to the sky, clashes from metal swords, and shields continued, more and more Garthian soldiers moved out of the star fighters to enter the war. Captain Acee is the least concerned, sitting upon his chair, keeping a sharp eye on the events out on the field. The fighting was intense all across the large field, what he thought would be only thousands of beings was now tens of thousands. Acee thought about the shield and its purpose, after looking all around him, there was another race of beings fighting alongside the original occupants of this world, as he began to wonder where did they came from, powerful creatures, which also used a powerful beam of light as a weapon.

Acee turned his sights to a western position to see his large beasts in battle with a beast of enormous power. He watched the beast catapult a six-legged creature twice its size skyward several hundred feet, crashing down to the surface. The powerful creature took hold of another beast's arm ripping it from its shoulder, then tossing its body into a patch of trees several hundred yards away as he begin beating the other beasts with the creature's arm. Acee's vision turned a bit south to witness a new being hit the ground from the air. In the midst of his fighting soldiers, holding a long thin weapon, the brightness of its tip could be seen from his position, Acee watched the being raise this weapon then push it into the soil. The ground shook violently then exploded outward in a wave of death 360 degrees. Acee looked as his men begin falling into large pits in the planet's soil. He begins to wonder if he had underestimated the beings of the planet. A flashing light caught his attention as something moved across the field quickly. He became alarmed for the first time, it moved towards two hover beam weapon ships. The ship exploded loudly, with fire and smoke. Acee then heard his soldiers screaming out in pain.

A female of this race of beings appeared on something that resembled a female of the new being race! Its fur hung down its back! Acee looked around the field for this same being! He noticed it again a good distance from where he first spotted it, fighting a large group of his soldiers, moving through his ranks as quick as the Garthians died all around it. Then the fire came from it connecting with several beasts moving all around the field, then Acee watched it disappear!

He turned his head left and right quickly, he said, "Release the signal of the gagetor beast to attack now!!! To kill everything but the Garthian soldiers below."

"Yes Captain, right away!" the Garthian soldier spoke in popping tones.

The soldier raced back inside the star fighter UVl. Seconds later, the ground all around the field began to shake as yelling came from all over the field from Garthians, Cravistines and Alkebu-lanians.

"Let's see what happens now," Acee smiled.

Out on the field, Tutannharmoon felt the rumbling of the ground, he turned and noticed Hutapsunnimoon standing beside him, then Ahknon struck out of the sky, hitting the ground loudly next to them.

"What is it?" asked Hutapsunnimoon, looking up at Tutann, then Ahknon.

"Well, I have no idea but whatever it is, it must be huge," Ahknon said, looking around trying to find out where the rumbling is coming from.

Tutann's huge body was covered in the alien creature, as he looked around before saying, "I don't have any idea, but whatever it is, it's bigger than anything we've encountered already." He clenched his teeth, hands balled into a fist, his eyes searched the Alkebu-lanian soil.

Hutapsunnimoon's long bow was already notched, Ahknon's spear firmly in his hand and Tutann stood strong! Many of the Garthians raced away from the field in all directions. Hutap noticed and said, "Look around, the Garthians are moving away from the field like they know what's sure to come."

Tutann and Ahknon looked around and agreed with Hutap.

The Alkebu-lan landside moved like nothing they have ever felt before, then the ground exploded in all directions and a towering beast head came from beneath the soil, its loud roar carried in the air! Thousands of Alkebu-lanians and Cravistines looked up covering their ears. The creature was tri-colored; half of its body was as dark as the Alkebu-lan soil, the other half turned blue, white, and green, like the trees and sky above. Its scaly body had spikes sticking out of its skin all around, it had nine powerful arms. Its under belly was that of the turtle shell, its mouth was huge with several rounds of teeth that would pull a being in, sharp but jagged teeth; large eyes searched the ground beneath it, as it breathed out deeply, it roared outward again, moving quickly down to devour one of the giant one-eyed beasts. Its teeth clamped shut on its victim, as it chewed, the victim's bones cracked; then the huge beast swallowed, quickly looking for its next victim, it spotted Cravistines and Alkebu-lanian fighters moving away from it, it began its attack.

Tutann wasted no time, he leaped at the huge beast landing a powerful, right hand to the beast's face to get its attention. It slowed its attack turning to its new victim. Tutann took hold of the creature's back as its several arms try to take hold of him.

Hutap was on the move, releasing shooting star arrows at the creature's large arms, each arrow sank in deeply cutting large chunks of flesh from the beast. She moved just under the beast and her star arrow exploded into the creature's flesh tearing a hole around its body. She moved quickly, leaping upward catching hold of its scaly skin. She moved up its side releasing several more arrows which exploded through its flesh. She continued to move upward steadily, releasing hundreds of star arrows, as the creature turned to meet its attacker. Its several limbs reached behind it scratching at its own skin. Its roar of pain carried to the air.

Ahknon took to the sky high above the creature floating in place, he spread his arms out wide looking to the sky above, words came from his lungs, as dark clouds gathered like a storm was brewing. Thunder erupted now in the dark skies, Ahknon's eyes turned the color red like that of fire. Tutann looked up smiling, but continued to extract punishment upon the huge creature, ripping out it

Hutap passed him, looking his way she released twenty star arrows that severed half of the huge beast's arms. Tutannharmoon, with power, snatched the arm off, it cried out in pain and rage. One of the creature's large arms took hold of Tutann and squeezed before tossing him to the ground. His body hit like another explosion several yards away, burying him one hundred feet below the soil, the beast rushed to consume him. Hutap looking upward knew what was next to come, she released thirty star arrows, exploding into the creature's back it reared back. Hutap leaped off! An explosion of lighting and thunder rocketed down from the dark clouds above lighting a trail on its path downward.

Ahknon screamed as the light went forth, moving at the speed of light. In seconds, it hit the large creature, as its body froze like it was trapped in a cage, ripping off several of its arms. Its spike broke off into every direction, its body danced in place, as the sparks of lighting cascaded around and through its body. Its hard armored body held fast; but Ahknon was not finished, he raised his spear. Then cascaded it downward at the larger creature, the lighting coursed through the spear glowing brightly as it moved down toward its target.

Ahknon screamed, "AAAAAAAAAAAAAAAA."

As the spear flashed through the air, leaving a trail of light in its wake. It descended down ripping through the air, Tutann moved out of the hole, witnessing the coming weapons Ahknon had released. The creature around Tutann's body was eager to feast. He leaped upward towards the beast's head rising off the ground. The weapon hit the beast and it roared across the landside, as the flashing of light exploded through it to exit its stomach. Hutap moved around the beast at the point of attack. She stopped to see Tutann make contact with the beast while the lightning coursed through the beast's body. She watched closely as millions of the parasitic creatures from Tutann's body entered the beast's wounds and began to consume it completely.

Ahknon flashed down beside her in seconds, she watched him come. Tutann hit the ground at their side as well, then he too turned to watch the insect-like creature consuming the huge beast.

"Where did all those parasitic creatures come from?" Hutap asked.

"I don't know, it seems like there is no end to the amount that is released," said Ahknon.

Tutann looked at the both of them then he shrugged his shoulders then gazed up at the beast being consumed. Cravistines and Alkebu-lanians begin to cheer as they rush out to the field where the Garthian was moving to meet the charging forces.

Captain Acee picked up his communicator, to contact the captains that commanded UV2 and UV3 that sat beside his star fighter, he said,

"Listen this is Captain Acee, ready the star fighter for lift off."

"Yes Captain, but what about the soldiers shouldn't we wait before we lift off?"

"No there's a branch in the shields, only days ago the force here was down to only thousands and tens of thousands fight on the ground, somehow they came through the shield and this time brought other. We are not fighting the normal forces here on this new planet; they have allies, very powerful ones. Get your ship off the surface, hover above ground until I find it safely," Acee finished.

"Yes Captain, UV2 and UV3 following orders."

"We can unleash the star fighter weapon while off its surface, and destroy them all, take defense positons to give our forces a bit of time to retreat before we bomb the enemy. There will be nowhere to hide! Contact the star cruiser, alert the commander, we will be needing reinforcements. Let him know that the shields have been branched and we need the use of the light weapons," Acee said.

"Right away, sir."

Seconds later UVl, UV2, and UV3 moved from the planet surface hovering over nine hundred feet off the ground. Garthian fighters raced away from the battlefield to find safety beneath the large hovering star fighter, leaving the Alkebu-lanian and Cravistine forces crying out a victory. Three hundred yards across the field the Cravistine's leader, Ick, looked on as the three ships raised off the ground and hovered at a few hundred feet. All around him Garthian soldiers were moving back toward their ship, away from the battlefield quickly, he looked at the ship then around to the force of Alkebu-lan celebrating a victory. He looked back up at the star ships and realized at that very minute that the star ship was preparing to fire down upon the forces of Alkebu-lan, despair and anger entered his old heart, as he screamed out as loudly as his voice could carry.

General Butann heard the Cravistine leader, Ick, yelling something out loudly, he and the other general, Ziko, looked in alarm, then they watched the Cravistines race off putting distance between them and the flying iron birds, they made the connection and Butann screamed out loudly.

"Retreat NOW!!!!! All men are to retreat now!" he said, swinging his arms jumping around the field.

General Ziko screamed along with General Butann. "Retreat!! Run for your lives, retreat!"

Ziko and Butann turned to run away from the flying iron birds.

All around the wide open plains, the sound of retreat went up. Cravistines and Alkebu-lanians moved quickly away from the huge flying iron birds, some through a dense patch of trees others towards mountains, thousands of fighting soldiers headed over the green landside. Ick moved across the large field.

Hutapsunnimoon caught up to the commander, racing at his side, she spoke, "What is it commander, what's happening?"

Ick began to give Hutapsunnimoon hand signals expressing that the ship was about to commence to unleash a powerful weapon to kill us all! Ick pointing behind him, he waved his hand, expressing for her to follow him. Hutap waved him on to cover. Thousands will die if she did nothing to stop what was about to happen, she turned and noticed Tutann and Ahknon not far from the flying iron birds, in second she move across the soil among them. They both turned around and looked down at her.

"Listen from what I see and what I've learned from Commander Ick, the iron birds are waiting for the Garthian soldiers to clear, those birds are ready to unleash some kind of weapon that will kill thousands of our fighting men," Hutap said.

At that moment, Ahknon and Tutann knew Hutap was telling the truth, they all turned to look up at the hovering huge birds.

"We need to give them something else to focus on rather than our people," said Tutann.

"Yes you're right," Ahknon said. "I could sense something beginning to happen, look at the flashing light aboard the iron bird."

"I need a lift," said Hutap, looking up at Tutann, "toss me to the top of the middle bird, after you do so go to that pile of large stones in the distance."

Hutap was now pointing behind the three of them, as Tutann noticed the place!

"Throw everything you can at the first ship."

"But what about you?? Will you be all right on top of the bird?" Tutann's rumbling voice stated.

"Yes," Hutap said.

"I think I can help," said Ahknon, "I have something I have not tried, I believe it's strong enough to work." He lifted his spear, as his body took to the sky flying high and quick, he landed two thousand yards away from Tutann and Hutap and right before the large ship. He stood in place as his hands begin spinning his spear out in front of him.

Tutann took hold of Hutapsunnimoon and tossed her upward into the air. She placed her hands at her side as her body moved quickly toward the center iron bird; the wind blew in her face as the sky was beginning to darken; bringing the first cloak of darkness. She was still moving until she sailed above the iron bird, which is much larger the closer she came to it. Her body began to descend downward, landing on the top.

Hutap pulled her long bow moving quickly across the top of the iron bird. She released thousands of star arrows; they exploded inside tearing through to its hide, she moved in blinding speed, releasing many more thousands. The star arrows tore through like the iron bird was made of flesh; the large part of the bird fell off, even in her haste she looked down into the crack of where the star arrows enter. There was smoke coming from inside; she could also hear the noise of the alarm. She continued rapidly, as the ring of her arrows continued to make contact.

After making sure Hutap made it to the top of the iron bird safely, Tutann leaped upward high above the tree and landside; he hit the ground among thousands of large stones; many four and five times his size. Many Cravistines and Alkebu-lanians raced away from the iron birds to find safety, he quickly took hold of the massive stones, one after another he tossed the massive gray stone to Hutapsunnimoon's right, the massive stone sailed through the air upward, ringing loudly at impact, smashing the ship's outer hide. The iron bird begins to move from side to side, as Tutann begins to toss even larger stones making contact. Moving to another location where more stones were in the ground, he pulled them through the soil, catapulting them threw the skies at its target, unrelenting in his efforts.

Ahknonkineton spins the sun spear quickly in a 360 degree rotation! Words of an ancient dialect spoke to him within his mind, the spear rotation moved much quicker, then faster, he looked down and he could not see his hand that turned the spear, wind begin to blow, and thunder crack loud above the skies. Ahknon noticed the sun was moving west. Then the loud crack of thunder again! Then lightning flashed down out of the night skies making connections with the center of the sun spear during its rotation!

A darkness darker the night skies appear as a circle at first then it begins to expand at the center of the spear where the lightning hit it. Ahknon noticed that wind begin to blow all around him much stronger. Ahknon continued to spin the spear! Now his arms had disappeared, the dark object grew much quicker now, it expanded ten times his size! The word Vortex entered his mind, and a dark hole appeared! Expanding every second, dirt and grass was being pulled inside, dead tree branches was being consumed. Then the winds got more powerful, Garthian soldiers that were hiding below the iron bird was being pulled across the soil.

Many of the Garthian soldiers were trying to take hold of something that would prevent their pull; hundreds sailed across the soil three feet pulled inside the dark hole disappearing from sight, it expanded now thirty feet! Ahknon looked inside this dark place; Garthians were moving away in the distance, in what Ahknon thought was the dark reaches of space itself.

More screaming commenced as thousands of Garthian soldiers were being dragged inside. Ahknon looked back behind him and noticed Tutann toss huge stones at one of the iron birds, one of the stone connected with the ship, then bounced off to hit the ground close to him. The huge stone was being dragged across the ground into the Vortex.

Ahknon watched as the iron bird to his far right exploded with sound as projectile was being released, he looked back toward Tutannharmoon. Tutannharmoon supplied large stones that caused the iron bird to crash into the center iron bird in which Hutap was upon! He stopped, very concerned for her safety. Tutannharmoon was hit, in which the ground and him exploded upward and back, his body crashed into another cluster of stones! Trees were uprooted as soil and other debris rained out of the night skies. More metal objects strike across the sky, he rose to his feet, taking hold of a large boulder tossing it in the projectile's way, it exploded on contact sending down a shower of smaller rocks.

Hutapsunnimoon was thrown off balance after the iron bird shifted quickly. She slid to the right side, taking hold using her left hand, held on to a piece of metal. Her long bow fell from her hand, it reappeared upon her back, as she held on to keep from falling to her death. She noticed that Tutann was hitting one of the iron birds to her left so frequently! It lost control and collided with the iron bird she was now upon, she pulled herself to safety. She heard an explosion of sound coming from the iron bird Tutann was attacking. She watched it release very large metal weapons that moved across the skies.

Hutap turned to look in the distance where Tutann was tossing large massive stones, the ground all around him disappeared into dirt and a cloud of smoke as another explosion hit that very spot. Hutap took hold of her bow, now in anger releasing hundreds of star arrows, which tore into the iron bird's side, small explosions came after the impact, the iron bird move away while she begin to worry about Tutann, she then continued her attack. Moving quickly aiming at various targets, as the star arrows reached their target.

"Unleash the weapon on the rebels now!!" Captain Acee said, looking out and down over the field, many of the Garthian soldiers moved toward the star fighters. Those that were injured were being assisted by following Garthian soldiers. Acee smiled, seeing the rebels fleeing across the fields into the tree lines, others found shelter down below, where the land sinks down out of sight, as still more rushed toward a mountain structure where a path through exist. Groups of rebels moved through it quickly, Acee whispered,

"Yeah run, find you somewhere to hide but still it's not enough to protect you from what I'm about to unleash."

Then warring lights flashed all around the control center, Acee looked around, angry eyes then, he said, "What is happening now?"

"Captain we are having a malfunction of the computer, this is one of the reasons the lights are flashing," said a female Garthian soldier, at her station, looking back at the Captain, then the siren blared loudly.

The female Garthian looked down at her computer, turning her computer towards Captain Acee, then said, "This problem stems from an attack of the star fighter from somewhere above us Captain."

"Are you serious, how could anyone reach the top?" said Captain Acee.

Out of nowhere flashing lights exploded through the ceiling, slicing through the floor and anything the light touched. Many more followed, flashing inches from his command chair, Acee leaped out of his chair as the weapon cut it in half, he rolled left and right as more came, other staff was killed several feet from him, where he lay in wait.

Somewhere a fire was raging, the detector was flashing off and on, as smoke begins to fill the room, Acee begins to cough loudly, others were coughing inside the room as well. He fanned the air with his hand, then said,

"Get up there and find out what's happening, if one of the rebels found a way to reach the top, I want it killed now! Do you understand?"

Several of his personal guards rush through a sliding doorway. Sirens blared loudly inside the compartment, other Garthian soldiers were working to place the star fighter on manual as the ship continued to take a brutal punishment, more flashing lights flashed through the compartment. Acee made it to his feet looking through the view glass of the star fighter, and noticed a huge rock structure was being flung high into the air to his left. He looked down into the direction the huge structure was coming from. Some kind of powerful being was tossing these structures from a great distance away, as many more of the large rock structures continued to move air ward. Then out of nowhere UV3 released its weapon upon the being tossing the rocks, the ground disappeared in a cloud of smoke and fire as the soil rained down in that spot.

Acee smiled, then he was knocked to his left; something very large crashed into his star fighter, he and many others were tossed against walls violently. Moving to his feet slowly now, he thought it had to be UV3 the other ship, he moved back to his feet, this time something caught his attention below him, a tiny single figure was spinning some kind of weapon, creating what looked like a black hole in space. Then Acee noticed that many of his fighting soldiers were being sucked inside, the hover vehicle followed disappearing completely. He moved to his chair noticing that for some reason the attack from above the ship ceased, he called over his communicator.

"Star fighter UV2, come in UV2, this is Commander Acee." A call came over the communicator.

"This is star fighter UV2, I hear you Captain."

"Release your weapons upon a single figure just below your craft, whatever it is, it has created some form of black hole and is killing a large percentage of our soldiers, destroy it now," Captain Acee said.

"Yes, Captain."

The vortex expanded as Ahknon continued to spin the sun spear, then something was happening, Ahknon watched panels open up all around the huge iron, what he thought was weapons was now exposed, the iron bird then tilted down in his direction. It was a serious possibility he wasn't going to make

THE EPIC SAGA OF ALKEBU-LAN

it, but he was glad that his people was somewhere safe, it was better that he was able to attract the iron bird's attention, lights begin to flash brightly as the moon reached the center of the night skies.

Then an explosion of sound came louder than any noise he has ever heard, fire projectile flashed his way, the same weapon that buried Tutann a short while ago, lights flashed behind the weapons, and Ahknon could smell a burnt substance in the air, as they got closer his heart rate excelled, he closed his eyes and begin to yell.

"IIIIIAAAAAAAAAAHHHHHHHHH!!!!!"

The huge Vortex expanded to suck in the explosive weapons, nothing escaped its powerful gravitational pull. He heard the projectile cutting the air towards him, everything around him got quiet, Ahknon opened his eyes and he was alive, at that very moment he felt invincible, he stopped its rotational spin. He planted his feet and threw the sun spear at the huge vessel, it cut through the air and expanded, its tip glowing brightly.

On contact it exploded threw the underside exiting the top, the sun spear reappeared back inside his hand and Ahknon tossed it several more times, as smoke exited the huge vessel all around it.

Tutann was angry now; the iron bird that attacked him must be destroyed. Then he thought about the dark sword mashed into his spine now, he leaped off the ground heading from the vessel, reaching behind him to pull the huge sword, its black blade shone brightly of oil. His second leap carried him closer to his target, his huge sword now inside his right hand, his body moved with activities as the insect-like creature covered his body completely. Hitting the ground, he leaped one final time, his huge powerful body connected with the haul of the vessel crashing right through it.

Inside now he swung the sword as it begin cutting through everything around him, insects leaped off his body at many of the Garthian that tried to flee. They begin their feast, Tutann crashed through walls swinging the large dark sword, everything it touched turned to smoke and fire, he leaped upward through the roof, crashing through and continued his raft of destruction swinging the dark blade in circles, then left to right, he went into a spin slicing Garthians, as he continued through the vessel. Tutann's loud rumbling voice yelled loudly throughout the vessel. Many Garthians rush at him at every turn but the large insects leaped from his body by the hundreds consuming their next meal, chilling screams came from every direction.

Tutann leaped upward breaking through to the next floor, swinging the dark blade as it passed through wall and ceiling like they was made of air, after running through another wall, he swung his dark blade, then a succession of explosions came and he was blinded by smoke. His body sailed through the skies downward toward the ground, the sword was still inside his right hand, when he hit the ground loudly. Tutann then looked up at the smoking vessel moving down from the sky toward the huge ocean, the entire vessel was on fire, he replaced the sword after taking a deeper look at its sharp blade edge, and it slid back into place easily.

The large insect-like bugs moved in to openings around his skin, he turn to hear another loud crash of another large vessel.

Ahknon struck across the sky to hit the ground next to Tutannharmoon, his powerful friend was breathing heavily, his sun spear firmly in his right hand. The last ship was in smoke but it floated in the air, Ahknon looked upward towards the dark skies where the moon reflected bright lights. Ahknon's facial features change which caught Tutann's attention, he looked upward quickly and noticed another large vessel was moving directly towards them.

"Where is Hutap?" Ahknon asked Tutann urgently.

"Hutap is still aboard the last vessel."

Ahknon looked at his friend and could now see the concern apparent in his facial expression. He heard the loud thumping of Tutann's heart, and then he heard a voice calling to them, as the both of them looked toward the vessel.

"I think that was Hutap," said Ahknon, "you go and get her, I will take care of this new threat, until you can get her free. I will keep the vessel busy."

"Ok," said Tutann.

Hutapsunnimoon looked down and seen Ahknon and Tutann standing together, just below the vessel she was upon, her voice got their attention, and as Tutann was searching for her, she noticed that they were pointing above her head and she turned to look upward and to her amazement another ship was moving fast towards her. She looked down at Tutann, who was preparing himself to leap; Ahknon held the sun spear above his head, then an explosion was heard above her head from the new vessel.

Hutap eye witnessed several large projectiles; she knew to be weapons cutting the air racing her way. Hutap leaped off the side of the vessel, her body sailed through the air picking up speed, she eyed Tutannharmoon, he was her only chance, she screamed!

"TUTANNHARMOON!!!"

Tutann heard her call to him, he watched her body falling from the large vessel, he left the ground quickly as his large body propelled through the air moving fast to meet Hutap's descent; expanding his arms wide, he noticed she was coming down backward, now he knew why she had jumped; several exploding objects were quickly moving towards the vessel Hutap leaped from. Tutann, found it odd of the vessel moving out of the dark skies to aim its weapons then launch an attack against one of its own vessels. Tutann captured Hutap in his strong embrace, wrapping her up tightly in the curve of his body. The vessel exploded with fire and smoke, lighting up the night skies. Fire covered him completely; metal objects smashed into his body, but the only thing he cared about was Hutap's safety.

Tutann's body now sailed downward toward the Alkebu-lanian soil. Tutann stayed in the curdled position, now a distance away from the fire, and when he was sure it was safe, he unfolded his body, wrapping his arms around Hutapsunnimoon, as the ground was moving towards him quickly; he hit using his legs to cushion her body from the shock, then leaped way from the fast moving iron vessel.

I mhotep broke through the Alkebu-lanian atmosphere, moving quickly, he was trying to remember what part of this large planet sat Alkebu-lan, then he noticed three star fighters just below him, firing upon the Alkebu-lan surface, he pushed the star fighter in that direction, after moving through large clouds, Imhotep noticed that the skies was dark it was now night just below him.

Imhotep targeted the center star fighter; he activated the weapon's locking device which appeared on a small screen at the arm of the command chair! Three targets were visible, then Imhotep watched one crash into the large seas, the other crashed upon the surface; his ship was now several hundred meters away. The locking indicator blinked red. Imhotep pushed the weapon button, as rockets release from the weapons bay, several power beams of light followed the explosive weapons, and he made contact as the rockets exploded with fire and smoke.

Nassir looked on in awe, from a seat just to the side of Imhotep. Nassir also noticed after the explosion the ship that was targeted by Imhotep was on the move. He looked at Imhotep, who said, "These small fighting star ships also carry shields, using their radar. They noticed me moving into the planet's orbit, they thought we were assisting them, after the first attack upon their star fighter. They raised their shields, but from the looks of the craft its shield will fail shortly! I have to keep up the pressure."

Imhotep was leveling the ship off to catch up to the last star fighter slowing its descent to the Alkebu-lan surface it was quickly propelling forward behind the damaged ship. Imhotep pulled the star fighter in to a steep turn, as many around the command center yelled in fright.

"Hold own, you all will be alright, just take hold of something," said Imhotep, concentrating on following behind the star fighter.

The vessel moved across the sky at lighting speed, turning right and left, passing over mountains into a dense dark forest, the landside was now completely dark, but Imhotep was quickly gaining on the Garthian leader's tail.

Imhotep turned a steep left as his passenger let out a low scream! He understood what they were feeling, it was the gravity of the planet pulling down on their bodies. Imhotep took another turn right, then the star fighter raised straight up behind the smoky enemy craft, it moved up higher then higher before leveling out. Imhotep noticed large canons from the enemy's ship turn his way, he looked down at his computer on his arm rest, he understood the Garthian word for shield, as he quickly pushed the button, laser lights ripped through the air at his vessel, a loud explosion came, but nothing happened, the shells did its job.

Nassir looked on, then down to the ground level, seeing the huge tree of his homeland looking like small spots below him, and in the distance he could see the snowcapped mountain, as they moved far northbound, the ship made him feel a bit sick, but it was a great experience, and something to talk about.

He gazed back at the passengers, whose eyes were locked looking through the large open glass window at the scene before them. He begins to wonder about his family, his wife, his daughter, hoping that the forces were strong enough without the strength of Imhotep. He looked back through the window, then whispered, "There always hope."

Imhotep stayed focused, he had to maneuver the ship without having the star ship damaged. The enemy star ship took a sharp left, striking through large clouds, he follow it through. Imhotep looked around the ship, all he ever dreamed about was now upon him. He looked around the ship at the people he loved, then his eyes moved to the female Aquanian, he learned her name was Aquantoria, looking at her now, there was more life in her eyes and face. She was just as passionate as he was in destroying their enemy! He can't possibly know what she has experienced all these years.

It was obvious she was a threat to the Garthians; why else would they keep her in a sedative state, frozen in time. She was the unbreakable one that could not be tamed. He smiled at the thought of how humble she really looked, but he knew she knew more about her inner power then he, unlike she, he has been on the new planet for over a thousand years with only the use of three of the planet's four elements. He also thought about, Ahknon, Hutap, as well as Tutann, it was easy to notice that they had put down two of the large star fighters, leaving only the one he pursued; powerful beings to combat a dangerous enemy. Imhotep was glad that only one star cruiser was use in its attempt to take the planet, more than one, would have made his journey to win less likely, and he knew very well the Cravistines fought hard against the Garthians. He hoped the Cravistine's leader, Ick, survived, along with E-Newtu and others.

Imhotep focused on the job at hand, he stayed close to the star fighter, as it continued to leave a smoke trail. The fire was consuming the ship and it could be long before the ship lost most of its power, his radar lock blinked red! He pushed down on the button, cannons lifted upward from just in front of the view window, a round of light exploded forward, on contact with the ship! The shield that protected it lit up, then faded.

Imhotep followed the ship, passed the northern mountain where the Cravistines lived, then the ocean, its vast water spread out farther north and south, as time passed the land was in the distance, and Imhotep was upon uncharted lands. He thought about his mentor, Ahknon's father, who traveled these lands, he noticed even in the dark of night the land's side was beautiful, the enemy ship turned a sharp left and Imhotep was upon it. The enemy star ship released thousands of rounds to destroy its pursuers, flashing lights and an explosion, as rockets, and lasers zoom directly behind it making contact with the shields. Imhotep closed his eye as the weapon exploded loudly! When he had opened his eyes, he watched as the shields faded away. Imhotep was very young when he first started flying space crafts, he was very good, but it has been some years, but he felt he was doing pretty well.

The enemy ship went in to a 145 degree turn heading back towards Alkebu-lan, as he followed. After coming out of the turn the radar lock sounded indicating there is a lock of its target. Imhotep realizes that the enemy ship's power was now faded, he armed all his weapons for release, the button flared as the indicator announced the weapons were fully operational. He looked one last time thinking about all the wrong this race of beings have committed around the multiverse, then to Aquantanita, who was looking directly into his eyes, a tear was there; he noticed and it was a reassurance that she was with him for all times.

Imhotep turned his eyes to the enemy star ship one last time, before pushing the firing button, every single weapon the ship offered was being released, explosive rounds fired from its cannons, laser lights flashed off alone with rockets reaching its target in seconds. Making contact with the enemy star ship, the huge ship exploded, as fire lit up the dark skies all around. Imhotep with his shells still in place crashed through what was left of the star ship to complete it destruction. The passengers and General Nassir placed their arms across their faces from the flaring lights. Then everyone on board the star ship begin to celebrate, hugging one another then calling out Imhotep's name, even Aquantoria looked at him very proudly. Imhotep smiled back looking; using the one good eye he had to look all around him.

The huge star fighter moved on a straight path for Alkebu-lan, then he had second thoughts, he wanted to show them more of their landside at the opposite side of their world, he knew this experience has changed their perception of things, and one day they will become teachers, to build their technology. They cruised the skies traveling over huge land, and massive, oceans that travel to new lands. They moved closer to the glass windows as the sun begins to rise.

All the passengers marveled at the world's creations, it was completely silent. After a short while, Imhotep turned the star fighter's head to Alkebu-lan, it wasn't long before he landed the craft in the middle of the battlefield, as the space craft touched down. Hutapsunnimoon was at one side of the craft's weapons aiming, Tutannharmoon took hold of the rear of the star fighter keeping it at the ground level, while Ahknonkineton stood just in front of the large vessel, the tip of his spear glowing white. A hatch opened as the soldiers of Alkebu-lan and the Cravistines marched to the large craft from all directions.

Imhotep stepped out first and the entire field of soldiers erupted in celebration, their voices raised to the blue skies above, many of the passengers begin exiting the craft down the hatch. Hutap moved closer toward Imhotep, still searching the crowd for her father Nassir, she looked at Imhotep sadly, who promised he would bring her father back! Then she noticed his injured face, it told its own story of struggle, Imhotep had noticed her for the first time and he smiled.

More and more Alkebu-lanians moved from the huge ship, Hutap continued to search the huge group moving out; Tutann came to stand at her side, knowing what she was going through! Somehow he figured, if there was any bad information to tell, Imhotep would have stated it already, also the bruises upon his face showed he did what was necessary to save the people of Alkebu-lan, and then he heard Hutapsunnimoon shouting loudly.

"Father, father, over here! Over here!" Hutap watched her father, Nassir, turning to look through the large crowd of gathering people. Hutap began to jump up and down like a little girl full of excitement. Tutann looked around behind him, his huge back preventing many from viewing others exiting the vessel.

Imhotep looked out across the land as every single man cheered! Nassir exited the craft last with the Zukufu female soldier at his side. Ick, the Cravistine leader, approached Imhotep stepping through the crowd to meet him. Stepping closer, their words became like music, only words they could understand.

"It's sure good to see you Imhotep," said Ick, taking Imhotep by the hand.

"I could see the ground attack went fairly well against the Garthians," said Imhotep.

"Well very brutal, we lost a great deal on both sides, Cravistines and Alkebu-lanians, and I must say the Alkebu-lanian woman, Hutapsunnimoon and the two others were very effective weapons in the war. We could have never have made it without the three of them, Imhotep," Ick said.

The female from Aquan exited the hatch moving to Imhotep's side looking at all the gathering people.

"Well what a suprise, your travels has found one of your kind, Imhotep."

"A great discovery after so many years of being alone," Ick said, looking to Imhotep then the female of his race, he bowed and said hello.

"Aquantanita, this is the leader of the Cravistines on this planet, powerful ally against a powerful race of beings, his name is Ick."

"Well hello Ick, its good meeting you," said Aquantanita, bowing as well in respect.

"She was a prisoner inside the star cruiser, I freed her and many other captives," Imhotep said.

Ick looked on in surprise, he noticed the injuries to Imhotep's face and wondered, after listening to his last words, to take over an entire star ship single-handedly was almost entirely impossible, but yet he has done it, and a ship large enough to travel the known Universe, making it possible to see what has become of his home world. Thoughts of seeing his home world died long ago, but now it was a reality, he smiled brightly showing rows of his many teeth then said,

"Are the Cravistines a part of the ships new crew?"

"Of course I would not have it any other way, we traveled towards Aquan, then the Cravistine's home world, we will circle the multiverse to find allies to join in the crusade to remove the Garthian control. We take a long and dangerous journey a head of us, if you are in, we leave in a few days," said Imhotep.

"Yes the Cravistines are certainly in and the few days will give me time to get all my people together for the travels, your name will be remembered among my people for eternity, someday I will repay you, Imhotep," said Ick, touching Imhotep softly on the shoulder.

"No, Ick you have been helping lead the force to victory, a victory that cost many Cravistines and Alkebu-lanian soldiers their lives, you have done a great service, the blood of our people lay within these soils," Imhotep said, touching the huge being on his hand.

Ick looked down on the one they called the wanderer; he was truly a man of wisdom, peace, and understanding. Ick said,

"We, Cravistines, head home to the mountains and prepare our travels through space, are the shields down?"

"Yes, I have cleared the shields, you can move on a straight path home Ick, have a safe travel and thank you," said Imhotep.

Ick turned around and moved away from the star fighter, he smiled, hopping away as hundreds of Cravistines followed, they moved north quickly. Imhotep watched them go.

Hutapsunnimoon moved into her father's embrace. She is a powerful soldier with extraordinary skill, but neither could she contain the emotions deep inside her, tears welled up in her eyes, as she tried to blink them away, Nassir held her tightly to his heart. Tutann was standing behind Hutap, towering over everything near him.

"I thought I would never see you again," Hutap said, looking up at her father.

"Well, I thought I would never see my home world, or any of my family, even the appearance of Imhotep as a captive brought me no real assurance of ever laying eyes on my lovely daughter coming home, but I've learned in such a short time," Nassir said, gazing into the eyes of his daughter.

"Well, Imhotep is a powerful man, father," said Hutap.

"Yes, you're right, Hutap, far beyond anything I could imagine, but like everyone, there is always some doubts. I guess I had to learn on my own." Nassir's eyes expanded then he smiled and continued, "I heard so much about you, I'm very proud of you Hutap, I should have known nothing could keep you away from the war, but know this, fathers wish to protect their young

Queens. I guess I was overly protective of you, because I just wanted you to live a normal life and find a man and be happy," Nassir finished.

"Well, father, I'm happy being the daughter of a war general, and I also have found a boyfriend," said Hutap, through teary eyes.

Tutannharmoon was listening carefully to Hutap and General Nassir's conversation, then he heard her say she found a boyfriend, it angered him at first, wondering who she was speaking of, then he heard her mention his name, as he smiled. Tutann realized that he would do anything for Hutapsunnimoon, even die to save her life. Hutap then introduced her father to Tutann. As they began to talk, he opened his hand to greet the general. Hutap took Tutannharmoon's hand while they talked.

Ahknon moved towards Imhotep, Imhotep smiled seeing Ahknon walking his way. The young boy who is now a man, Imhotep thought as the newfound powers radiated from the man's skin.

"You did it Imhotep, you saved our people as well as the land," Ahknon said, stepping close to Imhotep. Then he noticed a woman just a bit shorter than Imhotep but there was no mistaking the features of her face and skin was the same as Imhotep. He smiled in respect, giving her a bow of his head.

"No, Ahknon, it could not happen without you and the others, you kept them busy down here, less focused on what was happening above their heads."

Imhotep pointed to the sky, "You Ahknon, are a powerful force in the Universe, and there is much to discover about you Ahknon; not only do you have the D.N.A. of the King font and Qehec race running through your veins, you also have Aquan blood," Imhotep said proudly, but he continued.

Aquantanita looked up as her ears picked up the word Aquan, it was the only words she understood while Imhotep was talking! Her eyes took in more of the being before her, she recognized the Aquan features so she smiled.

"Sorry, Ahknon, this is Aquantanita from Aquan," Imhotep then turned and begin to explain to the woman who she was meeting, as she moved her head up and down in understanding, he looked back at Ahknon and continued his conversation, "You should travel along my side there is a lot for you to learn out there in the dark reaches of space, the Garthian battle doesn't end here. We must free the Garthian's hold around the universe, there are many places that need to be free of the Garthians, but other worlds are unaware of them; they may soon become victims. The universe is vast; it would take many lifetimes to concord each solar system. I will show you things of wonder, and you will see E-Newtu and Tu-ney again," said Imhotep.

Ahknon thought for a few moments, to see new worlds up there in space, it would be wonderful, he thought about the woman standing next to Imhotep. Imhotep has found companionship, how would he, Ahknon thought, so he asked Imhotep.

"May I bring a woman to comfort me on our journey? If it's her decision to go along," Ahknon said.

"Yes, she may come along," said Imhotep.

Ahknon turned quickly, racing away from the crowds then leaping up into the air, as his body sailed up and out in the distance. Imhotep and Aquantanita watched him go.

For the next several days, Imhotep spoke with Hutapsunnimoon and Tutannharmoon. Imhotep imposed the same question he laid on Ahknon. They both took time to bring him their answer. But Nassir and Butann agreed that the powers instilled inside them was for the purpose of doing good, and both generals agreed that it would be selfish of them to want Hutap and Tutann to stay here with them after what they all had experienced.

Hutap went home to see her mother and community for a few days. Tutann was beside her. She and he then headed to his homeland; his mother was very excited to see him and her husband, Butann. Tutann and Hutap reached the top of his mountain home, they spent time together looking all around the colorful landside and then out west toward the rolling seas, the air currents carried Hutap, blowing in the wind behind her, as her and Tutann stare, wondering what lay beyond the seas. They stayed there listening to the large waves crash upon the sandy shores, as the skies darkened from the coming night, a crest moon glowed brightly in the eastern sky, the huge shape of what Imhotep called a star cruiser, floated suspended in place near the moon. Tutann and Hutap gazed upward wondering where their journey will lead them.

Tutann and Hutap were satisfied that wherever the road takes them they will be alright, as long as they had each other! The next day, they swam in the deep lake above the mountaintop, enjoying every minute together, later that same day they descended the mountaintop, heading toward the star fighter where Imhotep was waiting.

Ahknon stayed in northern Kemet with Isis for two days, the both of them confessed their love! Ahknon explained the importance of his departure of the planet as Isis had become teary eyed. She pleaded with Ahknon not to go and to stay with her. Ahknon explained his need to help others, by using the powers sent to him across a vast universe and it would be selfish of him if he only used it for his people alone. Isis understood his point; but it did nothing to stop the pain deep inside her heart, then Ahknon asked her,

"Will you be willing to go along with me to be my future wife, to comfort me when I truly need you, and I will be there for you Isis for always, I promise."

Isis's tears stopped, as her heart beat rapidly inside her chest, there wasn't anything she wanted more then to be at Ahknon's side! She placed both hands to her mouth as her body shook a bit then her face brightened with joy as her eyes expanded, she said,

"Oh yes, Ahknon! Yes I will be your wife and I promise to be there for you forever more. You have chosen well," she smiled, placing her hand at her waistline, then she rushed into Ahknon's arms, wrapping her arms around his neck, squeezing him tightly, while kissing him all over his face.

Ahknon watched Isis run off to pack all of her things while he went to speak with his uncle, E-Newtu and his wife, Tu-ney, expressing his future plans; they both agreed with him that he was doing the right thing. They explained that when he got back they will be right here for him. They also expressed their love and that they wished him to be careful. The three of them hugged tightly as a family and to Ahknon it was the only family he had; none after the passing of his mother! When they released each other, they began to hear thousands of footsteps moving into their direction. E-Newtu exited the large tent, followed by Tu-ney then Ahknon, what they was witnessing was a huge gathering of Cravistines headed towards Abyssinia to where Imhotep was waiting. Large male and females carrying young were marching forward.

Many of them recognized Ahknon; they waved but kept their step steady forward, Ahknon looked on. He learned that the Cravistines were pushed from their own world by the Garthians and have been living here as long as Imhotep, inside the northern mountains for well over two thousand years. But now they were on their way home. Ahknon smiled looking at the powerful creatures. He continued to watch until they were out of sight.

Shortly afterward, Isis came upon them as she greeted his family! She carried a bag, Ahknon was sure that it held clothing items, he thought she was the most beautiful woman he has ever seen. He and Isis said their goodbyes as they walked away from his uncle's tent, out into the open ground, Ahknon stopped and said,

"I hope you're not scared of heights."

Isis looked at him then looked up, she said, "As long as I'm with you Ahknon, I'm not scared of anything," smiling, then kissing him on his face.

Ahknon wrapped his arms around Isis's waistline, lifting his spear to the clouds! As he and Isis rocketed upward leaving the ground far below, he leveled out, moving quickly into the eastern sky. Ahknon moved across the darkening skies, he was surprised how effortless it was to carry Isis in his arms, moving quickly over the Cravistine's leader, Ick, he looked ahead and his body motioned forward faster.

Isis looked around at the landside below, the view was breathtaking. The cool wind blew in her face, as her clothing wrapped around; the trees and lakes are so small, as the herds of animals raced away as they passed over. Isis often wondered what being so high would feel like while watching the large bird gliding the wind currents, and she had her answer as they continued onward.

Four days later Abyssinia

Thousands gathered to see the old wanderer, Imhotep off. The large star fighter hatch was open as Tutannharmoon moved into the ship, just behind him was Hutapsunnimoon, then Ahknonkineton hand in hand with Isis, Ick was in next waving his goodbye to the Alkebu-lanian people as the Cravistines followed their leader inside. Imhotep and Aquantanita greeted every one with a huge smile standing at the landing side as the passengers entered, everything the passengers would need was provided by the Alkebu-lanian people; food, water, plant life for growth of food, fruits and vegetables, will be grown in the star ship planetarium; many other things was brought along to aid those with injuries, after the last passenger entered the ship. Imhotep looked through teary eyes as he waved to the Alkebu-lanian people he has called his family, young children, women and men waved their goodbyes, many cheered for him and his crew. The war for Alkebu-lan was a long but difficult fight for its people, but they will carry on.

Imhotep took his last deep breath of the young planet's air, the Alkebu-lanians cheerful manor showed no sign of struggle just days ago, its people are more knowledgeable from their experiences, things that may not have be conceivable at one point in their lives. Now those experiences taught them to dream of the stars above. Aquantanita understood the emotion Imhotep was now feeling, kinda like the way she had when she first seen him enter her life, she held his hand close to her heart, as he and her waved to the only family he has ever known. They turned, heading up inside the star fighter. Seconds later, the ramp rose upward, sealing the doorway shut.

Shortly afterwards, Imhotep and Aquantanita took their seats inside the huge circular compartment with rows of seating around the large glass viewing window, where the images of Alkebu-lanian people were waiting. Imhotep sat in the commander's chair there in the center of the room. Ick was his captain and second in command and Aquantanita was third; other seats around the control room sat Cravistines. The older one who held experience at flying space crafts; they prepared the star fighter for lift off. Hutapsunnimoon sat to the right of Ick and a huge chair was constructed for Tutannharmoon, who sat beside her, a huge metal strap held in place. Ahknon and Isis sat to the left of Imhotep.

Imhotep gazed around at just a few of the star fighter occupants. The other several hundred were strapped down in seats in the lower levels, a huge ship to those who have not witnessed the commanding star cruiser; above, Imhotep smiled, then said, "Captain Ick, ready for lift off?"

"Yes Commander, awaiting your order," said Ick.

Imhotep looked around the room, it was his dream to fly through the Universe once again.

Imhotep said, "Prepare for lift off."

"Yes Commander," Ick said, and he continued prepare for lift off.

The star fighter rose off the Alkebu-lanian soil level, it moved upward quickly then gained speed. The ground below moved away very quickly and once again inside the compartment everyone was silent as they watch the ground fade away. It was strange to those that have never left the surface of the new planet. They watched the huge mountains, trees, and ocean change to nothingness, their faces held distraught looks. Imhotep's eyes looked upward as the star fighter went through thick clouds, then more clouds. Others begin whispering; the ship entered the dark reaches of space.

Imhotep turned right and then left to see Tutann, Hutap, Ahknon and Isis. Their eyes glowed in wonder at the sight of the huge, bright sun and the twinkling stars. He knew now he would have to tell them everything he knew about the universe. They, abroad, are his extended family, those who trusted his actions as well as his judgement! The star fighter moved quickly toward the large star cruiser.

"What is that?" Hutapsunnimoon asked.

"It has to be the large craft, Imhotep," Ahknon said, looking over at Hutap.

"That thing is gigantic," Tutann said.

"Well, this thing you're look at will be your new home for a long while," Imhotep said.

The Cravistine leader, Ick, began to bark out sounds looking towards Imhotep. His eyes looking, searching the huge space craft their star fighter was quickly moving towards.

"Yes, Ick! Everything you will need is inside that star cruiser, you will find books of all kind, some even in your own native tongue, we will be there in a short spell," Imhotep finished.

As the star fighter moved closer to the space dock of the ship, the space door begin to open revealing the inside, whispering began as bright lights exited the dock's outer doorway, to many inside the star fighter; they noticed that the ship they were inside was tiny in comparison, to the large ship. The star fighter moved inside, the bright, illuminating lights showed just how huge the star cruiser actually is. Hutap and the others notice there were many identical crafts stationed on the space dock floors, many of the occupants inside begin to stand to get a better look; many of those are young Cravistines.

Imhotep placed the star fighter down next to many other star fighters as the craft engine quieted. The hatch door opened and

Imhotep step out first. Hutap, Tutann, Ahknon, Isis and many others followed just inches behind him. Ick looked around tapping his chest from excitement. Then other humanoids caught their attention, creatures made from fire moved towards them followed by a horned beast as large as Tutannharmoon. Ick screamed out loudly moving toward the large beast, it recognized a being from its own planet, the large creature raced towards Ick with its hands spread wide.

Other Cravistines looked on in surprise as the huge, horned beast lifted the Cravistines leader in a loving embrace. Well, many begin barking loudly; Ick and the creatures began communicating, many of the Cravistines moved close, as the large creature bent down to greet many other Cravistines, native of his home world. The Elementals stopped before Imhotep, as everyone exiting he ship watched.

Imhotep said, "Is everything prepared aboard? Have you searched the entire ship for Garthians that I may have missed?"

"Yes, the ship is cleared of the Garthians, the ship is ready. Everything is in order," the Elemental said, then it bowed to its creator.

"Now show our crew to their quarters, we leave once everyone has familiarized themselves with the star cruiser, I have many items on this star ship. I need them moved to their proper places! If I'm needed, you can find me inside the control center of the ship," said Imhotep, he then turned to the gathering on the space dock.

"Ick, Aquantanita, I need the two of you to follow me, the rest of you find your place to sleep, you need to know everything about this ship, weapon room, places where we eat, conference room where most of the meetings will be taking place. I'm pretty sure you will find something that will accommodate each and every one of you, this ship holds many levels get to know them. It's my first command." Many of the Cravistines reacted to those words.

The ship's newest crew moved out behind the elemental beings. Tutann greeted the huge beasts from the Cravistines home world, it was the first large beast of his size; he could truly be friends with. Tutann moved out behind the large creature, looking for a room to accommodate his size. Hutapsunnimoon was fast on his heels followed by Ahknonkineton and Isis.

In a short few days, Imhotep's new crew found the space craft spacious, even Tutannharmoon, the largest on board at the moment, his sleeper was large enough that even he could roll over in bed comfortably and Hutapsunnimoon's room was just next door. Ahknonkineton and Isis's room was beautifully crafted, many tools inside, the room came to life; but Isis or Ahknon knew anything of the tools, some of the more older Cravistine males and females moved around the ship like it was second nature. The older taught the young Cravistine of the dynamic of their new living quarters. Each person on board held a position that will ensure the ship was clean, as others made meals daily. The transition for many went smoothly, it was the same as living in Alkebu-lan or atop of the large mountains.

After several, days, the ship was ready to depart for destination in the multiverse. Imhotep sat in the commander station proudly, then he looked around and noticed everyone was seated in there designated seating arrangement. Within the last few days, Imhotep has learned so much from Aquantanita; lost knowledge, but it made him much stronger. He learned of her escape and final capture, she was then place inside the sleeper cell for hundreds of years, only waked to be questioned by the Garthians. She remembered the killing of Aquanian occupants and truly thought she was the last of her kind.

Imhotep pondered everything he has been through in the last thousand years. He was happy to hear that Aquan thrives without its people. He plans to change all that! Imhotep touched Aquantanita's hand softly. She bowed in a jester of respect. She is a wonderful person like him and another key at him accomplishing his goal.

He called out, "Captain Ick, Aquantanita, are we ready to make our leave?"

"Yes Commander, the engines are at full capacity, light, hyper, drive cells are fully charged, just awaiting you order Commander," Ick said.

"Yes Commander, the ship's computers are set for ordinance 356 stellar region of the multiverse," said Aquantanita, in a voice only her, Imhotep and the Cravistines understood.

"Let's turn the ship around," said Imhotep.

"Yes Commander," Ick said, as the engines came to life.

The view screen of the young planet begins to shift to the right, each person in the command compartment ready for motion. The large ship engine rumbled smoothly.

"Prepare the ship for level one cruiser speed," Imhotep said.

"Level one cruiser speed," Ick repeated to the crew.

The crew responded, "Yes, Commander."

"All hands ready for take-off. Repeat, this is Captain Ick, prepare for take-off."

As a low pitched sound signaled their departure, the large star cruiser pushed forward; over the intercom, came instruction for those around the ship to take their seats. The huge vessel gained cruise speed, then even greater rate of speed passing several large planets, then all the passengers was experiencing something totally new, as all eyes stared. Even Ick looked on after two thousand years in Alkebu-lan. Young Cravistines marveled at the large planets, some with rings, and others large with many moons beyond their wildest imagination.

"Prepare for warp speed," Imhotep said.

"Warp speed," Captain Ick yelled.

"What is warp speed?" asked Tutannharmoon. Hutap, Ahknon and many others in the control center waited for an answer.

Imhotep smiled and said, "Hold on to your seats, you all are about to find out."

The ship's engine raved and the stars before their eyes became a million flashing lights, away the ship carried them, in seconds. Imhotep moved through space destroying Garthian battle ships, re-enforcing old bonds between worlds, to combat the Garthian's home planet. Tutannharmoon, Hutapsunnimoon and Ahknonkineton were a powerful force against the enemy. Others joined the fight after recognizing there planet champions. The saga continues but that's another story, as our companions are faced with war against unimaginable odds. As Imhotep seeks to relinquish Garthian hold around the Universe and re-establish the natural order of Aquan, the Cravistines home world and other planets are in need of their alliance.

The End

See Book 2# Alkebu-lan Conquest. Coming soon.

About the Author

Roosevelt Broadus III is a native New Yorker. He was raised by his father in Laurelton, Queens. While growing up in Laurelton, Roosevelt found himself very engaged in the streets. His life of mischief, drug selling, and crime finally caught up with him. Roosevelt spent most of his years in some of the most infamous penitentiaries in the United States. While incarcerated he took advantage of his time and found the love of writing. He wrote over eight novels in genres that

include science fiction, realistic fiction, mystery, and drama.

Roosevelt was released from prison under the President Obama regime in 2015. He spent over twenty years incarcerated. Today Roosevelt is the CEO of his own production company called SNJ Entertainment. During his spare time, he is heavily involved in community outreach where he speaks to young inmates about transitioning back into society.

www.ingramcontent.com/pod-product-compliance
Lightning Source LLC
Chambersburg PA
CBHW071140100726
47908CB00002B/192